Evelyn

8th Oct. 1950.

Dublin.

THE WATERS OF WALLA

Eden Phillpotts' new novel is a chronicle of the village of "Wallabrook" in Devon and of some of the people who lived there.

The loving care with which the author draws his characters has rarely been shown to better effect than in this delightfully human tale. Before the reader has finished he will feel he knows each varied figure as well as he knows his own next-door neighbour.

By the Same Author:

Novels

REDCLIFF
GEORGE WESTOVER
UP HILL, DOWN DALE
A CORNISH DROLL
THE GREY ROOM
THE JURY
THE RING FENCE
THE THREE MAIDENS
STORMBURY
"FOUND DROWNED"
BRED IN THE BONE
WITCH'S CAULDRON
A SHADOW PASSES
MR. DIGWEED AND MR. LUMB
THE OLDEST INHABITANT
PORTRAIT OF A GENTLEMAN
THE WIFE OF ELIAS
A VOICE FROM THE DARK
A DEED WITHOUT A NAME
PILGRIMS OF THE NIGHT
THE BOOK OF AVIS
FLOWER OF THE GODS
THE CHANGELING
THEY WERE SEVEN
A MUSEUM PIECE
THE DRUMS OF DOMBALI
QUARTET
THERE WAS AN OLD WOMAN
THE FALL OF THE HOUSE OF HERON
ADDRESS UNKNOWN
DILEMMA

Essays

A WEST COUNTRY SKETCH BOOK
ESSAYS IN LITTLE

Short Stories

IT HAPPENED LIKE THAT
THE TORCH
CHERRY GAMBOL
THEY COULD DO NO OTHER
PEACOCK HOUSE

THE WATERS OF WALLA

by

EDEN PHILLPOTTS

HUTCHINSON & CO. (Publishers) LTD
London New York Melbourne Sydney Cape Town

To

FRANK ROPER, M.D.

Though hopeful wishing be of small avail,
Yet am I sanguine you approve this tale,
But, failing that, my valued friend, admit
Devout good willing comes along with it.

BOOK I

CHAPTER I

WILLIAM BROWNE of Tavistock—a singer from the past, though surely most considerable of Devon-born poets—is no longer read and welcomed as when he wrote *Britannia's Pastorals* and delighted therewith a bygone age. His prime as an artist coincided with his youth and he accomplished the best that was in him when a young man of few cares, but abundant good spirits, wholehearted Nature-worship and a warm humanity pertaining to all his works. He haunted the wild, gleaning their varied magic from hill and vale, from moors and coombes, from rivers and rivulets. Indeed, music of Devon water-springs is never absent from the 'Pastorals'; their tinkle and murmur charm every page with its own proper melody; today their summer harmonies inspire him and tomorrow the verses quicken with shouting of autumnal spates, or thunder of winter storms, for greatly he loved our water-courses in every mood and he has set it down how once his purpose was to chronicle the glory of each and all:

> Yet when I shall return, I'll strive to draw
> The nymphs of Tamar, Tavy, Exe and Taw,
> By Turridge, Otter, Ock, by Dart and Plym,
> With all the naiades that fish and swim
> In their clear streams. . . .

It was Browne's use to link old legends and pagan faiths with the Devonian scene and set his mythic folk amid the dissolving views of the West country from season to season amid uplands and lowlands to the margin of the sea. The pathetic fallacy he handled with ingenuous imagination and carried human emotions of joy or sorrow, hope or despair, into every streamlet, stock and stone, thus often from unconscious things weaving a kinship of heart between mankind and his environment. His water music has warm blood in it sometimes, as when he tells the story of Tavy and Walla, their sweethearting, courtship and ultimate union. Tavy is the hero and Walla the heroine, upon whose brief but delicious wanderings the poet lavishes every image of virgin loveliness that he can think upon:

> Walla, the fairest nymph that haunts the woods,
> Walla, beloved of shepherds, fawns and floods,
> Walla, of whom sweet birds their ditties move,
> Walla, the earth's delight and Tavy's love.

Despite hazard from unmannerly satyrs and other dangers of her journey through fairyland, the maiden rivulet arrives safely at last:

> To Tavy's crystal stream her waters go
> As if some secret power ordained so,
> And as a maid she lov'd him, so a brook
> To his embracements only her betook.

Sedate, a woman now and quite grown up, she flows amid peaceful denes and dingles, valley groves and lawns, to keep tryst with her lover at the Mine of the Virtuous Lady; whence, united and sharing a new name, they proceed, 'where Tamar pays Her daily tribute to the Western Seas'.

Aloft, from the great watershed and urn of Devon rivers, both started on their diverse ways, and the masculine stream, leaving Tavy Head, refreshed by Rattlebrook and lesser tributaries from Great Kneeset and Fur Tor, wanders southward, amid the hut circles and cairns of the old stone men, through Tavy Cleave by Mary Tavy, Peter Tavy and Tavistock to waters-meet; while maiden Walla, enjoying a like journey from her moorland cradle, has scrambled and scampered and sung down her granite staircase by way of White Barrow and Greena Ball, ever southerly beneath Great Mis Tor to Merrivale and Huckworthy, where stepping-stones and fords tend to mar her hoyden loveliness, abate her speed and bid her take note of many strange things unmarked till now.

Henceforward Walla confronts the activities of man and she, who has yet known no other bridge than a rainbow, finds herself spanned with arches of stone carrying his highways, and shadowing her flood beneath them. Her liberty is threatened although as yet no mill-wheel beats her bosom, or sluice is stolen from her current; but now she moderates her carefree progress as the gradient grows gentler, widens her boundaries and loiters a little amid new valleys, mightier woodlands and the mystery of mother earth cultivated and tamed.

Upon her childhood's journey through the wilderness Walla was free; now her liberty is curtailed and powers stronger than her own whisper of tyranny beyond her ken. The crofts around her harbour other four-footed beings than she remembers; the black-faced, horned sheep of Dartmoor drink no longer at her fountains and the heavy-coated, shaggy Scots cattle from the hill-tops are gone, giving place to fat, slow-moving sheep and ruddy 'Devon' herds browsing together in green pastures and glimmering water meads; while—stranger still—humanity, so seldom glimpsed aloft, now becomes a common object of the bank-side and the wondering river glides among homesteads and hamlets, to marvel at their purpose and consider their reason for existing.

The still, broad reaches of her stream grow longer now and the stickles between them fewer. She turns west of south and becomes adult, more staid and orderly, yet not less lovely than of old; and then she quickens once more, narrows at a gorge and, for the last time since her upland pilgrimage, runs merry riot to a true waterfall, leaps downward in a cataract of foam, lifts her voice and pours her torrent into Walla Pool, there regaining composure, abating her volume and threading her placid silver among the abiding-places of men.

Walla Pool lies in a sylvan region treasured by painters, trout-fishers and picknickers. It pertains to the manor of Oakshotts and for many generations has been free to all; yet, with that perversity alone to be met with among reasoning animals, those who may love it cannot love each other. The artist dislikes those busy, inquisitive children who creep to his elbow and whisper views as to what they see; the angler detests both painters and pleasure-goers, whose shadows, or the tremor of their footsteps, have scared the trout beyond thought of his fly; even Walla herself perchance may be imagined as loving best her own loneliness, and the moonlit silences of midnight when all of them are gone, the sole music and movement her own and no eyes behold her enchantments.

Now, on a summer morning, where the river approaches Wallabrook, the hamlet that bears her name, upon a little strand of pebbles there stood a boy fishing. He pretended to no skill and cast a hook laden with nothing more troutworthy than a worm. Upon the western bank opposite to him a paddock spread and an old donkey browsed; while not forty yards from the water stood a white-washed and thatched cottage upon which from time to time the boy cast anxious glances.

Downstream, where Walla flowed through her name village, a venerable bridge spanned the river, while cottage homes spread upwards to west and east about it; and upon the bridge a police constable, catching a flash of sunlight upon the distant boy's fishing-rod, turned his very keen eyes in that direction. Walla was not under his jurisdiction, for a water-bailiff looked after the fishing rights demanded before any angler might wet his line; but, none the less, Peter Chadd considered action because this youthful native appeared unlikely to hold any licence whatever and, in that disorderly event, committed a misdemeanour.

Chadd was a Wallabrook man and, though very familiar with the theatre of his new task, had only just returned to it after many months elsewhere. When twenty years of age he fought in the Second World War and, returning from it unscathed and undistinguished, was able to attain his own lifelong ambition and join the Police Force.

Now, full fledged and welcomed home again, the young man rejoined a widowed mother, quickened old friendships, made new ones and picked up the threads of that peaceful rustic existence war had ended. His imagination was meagre and he had come through his tremendous experience without any convulsions of opinion; but his principles were sound and his mother-taught conscience still actuated Peter, for whom life at no time presented as yet any very tortuous dilemmas. He had done his duty faithfully enough and met with no temptations to shirk it; but war at least was responsible for a more open mind and juster estimate of values than the average country boy will be found to display, and an element of ambition began to suggest that he would outgrow his youthful environment and seek channels more likely to advance promotion. Police Inspector Manley, who was now his commanding officer, supported this opinion, but sounded a note of warning.

"A place like this don't at first sight offer much to draw an ambitious man," he said, "but we'll wait and see, Chadd. You'll often find a small spot quite equal to harbouring a big crime and if, which God forbid, you was ever called to pit yourself against right-down criminals and made a good job of it, then you'll find me the first to report to your advantage. The war's made England a hot-bed for the lawless and the standards I'd lifted to a tidy good pitch in Wallabrook, though they hold their own here, are sunk a lot in the neighbour parishes."

Now Peter, knowing every turn and twist of the river exceeding well, went his way, passed down a lane, crossed a meadow and presently emerged at stream-side behind the fisherman, then tramped over the pebbles and directly approached him. But the lad showed no alarm, appeared unconscious of peril, set down his rod and came forward with a grin on his face.

"Morning, Mr. Chadd, sir," he said. "You'll mind me. I'm Gilbert White, Mr. Chadd—him you used to learn in your Sunday School class afore you went in the Army."

Peter scrutinised his old pupil.

"Sure enough so you are," he said. "Grown from a nipper to a sizeable boy, Gilly."

"I've been terrible wishful to see you," declared Gilbert. "We've oft wondered how you was faring and felt ever so glad you wasn't killed. I'd have 'listed, but seven was too young to go. I'm fourteen now—very near old enough to join the labouring classes, mother says."

"And be a railwayman like your father, I expect. How's Mr. White and Mrs. White? I'm coming to see 'em one of these days."

"They're very well; but I don't want to be a railwayman. I pray for to be a gamekeeper some day up at Oakshotts. Father says I needn't to count on it, because there won't be no gamekeepers by the time I'm old enough to be one. He says the Socialists will put a stop to that sort of job and folk like Squire Fortesque and parson will be off the map in a few years' time and Labour top-dog all over the world."

"Brian White was always tolerable red," agreed the policeman. "Pity your father weren't called to fight for England, Gilbert. Might have done him good."

"He'd have fought all right," answered the boy. "He's the sort that loves fighting. I don't like my father very much, Mr. Chadd; but the war called for terrible hard work on the railways and he was commanded to bide. Why, even mother got a job up to the station."

"Women toiled at home same as we toiled at the war."

"And scores was killed in the Plymouth blitz—childer too."

"Yes," said Peter. "And now about your fishing, Gilly. The river's not a police business, but if water-bailiff was to see you here, what would he say?"

Gilbert felt on safe ground here.

"It's like this, Mr. Chadd: a very peculiar case, and Mr. Ponder takes a friendly view—not on my account, but because of his friendship with grandmother."

"What's your grandmother got to do with it? She wouldn't want for you to turn poacher at your age. The police are on the side of the water-watchers and the gamekeepers likewise, because poaching is contrary to the law. And whoever heard of your grandmother—such a one as her—going contrary to law?"

The boy considered this.

"So far as a small trout here and there, my dear grandmother, who's my best friend on earth, runs contrary to law then," he explained. "But grandfather's dying, Mr. Chadd. He's for it any time now, because his liver be a thing of the past, and nobody can carry on very long without one. And now the only food he fancies, or grandmother can get him to let down, is a trout now and again. Then, if she can coax a bit of fat out of anybody round about, she'll fry the trout and grandfather will eat it pretty comfortable; so Mr. Ponder will tell you he suffers me to catch a few."

"I hear your grandfather is very bad," said the policeman, "and I ordain to call and see him. He was always very kind and friendly to me."

"Well, you'd best to be quick then," advised Gilbert, "because he might become a goner any time now. And that's how 'tis, so you can't call me a poacher no more. Grandmother's the law and the prophets for me and I must fish for her, but it's only for a dying grandfather, not for lawlessness, Mr. Chadd."

"You can call me 'Peter', Gilly, same as you did. Have you took anything today?"

The angler brought one small trout from his pocket. It was little larger than a sardine.

"Undersized, I grant you," he said; "but a trout's a trout. I want to gather up three more and then take 'em to his house."

Gilbert's eyes lifted to the cottage beside the little paddock where the donkey grazed.

"Your grandparents still live there?"

"Yes, Peter. There's no Blanchards left but them."

"Fish on, then. If Mr. Ponder says 'yes', then all's well."

"He says it's 'for the duration'," pointed out Gilly. "I can fish for the duration of a dying grandfather so long as he lives; but I mustn't fish again after he's dead."

"You'll soon be old enough to earn your living now."

"So mother says. She understands all about labour and says, with the farmers and traders calling for handy boys just out of school, I ought to be worth more than a pound a week to her and father in a year's time. Five-and-twenty shillings she'll get by me, she says, and not a penny less."

"And what will you get?"

Gilbert was frank.

"Father's given me to understand I'll get a darned good hiding from him if I don't earn the money," he said. "The idea in father's mind is that mother and him have brought me up and now it's my time to repay a bit of all they've done for me."

The young policeman sniffed.

"Well, good luck and let the next trout be a bigger one. Better be fishing than talking; and tell your grandmother I'll venture to call tomorrow if Mr. Blanchard's well enough to see me."

Elsewhere, in the thatched cottage, Unity Blanchard sat knitting and talking to her husband, John. She was a woman of sixty, still handsome, sturdy, tall and well preserved. Her hair was grey, her face but little lined, her pale, grey eyes still bright and clear. A kindly expression marked them, but her mouth, though large, was firm, her teeth all her own. Frustration had been Unity's portion, and failure to reclaim her husband from a cloud that never lifted during her long and losing battle. She fought and lost and was now about to see her failures culminate in the early death of John.

Early it was not on Bible computation, for the departing countryman had seen nearly seventy years pass over him and human friendship, won again and again by an attractive nature, only lost through his own hopeless frailties. Lack of will-power was John Blanchard's bane, and if his wife's good sense had sufficed to take the place of his weakness, then he might yet have made good, for Unity possessed a strong character and a sense of humour to sweeten it. But even she proved impotent against the man's utter inability to play his part in a world that called for concentration, devotion and self-sacrifice from those who felt any desire to better it. So now the kindly drunkard was going to die short of three score years and ten, rather than face life as an octogenarian after the usual Wallabrook custom.

The pair had always been remorselessly frank with each other, for they belonged to a class that employs blunt diction. They never annoyed each other by this habit of saying exactly what they felt and the sharpest criticism or hardest words were accepted as a matter of honest opinion rather than any reason for anger. Censures that might well separate sophisticated people for ever do not scandalise the folk. They are accustomed to plain speaking and their meagre vocabulary favours it, for ugly truths can often be packed into very few and simple words. John Blanchard much regretted the harsh condemnation expressed upon his errors, but it never modified good-willing to those who blamed him.

He was very sick now and near his end. His face that had once been handsome, though never strong, had shrunk and turned flaccid and mottled; his eyes were grown dim and his voice feeble. He was clean-shaven still and a barber friend from the village operated upon him twice a week for his comfort. He had been a big man to match his tall wife, but now was bent in the back and shrunk to a drooping shadow. John left his bed but seldom, yet would sometimes crawl into the garden and sit within sight of the river. He still talked and listened to Unity and liked her near him, but he cared not for other voices, save that of one man—his most faithful and lifelong friend.

"Arthur Brimblecombe," John often said, "has been my mainstay all my days and I'm well pleased to hear him tell, because he picks out the best of the past and keeps his tongue off the nastiest bits."

But to the past he usually turned, and the pair, now about to separate after more than forty years together, discussed it. They probed after their custom, but neither hurt the other.

"I'm very near to the finish now," said Mr. Blanchard, "and, taking it by and large, claim to have had more frosty luck than my share."

"You was very apt to leave the door open to it, Johnny. You've got to mind that. I'm fearing 'tis near the end as you say; but fearing for myself, not for you. You was fashioned to your pattern by the will of God and will be judged according; but I'll miss fighting for you and be a very lone woman when you go under."

"A most faithful partner you was and had a lot to contend against. But good-willing don't always carry good luck along with it. The brain-power was yours, but I put a spoke in your wheel from the outset. I had one brain-wave because I had the wits to win you; but after we was wed, I didn't have no more luck."

"I wouldn't say that, John. I wouldn't even say we haven't had our share of luck. We've had enough good fortune to keep friends whether or no," so Unity reminded him. "The quality was always well disposed to us. We've had many good words and useful jobs from the better-most and, when you minded to work now and again, folk always said no man done it better."

"Their number's up now," said John. "The upper people are finished. Arthur tells me that, under the new dispensations, there won't be no more quality in ten years' time. The middle class is in the soup already, because Labour wants their money, but it don't want them. The 'Reds' will strip 'em to the bone and alter the law so as it won't be highway robbery, but honest-to-God statesmanship."

Mrs. Blanchard laughed.

"That's Socialism, John. More wages and less work."

"But who's going to pay the wages?"

"The State will find the money and look after the childer free gratis, John."

"I doubt if it can work that way. I always withstood the 'Reds' myself."

His wife nodded.

"You was often a very clever thinker when you weren't under the influence," she said. "I've heard you speak a tidy lot of sense in your time, my dear. If you'd took half the advice you offered to other people, you'd have cut a braver figure than ever you have done."

"The trouble with me you can put in a nutshell, Unity. I had a spot of brain, granted; but I was called to use my arms and legs, not my brains, and bodily labour ran contrary to my nature. Manual labour I never could stand up to, being born bone-lazy by the will of God. The skill was there along with a hatred to use it; but if I'd belonged in another rank of life and got education, then my brain might have fruited."

"You always knew what was right," said Unity, "but the will-power wasn't there for you to reach it."

"True by this hand!" he agreed. "I was like Moses and allowed to see the Promised Land, but forbade to get there. Nothing's worse than to have a will you can't count upon. If ever a man felt undying wishes to pleasure a woman, I had to please you, and yet how oft the deeds weren't there, but only the wish to do 'em!"

"'Twas sad for me to see you muck up your own life and lose your chances and be so untrustable to those ready and willing to trust you."

"You've stood the devil of a lot," he confessed. "Just the difference between me and you. You had the will-power to suffer me all these years and you done so without a murmur. How little you thought when you had to choose between me and brother James, where your love would land you! That was the only time in my knowledge when your judgment played you false."

"Who knows? Who knows what his life turned out when James went foreign? As to why I took you, Johnny, and not him—that's because I was true to myself really."

She smiled at past recollections.

"I liked you both. I liked you both so well I felt quite content to go to one or other. I measured you up and there was things about each of you that took my fancy from the first—quite different things. I admired James for his hardness and doggedness; and I liked you for your beautiful face and your voice and your queer speed to learn what pleased me and your way of making love. My mother wanted me to take James. She said he was worth ten of you, and so he was, of course. But I happed to be the sort that don't like playing second fiddle, and when I was seventeen I knew very well how your brother would rule over me; but I knew you wasn't born to rule and might be a lot easier to live with. Then there was James's beard. I hated that and always felt he'd be a more trustworthy object without it. You never know what a man may hide behind his beard—not that James was ever at the trouble to hide anything from anybody. But I went so far as to ask him once whether he'd cut it off for love of a maid if she wanted him to. That was before he'd declared himself. And he said that if a woman ever dared to advise him how to wear his hair, he'd tell her to go to hell and mind her own business. I dare say his beard decided me against him really, because big things often turn on little things like that."

"They do," he admitted. "If you'd took him, he'd have been well content to stop home; but the instant moment he heard your mind was made up against him, he went foreign and never came back. He had the will-power to cut his losses."

"He took it very well and very brave," said Unity. "I can see that now clearer than what I did at the time. But it was best for him really. I wouldn't have been to him what I've been to you. He was an ownself man, very well able to make his way without any woman's help."

"I wonder what fashion of childer he'd have fathered if ever he married an Australian girl," mused John. "Something a tidy sight better worth the trouble than our blasted Maude, no doubt."

"Our Maude was always a disappointment to us and always will be," agreed Unity. "Belike, if we'd had any more childer, something hopefuller might have come of it; but Maude never favoured you nor yet me from her cradlehood upward. Not a pinch of your loving-kindness and thought for other people in Maude, and, whatever else I was, she never got her sly and shifty nature nor yet her love of money from me."

"You was the top flower of the basket in the Prince family," agreed the sick man.

"The Princes of Tavistock never showed in Maude," confessed Mrs. Blanchard. "They used to say there that we were well named, because we stood high and took our place among the folk and never a black sheep known among us. And now they are all gone save me, and the Blanchards all gone but you, John. But there's good Prince blood in Maude's boy, though none in her; and good Blanchard blood in him too. I can see you in him—the best of you."

"Pray for him to be a better man than his grandfather whether or no," sighed John.

"So I do," she agreed. "I feel Gilly to be a bit of my duty still: that's why I ordain to go and live with Maude and Gilly's father when you've gone, my dear."

"Yet I hate to think of you along with them," he murmured.

"So I do," replied Unity. "But it's for the boy's own sake. I can watch over him a bit closer there and see him launched. The bad's oftener handed down to the next generation than the good, and his father might be a bit of a handicap in Gilly's blood. Brian White's a poor thing."

"Anyway the lad can't leave his parents too soon," summed up John Blanchard, "and when he gets work—the farther off his mother the better."

Silence fell between them and his wife saw a familiar look in his eyes she had long learned to read.

"I know you're thirsty, my love, and you shall have a proper tot very soon now. I'll scramble an egg and give you the whiskey to help it down."

"You told Hannaford how grateful I am to him?"

"I did. It's a job to get it at all these days. All, or nearly all, goes to America now, but Amos Hannaford says that such a customer as you have always been shan't stint so long as he's got a bottle left."

"A right Christian man in all his dealings is Amos. I won't drink much more, be it as it will."

Then came an interruption and Gilly plunged into the room. He was free to come and go as he pleased here, and now kissed his grandmother first and then his grandfather.

"I've took four trout for you," he said. "Three's small, but one's sizeable, Grandfather."

Unity inspected them and then applauded.

"Just the right minute, Gilly! Now you'll have a trout instead of the egg, John. I'll fry 'em this instant moment and you can stop, boy, till I come back."

"Be quick, then," begged Mr. Blanchard, and when Unity hastened away, his grandson chattered to the sick man.

"I felt feared of my life just now," he said, "but didn't show it. Peter, the new policeman—Peter Chadd—was on his beat and he catched sight of my fishing-rod and came down to see who it might be. But when he saw it was me, he minded I was a Sunday School boy before the war and turned very nice. He looks grand in his uniform."

"You told him Mr. Ponder let you fish for me?"

"I did, Gran'father. I said I was suffered to catch what I could for the duration of your life; and Peter felt terrible sorry that you're going to die any minute now and hoped he might be allowed to call, and said he well remembered what a kind man you was."

"He pulled his weight, no doubt, in the war," said Mr. Blanchard.

"It must have been a tidy heavy weight, too," declared Gilbert. "He's a topping big chap."

"So was his father before him, and a topping bad chap. Great feats of strength he could perform and made money by it," said Mr. Blanchard. "Such was the might of Aaron Chadd's right hand that he could squeeze a pewter pot flat."

When Unity returned, her grandson left the cottage and went home, where dwelt Brian and Maude White well above the village, midway between it and the railway station, a quarter of a mile higher still. Here laboured the railwayman and worked hard enough, but without gusto or enthusiasm. He was discontented by nature and must have displayed that quality, whatever his calling or status.

His ambitions were vague and he always declared himself underpaid and overworked. Sport had long become his particular distraction, but opportunities to enjoy it at Wallabrook were small and, in their leisure, both he and his wife escaped from home and sped together to Plymouth, or Exeter, or Torquay, that he might enjoy dog-racing, or a football match, while she could go to the pictures. They had long since ceased to care greatly for each other, being egocentric beyond common, and over-given to the original sin of human selfishness. They were exceedingly indifferent to the claims of community and in consequence unpopular; but experience had shown the pair of them that the fewer our friends, the less our distraction from the cuckoo-call of 'self'. Together they faced life and evaded any obligations it was possible to incur save those demanded by the law. The test of their principles yet awaited them, along with the dangers that promised to accompany it.

Maude White rated her son for coming so late to his dinner and thrust his midday meal before him. She resembled her mother but she lacked the placid and not unamiable expression of Mrs. Blanchard; her grey eyes were sharp enough, yet neither humour nor truth shone out of them. Her hair was Maude's sole beauty—lustrous, auburn, ample and shining. She had tried to sell it and failed to get her price. She was not vain or plagued with petty vices, but a great opportunist, always on the lookout to make money, exceedingly fond of it and avid after a bargain at any time.

One friend had Mrs. White and only one—a childless, Wallabrook widow in easy circumstances, who looked at life from a wider angle than Maude and took her pleasures differently. Thomasina Parsons enjoyed limitless leisure and her first interest and amusement centred in the affairs of her neighbours. She always appeared to know everything there was to know about everybody else—men, women and children. Little was hidden from her investigations, except their mysterious sources; but annoyance often accompanied Thomasina's revelations for those who listened to them—in amazement or exasperation, as the case might be. Her curiosity made her unpopular; yet some admitted its occasional value and, as the prime intelligencer of Wallabrook, she received a guarded measure of respect, usually combined with dislike.

Gilbert ate his ration and told of his morning experience while he did so.

"I went fishing for gran'father and catched a good eatable trout for him this morning, Mother, and Policeman Chadd saw me and came down on the water; but I told him I was in order."

"How's your grandfather?" asked Mrs. White.

"Looks awful. He was thirsty, but going to eat the trout before he drank his whiskey."

"Where he gets the stuff and who pays for it I'd like to know," said his mother.

Gilbert could throw no light on that matter and she spoke again.

"Come he goes," she said, "your grandmother is to live along with us and you'll have to sleep in the cubby-hole under the stairs."

"I'd do all in my power for granny whatever it was," promised her son.

"She's got a good few friends among the farming people and there's Arthur Brimblecombe, the market gardener—a very special friend of hers," his mother told him. "Among them I'm hopeful to find tidy work for you next year."

"So long as it lies in the open air I don't care what I'm going to be," he said. "The only thing I'd hate above all else is butchering."

"You'll do what offers for you to do," she answered.

Brian White entered at this moment. The hours of his activities were uncertain and he came and went from them at all times, but it was not often that he returned at one o'clock and he usually took food to the station with him.

"What are you doing at this hour?" asked Maude. "You don't want anything to eat, do you, Brian?"

"No," he said. "There's a hitch at Tavistock and the down won't be through for an hour. Time for a drink and a smoke."

The porter was a sandy-headed, not bad-looking man of five-and-thirty. His eyes were blue but small, and the lashes yellow, his mouth and chin assertive and his expression sulky. But he was in a good temper.

"Now we're in the saddle, Labour will know how to bide there," he told Maude. "I shan't be a porter on the Great Western Railway much longer, but a Civil Servant attached to the National Railways."

"With better money to it?" asked his wife.

"Surely. More wages for less work. What used to go in dividends for the idle rich will come into our pockets now."

"With tickets cheaper, I should hope," added Maude. "It did ought to be more piled on the first class and more took off the third."

"Higher wages though fewer tips from travellers," explained Brian. "Next thing will be to shut down on the omnibus companies and get them off the roads along with private motor traffic, so as everybody will be forced into the trains. Soak the rich—that's the Government's first job now, to recompense us that put 'em in power. Men like me will work for the State in future; but no more slavery—

just a five-day week and a tidy pension before we grow too old to enjoy it."

"Them that fought the war are getting wonderful gratuities when they're demobbed," Maude told him.

"And so ought the railwaymen," declared Brian. "We sweated for England night and day, same as the soldiers. But what thanks have us had? When I think of the winter nights . . ."

There came a whistle from the great viaduct down the valley and Mr. White rose.

"She's through and on her way," he said, then hastened off.

CHAPTER II

AMONG the last coherent reflections of John Blanchard was a matter concerned with his interment.

"It will be a walking funeral, my love," he said to Unity, "and not much beyond half a mile to carry me. Six men I count upon."

"And plenty ready and willing to do it, Johnny."

"You're right. Though of no account, I can number friends enough to do the job, and if I name them in advance there won't be no bad feeling. I wouldn't like undertaker's men that didn't know or care."

"It will be a compliment for the chosen ones," said Mrs. Blanchard.

"So I intend it, and the well-wishers will understand I couldn't name but half a dozen. There's some have a right to bear me and they must come first."

Unity reflected.

"Arthur Brimblecombe, of course."

"Before all others, Arthur."

"Then Brian White, I suppose. He's your son-in-law and he ought to be there."

"And Gilly. A dour task for a young youth like him; but it will be an adventure for the boy to remember when he grows up."

"I think he ought to be there. It's becoming for him."

"That leaves three and I'd wish Amos Hannaford to be one of them."

"He'd wish it too. Last time I was in the 'Fisherman's' on your account, he hinted, when the end came in God's good time, he'd like to pay his respects that way, being the last honour he could pay to an old customer and valued friend."

"Did he? So he shall, then. Now there's only two called for. I couldn't tell you for why, but I've got a feeling Matthew Owlett might be one of 'em. There's two opinions touching Matt, and some hold he's doubtful, with a lot more to him than meets the eye; but I've found him a very good neighbour of a dark night now and again when I wanted one."

"He's seen you home scores of times, my dear, and he'd think it a nice thing for you to invite him. I've always found Owlett to be a very good man, and he's a lot cleverer than most of the others round about."

"They say he uses his friendship with Sir Gerald for his own ends and, because he's free of the woods and river by night, he's very apt to poach there."

"I don't believe it," declared Unity. "He's friendly with Sir Gerald because he's a great one for natural history and very smart to catch the insects and find the queer creatures Sir Gerald's interested in. That's why the keepers are told that Matt's free to adventure where he will in Oakshotts. But the talk about him stealing game I won't believe in. He's not that sort."

"Even if he was, who am I to feel doubtful about him?" asked John. "I'm come to a time when I ought to think the best possible of all my fellow men now I'm going to part with 'em for evermore. You can tell Matt it will pleasure me if he helps to steer me home again for the last time. And that leaves but one."

Such conversation was giving Unity more pain than Mr. Blanchard imagined.

"We'll decide for the other tomorrow," she said. "Think on something else now."

"I picture it in my mind's eye—nice burying weather and all going very suent and orderly. And a brave lot of flowers, I hope. Naught rounds off a funeral like a good dollop of flowers."

"I'll hurry up with our tea, John," she suggested, and left his bedside, while he found a sort of pleasure in following the familiar details and wondered as to those likely to be present.

"I've been turning over in my mind as to how many's like to see me put away," he said to his wife when she returned. "Not a lot, Unity."

"There very seldom is, John. Folk are busy; but there's a tidy big number are like to bear you in their memory."

Before they had finished, one of whom they had just spoken came to visit Mr. Blanchard, and heard for the first time that John wished him to be a bearer.

Matthew Owlett tapped gently at the door and waited to learn whether the sick man might be seen.

The native presented a challenging figure by reason of his indifference to convention and a gipsy-like love of colour that led him to bedeck himself in brighter fashion than his neighbours; but, for many of them, his circumstances, interests and manner of life were a perpetual theme of argument, and while his raiment no longer surprised, certain antecedents of Mr. Owlett's existence continued to form pleasant material for debate. Some respected him as an original, able and even distinguished man; while others held him to be crafty, cunning and probably dishonest, yet blessed with such mastery of stratagem that, like the green bay tree, he continued to flourish beyond his deserts. For those who took this gloomy view, the very summit of Matthew's turpitude existed in a single, scandalous fact which, once admitted, revealed too certainly the truth of him. A very exceptional accident was responsible for his good fortune and those numbered against him stoutly believed the extraordinary, personal friendship existing between Mr. Owlett and the lord of the manor was repaid by secret infamy.

Others denied this unfriendly conviction and declared that nothing save jealousy inspired it. They granted that Matthew possessed a mysterious side and lived in a world of his own which none, save perhaps Sir Gerald himself, was permitted to enter; but they denied any proof that sinister and unsocial motives inspired him and argued that, if he was in truth a scamp and actually concerned to betray his benefactor, then the baronet would long since have discovered such a thankless line of conduct, withdrawn the light of his countenance and punished Mr. Owlett according to the measure of his offences.

Matthew was an old sailor, and during thirty years in the Merchant Marine had visited many South American ports, and gratified his passion for the wonders of Nature to the best of his powers. After every voyage he came home with a full ditty-box of strange odds and ends gleaned in strange places. Best he loved birds and insects, returning with the skins and feathers of tropic fowls and the entire corpses of butterflies, moths and glittering beetles.

These things he dearly loved, and though, while she lived, Jane Owlett kept a restraining hand on his specimens, now that she was gone they emerged from their drawers and cabinets to cover the walls and tables of his parlour and turn the old traveller's dwelling-house into a museum. It was after he left the sea that Matthew's friendship with Sir Gerald came about, and his own enterprise had to be thanked for this important event. Like everybody else he knew the lord of the manor's real fame arose from a lifetime of devotion to certain branches of natural history, and none had ever more respected and admired the squire's importance as an eminent entomologist than Mr. Owlett. Upon the strength of it he had long ago ventured to approach Sir Gerald by letter and invited him, if the idea were welcome, to visit the Owlett home when next in Wallabrook and cast his accomplished eyes over the mariner's hoard of treasures.

No reply came to this invitation and Matthew feared that he had been too pushing; but a week later the man of science appeared one afternoon in his motor-car and declared that it would give him pleasure to inspect Matthew's collection. The old and crippled baronet anticipated no great pleasure from such a survey; but he did not as yet know his man and now quickly discovered great possibilities, for Matthew revealed more wisdom than the sea could teach him. He was indeed highly intelligent and possessed just that ardent love of Nature missing from most of Sir Gerald's local circle. Among the many strange objects that the old sailor had to show were rare and well-preserved insects from afar, and amidst many other specimens he submitted examples of just those things his guest best knew and valued.

"Out foreign the moths and butterflies run a lot bigger and brighter than what they can reach to in our climate, your honour," explained Matthew. "Here's fine creatures I took on the coast of Honduras—the butterflies by day, the wondrous night-moths after dark. I was free to sugar a palm tree or two at the jungle edge and so got 'em."

The visitor's fading eyes glittered at an insect of large size—a butterfly with fore wings of royal purple streaked with white, and hind wings also deep purple, but surrounded by a deep border of orange gold.

"*Caligo uranus!*" murmured Sir Gerald, "but what a *Caligo*! And this remarkable moth! *D. Elpenor*—a tropic variant of our familiar Elephant moth. Gorgeous! I salute you, Owlett! You will certainly not wish to part with these things while you live, for they must be a marvellous addition to your life; but be careful to bequeath them to the nation. They are priceless and that is your sacred duty."

The old man stayed an hour and found no little to delight him, while his host presently ventured to ask whether he might some day be privileged to see Sir Gerald's world-famous collection. He was invited to do so and, much pleased to find his hope gratified, on a future occasion he took with him to the manor both the Caligo and Elephant moth as gifts for this new and eminent friend. Thus had begun that strange union of kindred spirits, and when the old scientist desired to pay for trophies so outstanding and suggested twenty-five guineas for the pair of them, Matthew begged that no such things should be mentioned.

"I'm very well recompensed by the pleasure of having 'em accepted, your honour," he declared, "and if there's aught else I can do to serve you, you only need to name it. I'm a bit of a night-bird and tolerable clever at treacling for moths by night. It was always a hobby of mine, so I could work for you in that matter if the fancy takes you. Then, again, you're famed for knowing a lot about the fungus family, and I'd be very willing to work at them in season and fetch along anything outstanding I might collect. At your age you wouldn't poke about much in your woods and stream-sides after fungus; but unless you've got understanding men around you to explore on your account, I'd be ready and willing to serve in that fashion."

The prospect of an enthusiast at his service pleased Sir Gerald. He was eighty-two years old now and beyond the physical activity of a collector, but his ardour continued undiminished and Matthew promised to be a useful minion. The lord of the manor seldom met anybody with his own proclivities and was indeed aware that the county not only lacked all interest in them but thought no better of him for devoting his life to matters of such unimportance.

He had agreed to Mr. Owlett's suggestions and the old sailor responded faithfully enough, proved exceedingly skilful in catching moths and butterflies and in discovering obscure fungi hidden among the depths of the Oakshotts woodlands. He learned quickly, studied the books his employer directed him to read and was now become not only a paid servant but personal friend—a man capable of giving Sir Gerald considerable pleasure. The veteran entomologist had never married and his lonely old age found satisfaction in Mr. Owlett. Matthew was amusing and that element of mystery about him, although it irritated his neighbours and made them suspicious, entertained his new and exalted friend. The union between master and man itself excited curiosity in Wallabrook when first established, and, in the case of Tobias Trimble, the head keeper at Oakshotts, created profound distrust and dislike. But his animosity was all on Toby's side, for Matthew quarrelled with none.

"Mysteries I may hold," he said on one occasion, "but none to throw a shadow on my honesty, and when Toby in his tantrums says that I'm a poacher and not trustable, then, if I was to name such slanders to Sir Gerald, he might send the poor man flying without a character; but we must be patient with Trimble. Where there's game there's poachers, and, where the head keeper haps to be a fool, birds will be stole. Once a man proves himself weak in the head, then allowance must be made, and though Sir Gerald cares little for his game, he did once care a lot for Toby's father, because that man saved Squire's life, or he thinks he did, half a century ago."

Now his only child, Nancy, looked after Mr. Owlett. She was two-and-twenty, heart-whole and fancy free as yet; but she often declared that a home of her own without the eternal memorials to her father's industry would not prove unwelcome. She was a dark, lithe young woman, three inches taller than her parent and devoted to him, but not averse from the thought of leaving him some day.

Matthew now learned from Mrs. Blanchard that his dying friend would like to see him for a few minutes and ascended to the sick man's bedside. He was clad with his usual contempt for convention and wore knickerbockers with blue stockings beneath them. An apple-green sweater clung tightly to his lean body and his grey head was bare, for a hat he never favoured except in the coldest weather. In his ears glimmered little gold rings—a relic of seafaring days. He shaved clean and his crinkled and deeply lined face was full of animation, his dark brown eyes revealed ceaseless curiosity and a questing mind forever on the move. The lid of his right eye was partially and permanently lowered, but it did not interfere with exceptionally keen sight.

John smiled wanly to see him.

"I had you on my tongue not a minute ago, Matt," he said. "Me and the missis were thinking upon my coffin-bearers, for you've got to settle little things like that while your wits bide clear. And I'm wishful for you to be among 'em."

Owlett's quick glance darted from John's face to Unity and she answered his unspoken question.

"I hope you'll see your way, Matt," she declared.

"A most proper task for an old friend, my dears," he answered. "I've took your weight now and again, John, and helped to steer you home, same as you would have lent a hand if it was me. Nobody will miss you worse than I shall, except your partner herself."

"I should wish for you and Brimblecombe to take the lead and the others follow after," explained John, "and I should like for you to go all colours of the rainbow, Matt, same as the butterflies and toadstools you're always after."

"Nobody's ever seen you in blacks, Matt," so Unity reminded him. "Have you got any blacks?"

"No, but fear nothing as to that. I'll show up as black as a crow, I promise you, though the feathers will have to be borrowed. But don't you dwell on no sad details, John. Leave them to those ready and willing to undertake 'em when the time comes. Sir Gerald's prone now and again to dwell upon his latter end and what will happen after; but I always strive to change the subject and bring him back to his fungi or what not."

"Does he ordain to lie in the Fortesque family vault?" asked Unity.

"No, my dear. Sir Gerald's all against going to ground at all. He says he had enough of his relations when they was alive and don't want to keep company with them till the Last Trump. He's going to be cremated first and then his ashes scattered where Walla comes down over the waterfall. I ventured to tell him it was a morbid subject and better left alone. But he soon throws off his gloom and grants that the world's no place for the old nowadays, and often the most dignified thing for a man of his years is to pass out and make room for somebody usefuller."

"In his case there's none to follow him," said Unity.

"No, his title will be done for, and he says, when his death duties are paid, Oakshotts will be done for too."

"Do he hold any views on the hereafter?" asked John. "That's where my own thoughts turn now and again of late."

"His honour keeps an open mind as to that," explained Matthew. "It ain't one of his favourite subjects for discourse, but he told me once that where you've got no data for speculation, then it's waste of time to speculate. He said how, in his eighty years and over, he'd lived to see the parsons give up hellfire, and that was a good move in his opinion, because he'd never found any definite data for hellfire; but as to the future, he put it like this: 'If a conscious future awaits us, Owlett,' he said, 'then the child that dies at five years old knows more about it than all the wisdom of all the ages has yet discovered.' He holds we'd do best to go about our business and justify this existence, which is better than wishful thinking about another."

"Comforting in a way that a clever man like Sir Gerald don't know any more touching heaven than us common people," suggested John.

"Data's the thing, my dears. We must have data with a scientific mind; facts is what counts. Butterflies and moths are facts of Nature; angels may be also, but we don't know, so 'tis vain to waste much precious time upon 'em. If ever the baronet lives to see 'em, he may find they belong to an upper range of the lepidoptera beyond human knowledge; but he'd be the first to welcome such glorious creatures. One thing looks to be certain for Sir Gerald: if there's no insect life up over, the gentleman will find he's drawn a blank."

"There will be plenty get there only to feel what they find ain't so precious to them as what they've lost," said Unity. "You for example, Matthew, because no proper sailor likes to feel he's going where there's no more sea."

"I don't worry. There's no data," replied Matthew stoutly; but Mrs. Blanchard withstood him.

"That won't do," she said. "There's the Word, and if the Word ain't data, where do you and your master to Oakshotts think to find yourselves?"

"Now you venture on ticklish ground, which is neither land nor water, Unity, and best given a miss," he replied; "but one man's data may turn out another man's delusion and when faith's up against facts, where are you?"

"Good's one thing and evil's another thing," said Unity, "and that's a fact."

"Surely—with plenty of data to go upon," agreed Owlett.

They pursued their conversation in undertones because John was sleeping peacefully, and now the visitor rose and took his leave.

"Us won't wake him, but time I slipped off," he said. "Just popped in for friendship to the pair of you. Tell him I shall hope to see him again before he's finished and, in any case, will be along with the bearers at the end."

"Good night, Matt, and thank you for looking him up. You was always one who saw the best of him," said Mrs. Blanchard.

"I did that,"admitted Matthew. "He was a big-hearted, kindly soul, friendly disposed and trustful of human nature and never heard to speak evil of none. And, given heaven, you'll meet him there some day as sure as eggs is eggs, my dear."

"So I hope and believe," she said.

"Oh yes. And the first thing John's like to tell you will be that it was your good work saved him and got him up there. You'll traipse the golden streets together so bright as peacock butterflies some day, I shouldn't wonder. No data for it, mind you, but——"

The old woman looked at him shrewdly and interrupted.

"Go home and don't laugh at holy things, Matt," she ordered.

Owlett went his way into the June dusk and marked a mist

rising off the river as he prepared to cross the bridge, where he fell in with Arthur Brimblecombe, the nurseryman. They were both undersized men, but while the old sailor carried no spare flesh, being lean, wiry and active as a weasel, his friend happened to be built on a different pattern. Stout and florid, he moved slowly with a dignity all his own. His round face was well filled out, his 'newgate fringe' well trimmed, his eyes of a pale brown and his brow but little wrinkled. He carried himself upright, despite his stuggy frame, and loved hard work. Concerning vegetables and rotation of crops he knew everything that there was to know. Arthur never failed of good-willing to those he regarded as personal friends, and among them the Blanchards always came first. Indeed Unity had excited his attention while he was yet a lad, and when she married, the spectacle of her devotion to her futile husband was so steadfast and beautiful that it had long wakened in him a genuine admiration.

For Mr. Blanchard, without the light that Unity threw upon him, he might have shared the general opinion, that John was no object for sympathy at any time; but she had explained her partner's unhappy weakness and lack of will-power, dwelling rather upon his invincible good nature and generous disposition, and Mr. Brimblecombe thus came to regard poor John with affection and take a sort of proprietary interest in him. His regard was repaid with devotion and the weakling felt proud of a friendship so undeserved. Now Matthew Owlett noted the basket that his neighbour carried.

"You'll be going just where I've come from, Arthur," he said. "Blanchard let me wait on him after his tea tonight and I talked him to sleep and never asked Unity what the doctor thought last time he looked in."

"I take John the best that's offering," explained Mr. Brimblecombe. "I've got some early peas tonight to surprise him. I always say the dying should have first call on the fruits of the earth so long as they can digest 'em. Every second day I go, Matt, and he looks forward to seeing me, and I lay he was very pleased to see you. As for doctor, I wouldn't go so far as to say he's mishandled John; but perhaps a younger man might have made a braver fight for him."

Owlett shook his head.

"Dr. Bridger's old, but his experience atones for it, Arthur. I know what you feel as to Blanchard and you have been his mainstay and godsend for twenty years, if not more. I'd even go so far as to say you have lengthened his life. But touching Bridger, feel no fear. Bridger always knows what a sick man hasn't got and frees your mind as to that; but I grant he doesn't always know what we have got. When he says you may safely leave a patient to Nature, then you know he's beat and can't tell for Adam whether your innards are off the rails, or only just sulking for a day or two. Sir Gerald likes him very well and tells me that half an hour of the doctor's company will often do you more good than a month of his medicines."

"I couldn't wish for a nicer man than Bridger when there's nothing the matter," admitted Arthur, "and in Johnny's case no doubt there wasn't no lasting cure. He's due to pass out any time now."

"And keeping a stiff upper lip about it, I was glad to see. Very wishful for you and me to be bearers at his funeral. You, of course, first and foremost, but I was a bit flattered he fancied me for one."

"If he's got so far as the bearers, then the end looks to be close," said Brimblecombe. "I've told Unity to trust me for the funeral details. She must be spared all that's possible."

"There won't be no great rally of neighbours, but trust you to do what's fitting. Call on me if I can lift a hand, if only for his partner's sake," promised Matthew.

The other regarded him suspiciously. Arthur cherished ideas as to the future; but a sudden fear that Owlett hid ambitions of like kind now caused him to make abrupt departure.

"I'll be seeing you, no doubt," he said. "Good night."

The nurseryman marched off and soon reached his destination.

"And how's Johnny tonight, my dear?" he inquired of Unity as she opened the door to him.

"He has had a good day and a comfortable one, Arthur. Your basket I see, filled as usual to overflowing. Never was such a generous chap as you."

"Some early peas and even a carrot or two—small, of course—in fact no bigger than radishes—still, carrots. Where greenstuff's concerned he shan't suffer no lack. And a tidy lettuce or two for you, Unity. I always say what serves a rabbit will always be enough for you. You don't miss red meat in these bleak days, same as I do."

Mrs. Blanchard smiled.

"The times are hard on working men," she admitted.

"Worse for us masters who employ 'em," he explained. "Labour's got to such a fantastical value that I tremble and dream ugly dreams. Shall I go up to John?"

"Not now. He's in a very fine patch of sleep and it will build him up against the night-time."

"Then you ought to be asleep also; but I can see in your face you're cruel short of it. Why don't Maude come down and do her bit and give you your proper rest?"

Unity shook her head.

"She's always hated her father, to be honest, Arthur."

"Never saw the goodness and even greatness behind his fatal weakness."

"She's built so. Weakness is the one thing she won't forgive in anybody. She says we owe it to ourselves to be strong."

Mr. Brimblecome came in, sat down and lighted his pipe.

"I'll bide half an hour against Johnny wakes up," he said. "And as for your Maude, I dislike her more than any living creature in my acquaintance. She's a mark on what she owes herself, no doubt, but them that bleat loudest about that are the first to overlook what they owe other people. How you and John ever got the creature is an undying mystery to all that know you."

"She's built so. Very unfortunate for her as well as us, Arthur. Folk say 'God help her husband', but never 'God help her'. I reckon it was Brian White went far to make her what she is."

"No, Unity, she was always a blot on your family long before she took White; and while we are on this painful subject, I may tell you that I properly hate your intentions to go and live with them."

"I properly hate my intentions too," confessed Mrs. Blanchard, "but it's my duty and I must do according. First there's John's wish in the matter. He don't see me in one of the manor almshouses, though I could get one when number three's vacant. Which will be soon, Widow Toozey being ninety-four and fading fast; and secondly seeing that John will leave no money, the old age pension's all I've got and so it's Maude's duty to look after me. But there's a lot more to it than that: there's my grandson. I care a great deal more for Gilbert than what his parents do. The boy isn't fashioned like her nor yet his father, and I'm glad of it. He's got to keep school for a bit longer yet and then he'll be marketable and Maude will market him to the highest bidder. Till then it's my duty to watch over him and I'm very well capable of so doing. And never better than if I live in the same house with him. His future means a lot to me, Arthur, and not until his mother, or me myself, has got him a good sound job of work, with trustworthy people, shall I lose sight of him."

"And what about your comfort and convenience meantime?" he asked.

"It won't be comfortable nor yet convenient along with Brian and Maude; but most like it's only for a year," she answered, "and then by the rights of Nature Mrs. Toozey will be on her way and I'll seek first refusal for the almshouse."

"That's how you figure it; but I may tell you there's somebody else is like to figure it differently. However, the future can look after itself, as it always does and always will do. It don't often go according to human plan and I hope and trust it ain't going according to the new Government's plan, else all my customers, and myself along with 'em, will be in a mess before next Christmas, if not sooner. Your John knows that. Seeing where he lies, it's wonderful to me how clear his intellects remain."

"He always had a very good brain away from the drink, Arthur."

"He had, and skill likewise. There was nothing he couldn't do when he gave his mind to it, but quite a lot of things he wouldn't do and money wouldn't have made him do 'em."

"He never could grasp the ways of money," said Mrs. Blanchard. "Talk on that subject made him impatient. Patient with humans and always ready and willing to pleasure them when able on his clear days; but money; he hated the name of it and never could see how your credit depends upon how you handle it. Maude has tried over and over again to make it clear to him, for nobody respects money more than she do; but again and again, when she'd cornered him with the bitter truth about money, he'd only tell her to shut her mouth. 'It's agreed to be the root of all evil,' so Johnny would say, 'and being so, the less any honest man have to do with the beastly stuff, the better.' "

Unity laughed at the recollection.

"Poor dear, he didn't have much to do with it, sure enough," she said.

"Will he leave any debts calling for cash?" asked Mr. Brimblecombe, "because if so——"

"No, no. Nothing to name, Arthur."

The nurseryman looked at his watch.

"Must be pushing off to lock up. I've missed four cucumbers from under glass lately and can guess who lifted 'em. Some of us ain't so honest as you could wish, nor yet so god-fearing."

" 'Tis the war and the shortness of everything that have done it, Arthur."

"The black market looks to be worse than what the black-out was," he assured her, "but they say in Tavistock it's a very convenient invention for the Government and they ain't fretting overmuch against it."

CHAPTER III

WHEN Peter Chadd returned to his mother and his new labours in the police service of Wallabrook, Mrs. Dinah Chadd became a changed woman and began to regain her youth. While he was absent, first at the war and then in training for his chosen task, she had missed him sadly; but now, with Peter under her roof once more, Dinah's anxieties diminished, despite the sinister possibilities that ever lurk in a policeman's path.

"It shows the queerness of our common nature," declared Mr. Owlett, when his daughter Nancy called attention to the fact. "After Dinah lost her husband, who was always a thorn in the flesh of the law till he got his last sentence and died in gaol before he'd served it, then the poor woman blossomed out again and was happier than she ever had been since she took him. Aaron Chadd only wanted one more year to go before he died, and the parlous thought of him coming back to Dinah aged her till she looked seventy, though still short of forty; and then when Peter left her, she withered again; but now his coming back has bucked her up once more. That's how fate worked upon her well at last. Against that you need to remember there's bad blood in Peter's veins and only time will show the truth about him. I've warned his mother as to that, but she feels very sure there's no weak spot in his character."

"We'll hope he's so honest as he's big," declared Nancy.

"Yes, he gets the size and strength from his father and naught else, I trust. I'd say he lacks Aaron's brain-power, which may turn out to be a good thing."

"Learning to be a policeman has brightened him up, perhaps," suggested Nancy.

Mrs. Chadd was a gentle soul and by nature retiring. None ever quarrelled with her and all respected her—not for any outstanding quality, but because she was well-to-do. After her husband's death she had inherited money from an uncle and now lived a quiet, self-contained life without enemies or many close friends. Matthew Owlett enjoyed her confidence and she relied upon him for advice when it was needed. He told her that she was like the nocturnal moths.

"You ain't the top flower of the bunch, Dinah," he would often say, "but the better folk get to know you the more they recognise your good parts, if they have got the wit to do so."

She was indeed moth-like in her attire and favoured greys, browns and blacks, while Mr. Owlett's love of colour often reached a pitch to cause her uneasiness. Her face was naturally pale and her blue eyes reflected early spring rather than summer. When a girl, Mrs. Chadd was considered beautiful. She had run away to be married at the age of seventeen, for in those bygone days Aaron Chadd's character was already well known to everybody but Dinah herself, yet, defying her parents, she had sped joyfully to her doom.

Six weeks were past since her son returned from a routine duty at the churchyard, for in the event of a funeral Inspector Manley always sent one of his constables to attend it. Now Peter came back to dinner after the interment of John Blanchard and his mother asked a question.

"You needn't tell me the details, Peter, because I shall get 'em from Mr. Owlett next time we meet, no doubt. Matthew hates black and, though I couldn't name it to him, of course, I did pray he might be doing something about it today. Poor John marked him for bearer and I've been wondering what the mischief he donned for his sad task."

"He was in funeral black, Mother, like all the rest. He took the head of the coffin along with Mr. Brimblecombe and then came Mr. Hannaford along with Brian White, and Gilly White brought up the rear with another young boy—a friend of his—to keep him company. I couldn't say who he was. Mr. Blanchard didn't want but four, really. He was gone so light as a windlestraw before his end, so I heard."

"Thank God Owlett went decent in any case," said Mrs. Chadd.

"Plenty of bright colour there without him," explained Peter. "Lots of flowers, but only a very small sprinkling of folk. He's put along with the Blanchards."

"They were a family very apt to cling together in death—all but John Blanchard's brother James, who went foreign and never came back," said Mrs. Chadd. "All gone now but Unity, and she tells me she'll lie beside John, and not a Blanchard left after that. She was one of they Tavistock Princes by birth."

"All went very suent and the few gathered together soon sped away after," continued Peter. "Mrs. White took her mother home, and when I left there was only Gilly White and his boy friend watching sexton fill up the grave and pile the flowers upon it."

"There won't be no funeral sermon come Sunday, I'm afraid," sighed Mrs. Chadd. "Parson only preaches for the outstanding ones, and there was nothing special to poor John's credit where the reverend could pin a discourse."

She heard a day later from Mr. Owlett how he had come by his funeral garments.

"The butler up to Oakshotts lent 'em to me," explained Matthew. "Mr. Chave's a very good friend of mine and it lies in my power to favour him and save him trouble now and again. He was very willing to lend me some of his clothes, which came near enough to my body after Nancy had took 'em in and fitted 'em on. Everything went orderly at the graveside. No pretence of weeping and wailing, or nothing like that. Unity was white as a ghost, poor lass, but firm as a rock, and the flowers from the well-wishers made a cheerful blaze. Weather genial and all passed off without a ripple, same as Johnny would have liked for it to do."

So departed the last of a long Blanchard line, and if undercurrents of feeling or eddies of distress existed in Unity's heart, none saw them. She was a realist and respected her friends the more that none among them approached her with unreal sympathy. For her, few readjustments needed to be made. The future would see her in her daughter's home at least until her grandson left it, and that was far enough to look forward over an uninviting prospect. By anticipation its probable realities were already accepted.

"I know precisely what I've got to expect," she told Mr. Brimblecombe, "so there's nothing coming to hope or fear."

He was less sanguine, however.

"There's always going to be two to one against you at 'Laburnum Lodge'," he said. "Remember that."

"I shall be there to keep an eye on Gilly," she reminded him. "But the boy mustn't favour me above Maude, because she would be jealous if he showed he liked me better than her. He does, of course, so I'll need to make him guileful in that matter. She's an uncommon clean woman, Maude is, and everything will be nice in that respect; but how much she may expect me to do for her, one way and another, I've yet to find out. There'll be lots of time on my hands for chores and we shall neighbour all right, most like."

Mrs. White described the situation from her point of view on an occasion when she met her first and only friend, Thomasina Parsons, at the village grocer's, some six weeks after John Blanchard's death. Mrs. Parsons was a full-bosomed and expansive personality with a high-coloured countenance, an unusually massive nose and large, inquisitive eyes. But of the senses, her hearing was by far the most acute. Her ears never missed anything, and they handed on the least breath or whisper of information to her wits, where every item of importance would be digested and its implications duly considered. Her deductions were sometimes incorrect and she hushed them up accordingly; but not seldom they resulted in a triumph and were proclaimed to all who would listen. As a cloak to this insatiable curiosity, Mrs. Parsons affected a lighthearted, merry manner, treating her discoveries with a humorous touch and laughing even at the most sinister suggestions.

"Probably it isn't true," she would often conclude, "but if it is, then of course one oughtn't to be amused."

News was her sole devotion. A few admired her as a mistress of racy novelties; many disliked and held her a bird of ill omen; pointing out that, whatever the woman might tell, it always boded ill for somebody. A wit in the public bar of the 'Fisherman's Welcome' had once called her 'Peeping Thomasina', and even those well disposed to Mrs. Parsons henceforth so proclaimed her behind her back. She herself was long familiar with this jest and roared with merriment when first she learned it.

"And how's it going at home, my love?" she asked Mrs. White as they proceeded together. "D'you find your old lady settling down to your nice ways and punctual time-keeping?"

"Tolerable well, Tommy," answered Maude. "I said, when mother came, that it would be a wise thing to go on as I was in the habit of going, and she agreed it was wise to be steadfast especially if you've got a working man to look after who's got to keep his hours. She's a poor riser and always was, and I allow for that because my father's illness has put a tax on her and she's still short of sleep. Most days my husband takes his breakfast at seven, if not earlier, but mother can't make it, and don't, or won't, show up till after eight. I'm driving her quiet and steady to better her hours and she will presently. She's very well in her health yet don't take life in general so serious as it ought to be took. A strong will, but not so strong as mine, nor yet Brian's. She's active for her age and tiresome of course. I never heard of any old person that wasn't tiresome."

"Especially they old ones who must be doing, and won't understand their ways and silly habits are all no more than a nuisance for us who bear the burden, Maude," said Thomasina. "How is she on the rations?"

"She gets her share same as we do, and no more. Mother is prone to grumble at her breakfast, for she's always greedy after she gets up. Arthur Brimblecombe toddles down twice weekly with nice vegetables for her, and mother sees that she has 'em; but when it first came to new potatoes, Brian helped himself and me out of her dish and she didn't raise any objection to that."

"Old Brimblecombe always had a soft place in his mind for Mrs. Blanchard. Long before your father died I was the first to notice it. You watch him, Maude. He may dream of putting in his oar now."

Mrs. White gave one of her rare, snappy laughs, like a terrier wakened from sleep by a sound none hears but himself.

"No fear there. Mother's pretty well played out. She's had enough of men. She thinks a lot of Arthur because he's a reminder of the past; but the past is all that much interests her. The present bores her, except for her attachment to Gilly, and she's a bit downcast these days and don't feel to no great hopes of the future."

"No chance of her cutting her own thread, or anything suchlike?"

Maude considered.

"Funny you should say that. Brian's sick of her because she contradicts his politics. He's said more than once to get rids of her would be a good job. I said the only thing might make her consider going would be if she found herself too uncomfortable to stop. He hates her naturally. She gets on his nerves and don't see the salvation of socialism for the labouring classes. She laughs at what he says, and if there's one thing Brian gets in a rage about it is to be laughed at. Even I never do it, though a woman can't live with a man unless she laughs at him or cries at him sometimes."

"So I found. And then there's her money. She wouldn't have much saved, but no doubt you'll get it when she goes."

"We don't know. When I asked her about her money, she was short and told me to mind my own business."

"It is your business, Maude. You've been a good, faithful daughter to her and it's your right to know where she may will to leave it if she's got any."

"She gave my father most of what she had while he was well enough to spend it, and she spent it on him when he wasn't. But Brian has an idea she may have three figures hidden somewhere. He knows I'm a hoarder and says I got the habit from mother. But I say that if she had any money to name, she wouldn't have thrown in her fag-end of life with us."

"Very interesting. Perhaps Mr. Brimblecombe knows. I always wondered myself why Mrs. Blanchard ordained to settle with you."

"So did I," said Maude. "She told me it was my father's dying wish she should, so she came according. I expect that's the truth about it. Father never liked me because I spoke too straight to him about his bad habits, and so did my husband; but he was very fond of Gilly, and mother's silly over him. She'd spoil him and bring him up a rotter if she could."

"He's a dear boy, but don't take after you nor yet his father, so I've noticed."

"He don't. He's a poor thing without a spark of cleverness and only wasting his time at school; but he'll be quit of that soon now and earning money, if I know anything."

"I'm sorry for the boys," declared Mrs. Parsons. "They are anchored to the schools, whether they are learnable or not, and then, once they are free to make themselves useful, there's conscription hanging over 'em and the chance to be shot, same as their poor fathers were—growing nearer and nearer every day, by all accounts. Some understanding men say England begins to look parlous like it was done for."

"The upper classes are done for," agreed Mrs. White, "but not the labouring classes. I forget how many millions and millions of money the labouring classes have saved by now and no Government would dare to lay a finger upon their money. But the upper-class money will be took for the State, so soon as they've passed laws to take it."

They discussed the situation as indicated by Maude and her friend declared some doubts.

"It will be a nice question where to draw the line between capital and labour," she said, "because if all savings is going to be took except labour's savings, then who's going to pay the labouring men their wages?"

"That's easy enough," explained Maude. "Labour's to be paid by its own fruits of industry. Instead of going to the capitalists and sweaters and tyrants, it's coming to the earners. They'll get what they earn instead of having most of it stole from them. You ask Brian to tell you how it's going to work. He's got his faults, as you know, but he do understand politics."

"He's clever about dog-racing and football pools too," said Thomasina.

But Maude was not prepared to admire these activities.

"I don't hold with pools and he knows it," she answered. "Brian won't be no playboy so long as he's under my command. There's only one way to save money, but a darned sight too many ways to waste it if you're built like what he is."

There came a night when the railwayman's wife found him disposed to discuss their private affairs. He had heard something and it had cheered him. He was apt to be noisy about his grievances and not much concerned with those of anybody else; but his woes resulted from no fanatical desire for a better world. Only the need to earn a living in this one troubled him. He resented his work, loved his pleasures and was under a hazy opinion that coming changes were going to lessen the first and greatly increase the second. No moral or social considerations bothered him; but money in his pocket he ever desired and, while he respected Maude's thrift and able control of his wages on principle, he often deplored her extreme parsimony when it came between him and the attractions of the moment. She was stronger than he and dominated as a rule, while in his absolute indifference to principle and common traditions of behaviour he proved more potent than his partner. They influenced each other, but for the worse in either case.

Brian waited that night until Unity and his son had gone to bed, as they usually did an hour earlier than himself and Maude. Then he spoke what was in his mind.

"I met Mrs. Mudge going down to Plymouth today," he said. "Just had half a minute before her train came in. She saw your mother yesterday for the first time since John Blanchard died, and she was properly shocked to mark the change in her. She looked to be a lot aged and broken, so Mrs. Mudge thought. I hadn't considered the serious chances of your mother's going, Maude, but she may be petering out faster than we think for. To be honest, nothing would suit us better than if she went. Then you'd have her money and I'd have peace. You think there's no money to name; I reckon there may be a bit, but, apart from that, I'd be a lot more comfortable if she was away and you'd have our spare room you could let for more profit than she's worth."

"She'll abide by what father wanted to happen," said his wife. "Mother's here for her lifetime anyway—long or short."

"Freedom was banished out of my house when she came in it," he grumbled, "and what's a man's life without freedom in his home? Everything I say is wrong and I can't let myself go and talk straight before her."

"If she heard you say some of the things I've heard, maybe that would fire her quicker than anything," suggested Maude.

"As to her life being long or short," he continued, "we might do something about that on a sideline—just something with no name to it. You could tighten up a bit in the matter of food and comfort to make her feel doubtful if her life's good enough. A bit of underground work to weaken the woman. She's a blasted bore, money or no money, and she hates us anyway."

Mrs. White regarded these suggestions without emotion. Brian never concealed his opinions, however dissolute, from her, but she knew they meant nothing and she seldom troubled to argue against them. When herself disposed to attack, she always knew the right weapon. Ridicule invariably angered the railwayman, and she found an easy subject now.

"I'd say mother angers you a lot worse than she bores you, Brian," she suggested. "I wish you'd heard what she told me yesterday. She thought you might make a very good wolf in a pack along with others like yourself; but hadn't the guts, nor yet the wits, to lead a pack. All thunder and no lightning you are—so mother said."

She laughed and her husband became instantly enraged.

"Then you can tell the old bitch to watch her step!" he shouted. "I don't take that sort of damned insolence from man nor woman neither!"

It was Maude's habit to make him furious, then calm him down again.

"So I told her," she answered, "to accuse you of weakness is just the right way to make you show your strength. I know that very well and I warned her that she would go too far some day. 'He's a fierce and passionate man, Mother,' I said. 'He's got his convictions and might show up to surprise you and terrify you if anything happened to make him go off the handle. And if you are called to live in a lion's den, then you'd best to treat the lion civil, whatever your opinion happens to be.' We can tighten up a bit as you suggest," she went on. "Mother ain't all regatta and fireworks, I grant you. I don't like living with her any more than you do. I never liked her and she never liked me, and I was thankful when I escaped from my home and came to you. But it's no use just bullying her. I'll think how best we can shift her on to somebody else. She knows she's far from welcome and we might rub that in a bit more, but there don't look to be any urgent need to do anything about it for the minute."

"For two pins I'd poison the old devil and chance it," he said.

"No need for you to talk like that, Brian. There might come conditions in life when a man would find himself tempted to do a crime for his self-respect and if he wanted to go on calling himself a man. And if you was faced with anything like that I'd be sorry for your enemy. But a powerless old soul like mother ain't going to make such an enemy. She's quick on the uptake and will let her tongue run away with her, and she ain't the only one to do so; but she's got a queer idea of what's funny and will often talk rubbish for a joke, though most time nobody sees the joke but herself."

"I hate like hell to see her looking at me and laughing at what I've got to say."

"So do I," agreed Maude. "It's beastly of her, but she's too old to change now. Just bear with her, same as you would bear with a machine on the railway past its work. Time will scrap her soon enough. Living along with mother may blind us to the changes in her, but if other people, like Mrs. Mudge, mark 'em, be sure they are there. Time's our side, be it as it will."

"What are you gaining by her per week?" he asked.

"Three to five shillings profit. And every penny saved. Trust me for that. So you can pacify yourself for the minute."

He subsided.

"If I thought she was putting on you——"

"Nobody puts on me, my dear. She always lends a hand when I call upon her and often wants to do things I choose to do myself."

Brian was on night work and now prepared to go to it.

"So long as you know my opinions, enough said," he answered, then left her.

Elsewhere that night, under the light of the moon, another resident of Wallabrook had accomplished something of note and captured an exceptionally fine 'Death's-head' moth, the largest of European Sphinxes. The creature's passion for honey had proved its undoing and, on the morrow, Matthew Owlett, conscious of achievement, conveyed it to Oakshotts. Sir Gerald greeted him with friendship and warmed into enthusiasm before the moth. He was an interesting old man upon his subject and entertained definite though antiquated views on most others. Inheriting strong conservative opinions, the baronet changed them when he was still a youth, but returned to them again in middle age. Now he remained a Victorian 'die-hard', though in truth no subject save his own greatly attracted him. Political, international and social questions passed him by.

As a Justice of the Peace he insisted on doing what he believed to be his duty and was exceedingly stern with all who dared to traverse the game laws—so much so that Mr. Westover, clerk of the local Magistrates' Bench, would sometimes be constrained to point out the limited extent of his powers; but for the rest, as a man of science, Sir Gerald recognised the adamant law of change and, while lamenting the universal upheaval, accepted it for the most part as inevitable, and only regretted that he had lived to experience its full severity.

There was a sub-acid flavour in his comments on life in general that did not add to the number of his friends; and now, still active-minded, he pursued the more difficult and abstruse problems of entomology with his old ardour. But he had become very lame and his eyes began to fail him. In person the ancient man was tall, white-bearded, and with an abstracted but amiable expression. The hair of his beard grew thin and his high-domed brow had lost its covering, but he wore a black silken cap upon it, and when he took the air, in his Bath chair, or a small carriage impelled by himself, he would wear a soft black felt hat with a broad brim and lofty crown. His clothes were of loose tweed, well worn and shabby, but he was particular in this matter regarding other people and liked his attendants to come suitably clad, smart and tidy before him.

Sir Gerald now donned another pair of glasses and paid some silent devotion to the great dead insect. Then he addressed Matthew.

"You have done well," he declared. "This is somewhat rare in the West of England, though I have taken it at Oakshotts on various occasions in the past. *Acherontia atropos*, at its best. For many generations this moth has been an object of ill omen and a harbinger of evil to the vulgar. Incidentally it is the swiftest flying insect known to science and the only one that emits sound. Did it utter a sort of subdued squeak when you took it off your smear?"

"No, your honour. It hated being caught but didn't say nothing. You may say you caught it yourself, because it was your directions that I followed. Speaking of 'Death's-heads' in general, you told me that they loved honey and would even go into hives and brave the bees for it, and you said the female was given to laying her eggs on the potato plants. So last night I smeared a trap with honey from the comb and set it up alongside Mr. Trimble's vegetable patch behind the south lodge where he lives. And darned angry he'd have been if he'd seen me; but he was long since in bed and asleep by then. And sure enough, round two o'clock of the morning I got it."

The scientist sat apparently lost before the sinister beauties of *Acherontia atropos*. He had a way of paying no apparent attention to a speaker and concerned with some private matter. It was a habit that caused indignation sometimes; but Sir Gerald usually registered any remark correctly enough, and would often surprise a speaker by returning to it long after he had spoken. He did so now, for, following further comments on the moth as an arrival worthy of his collection, he reproved his visitor for a recent remark.

"You spoke of my head gamekeeper just now," he said. "Be careful as to what you may report concerning Toby, no matter what you may think of him. I feel no personal admiration for Trimble; but tradition and the memory of his father have always made me jealous for his well-being and good repute. Andrew Trimble saved my life on Berry Head above Torbay in eighteen ninety-four, Owlett. He always attended me on my expeditions and was my body-servant at home. I had risen a moderate-sized diurnal moth on Berry Head, somewhat near the edge of its eastern precipice, and, pursuing it with butterfly-net before me, struck and captured it successfully, but at the same instant fell forward on my knees. In another moment I should have descended some three hundred feet or more into the limestone quarry beneath and so perished; but Andrew, who was close at my heels and saw the danger, grabbed me, held on and saved me. Meantime the moth along with my net, caught by a strong breeze, fell far off into the sea and, whatever the creature may have been, that specimen was for ever lost to science."

"Thank God you wasn't lost to science yourself, your honour," murmured Matthew, who had heard this story many times.

"I have done my best to justify my deliverance," admitted Sir Gerald. "But at least I repaid the debt to Andrew Trimble. He married soon afterwards but never left my service and, for his sake, when his eldest son, Tobias, was old enough, I gratified the boy's ambition and let him join the gamekeepers. Toby is sound, but never was brilliant. However, he knows his business, and has always proved an honest and faithful man, but without imagination. He utterly lacks those gifts of strategy and prevision necessary when dealing with the poachers of game."

"I've heard it said he hates for me to be free of Oakshotts, your honour," sighed Owlett.

"He does, and long ago went so far as to express his regrets to me personally, thereby casting a very insolent reflection upon my own intelligence. To be frank he suspected that you were a thief in disguise and put some abominable charges upon your shoulders. He implied that you had deceived me, Owlett, and were robbing me in secret while pretending a devotion to my interests that you could not possibly feel. He slandered you to my face, actually daring to suggest that he was a shrewder student of character than myself! But keeping his father in my memory, I was patient. I chastised him pretty sharply with my tongue, however, and gave him a glimpse of himself that caused him considerable pain. So much for him, and if he is defaming you in the public ear, and you have evidence of the fact, then report the man to me, not sooner."

"Thank your honour," answered Matthew, "but it don't signify a button what the keepers say in their ignorance."

"While there are landowners left to preserve game, there will always be poachers to steal it and gamekeepers for the rascals to delude and hoodwink," said Sir Gerald. "Crime of every sort is on the increase for various sad but sufficient reasons. Many exceedingly clever and desperate people are reducing theft to a mere routine, with technique so accomplished that the Police Force quite fails of its salutary purpose. The Government is largely responsible for this, because they have long ceased to take the Eighth Commandment seriously, and what our Parliamentary leaders practise on a large scale under nationalism, they must expect to see developed in more modest and secretive fashion by those who elected them.

"The fact that no substantial efforts are being made at present to strengthen our meagre and inadequate constabulary seems to show that our masters attach inadequate importance to those sacred rights of property respected in the past. Fundamental principles have gone by the board, as you seamen say, and in their place are rules and regulations, exactions and demands all aimed at the destruction of any property rights whatever—either in our purses or our securities, whether of land or cash. However, my dear Owlett, as I have always declared and observed, a nation usually gets the Government it deserves to get."

The old man paused to take breath and Matthew ventured on a protest.

"Surely to God the nation never deserved Mister——" he began, but Sir Gerald cut him short.

"Name no names and be off, my friend," he ordered. "You have once again drawn me into my fatal propensity—that of uttering prolix platitudes. Go about your business, Owlett, and try again some night by the gamekeeper's potato patch. But conceal your enterprise from Trimble. He and I are mere passing survivals of an old order and should soon take our places in the Natural History Museum as specimens of species now extinct."

CHAPTER IV

THERE came a morning of July when Mrs. Blanchard was unusually late in rising and returned no answer to Maude, who had twice bawled up the stairs that breakfast was over and her mother's food growing cold. Gilbert had eaten his meal and gone to school, and Brian, commenting upon his mother-in-law's delay, spoke freely. He was very weary of his incubus and much wanted her to be gone.

"If only the old woman would peg out!" he said. "Some days it looks as if she was heading for it, thank God."

"She don't show her old fighting spirit so much as she did; but it flares up now and again," replied Maude.

"It didn't ought to take much to snuff her out," he said. "She was tolerable down yesterday and thought there didn't seem no great call for her generation to carry on."

"I've given it out to a neighbour here and there she's pretty weary of being alive," explained his wife. "And that's the truth, so no harm done."

Unity entered herself a few minutes later and the railwayman prepared to rate her for keeping bad hours; but it happened that she carried the war into the enemy's country before he could begin. Her eyes caught sight of the remains of Brian's breakfast and she was always at her fighting best when she was hungry.

"Your bread-and-milk's cold and it's your own fault, Mother," grumbled Maude. "There won't be no more oatmeal for porridge till next week."

"I thought the war was over," said Unity. "But Brian has had a duck's egg, I see, while there's only skim milk and bread-crusts for me."

"Don't be a fool!" burst out the man. "If you've got to work, you must eat."

"The saying was 'men must work and women must weep'," smiled Mrs. Blanchard. "Now it's 'woman must work and man must guzzle'."

"Don't try to be funny," he answered. "There's nothing to be funny about."

Then he turned to Maude.

"Get my dinner packed. Time I was away."

She left them in the house-place and Mrs. Blanchard began her breakfast and spoke to her son-in-law.

"Pour me a cup of tea if there's any left, my dear. You're quite right: there's nothing to be funny about bread-and-milk on an empty stomach. But the circus comes to Tavistock next week; then you'll get your chance for a bit of fun. 'Twas only greediness made me mark the shell of your blue egg. I wish you could have eaten two and a pat of butter along with 'em. The railways did a mighty fine job of work in the war. I grant you that."

"Yes," he said. "Now they're going to nationalise the railways, it's our turn."

"Labour will think more of the porters than the passengers then, I expect," she suggested mildly.

"We put 'em in power to do it. It's the workers have got the whip-hand through their Unions," he explained. "And we rule the Unions. We're the big noise now and shall so continue."

"If still alive, I'm going to vote against you next time notwithstanding," promised Mrs. Blanchard. "The Prince family was always Tories and so was the Blanchard family."

Maude returned with her husband's food.

"You'd better push up the hill," she said, "else you'll be called over the coals again. It's half after seven."

Brian grabbed his frail and hastened away while Unity commented upon him.

"He'll be happier soon with more wages and shorter hours."

"So he thinks, poor idiot. Finish up your breakfast and don't be talking, Mother. I want to clear. Will you sit in the garden this morning?"

"Yes, I'll sit in the garden and peel the potatoes and think."

"Better bury the past. It don't do any good to feel your life's ended so far as this world's concerned. I often do myself, all the same; but I've got my husband and Gilly. They are my duty; but for them I'd take leave of the world and be thankful to go," said Maude.

Mrs. Blanchard surveyed her daughter thoughtfully.

"The past takes a lot of burying after a war," she said. "The eagles gather together over the dead men and quarrel which shall have the spoils and lay their eggs to hatch the next war. So your father used to say——"

"Shut up about my father, for the Lord's sake!" cried Maude. "Have mercy on me and stint your eternal brooding on him and his friends. If you can't do without 'em, go after 'em and be done with it."

"All in good time," answered her mother quietly. "My dear

husband, who was your father, deserved better fortune than ever he got. He deserved a better daughter than ever you was, for one thing. He wouldn't have left me to your mercies on his death-bed if he'd guessed how tough you and Brian were going to serve me. You were our only one, well married to White as we thought, and what more natural that you should take your widowed mother in your home? And Gilly was your only one, and what more natural I should feel kindly to him and think kindly thoughts about him?"

"The boy likes you a deal better than he likes me, or his father. But that's only because you've told him he's going to get your savings," answered Maude, and her mother laughed.

"My savings! Sixty-five pounds and my burial expenses to come out of it," she said. "Gilly never heard a whisper as to that and well you know it. You get my old age pension so long as I'm alive, and I'm in my rights to call for more consideration and more food in consequence. And now I'll go in the garden and peel potatoes, or else shell broad beans, as you may ordain. No use for us to waste our wind snapping, Maude. We don't like each other and never have done since you were weaned; but we are Christians, or claim to be, and we did ought to love each other and act according."

"I don't want to quarrel. I only want your peace, Mother. You've got your latter end to think of now, and I almost wish sometimes you could find your peace, where we all shall find it soon or late, and slip away out of this beastly world to the next without any more fuss or fret," whined Mrs. White.

"You'd miss me if I was gone?" suggested Unity.

"Yes, I would," admitted Maude. "And so would Brian and so would Gilly, and so would Arthur Brimblecombe, who sets high store by you and liked father very well, or always said he did; but if you passed over we'd know you was at rest and in your glory along with your old friends."

"No, Maude. A pretty picture, and sometimes I feel a will to be gone, same as I did just now when I saw bread-and-milk for my breakfast again; but I've got my manners still, if nothing else. I can't go to heaven, my dear, unless I'm invited, can I? I'm mighty well in health and take my exercise and let down my food, when there is any, and keep the wits and will to carry on. But if you and Brian want me away, you'd best to ask him to knock me on the head in a gentlemanly manner, or put rat poison in my bread-and-milk."

Mrs. Blanchard laughed and Maude showed signs of bursting into tears. She restrained her sorrow, however, and took down her mother's bonnet and shawl from a peg where they hung behind the door.

"Here's your clothes, Mother. Go out in the sun and don't say wicked things like that," she begged.

"Get my work-bag too," directed the elder. "When I've done the veg, I'll go on with Gilly's pullover and smell the rose blossom."

Maude obeyed. The hour was still early but a cloudless July morning made the little garden of 'Laburnum Lodge' pleasanter than the kitchen. Nor was the hour too soon for a caller, and hardly had Mrs. Blanchard settled in her favourite nook when somebody arrived, entered the wicket gate, and beamed upon her.

"Good morning, Granny!" cried Mrs. Parsons. "You're an early bird like me."

"But not the early bird that catches the worm—not this morning, Thomasina. You'll be wanting Maude, no doubt," said Unity; and then Maude, who had heard her friend's familiar voice, appeared from the house.

"'Lor, Tommy! What brings you out of bed so early as this?" she asked.

"You, my dear—a message for you I was to deliver so quick as I might, before he opens his shop. Mr. Cobley says he's . . . Well, you're one of his pets."

"Something worth while to be the butcher's pet nowadays," declared Unity. Then she turned to the visitor.

"You cheer her up, Tommy. She's not quite herself this morning."

"I'll fetch my hat," said Mrs. White. "I know what Cobley means—very kind, I'm sure; but it's mother he's thinking on, not me."

Maude returned to the house and her friend praised her.

"A proper wonder you've got for a daughter, Granny. So patient and good and brave and hardworking. I always tell people they don't make enough of Maude. A proper picture her house, I tell folk. A lesson to the untidy ones."

"Yes, a clean, tidy-minded woman," agreed Unity. "I wonder sometimes why she's got so few friends."

"Just the opposite of me, because I often wonder why I've got so many," explained Mrs. Parsons. "But there's something about Maude's appearance that looks to be against her in the eyes of small-minded people. Not for me: I don't measure a fellow creature by their outside pattern."

"She'll like to know that," declared Unity. "Time has been rather hard on Maude. She was fairly personable when she was young; but she's the sort that don't wear too well and looks more than their age."

"If she's got a failing, to say it kindly," suggested Mrs. Parsons, "it is that she's a thought closer than need be."

"Nowadays we've got no chance to be anything but close, have us? But she was always the same even before she married my son-in-law. A good thing for him she is."

Maude returned and the companions went off together.

"Dear old granny," sighed Thomasina when they were out of earshot. "I was praising you, same as I always do, but no response. She thinks you're mean, Maude! Must be a thorn in your flesh sometimes, I fear, but no cross, no crown, they say. She's got her good points. She's always cheerful."

"Not always. She has her dark days."

"When she thinks what you and your husband have got to bear, then her conscience pricks her, no doubt. She'll be on your hands a good few years yet, I'm afraid. Strange how the ancient ones worry the middle-aged to keep 'em out of the workhouse. But if granny feels she's in the way——"

"The last thing she ever does feel, or any other old one," answered Maude. "They don't want much; but they stick like grim death to what they do want."

"I know: a feather bed for their aches and pains, a mite of food or a pinch of tobacco to keep 'em going, and a sound roof over their heads. That's all the contentment they hope for. Happiness—what we call happiness—they don't expect."

"That's only a dream for children nowadays," declared Mrs. White. "There ain't enough happiness to go round, Tommy."

"My dear love, there ain't enough of anything to go round!" cried the widow. "Come on down to the village and see Cobley. He ain't got enough to go round neither: he lost the last chance of that when he married Susan French. But he's a big-hearted toad and keeps a pinch of happiness under the counter sometimes for his favourites."

They went their way and Mrs. Blanchard peeled her potatoes, and then turned to Gilbert's pullover. She knitted in masterly fashion, and of old days had taken prizes for accomplished work; but now she got not far. There arrived a second visitor—this time for her.

Mr. Brimblecombe came to the wicket and marched in.

"Yet another early bird!" cried Unity. "Good morning, Arthur. Haven't seen you for a month of Sundays."

"You saw me last Wednesday, my dear; but that's by the way. Then you called me 'your cloud with a silver lining'. I shan't forget that."

"Sit down, Arthur. There's some clouds with no silver linings, however."

The market gardener fell into a tattered basket-chair and mopped his forehead.

"I saw her down the village with Peeping Thomasina," he said, "so counted to climb up and have a look at you."

"Better you was having a look at your vegetables and keeping the birds off your green peas and butterflies off your cabbages, my dear man."

But Arthur appeared annoyed about some concealed tribulation. His face had lost its customary contentment and he still panted a little from his speed up the hill. After a pause he spoke.

"There's some folk can't be Christians, try as they may, Unity," he began. It was a favourite sentiment with Mr. Brimblecombe.

" 'Tis the old Adam conquers you men, same as the old Eve beguiles us women," suggested Mrs. Blanchard, dropping her needles. "You ain't come to talk against Maude, I hope?"

"No, I ain't. I hate her worse than Satan, but I want to talk about what she said to Ruby Manley, the inspector's wife."

"Bless my soul, Arthur! Maude hasn't been saying naught against me to the police, has she?"

"She's been saying how you were failing in her opinion and can't get over John's death. She's fearing you may sink under it; and now Mrs. Manley will tell all the village you're fading fast."

His friend nodded her head; then she laughed.

"All Maude's kindly affection, Arthur. She's only wishful for my merciful release and so as I shall go in comfort. Once dead, always dead, and there's no more tribulation nor household worries in the grave. It's true I can't get over John's death; but I ain't fading under it. When you marry, you've got to face the chance of widowhood, along with a lot more chances; but widowhood don't wash you out. It may do quite the reverse and make life worth living again. John's all right now, and I'm all right with Gilly to fend for."

"He'll be worth good money when he's free to work," suggested Arthur.

"He will. I've asked schoolmaster how the boy's shaping and he says he's shaping for a good, steady day-labourer at present and wasting time at his lessons. Gilly ain't simple but just kindly-natured and willing to please, like his grandfather was. No bats in his belfry, nor ever likely to be, though many of the poor young creatures of his age ain't kindly-natured, nor willing to please anybody. That's along of their loss of fathers and being evacuated and so on by the war. So my grandson may seem odd only because he's amiable.

"But you can't damn a boy out of hand because he's a well-meaning, obedient sort of boy. Gilly haven't got a high-powered brain—how many have? But he's mighty strong, like his father, and I don't want for him to be like his father in any other respect. His parents don't favour him and so he don't favour them. They look on their child same as a farmer looks on his stock—just something he's reared to sell again as soon as it's worth money. So I've ordained to watch over the boy until he's clear of them and along with somebody trustable and fair, who will presently find he's a dear boy and get fond of him. Before all else he must be taught to think well of himself and self-respecting. 'Tis a wicked thing to learn a child he's no good: that's only like to make him so."

Mr. Brimblecombe nodded.

"If you're on his side," he said, "then the Lord's on his side and all should be well with him."

"Talk about yourself now," suggested Unity. "They say you're going strong and I always like to hear that."

"Lucky in life, unlucky in love, according to the old proverb," answered he, "but hope will keep at me yet. I can't see no impediment why you shouldn't take me, and the more I hanker, the less I find any reasons against. Quite the contrary, in fact. Your face don't flatter you and tears leave their mark on every woman's if she's been called to live a past same as yours; but the will and the high heart and the zest of being alive are still all there. You could face the married state again without fear along with a man like me."

"Me in sight of seventy and you in your early sixties! You must draw the line somewhere, Arthur."

"But look at it," he begged. "I stand to work and you would go to market with my stuff once a week instead of the middlemen that rob me and the public alike. Greengrocers are the scourge of my business, and their misbegotten profits properly cry to heaven."

"I know that," declared Mrs. Blanchard. "I've told you it would pay you well to have your own stall at Plymouth, or Tavistock market. But that's another story, my dear, and don't call for a wife unless she was a lot younger than me. You mustn't lay your heart at my feet no more, Arthur, else the people will be laughing at us."

"Let 'em laugh and be damned to 'em," he said. "I ain't offering so much as they think for that matter and I ain't so well-to-do now as I was before the war neither. With you things might mend, but at present under the new dispensation, what with rules and regulations and the snoopers always poking and prying and the price of labour, my business ain't no bed of roses no more, nor yet a bed of anything else."

"They say the farmer that cut his throat at Little Pedlington last week did it on sole account of Government officials calling and driving the poor chap out of his mind," sighed Mrs. Blanchard. "I couldn't believe it."

"Perfectly true all the same, Unity; and he's not the only unhappy wretch has done the like," so Arthur assured her.

They were still speculating on this gloomy subject when Maude returned with a parcel wrapped in newspaper.

"Ah! Cheering my old dear up, Mr. Brimblecombe? That's kind, I'm sure, and I hope he's done you good, Mother," she said.

"Pity others don't try to do the same," he answered sourly and rose to depart.

"I've got something to cheer her this minute," replied Maude, "but I ain't going to tell you what it is."

He stumped off without more words and her daughter turned to Unity.

"A lovely bit of calf's liver, Mother! Mr. Cobley sent it to you. But he charged enough for it."

"Keep it against Brian's supper, Maude," said Mrs. Blanchard, "and serve they spring onions Arthur brought me last time he was up before today. I'll have a taste too. Such good things are rare as white moles nowadays. What you took for granted before the war, you can't buy for money since. Charity don't begin at home no more: it have got to be exported like everything else worth having."

"That's what Brian don't like," said Maude. "He says we won the war and we ought to treat the Germans same as Russia treats 'em and starve 'em. He says the Russians have got a longer memory than us."

But her mother possessed an instinctive and traditional distrust of all things Russian.

"If so, Maude," she declared, "let 'em carry their long memory back to them that saved 'em from losing the war."

Mrs. White turned to a more interesting subject. She set down the luxury from Mr. Cobley and mentioned her approaching holiday.

"Brian was reminding me last night that he gets his fortnight off as usual come presently, Mother, and we're both of a mind that we'd like to go to Plymouth, same as last year. There's the sea for him and sea-fishing along with the fisher-folk that harbour down by the Barbican, and the pictures for me and 'Chara' rides all round about and a stroll on the Hoe sometimes. You'll remember last year you took Gilly while we was away and 'Laburnum Lodge' shut up; but this year, if you're willing, you'd carry just on here and look after the boy. He'll be back at school after his own holidays and no more of a nuisance than usual."

"Certainly, but on one condition, my dear," replied Unity. "They say there's bounteous mackerel being catched this year, so when Brian's took all that you and him wants out of the sea, he must send Gilly and me a good few now and again. You keep him up to that."

Maude promised to do so.

"'Tisn't as if you'd be lonely without us," she continued. "Friends will drop in on you and you must have a care for your health and put no tasks upon yourself you ain't suited to bear."

Unity made no comment upon this change of heart. Her thoughts, arising from the mention of the mackerel, were elsewhere.

"The last mite of food your father swallowed was a little trout Gilly caught for him. Very fond of his grandson and saw great promise in the boy, same as I do."

"So do I myself, Mother, and I won't have him under-valued. He's strong as a pony already and there's a time coming when a powerful day-labourer is like to be more valuable than the poor, skinny, black-coated creatures, only good for sitting on a stool and casting figures."

"Very like," agreed Mrs. Blanchard. "When you think of it, half the men who govern the country today began in the mines and workshops. But they had the brains to get to the top when the time came. You may be a machine-minder today and boss of the machine tomorrow; or you may work on the coal face when you're a lad and command all the coal in England come you grow up."

"That's Socialism," said Maude triumphantly.

In this amicable spirit mother and daughter proceeded for some weeks, and, on his next visit, Unity assured Mr. Brimblecombe that Maude had become moderately reasonable in sight of her annual vacation.

"She's left my approaching death alone of late," explained Mrs. Blanchard. "The thought of her holiday and the picture palaces to Plymouth has cheered her up."

But other matters than Maude occupied Arthur's mind on hearing this news.

"I'm properly glad at what you say," he answered, "for that's very good hearing, and you'll be at peace for a fortnight, free of vexations. You must visit my gardens and cast your eye over 'em, especially the small fruits, and eat your dinner and drink your tea with me now and again. Furthermore, the boy can come also if he must, though I'd sooner have you neat. You promise that much—whatever else you don't promise?"

"I'll come for certain, Arthur. It's an item for me to look forward upon," said Mrs. Blanchard.

CHAPTER V

In the practical and sagacious society to which Police Constable Peter Chadd belonged few conventions intervene between its members. Nothing prevents them from winning each other's acquaintance and social intercourse can be enjoyed without the least difficulty. In Peter's case, indeed, an obvious opportunity occurred for seeing Nancy Owlett, who was a farm girl engaged upon a field beside his extended beat, and, remarking that she found herself in some trouble with a tractor, he got over the hedge and strode to her aid. Already he knew her quite well by sight and name and had already considered Nancy's promise as a possible feminine friend, but decided, when he now approached, that he liked her better in a skirt than the breeches proper to her calling.

Young men of his status are prone to seek maidens apt for companionship of a purely platonic character; they like to walk out on occasions of leisure with a girl, and the unwritten law of every countryside ordains that this practice involves no obligations whatsoever. In other ranks, when advanced to a punctual, weekly rite, persistent 'walking out' would indicate a frame of mind upon both sides tending to more than mere amity; but both Peter and Nancy well understood that they ran no risk from an occasional stroll of this character. As for him, he did not even know whether she was already committed to such perambulations with another but, in that case, she would tell him so.

Now he attended to the tractor, praised her skill in handling the monstrous thing, inquired as to the work it was competent to do, and then, after receiving thanks, ventured to wonder if, when they were both at liberty some Sunday, she would take the air with him in any direction agreeable to herself. To his gratification Nancy declared this not impossible. She was flushed with her exertions and her hair escaped from under her cap in a wild and attractive manner. Peter had never been so close to her before and he admired her much. He also found her voice of admirable musical quality and her words well chosen. She paused a few minutes before speaking and regarded his massive dimensions both thoughtfully and frankly.

"You'll be Mr. Chadd, of course?" she suggested.

"That's right, Miss Owlett."

Nancy nodded and showed an inclination to be evasive. She laughed and entered on a side issue.

"We was wondering back along—me and some other girls—how tall you stood, Mr. Chadd, and I said you topped six feet by inches, but t'others said you might be six feet and no more."

"You came nearest," declared Peter. "I stand six foot three. What about it, miss? I must get back on my beat. But if there's naught against, I'd be very wishful for a walk."

"Nice of you, I'm sure. There's nothing against to my knowledge, for the minute."

"Good—name the day and I'll heave up where you ordain."

Nancy considered, and Peter, conscious that this interchange was no part of his duty, looked at the empty road.

"All for law and order, ain't you?" she said, perceiving what was in his mind. "You go back to work and I'll do the same. Not next Sunday, but the one after, round three o'clock. Then we'll go up over perhaps. You know where I live along with father."

"Right, then. Sunday week. Time three o'clock. Wishing you well till then."

They parted, with peaceful satisfaction on Peter's part, but secret animation in the breast of Nancy, because, for her, this amounted to a minor triumph. She and certain of her fellow workers were quite aware of Peter's return to Wallabrook and his impressive and attractive appearance in uniform. They had speculated on much more than his height or weight, but considered his handsome looks and argued as to his inner nature. Some guessed that he was of mild disposition and probably easy to manage in private life; others inclined to think this improbable, because a young man does not enter the Force unless possessed of determination, nerve and quality to face any challenge. But all agreed that he was bound to fall in love at no distant date, seeing how policemen almost invariably marry, and all wondered which, if any, among them might presently be called to follow custom and interest Peter as a preliminary to greater things.

Nancy, like many others, was familiar with these tentative excursions. Twice she had walked out, and in one case been abandoned by the boy after some sharp and shattering exchanges of opinion; in the other she had sent a lad packing for certain criticism of her character she felt to be unjust. And now she was entering upon a third hazard and in a position to tell her friends of the fact.

The relations between Miss Owlett and her father were free and easy but none the less devoted. Matthew thought the world of Nancy and reposed absolute confidence in her good sense and ability to conduct her own affairs; while she felt admiration for his varied gifts and his opinions on every question of the hour. That he should have won the friendship of Sir Gerald was also a source of pride and reflected glory. Her father knew well enough she would marry, but experienced no shadow of fear on that account and doubted not she would seek his opinion when the time came, yet felt confident that her own judgment might be relied upon. In any case he trusted that her departure would be long postponed and had no present desire to consider the domestic alterations in his home after she left it. When she had decided to become a farm-hand at the demand of the war, he raised no objection and declared it an excellent way of answering the national call; nor did he protest when she chose to stick to her work and go on earning her money after the war was ended. She was strong, enjoyed the open air, and farm work kept her fit and cheerful.

That night, without any emotion, Nancy told Matthew of her adventure and he raised only one trifling and humorous objection.

"Don't entangle me with the police; that's all I ask," he said. "For their own silly reasons Inspector Manley and his constables have always been a bit against me. They've caught the infection from the Oakshotts gamekeepers—Toby Trimble and his gang. Just an amusing fad they display, because their master favours me and makes me free of the coverts; though why, because there's a lot of godless poachers too clever for 'em, they should dare to say I'm the ringleader, is hidden in mystery. If I had liberty to do it I'd summons Toby for libel. But Sir Gerald wouldn't like that. He's sentimental in that quarter, though he knows his head outdoor man is a fool as well as I do. But it's funny my own daughter thinks to walk out with a policeman, though young Chadd didn't ought to be tainted against me yet."

"If he said a word against you, it would be the last ever he did say to me," promised Nancy.

"He won't, my dear. He'll know from his mother that I'm an old and valued friend of hers. She'll give me a good character and he's more like to take her word than another's."

But when the time came and Nancy started upon her ramble, Peter proved to be quite sound in his view of Mr. Owlett's moral principles. Other topics, however, occupied his preliminary moves and he concerned himself with the land girls in general and his companion in particular.

"A proper fine job of work you young women have done in the

war," he said. "The wonder of the nation, to see females doing men's work and carrying out their tasks in all weathers, so well as ever the men do."

"There's some think we demeaned ourselves, all the same," replied Nancy. "A young schoolmaster I walked with, back along in the war, turned me down when he came across me pulling swedes in my breeches. Showed a cheap and nasty mind, I thought."

"No mind at all, and I hope he didn't advance his opinions in his school. When England was up against the chance of destruction it didn't look the time for men to quarrel with women's clothes."

"A girl here and there may be built to look fantastic in slacks," she admitted, "but none of us went on the land to show our figures, and we were content to wear the properest garments for the job."

"Without a doubt," he agreed. "It showed what maidens is mostly made of. For pluck nobody else could beat them. Notwithstanding, to the male eye, you're a grander sight in a frock than otherwise."

"You get used to everything," declared Nancy.

They changed the subject and she invited him to tell her why he had chosen his business.

"I've often wondered myself," he said. "My mother always says it was because, when a child, I heard such a lot about the law and prisons and verdicts and sentences and suchlike. She had the misfortune to marry a very lawless fashion of man. My father was always in trouble, Miss Owlett. All his pleasures—everything that seemed worth while to poor father—brought him up against law and order; but sometimes he escaped and was encouraged to try again on a bigger scale, and sometimes he didn't escape and got locked up for his misdemeanours. He served sentences for various crimes, mostly burgling, and died under lock and key. I always felt cruel sorry for his way of life; but, to say nothing uncharitable against him, you couldn't but see he wasn't a very helpful father for a young boy. He did one thing, however; he made me hate crime from my youth up. Some lads might have been dazzled by his wickedness and, if he'd been successful oftener, perhaps I should have followed in his footsteps, too, same as youngsters take to bad ways from seeing the gangsters in the pictures. But not me."

"I see," declared Nancy. "That makes it plain why you went for a policeman. I'll bet Mrs. Chadd always told you that honesty was the best policy and things like that, and your father's career showed you she was right. So, when you grew up, you went to the other extreme and joined the Force, because you felt you might be able to atone for your father's lawless manner of life."

Peter praised this theory.

"What we call deduction," he explained. "Very clever of you to think it out and I'll bet it's true. In a manner of speaking, you might say law and order's my god."

"I expect a policeman couldn't have a better," agreed Nancy. "You don't often hear of a crooked policeman, do you?"

"Not often. They do happen, just as crooked lawyers and even crooked clergymen happen, but only at long intervals."

"What my father calls 'sports' or 'exceptions', when he's talking about beetles and butterflies and suchlike," she said, then changed the subject.

"Do you count to be on duty in Wallabrook overlong, or is this only a set-off for a bigger job, Mr. Chadd?" Nancy asked presently. "Are you an ambitious sort of man, or all for peace and quietness, like Inspector Manley?"

Peter laughed at this question.

"Inspector's got his own views and it wouldn't be orderly for a constable to question 'em, still less such a young one as me," he replied. "The inspector says the proof of the pudding is in the eating and that our job is, firstly, not to catch criminals but to prevent crime. To prevent crime before it's committed sounds all right; but the advantage is always with the criminal, for how the mischief can you nab him until he's broke the law? Take the man red-handed by all means if and when possible; but even if you know he's a wrong 'un, how are you going to stop his nefarious practices before he commits them and before there's any evidence against him? But Inspector Manley goes on a higher plane than that. He says that good, watchful police, like he is himself, create a high and orderly spirit in a place and set such a fine example of well-doing that there's no breeding-ground for crime where they rule over the people. He says, if you take Wallabrook from the day he was appointed inspector, there hasn't been one capital crime in the parish, whereas there's not a single adjoining parish where you'll find a clean bill."

"Got a sort of feeling crime can't breathe the same air with him and his constables," suggested Nancy.

Peter laughed again.

"Yes. He says his system cleans the air for the rising generation."

"If that's true, you're going to have rather a tame time," suggested Nancy, and Peter laughed again.

"I see his point, of course, and I wouldn't go so far as to hope he's wrong; but I don't want to waste what I've got in wits and strength doing naught but pad a country beat."

"I should hope not, I'm sure. All very well for Inspector Manley, looking forward to his retirement and his pension in a year or two. You can understand him wishful for peace and nothing to put Wallabrook in the newspapers."

" 'Seek peace and pursue it, Chadd'; that's what he says to me."

"The more peace the less preferment in your job," she said. "I should think, if you want to make good, you would rather like to handle a spot of crime, for Scotland Yard to see what you're made of."

"If you look at it like that——"

"Well, how d'you look at it? Wouldn't you say, with all your advantages, you ought to be keen to make your mark?"

"The questions you ask, Miss Owlett! I've scarce settled down yet and no time to look very far ahead. But I'll do so, no doubt. For the minute I just feel the pleasure of being back home again among old friends and only wishful to make new ones."

"I understand that," she said.

"Things is on a bigger scale in other parts of the country," he explained. "Bigger surroundings, tons more people, bigger rivers running and more news and more noise in the air—more bustle and stir and quickness and cleverness. But I was darned glad to get back to Wallabrook and mother and the earth and the old smells and familiar food, scamped though it is, and earn my living amongst 'em."

"To seek peace and pursue it, in fact," summed up Nancy.

She admired him immensely, but considered, as one who had fought in the war, his outlook should be a little more valiant. 'Valiant' was the word that came to her mind, yet she felt it too early to express this wish.

"Well, it takes all sorts to make a world, don't it?" she asked, and they walked forward in silence for half a minute.

"I always think this is a very fine sight," he said. "That great hill t'other side of the river, where the goats used to graze, and there they are still, I see."

"Farmer Melbourne's goats, and he makes a lot by their milk."

"Doubtless he would, else he wouldn't run 'em. Then the rolling country beyond and Dartmoor up over to the north-east. What you might call spacious."

"And Oakshotts away up Walla valley, and Lady Champernowne's estates alongside it. Father says that Lady Champernowne was wishful to marry Sir Gerald Fortesque; but he never had any use for her."

"Mr. Owlett tells mother all sorts of things about the upper people and his friendship with Sir Gerald," said Peter. "Mother's very proud of your father's friendship with her too. Mr. Owlett used to know my father in the old days. He told her once that to know all was to forgive all, and it touched my mother's heart a lot that he could forgive father, because nobody else would."

"Father forgave your father for everything but one thing," explained Nancy. "He never forgave him for being cruel to Mrs. Chadd."

"There's nothing better than the power to overlook other people's weaknesses, and Mr. Owlett has a name for being that sort of man."

"Yes, he has; but I shouldn't have thought that was much of a stronghold for a policeman," suggested Nancy. "If you were in such a hurry to take a kindly view of anybody caught doing wrong, the weakness might grow on you and spoil your credit. Would you say to a house-breaker, or perhaps a murderer, that you were going to overlook it this time, but it mustn't happen again?"

Peter's mind was occupied with her father and he made no reply to this insulting question.

"You may know, or you may not," he replied, "but I've found quite a number of responsible men about here that don't take Mr. Owlett at his face value. The keepers up to Oakshotts hold he's untrustworthy and the head keeper goes so far as to say he's responsible for breaking the game laws—otherwise poaching. And from the keepers this opinion has spread to the police, because it's well known the Force can be called on any time against poachers—to oppose 'em and arrest 'em when a situation calls for it. I'm talking in confidence, of course, but Inspector Manley's a friend of Mr. Trimble's and believes he's most likely in the right. And I tell you these things to show what I said was true."

"What did you say?" asked Nancy.

"That it is a very fine thing to have a forgiving nature, which Mr. Owlett has got, because, when he hears these opinions and forebodings against him, he just laughs at 'em and treats 'em for the lies they are."

"And how do you treat 'em?"

"With contempt," answered Peter. "I don't believe a morsel of it because I've got wisdom at my elbow in the shape of mother. She knew Mr. Owlett before you were born and before I was born and, when ashore, your father was always a good and kind friend to her and everybody else. It isn't my place to contradict Inspector Manley and tell him he's talking through his hat when he utters doubts against your father, but I well know he'll live to find he was mistook."

"I'd like nothing better than to see father have the law of Trimble, and Samuel Manley, too, for that matter," declared Nancy.

"Your dad's way is the best," he assured her, "and in any case my chief stands for law and order and you can't outface the majesty of the law."

"I'd say he stood for his silly self and nobody else," she answered. "I'd say he was the servant of the law and no more. However, he don't matter the flip of a duck's tail either way; but I'm glad you haven't let any wicked chatter influence your opinion of father."

"Certainly not, Miss Owlett. He's a very outstanding fashion of man by all accounts and nobody respects his learning more than me and my mother."

"Because if you'd thought otherwise," continued she, "our first walk would have been our last, Mr. Chadd. He served in the Merchant Navy and he says that as a rule sailors know a lot more general knowledge than landsfolk and have got larger ideas and bigger brains to hold 'em in."

"That's true, no doubt," admitted Peter. "A seeing man who's gone round the world once or twice must have learned a lot he never could have picked up in Wallabrook."

"If you come to know father, you'll be dazed to find what he does know. I often tell him he could write a book."

"So mother says."

"And some days he admits it is so; but other days he doubts he has enough education."

"I expect you'd have enough education to do the writing if he was to dictate it to you."

"I did all right at school; but I'd sooner be active and in the open air than chained down to pen and ink, or anything like that."

Nancy had found matter for considerable satisfaction combined with doubt during these interchanges. Peter's general opinion satisfied her in the main and his respect for her father pleased her;

but his lenity of spirit and inclination to an all-embracing tolerance made her feel distrust. His person she approved. She fell silent now, and he welcomed the silence while he considered and told himself that here was a spirit quite beyond his experience—a spirit that knew its own mind and was impelled by stern but just principles. To discover so young and beautiful a person fixed in such severe values struck him as remarkable; but none the less they created great respect and awakened interest. After a pause the girl announced a decision.

"You must come and meet father one evening when you're free of work," she said. "He's a most approachable sort of man and very sociable when he takes a fancy, though apt to be short and sharp where he don't. He likes going over his curiosities, especially with a stranger that hasn't seen them before; but he never gets to the end of them, and sometimes hardly goes further than the beginning, because every queer thing, or specimen of a foreign creature, starts him on a tale of how he came by it and the adventure that went to it. Then suddenly he finds the visitor has to go before he's more than started."

Nancy smiled and hoped that Peter would echo her amusement, but his attention had stopped with her unexpected invitation. This impressed him beyond measure, though he had already dreamed of such a possibility in the future; but to find it actually offered on their preliminary ramble astounded him. He failed to understand it. The obvious explanation, that she might like him, did not occur to Peter. He guessed that Nancy wished to learn her father's opinion of him; but abandoned this theory, because he was already convinced that she would never let even such a parent as Mr. Owlett make up her mind for her. He was still pursuing this problem, and ignorant of the time that had passed since his companion's last remark, when she showed impatience.

"If it would bore you, of course don't come," she said abruptly.

"Far from any such thing," he declared. "It surprised me such a lot to get such a fine offer that I forgot to answer. D'you mean it? I expect it's your father would be bored, not me."

"He wouldn't be bored if you showed you was interested and asked him a bright question now and then that he thought worth answering," she said. "He was rather amused when he heard I meant going for a walk with a policeman, but, being what he is and all for live and let live, he hoped I'd enjoy myself."

"I'm sure I hope you have," said Peter.

She did not answer this but spoke again.

"Then you'll come? Morning's the best time when you've got a morning. Of an evening just now he's busy after the night moths."

"The gamekeepers are whimpering that a lot of pheasant chicks have disappeared, so I hear."

"Then Sir Gerald ought to sack the fools. If a parcel of grown men calling themselves gamekeepers can't look after the job of feeding pheasant chicks, then best to engage some land girls who could. And now we must be turning back, Mr. Chadd, else I won't be in time for father's tea," declared Nancy. "I won't ask you in, if you please, but maybe some day, if your mother can spare you, I will."

"Same here," he said. "I'll be very proud to plan a tea for you if you're so inclined, but mother would like a spot of notice to prepare one of her famous cakes."

"I like Mrs. Chadd and she likes me."

"She knows a good piece when she sees one, if I may say so."

In this amiable spirit they retraced their way and presently parted, shaking hands before they did so.

Mr. Owlett was making ready for tea when his daughter returned at five o'clock. She had few secrets from him and proceeded to relate her recent experience.

"He was very smart in a suit of grey flannels and a straw hat with a dark blue ribbon and a showy tie, brown shoes and what looked to be a silver watch-chain across his waistcoat."

"A fine sight, evidently," agreed Matthew; "and did his remarks come up to his appearance?"

"We were very much of a mind on things in general," admitted Nancy, "though not in some directions. Mercy looks to be his strong suit."

"Good in itself, but won't get him very high in the police. With a grand frame same as his, Chadd might have risen very high indeed as a wrestler. In proper hands he could have become heavyweight champion of the West country, as like as not; but he'd be too slow and muscle-bound for a fighter. Too late to learn boxing now."

"And too tenderhearted, I'd say."

Mr. Owlett nodded.

"In the ring you must learn to give it as well as take it," he explained. "Many a silly man, seeing his opponent in pain and trouble, have held his punches and given t'other a chance to weather the storm. Then he's lost—just when he'd thought he'd won—and deserved to lose."

"I wouldn't say there was much tiger in him," admitted Nancy.

"A pity in a way. There was tiger enough in his father. Still, a man can shine and earn his living without it if he chooses a walk of life where it's unlikely to be called for."

"You showed plenty of tiger according to the tales you tell, Father."

"Oh yes; but craft along with it."

"I wouldn't say there was much craft in Mr. Chadd; yet one thing pleased me. He despises Inspector Manley for daring to doubt of your character, and he reckons the gamekeepers are a feeble lot."

"He's right there. Losing chicks, now. Sometimes—on Sir Gerald's account, not his own—I'm half in a mind to give Toby a useful tip or two."

"Don't you do it," advised Nancy. "If anybody was catched, he'd take all the credit."

"I expect he would, my dear. And I shouldn't mind."

"Are you coming to church tonight, Father?" she asked when their tea was finished.

"No, my love; not tonight. I'm for Oakshotts this evening and under the master's direction. I also want some willow leaves for the puss moth caterpillars."

"Mr. Chadd's on night duty tonight. It takes him on his beat round the woods to the west."

"If I fall in with him, I shall tell him he may consider himself worthy of your attention."

"Don't you dare, Father!"

"No, no. He's got to prove worthy of my attention first. I'm all against changes at present."

"So like as not he didn't find me what he hoped," said Nancy.

"Quite possible, and he wouldn't be the first. Keep your standards high when you're walking out, and if they frighten a chap off, then he's no loss. Same holds good for the young man, of course."

She considered this.

"If ever I was really to fall in love," she said, "I'd think of a lot of things before I let myself go, Father."

"Too late then," he told her. "Think before you fall in love. Too late after. Once in love, then the game's up and thinking ain't going to save you. Watch out for the first symptoms in time to nip 'em in the bud if that looks the wisest."

She was scornful.

"That don't sound very bright to me, Father. How the mischief do anybody know the first symptoms if they've never been in love before?"

"Nature won't leave you in any doubt of her intentions. Or so I found it," he answered. "But don't think Nature always tells gospel truth, by any means. She's a downy bitch and never gives a damn for our peace of mind, or our good, or evil, so long as she has her own way."

"I'm going to church whether or no," said Nancy. "I've promised to meet one of the girls after and take supper along with her. She's quitting and going to live in Tavistock, because her young man seems to be in line for getting a house at last. And if he has, they'll marry instanter."

"No doubt Nature's impatient over the shameful lack of houses. Civilisation would have broke her heart long ago if she'd got a heart to break," replied Matthew.

CHAPTER VI

MAUDE WHITE prepared to take her holiday and enjoy in her own way the varied pleasures that Plymouth could offer. She was a woman of brooding disposition, ever ready to blame unkindly and undeserved fortune for leading her into lifelong bondage with a man she had accepted from no better reason than his declaration of desire for her. She had welcomed a chance of marriage as proclaiming to the parish she was not of the neuter species whom no male wants; while the railwayman, having won her without much effort, strove for their common self-respect to appear as a well-contented suitor when he announced their engagement. Both, from some dim sense of how betrothed persons are expected to behave, assumed a shared happiness quite unreal in two such selfish souls, and devotion to their personal interests continued to be the ruling spirit of them both.

Brian had only sought a woman for his comfort and domestic convenience, while Maude's prime purpose was to secure a home of her own and confound the general conviction that she must never expect to do so. Now, taking the railway worker's measure correctly, she ruled from the first in all material matters, seeing to it that he should work, inhabit a respectable dwelling and present a seemly appearance before the little world of their neighbours.

Maude was the less happy of the twain, because her husband could still take life as it came and trust in a vague fashion that socialism was going to better his fortune some day. She had enough sense to realise his limited capacity and perceived that Brian was of very modest mental standing and beyond hope of much increased prosperity under any social changes. She knew herself, too, and sometimes felt herself to be commonplace. Such introspection was rare, however, and only in company with her friend, Thomasina, did she ever confess to it. But Mrs. Parsons proved always ready to express sympathy and declare Maude much mistaken.

"No, my love," she would say. "Far from it. You're not a stupid creature by any means. You're a mighty clever woman and handle White to perfection, and you'll get your reward some day. He's a difficult chap and you've made him into a trustable one, so far as any man ever was or could be trustable. You've got a will, and a strong will is a lot better to have than a high education. There's very few women I've known that would have drove your husband so steady and watched out he didn't kick over the traces; and he knows it."

"There never was much love lost between us, as you were the first to point out when I took him."

"And a good thing too, because you can't hurt each other worth mentioning," answered the widow. "But though he don't exactly love you, any more than you love him, he respects you and knows you've been the making of him. It would have been very nice if you could have respected him also, but you're too clever for that, of course."

"A man and his wife have got to sink or swim together," agreed Maude. "Anyway, for my own credit, I'll see he don't sink."

In practice no vital difference separated the pair, for their selfishness took different shapes and seldom clashed. Indeed it tended to make them see alike, because Brian rather admired Maude's thrift, her aversion from spending money and her peculiar power to get exceptional value for it when she did. He admitted that she was the smart one and he knew, when their annual holiday came to break the monotony of life, that she would relax somewhat, never grudge him his amusements and not hesitate to make some outlay on her own. Thus, when autumn returned and their fortnight of pleasure awaited them, they went to it in tolerable good spirits, prepared for the necessary dip into their savings. Maude cherished no private vices and though Brian in earlier years had yielded to his love of a gamble, when certain misfortunes made it necessary to place his bad luck before her, she had adopted drastic measures and now he betted no more.

At Plymouth they pursued their own ideals of a holiday, which often parted them all day, though they usually joined forces at night and went to cinemas or racing tracks. Brian liked the dogs, while Maude preferred the motor-bicycles. The weather was fine and, renewing old friendships, the man spent most of his days on the sea, helped to lift lobster-pots and caught plenty of fish, while Maude surveyed Plymouth rising from its ashes and taking new shape. She studied the shops, drank an occasional glass of port wine and lunched with holiday abandon in the better sort of eating-houses.

Returning to their lodgings one evening with ample spoils, Brian amazed his wife by a suggestion that an exceptional crab should be packed and posted home to her mother. He modified this gesture of friendship somewhat by the hope that Mrs. Blanchard would be poisoned as the result; but Maude, in high holiday mood, applauded the notion.

"It will be the surprise of her life," she said, "and cost nothing, because Tommy's coming tomorrow, to put in a day with me and see the shops. So she can take it back with her and leave it at home."

Brian, who cared little for Thomasina, made no comment on her approaching visit, but arrangements for it were already complete and she duly arrived from Wallabrook by the earliest possible train, to find Maude upon Millbay platform ready to welcome her. They kissed and Mrs. Parsons praised the younger's appearance.

"You've took the sun, Maude," she said, "and look a lot richer in your complexion, my dear. How's Brian? Did he cuss when you broke it to him I was coming?"

"No. He's in a very good temper killing fish and drinking beer and seeing a lot of dog-racing."

"Quite the gentleman at large, I expect."

"For the minute, yes. On a holiday he's generally pretty amiable. Born to hate work, he was."

"Like most men," agreed Thomasina. "But they're a lot safer working, all the same. I always kept my late husband up to the collar —for his own good, you understand. Let 'em be idle and nine out of ten turns to their nasty amusements, like a duck to a puddle."

Maude uttered her rare laugh.

"I see he holds down his job," she said.

Mrs. Parsons was full of news and at breakfast Brian congratulated her.

"The early bird catches the worm sure enough," he told her. "Surprising what a lot you find to happen even in a god-forgotten hole like Wallabrook."

"News flies to her, sure enough—good and bad alike. Tommy don't miss nothing," declared Maude.

"Yes, I've got a knack to pick up items," admitted Mrs. Parsons. "It comes natural to me to inquire. The way is to pick the right one to inquire of. You get snubbed now and again and draw a blank. I've kept my tit-bit to the end. Old Joshua Tibbets has gone at last! Went day after you came here. A proper landmark took though, no loss in reality because all his generation was gone by now. And yet how he clung to life, though over ninety!"

"Not him," replied Brian. "He was a born liar and years younger than what he pretended. A proper old scandal-box—so bad as you, very near."

The visitor laughed.

"Yes, I had many a tell with Joshua. He'd begin every sentence he spoke the same way. 'Of course there's not a word of a lie in what I'm telling you,' he'd say, and then prove out of his own mouth he was the biggest liar in the parish. But his health was always his favourite object of conversation. He watched over his flesh and bones like a mother watches over her children. 'I can bear with the old evils,' he'd say, 'because I'm schooled to do so and I know their torments will lift soon or late; but when I get a new pang in a new place where I've never had one before, then I'll be up in arms in a moment and fear 'tis the beginning of the end.' "

"What took him?" asked Maude.

"I asked Dr. Bridger that question, because I could get no light on it from any place else, and he told me 'twas just old age had worn Joshua out. He crept in his bed as usual to sleep and didn't wake up again. No fuss, no worry for anybody and not a twinge for himself. You couldn't wish nothing better for yourself or your dearest friend."

"You went to the funeral—trust you!" said Maude.

"Oh yes. I was there. Not much of an upstore about that. Blowing cold it was and rain down off the Moor. I met Billy Fern after it was over and he said he was a fool to have gone, but done so out of respect to Mr. Tibbets, because he's given him worki n the past when nobody else would. Then he said that, be it as it might, funerals are proper death-traps for the living, especially if the wind blew from the east; but of course worse in winter than in summer. 'At a winter funeral,' so Fern said, 'the only safe ones be the corpses.' "

"You can get a spot of fun even at a funeral, seemingly," suggested Brian, and the remark suggested another experience to Thomasina.

"I always like the cheerful news best, myself," she said, "but you've got to face up to the bad news also—not because you like it for anybody, but because there's mostly such a lot more of it nowadays. I'm not like Ruby Manley, the inspector's wife. Good items don't interest her; but she scents the bad ones like a game-dog scents partridges and pours 'em out gratis for all that will listen. As a result of that she's a lonely woman, because her failing is known and folk give her a miss. I've tried a bit of good news on her once and again, but she never rises to it."

"If you've got an appetite for woe, other people's luck don't wake your interest at any time," suggested Maude.

"The dark view comes natural to some people, same as it is to moles and owls and night-birds in general," explained Mrs. Parsons. "I believe good news dazzles that sort and offers 'em more pain than pleasure. You get to read people if you've got an inquiring mind like mine, and one of my amusements is to read between the lines and guess what's hid behind the spoken word. There's a lot of humbug in some of us to Wallabrook, but you can always see it peeping out if you've got the seeing eye. Take last Poppy Day. I carried poppies as usual, being very fond of accosting strange folk any time, and it's easy with a tray of poppies for a good cause.

"Well, I met Blades, our carpenter and undertaker. He saw me coming and tried to dodge me, but I cornered him and said I knew he'd like a half-crown poppy, so as he should feel he'd done his good deed for the day. Just the light touch and a pleading smile you've got to put on, you understand. But all in vain with Blades. The dirty little twerp wouldn't part with a copper! 'Can't favour you just now, Mrs. Parsons,' he said. 'The spirit's willing and I often wish it was in my power to be generous, but that's one of the things I'm denied to practise.' Spoke as if he'd got all the virtues but generosity and that was beyond his power, through no fault of his own. I laughed in his face! 'Don't you think to come it over me with that stuff,' I told him before he scuttled off."

"Beastly miser!" said Brian. "And him the richest man in the village. Stinks of money."

"Of course he do," agreed Maude. "Whoever heard of a poor undertaker?"

In this agreeable fashon they ate a handsome breakfast and then planned the day.

"Brian's going fishing as usual," explained his wife, "and we'll poke round the shops and sit on the Hoe if you're so minded and it don't rain; and if he gets a tidy-sized lobster, as he mostly does, he'll give it to you. Won't you, Brian? To pay Tommy for taking the crab home to mother."

He agreed that would be fair and, after an agreeable day, when her outing was ended, Mrs. Parsons returned to Wallabrook encumbered.

It was dark before she called at 'Laburnum Lodge' and told Mrs. Blanchard of her adventure.

"I'll come in and sit down for half a minute, my dear," she said, when Unity opened the door to her. "I'm just back from a very nice day with Maude and Brian and I've got a present for you. They are both a lot more lighthearted than is usual with 'em at home; or so I thought, and they've sent you a Plymouth crab that very near broke my arm bearing him along. And Maude said that Arthur Brimblecombe ought to furnish a nice cucumber to go along with it."

"Fancy!" said Mrs. Blanchard. "They must have been lighthearted, as you say. Shall I get you a cup of tea? You'll be tired."

"No, no—just ready for bed, no more. They done me very well and I've had a thimbleful more port wine than usual, me being teetotal except now and again. And you'll be glad to hear they are on very good terms, Granny—not a cross word between 'em in my hearing."

"The sea air," suggested Mrs. Blanchard. "It acts like a balm on some people."

"Yes—and my company. I always feel I've got the touch to cheer Maude. She's such a proper good sort, really. Never was one to give her friendship to anybody—not like your dear husband—but once Maude feels she can trust another person, then she's a friend for life. Or so I've found her."

"I'm glad you like her," said Unity. "And I'm glad her holiday is doing her good."

"If she could only find that Brian ought to be a pleasure to her as well as a duty, that would be a tower of strength," suggested Mrs. Parsons, "but I grant you in a general way he ain't pleasurable."

"Not in a general way," agreed Brian's mother-in-law. "What he may be along with other railwaymen, I couldn't tell you. At home he's very apt to see trouble, but blind to all the needless trouble he gives other people."

"No outstanding news here today, I suppose?" asked Thomasina.

"None that I've heard of," answered Mrs. Blanchard.

When Thomasina was gone, Gilly opened the parcel she had left behind her and exclaimed at the size of the crab and the wonder of his father's gift.

"To think Dad got hold of such a hugeous creature and didn't stick to it himself!" he said.

"A most kindly thing for your father to do," declared Unity.

"Shall you be up to cooking it and eating it, Granny?" he asked.

"To cooking it, yes, Gilly; but not to eating it. I don't eat shellfish even when I get the chance. Turned against 'em after some wrong cockles I had round about forty-five years ago."

"Oh dear!" sighed the boy.

"Don't you fear. I know somebody will like it—somebody will be very pleased to see you join him when he sits down to it. That's Mr. Brimblecombe. It just fits because we're going to midday dinner along with him tomorrow and we'll take the crab with us."

"Won't he properly love it, Granny!"

"I hope so, but I never heard his views on the subject. He may agree with me about crabs, or he may not. Most men like 'em."

Arthur had planned an unusual meal for them. Unity's condition was that her grandson should accompany her and the day be Saturday; and Mr. Brimblecombe had agreed to it.

"Bring him by all means," he said. "Then, after you've broke bread under my roof, he can go out and do a bit of weeding or what not, while we have a tell."

His visitors arrived at noon and Mr. Brimblecombe stood at his gate to meet them. He felt pleased to mark that his entertainment was taken seriously and his guests were clad in their Sunday clothes. But a melancholy piece of news awaited Unity's grandson: their host shared her aversion and the crab was no use to him. He thanked her but shook his head.

"Not manners to look a gift-horse in the mouth, my dear, nor yet to doubt the age of a gift crab," he said. "It looks to be fifty years old, else it wouldn't be so huge; but in any case I couldn't eat crab for money. I'm funny that way. If the outside of a bit of food's properly hideous, then I'd rather starve than put it in my mouth. How any man that has looked on an oyster can swallow an oyster I never could imagine; and the same with a lot of other queer things that come out of the sea. An honest-to-God fish—yes, certainly; but naught fantastic."

"So long as you're sure it ain't because it came from my daughter," said Maude's mother.

"No, no—I'd take it for granted that she meant well for once."

"What have you got for our dinner, Arthur? I'm with you about shellfish; but I like a bit of red meat still, though very near forgot how it tastes these days."

"No red meat, but one of my own chickens—game-birds they are, as you know. Poor layers, but on the table you can't beat 'em."

"You didn't ought to have killed one for me; but a proper treat, I grant you."

"The liver, wing and so much of the breast as you can feel to enjoy," promised Mr. Brimblecombe.

At dinner their talk ran on fruit, which was one of the nurseryman's favourite subjects.

"You were always a vegetarian at heart, Arthur," said Mrs. Blanchard; "and your pet eating plums and pears."

"That is so," he agreed. " 'The kindly fruits of the earth', as they say."

"An orange was always my choice in fruits," declared Unity, "and after that a banana."

"To my mind we're far ahead of foreign countries and there's no such quality as our stone fruits grown in England," he said. "Likewise in apples and pears. You shall have your choice presently. I picked over my 'Golden Drop' plum for you this morning. As for bananas, there is a rumour they are in the Tavistock shops, but I haven't seen none myself so far. If I do and my friends have got a bunch, I'll see you get some. As to oranges, far too early for the Jaffas yet and I see in the papers that, along of the fierce wars out there, Jaffas are likely to be scarce this winter. Speaking in general on fruit-growing, the mischief is that when you've got a bountiful harvest everybody else have got the same and prices turn so low they scarce pay for picking. A glut for market amounts to little better than a famine for the grower."

Unity listened with interest to these facts.

"You can have too much of a good thing, seemingly," she suggested. Then she stopped Arthur, who was about to pour out another glass of beer for her. He had offered her cider and she had chosen beer.

"Not another drop, my dear," she said. "That's another good thing you can have too much of."

Mr. Brimblecombe himself was a cider-drinker, but frugal in all matters of food or drink. Today his thoughts soared far beyond the table and, when dinner was done, he returned to the dream still dominating them. Having despatched Gilly to the pleasant task of picking dessert apples from a certain tree, he conducted Mrs. Blanchard to a little summer-house, seated her in comfort and tried once again to win her. She had hoped that he might avoid the subject on this occasion.

"Well," he began, "here we are, my dear woman, and I've got the satisfaction of seeing you in my nursery once more. And I may say it gives a fine finishing touch to my establishment when I see you in it. You fit in the picture something wonderful, and I've often figured you in that identical chair and I much wish you could see your way to stop here. It would reconcile me to a most difficult life if you found your way to share it, and I may tell you the more I go over your objections, the less I find in 'em. If I was outstanding ugly, or an unbeliever, or woke doubts in you as to my character—well, if I was any such thing, or had a screw loose unbeknownst to anybody but you and myself and my Maker—then the case would be altered; but there ain't no such charges against me. You've gone so far as to praise my record of work and clean living yourself. You don't find me passing plain, nor yet showing qualities you couldn't abide to live with. I've heard you say more than once that it was light in your darkness to know poor John had such a respectable man as me for his friend and well-wisher.

"Then, feeling that way, I'm bound to go on hoping you'll see you'd be safe with me and entitled to my affection. I'd give you more power than ever you have had in your life. You'd be somebody along with me instead of nobody, and I'd be a darned sight bigger man than ever I was, or hoped to be, with you by my side. This ain't romance or any silliness of that kind: it's a business bargain built on circumstances. I'm the gainer and my nursery's the gainer on the one hand, and you're the gainer by having power and comfort and a proper reward for all your high qualities. If there's one thing about your fate that makes me mad, it is to see such a woman under the dominion of her own child; and though Maude is your daughter by the freak of God, I still say so and will repeat it."

Here Unity took him up.

"Stop, stop, Arthur. Get your wind and keep your temper, my dear. Maude is what the Lord ordained she should be, and when any fellow creature happens to give you the creeps, always remember who made 'em. As you well know, I'm most fond of you and you're my greatest man friend these days. A good friend, and if it was only to pleasure you I'd come and look after you and you'd be a great interest and satisfaction to me; but I'm too old by ten years, if not more."

"You ain't so old as you feel to be," he said. "It's only your relations make you feel old. You didn't ought to dwell with them that want you to be gone, but with a man like me who would like you to live for ever. You'd lengthen your life by years if you was to spend the balance of 'em with me; but what you're doing now is to let that pair of vipers rush you into old-age years before your time."

"That's a good point," granted Unity. "A clever thing to say, Arthur, and a pinch of truth in it, I shouldn't wonder. 'Tis ageing to live with Maude and Brian; but they don't plan nothing vital against me, to my knowledge. Meanwhile there's Gilly and I'll promise this much, that once he's free of the School Board and got a job away from his parents, then I'll leave 'Laburnum Lodge'."

"You know I'm ready and willing to take the boy," said Mr. Brimblecombe. "If I'm still here and ain't driven out of business by this hateful Government, I'll take Gilly; and what more conveniently and vitty but I took you too? Then you'd have him under the same roof with yourself and watch me bring him up to be a god-fearing hard worker. If you're so powerful quick to see the hand of Providence lifted, then surely you can see what's ordered for yourself and staring you in the face."

Mrs. Blanchard laughed.

"Your own interests make you a very clever argufier," she said. "You can be as sharp as a needle when you mind to, but don't feel too sure what your own interests are. A time might well come when you looked at me as the biggest mistake of your middle age, and find yourself wondering what the mischief ever made you hanker for me. Friendship—even such a fine friendship as ours—don't get to the bottom of all things and, just for that reason, may run smooth and happy through a lifetime; but marriage goes a darned sight deeper than friendship and probes to the root of man and woman alike. You think amazingly well of me, same as I do of you, Arthur, and long may you continue to do so; but if you was to marry me, you might find to your horror and your sorrow that you never knew a thing about me and had made a fearful mistake when you thought you did."

"In the case of young people I grant you that might happen and often does," he admitted; "but not in our case. We shan't do nothing to breed horror, nor yet sorrow. A woman of your age would have declared herself if ever she's going to do so. Same with a man of my age. Our characters are well known to the public at large and to each other. If ever a woman deserved to spend her latter days in peace, 'tis you, and I'd go so far as to say you'd have the peace that passes understanding along with me."

"I don't favour peace when there's any proper thing to fight about," confessed Unity. "There's a warlike strain in me that might surprise you. I fought for John all his life and I miss the conflict now he's gone. But I shall fight for my grandson if needs be and I wouldn't wish to be under submission for ever same as I am just now."

"There won't be no submission with me."

"No—nothing to fight for with you—except fight for you, if need be."

They chattered on to no purpose and presently the boy came back; tea was taken and the visitors left their friend with many expressions of gratitude. Gilly clung to the discarded crab and, as soon as they were beyond Arthur's hearing, put an anxious question.

"What happens to this now, Grandmother? 'Twas a great set-back to hear Mr. Brimblecombe didn't want it."

But Mrs. Blanchard had already considered the incident.

"I know, Gilly. I've taken thought," she said, "though I wouldn't say I've decided. There's two people in my mind for that crab. In either case I've remembered you, so you needn't think it's lost. My first idea was Mrs. Chadd, because it would give her a lot of pleasure to see her policeman son eat it, which he would do no doubt if I make it over to her. And my second thought was Mr. Owlett, him that catches insects for Sir Gerald. He's an old friend of mine and he was a good friend of your grandfather too, and Nancy Owlett would help him to eat it."

"A lover of curiosities would never turn against a crab like this," said Gilly; "but where would I come in once it's lost to you, Granny?"

"You'd come in like this. I'd say to Mrs. Chadd or Mr. Owlett, as the case might be, that one condition went along with the crab and tell that I wanted you to help eat it. Then either would see you was there at the appointed time to have your share."

"Make it Mr. Owlett," begged the boy.

"Why him over Mrs. Chadd?"

"Because, if I had to go in his house and pleased him, he might give me a peep at his wonderful curiosities," said Gilly. "I'm always hoping for a chance to do that. A proper eye-opener—so a boy told me. He'd took a huge green grasshopper to Mr. Owlett, thinking the creature was in his line, and Mr. Owlett was so pleased he let the boy see a feast of wonders."

"Then you shall offer the crab to Matt tomorrow," promised Mrs. Blanchard, "and I'll dictate to you a letter for him to read. Then, if he's game for the crab, he'll tell you when to come; but if he's no crab-eater, then you can bring it back and I'll try Dinah Chadd."

Mrs. Blanchard was not given to the pen and, if she had occasion to use one, generally called on her grandson to write for her. He carried her letter to the Owlett home next morning and all was well, for Matthew commended the gift and decided it should be eaten that same evening.

"A very fine decapod," he said, "but it wasn't born yesterday, though just right for eating at present. You can't dawdle over a crab. 'Tis now or never with 'em. And today, being Sunday, Nancy's home and you can come to the feast round about eight o'clock, Gilly."

He smelled the gift thoughtfully and spoke again.

"I may or may not ask one more to share it, but most like us three will be enough."

Mr. Owlett enjoyed to talk and, though there was nobody greater than Gilly to listen for the moment, he continued:

"Today, my lad, though but few in Wallabrook know it, is Sir Gerald's birthday. Though gifts from the parish to such a man might be pushing and not acceptable, I'm different and I shall go up over presently and wish his honour well and take him something he will accept."

"A most proud thing for you to be able to do, Mr. Owlett."

"It is, and it comes out of my far-famous collection. He's seen it and thought very highly upon it, and he'll go to his rest tonight knowing one more treasure out of it have become his own property."

"Would it be asking too much for me to look on such a treasure, Mr. Owlett?" ventured the boy; and then the morning teemed with richness for him and the thing that he had desired fell out. Matthew bade him enter his inner sanctum of curios, and there behold a glorious Brazilian butterfly of great size, nobly clad in shining amber and russet with huge black spots like eyes upon its plumage and a touch of crimson at its throat. Gilly's mouth fell open and he gazed for a moment stricken into silence while the old sailor admired his admiration.

"Lord save us! More like a bird than a fly, Mr. Owlett. Do such things home where you've sailed in your time?"

"They do, my lad, but ain't often taken by the hand of man, I promise you. However, I was one too many for him and I've cherished him a good few years since then. Now you can look round if you've got the proper nature to take wonders in a right spirit."

"Oh, may I? Thank you for your gracious goodness, I'm sure, Mr. Owlett! And Granny will forgive me for not going to church with her when she hears tell."

"She will, Gilly—if I know her. You may look round and take in what you can, and I'll throw light on what's beyond your understanding."

In this fascinating manner Gilbert spent his time until it was near midday and Matthew told him to go home. He had illuminated many a dark specimen, rehearsed not a few of his favourite stories and enjoyed the entertainment as much as his visitor.

"You look to have enough mind to value new knowledge," he said, "and I'll tell you a wondrous tale about giant crabs tonight when you are eating this one along with me. Thank Mrs. Blanchard for her gift and now hook it back to her, else she'll be fretting what's become of you. And tell her that I'm going up over to wish Sir Gerald many happy returns of the day and taking him a gift."

"And what a gift, Mr. Owlett! For all his greatness he never had such a gift before, I expect."

"A great gift," admitted Matthew, "and he'll make a fuss over it for its own sake, because he'll know, though it didn't cost me a penny of money to give it, yet it demanded good-willing, which is above money value to Sir Gerald."

Mystified by these reflections, but overflowing with happiness, Unity's grandson now thought upon her. She would just be coming out of church and he resolved to hasten in that direction and accompany her home. He thought about his parents also. "When father and mother hear tell of this triumphant day," he told himself, "they'll find out I ain't the zany they think I am."

CHAPTER VII

THE ritual of Mr. Owlett's approaches to Sir Gerald was punctually observed and had been ordered by the baronet himself. On the occasions when they were to meet, Matthew took his midday meal with the staff and then entered the presence and remained for precisely half an hour. His friend was ready for him at two o'clock and always bade him farewell at half past; but he would not let the visitor depart a moment earlier and occasionally, if the matter in hand was already settled, detained him until the appointed hour.

Now the old sailor arrived in due course bearing his birthday present. He was popular at Oakshotts and regarded as an exceptional man and worthy of special attention. The butler had become a personal friend and found, as he told the housekeeper, that Mr. Owlett possessed very unusual knowledge, great good sense and much else to commend him. "Otherwise," said Mr. Chave, "the master would not favour him same as he is apt to do."

Today, however, Matthew felt a little uncertain of his ground. He had never received any order to appear on a Sunday, for, although he rarely attended worship save on special occasions, Sir Gerald made a point of respecting the day of rest at Oakshotts and the leisure it demanded for his people. Therefore Mr. Chave declared doubt at Owlett's arrival, but when he learned the reason for such an intrusion, expressed hope that all might be well and, after Sunday dinner was over, presently reported that Sir Gerald had displayed no uneasiness and was willing to see the visitor.

"He said that, knowing you, he reckoned some incident of importance must have prompted you to break the rules, Matt," explained the butler, "and I was minded to tell him you knew about his birthday and had brought him a gift; but I didn't: I thought you would like to spring your feat upon him, so I drew a mystery over it and couldn't hazard any reason for your coming."

"Haven't the staff done nothing to celebrate?" asked Owlett.

"We did on one occasion in the past," replied Mr. Chave. "We subscribed for a very fine cushion for his run-about chair and he thanked us, but hoped we'd pass over his birthday in future without any outward or visible sign of our inward good feelings. He also said that, after a fellow creature has turned eighty, his friends should keep quiet over the fact and not rub it in. 'By rights,' he said, ' 'tis the octogenarian should give presents to his remaining friends on such future anniversaries as may be spared him.' So we hushed it up next time and was careful to take no note of it. He forgets it himself now and again in my opinion and I shall be rather interested to hear what he thinks of you for remembering it, Matt."

"It turns on this fine insect," explained the giver. "The creature's outstanding, else I wouldn't have thought upon what looks to be rather a rash act, seemingly."

"A butterfly would stand a better chance of success than most things you would offer to him," admitted Chave.

But the dead Brazilian enjoyed a complete triumph and Sir Gerald, on hearing of Matthew's emotions and desire to please, became himself somewhat moved. He had shaken his friend's hand on entry and inquired somewhat sternly what exceptional incident could have induced a visit so irregular; but, learning Matthew's errand of goodwill, shook his hand again. Then he fell into a complete silence while he gazed upon the gift. It was as though this very beautiful thing had robbed him of speech. Owlett said nothing until the elder wakened from his trance and then he expressed a hope that the gift would be accepted.

"Few men of science can ever have received any more gratifying token of friendship," began Sir Gerald. "This is one of those overwhelming acquisitions quite beyond the recipient's powers to repay or requite: one accepts it as one accepts the blessings of Providence —with heartfelt thanks and utter inability to return any adequate evidence of gratitude. I have often thought upon this insect since first I saw it in your collection, but never, in my greediest and most selfish moments, pictured it my own. You are indeed a generous friend, Matt. I accept the gift and, more gratefully than this wonder itself, I accept the thoughts that inspired the giver. You have a large heart, my dear fellow, and nothing could have better served to get me over my birthday, and the melancholy reflections arising from it, than this noble specimen and still nobler spirit that has prompted it."

Then the old man entered upon an explanation of such a present's exceptional value.

"Knowledge does not always come to us in such a delectable shape as this," he said. "Indeed, many denizens of the insect world, though generally instructive and therefore precious, awake no aesthetic emotions whatever. Some, indeed, to the ignorant create loathing. I have seen actual aversion displayed by persons, otherwise intelligent, when they watched me handle a live spider, earwig or woodlouse; but here is a revelation of beauty which must render any rational being wiser and happier for seeing."

It appeared that no more remained to be said and an agreeable incident was closed; but Matthew ventured on one further thought.

"If the creature cheers you up, your honour, then I'm properly glad to think so. And, though you don't feel your birthday to be a gladsome event yourself, I'm sure everybody in Wallabrook will be happy to think you've come to it in good health and will long so continue."

These interchanges had occupied but five minutes, but Sir Gerald was not prepared to dismiss the Sunday caller until his regulation half-hour had passed. He talked upon the disabilities of the octogenarian and then, during a pause, Matthew changed the subject and mentioned an incident that had amused him. He was fertile of trifles that often gave his learned friend an opportunity to build interesting information upon them.

"You've sometimes marked the small things that surprise small minds, your honour," he said. "I was having a tell with Mrs. Chadd a bit ago—the mother of Peter Chadd, our youngest policeman. Peter got a letter directed to 'P.C. Chadd' from an old friend—another young man who trained to be a policeman same time that Peter did. And the letter puzzled him. 'Why does he put in a "C" to my account,' he asked his mother, 'when he knows my name is Peter and no more?' She couldn't tell, but I could. 'P.C. stands for Police Constable,' I told her. 'That's what your boy is, and his friend named him according.' "

Sir Gerald rose to the bait, for it was never difficult to find a subject on which he would talk if in the mood.

"I can tell you another and more interesting thing about those identical letters," he said. "If they prefix a man's name, then they certainly proclaim him a police constable; but should they be suffixed to it, then what do they stand for?"

"Still a policeman, I'd venture to think, your honour."

"You would think wrong. In that event they declare their bearer to be a member of His Majesty's Privy Council—quite another pair of shoes. To be a policeman is probably to your credit; but to announce yourself a Privy Councillor earns you outstanding respect. Such a man has done the State some valuable service, devoted himself to important work, subscribed to high causes and, as a rule, deserved his honourable distinction."

"I'll bear it in mind, Sir Gerald," promised Matthew. "We live and learn."

"Many such compliments are of little account," continued the speaker. "Our fountains of honour spurt them so lavishly that they cease to command our salutations. Some actually possess a market value and can be purchased by those wealthy enough to pay for them; but there are others whose worth is above rubies and within reach of few. Rank may become, as in my case, a nuisance when the hereditary holder is expected to follow certain standards of conduct and imaginary obligations only existing in the traditions of the past. Idiots will exalt a man above the norm of mankind because he happens to be the son of his father. Many, for example, consider me to be an utterly inadequate baronet, for the reason that I fail of those pre-historic ideals as to how a right baronet should comport himself.

"Now *Respondete natalibus*—live up to your birthright—is a noteworthy command, and I am the first to respect it; but Nature, not heredity, must determine what your birthright happens to be. The county is incapable of grasping this elementary fact. That an ancient baronetcy should have ended in an eminent entomologist certain persons in my acquaintance regard as a scandal—a dereliction of duty on my part, a contempt for a family which I should have made efforts to prolong rather than terminate, a deliberate and godless disregard of ineluctable principles. They hold apparently that the activities and sleepless search for truth proper to a scientist become almost indecent if displayed by a man of title.

"My own respected father subscribed to this grotesque opinion and viewed my adolescent attainments with dismay. He would tell me that never in the annals of my race had the head of the family failed of God's divine purpose as I threatened to do. I promised in fact to become a hopeless baronet—a tare sprung up in the wheat-field that for centuries had yielded a seemly harvest of manor lords."

Matthew listened with the grave interest that this confession demanded, and then Sir Gerald uttered his deep, abdominal laugh.

"Yet consider these circumstances from another angle, my friend," he continued. "My father, Sir Eustace, was human, just as you and I are human. He was the fifteenth baronet; I am the sixteenth, and each in his turn developed a most human ambition. Both of us desired something within the power of our fellow creatures to bestow upon us; a distinction familiarly known and recognised in the shape of three letters. But not the same letters. My father's were only to be obtained by the possession and practice of his own special endowments and we both lived to see our ambitions gratified. His triumph in no way sullied his condition and repute. He was a pre-eminent sportsman and, as you may have heard from the aged among us, when he became a Master of Hounds, none was more capable and accomplished than himself in all that pertained to such a mastership. Those who yet remember him will tell you that, in his great years, he proved the most accomplished M.F.H. it is possible to imagine, and I have no doubt whatever that they are right."

Sir Gerald paused a moment, then proceeded to discuss himself.

"How different my ambition! What a lapse was there, Owlett! What a gulf divided my three coveted letters from those that Sir Eustace so worthily achieved! You know them, I suspect?"

"The Lord forgive me, your honour, I've no idea whatsoever," said Matthew.

"F.R.S., my dear fellow! I am a Fellow of the Royal Society, and that, let me assure you, is also a recognition of some moment. It declares the holder to be a successful and original servant of truth and sets him on record as having served science with devotion in one or other of its myriad activities. There for ever beckoned my apex and pinnacle of ambition, and such was my natural bent to those uncharted and unfrontiered fields of entomology that I concentrated and dedicated my life to the moth! A thousand byways and lesser channels to truth opened before me as I proceeded; but the eternal quest for all pertaining to the moth commanded my first devotion. And what was the result, Owlett? Those endowed to appreciate and comprehend my labours combined to bestow upon me this unique recognition, before which all others, in my judgment, pale to nothing. I dreamed of it and chid my own vanity for so doing, and yet——"

Sir Gerald broke off and silently pursued his own reflections for a moment. Then he boomed on again:

"And yet, long after the last haunting aspirations for such an honour had ceased to trouble me, my youthful dream was turned into reality."

"A proud moment, master."

"Not in the least! Its advent found me long past the psychological moment to appreciate it. To have seen it bestowed upon certain younger men for whom I entertained admiration would have wakened far more pleasure and satisfaction; but, coming to me at fifty-five, I found the gilt worn off the gingerbread. Fame in truth seldom reaches a man of science until he has long ceased to set any store upon it."

These subtleties were beyond Matthew and he prepared to withdraw as swiftly as possible. He rose to indicate that he was going.

"Thus time has its revenges," summed up Sir Gerald, "and if enough time is placed at your disposal, Owlett, as in my case, you will see the saliences of the past reduced much to the level of the beaten track. But you have created for me today a very considerable elevation. And when I go to earth—not in our deplorable family mausoleum, but under the good greensward—I could wish nothing better than that the ghost of your wondrous gift might occasionally spread its wings on moonlit nights above my resting-place."

Bewildered and scarcely knowing whether to laugh or shed a tear over these vapourings, Matthew shook the lean hand extended to him.

"Even its ghost wouldn't stand up to our climate; but be it as it will, your honour's goodness, I'll always continue your faithful bedesman," he said.

"Excellent, Matt! A beautiful word we seldom hear nowadays. Lift an occasional petition on my account by all means. It is interesting to reflect that some everlasting and potent entity may be responsible alike for Matthew Owlett, this glorious *Caligo brasiliensis* and myself. But I will leave the thought with you until we meet again and then learn if you can make anything of it."

Before leaving Oakshotts Matthew uttered a word of caution to Mr. Chave.

"The master's in one of his most fantastical moods today. His birthday looks to have gone to his head, so you'd best to watch out; but he's properly pleased over the present."

"If he said he was pleased, then he is pleased," declared the butler. "You can always take the gentleman at his face value, Matt, because the whole truth and nothing but the truth has been his watchword so long as I've known him."

When evening came, Gilly White arrived in good time for the crab and ventured to ask whether Sir Gerald had been properly rejoiced at Mr. Owlett's gift. Nancy cooked the crab, and her father created some slight disturbance in her mind by jesting upon a subject that admitted no levity in his daughter's opinion. She had spent the afternoon in companionship with Peter Chadd, and he continued to command her interest and attention. They not only walked out when time permitted, but he had once taken her as far as Tavistock and been allowed to give her a very good tea there. Now, as the three ate their crab and Matthew directed Gilly in the technique of this operation, he made his ill-timed remark.

"I was going to ask Mrs. Chadd to join us tonight," he said, "but then I remembered she'd be safe to bring her policeman, and what was one crab to the likes of him? A man his size would think no more of it than eating a prawn, and we should all be forced to sit with empty plates while Peter wolfed the lot."

Gilly laughed and Matthew laughed, but Nancy did not, and after supper was over and the boy had gone home, she returned to the subject.

"You may think what you said about Mr. Chadd was funny, Father," she began, "but it wasn't really, because Peter's got rather a small appetite for such a big man. And, as he's coming to supper with his mother next Sunday, I hope you won't say nothing like that again—not in Mrs. Chadd's hearing anyway. If you want her friendship, you best not be vulgar about Peter, because she puts him in a place of his own and wouldn't stand no undervaluing even from you."

"God's mercy! Who am I to undervalue Peter Chadd, or anybody else?" asked her father. "Don't be so sharp-tongued, Nancy, for I won't have it. I was only cracking a joke same time as I cracked the crab. So far as I know I'd say the police constable was a very outstanding, modest man and as trustable as he is handsome. I admire him very near as much as his mother does, I shouldn't wonder."

Nancy was mollified.

"I know him better than you do and he says I know him better than his mother does in some respects," she said. "He's got opinions that go a bit beyond Mrs. Chadd; but I see what he's driving at all right."

Mr. Owlett also saw what Peter was driving at and perceived that, up to the present, he appeared to be making reasonable progress. Nancy's father had hardly expected this particular young man to challenge her seriously, but of late began to view the situation as growing more tense.

"I shall get better acquaint after next Sunday," he said. "And fear nothing, my lass. There's some people who laugh even when the joke's against themselves, and there's others like nothing less than having their legs pulled, and there's others again you wouldn't dare to pull their legs. Our police inspector, Samuel Manley, is such a man as that. You might poke fun at him, but only to waste it. It would be beyond Samuel's imagination that such a thing was attempted; but Peter—I don't know yet: I must know him better."

"He's high-minded, though never much one for the amusing side of life, like you and me, Father."

"No quarrel with that, my love. I wouldn't say for a police constable there was any great advantage in making jokes. Nothing particular comical in their job of work as a rule, and them that fall into their hands and find they've got to stop there ain't often in a mood for backchat."

Nancy agreed.

"You'll find Mr. Chadd is large-minded about criminals," she explained. "Inspector's different. He's down on ill-doers like a ton of bricks, and when he sees the first spark of wickedness dawn in a child's eyes, then he starts to put the fear of God and himself into that child's mind; but Peter says that if a child was born in sin, it weren't the child's fault and you've got to make allowances."

"Nobody's more willing than myself for even-handed justice to be done," declared Matthew, "and in some cases I might tip the scales a trifle for any poor devil who found himself up against the law; but I'd need to understand particulars and look beyond the facts to the situation behind 'em."

"Then you'll mostly find Mr. Chadd's the sort to satisfy you," promised Nancy. "He's great on deduction, but he says that once that's done, then you ought to go on deducting into the reasons that made the culprits to be wrongful-doers and sometimes find yourself in two minds as to whether they were wrongful-doers at all."

Mr. Owlett laughed heartily.

"Your Peter—so to call him—sounds a bit out of the beaten track," he said. "He takes his job seriously, sure enough, and I'll be glad to hear him on it himself come Sunday. He sounds as if he might be a bit heavy in hand, however."

"He's not 'my Peter', Father, but I respect his opinions when I can grasp 'em, and he respects my opinions. I don't find him heavy in hand as a rule. What he says and thinks might bore some girls to tears, but he don't bore me. He ain't one of those chaps who will be talking though the heavens fall—mostly about himself. But he don't talk much about himself. He's just willing to live and let live and likes to hear me talk and most always agrees with my views."

"And right to do so, Nancy. Nobody's got better sense than you as a general habit."

"If there's one subject on which he'll weary me now and again," she confessed, "it's his mother. He's got a mad affection for her and he'll run on about her till the cows come home."

"She's a very likeable and nice woman and a most faithful mother to Peter."

"I know. I know he's right to set a lot of store by her, same as I set store by you; but I don't jam you down people's throats and praise your gifts and your greatness in season and out, like Peter praises Mrs. Chadd."

"Dinah's very well in her way and she's had the deuce of a bad time and stood up to it amazing brave. Peter was too young to understand all she had to suffer; but, if he'd known the ugly truth as to his father, he wouldn't have felt cause to make any allowances in that quarter. There's a challenge there, Nancy, because however trustworthy and above suspicion Peter may be on the surface, you've got to remember he's the son of an out-size scoundrel without the bare bones of a conscience in him. Nobody ever did evil with a better appetite than what Aaron Chadd did."

"He knows that only too well, Father. He pointed it out to me himself. He said that when a boy's old enough to be told his father is a drunkard, then it's that boy's solemn duty never to touch a drop of drink so long as he lives; and he also said in his case, when he understood the fashion of man his father was, he felt the danger and strove, with all his heart and soul, to go straight no matter what the temptations to go crooked. He told me that, if he'd been in a higher walk of life with money behind him, he'd have tried to get into the Church and become a minister as a safeguard against the blood in his veins; but seeing he couldn't reach to anything like that, he went in the police force, feeling no course of life was more like to make him hate wickedness."

"Sounds almost too good to be true," said Matthew. "And all credit to Dinah for bringing him up with such fine opinions. She must be thanked for her share in the young man. Life will prove him some day. You can always trust your life to show up your character soon or late; but if all you tell is true and other sides of Peter haven't shook your judgment, then I should reckon he ought to make a respectable business of being a policeman. We'll wait and watch."

"It's a bit tedious waiting and watching," said Nancy, "but you've waited and watched oft enough, Father, over your natural history, and I'll do the same—at any rate for a bit longer."

"Nothing like marking time, and nothing harder at your age. But it may come easier to him than you. Half a policeman's job is marking time."

CHAPTER VIII

WHILE his daughter was throwing light on the complex attractions of Peter's character to her father, the policeman himself, who had spent the afternoon with her, dwelt upon Nancy's unusual qualities, after Mrs. Chadd herself had opened the way to views on this delicate subject.

"You wouldn't say you was making too much of a habit of Nancy Owlett, would you, Peter?" she asked. "You know I've got a high opinion of her, same as I have of her father, but what you are doing along with Nancy leads to create a public opinion, my dear, and folk get to think there might be more in it than meets the eye."

"She isn't one to worry herself a lot about public opinion, Mother, and no more am I," he answered. "We've reached to a stage, I'd say, when we find ourselves enough interested to inquire further. We see a lot alike and my idea of Nancy looks to be much the same as her idea of me. We haven't come to a showdown, so to speak—not yet. Nancy's above any craft, being one to lay all her cards on the table—so far as you can say any woman ever do lay all her cards on the table. That's their protection against us and, though I don't know a thing about 'em in general, I can see now and again, even with Nancy, that she'll always keep a card or two up her sleeve."

"What's your feeling to her when you look ahead, Peter?" asked his mother. "Excuse me asking, but do you feel walking out satisfies your nature so far as she is concerned, or don't you?"

"I feel it a very important part of my life to walk out with her," he admitted. "She leaves me with a sort of general conclusion I ain't up to her standard, but against that you've got to argue she hasn't changed her mind as to walking and, so far, gives me to understand it suits her. She says she can always rely upon me, because I look to be about the most steadfast object she knows in a changeable world. That's the most personal remark she's allowed herself to make so far as I'm concerned, and though she's apt to talk very freely about other people and looks to be a very good judge of human nature for a young girl, yet she's fair and don't often say anything to be called unkind."

"You haven't got no idea what she really thinks of you?"

Peter considered this.

"No; I wouldn't venture to put it in words, Mother. I'd say she ain't dead sure what she thinks. What she's really thinking depends upon clues outside my knowledge. Some days she'll be a lot more oncoming than other days. Some days I find myself nearer to her understanding than others. There's nothing puts her off me quicker than the days I'm oncoming myself, and then, when she looks to be oncoming and I respond, the result is that she stops being oncoming and goes to the other extreme and even gets a bit chilly."

"That leaves you with a lot in doubt," agreed Mrs. Chadd. "Then you'd say there was nothing serious doing between you in sober truth—at any rate so far?"

"No, I wouldn't like to say that," he answered. "Too bleak, that is. What may be doing—if anything—in her mind, I couldn't guess; but what's doing in my mind I do know. My general deduction is that she's a lovely piece and long ways the prettiest and cleverest woman ever I spoke to. You've only got to pass the time of day with other girls to see the difference between them and her. But, being so outstanding, then she must know it herself, and if she knows it, she may well ask herself if she isn't wasting her spare time along with a man that isn't outstanding but just ordinary."

"She's quite bright enough to know you ain't ordinary, Peter, and if you're too humble to see why she's taking this line, then I can tell you. Nancy has got her ideas about you and most likely finds you quite as different from other males as you find her different from other females. From what you say I should reckon you could make her fall in love with you if you want to. But, in that case, you'll do well to stop singing small, because the humble and meek fashion of man is the last to take any pushing and hopeful young woman's fancy. She expects to have a good trustable husband some day and reckons she deserves one. She don't think small beer of herself—quite rightly. She's a very fine girl and might have wed long before now if she'd been so minded. A rich man once offered for her, to my certain knowledge, because Matt Owlett told me so; but she turned that man down because she didn't love him, or ever see her way to do so. Which proves she's got proper principles and respects herself."

"She wouldn't marry any man unless she loved him, I know that," agreed Peter; "but you mustn't let your affection for me make you one-sided, Mother. She is ambitious and hopes for a position in the future, as you say; and what sort of prospects would arise for that if she married a police constable?"

"A poor man in love has got one great advantage over a rich man in love," explained Mrs. Chadd. "The rich man will never know to his dying day whether his wife loved him or his money, and whether she only took the one to be sure of the other; but a poor man without any chances of being a rich one, if he wins a girl, knows that he was took for love only, there being nothing in his favour but himself."

"I expect that's true," he admitted, "and when you put it like that I doubt if any such huge thought has ever entered her mind in connection with me. She'll say things bearing on marriage but only with a light touch, whereas, if she'd ever felt any inclination to the state, she'd very soon see the darned solemn side to it."

"That's the sensible way, no doubt, my dear," declared Dinah, "but love has a trick to make you light-hearted, just for the joy of being in love, and most lovers take that way and never see no serious side till it's too late."

Peter was tired of the subject and a night's beat awaited him.

"Well, we must leave the matter to unfold as it will," he said. "I don't see Mr. Owlett without Nancy and he might not see her along with me instead of him."

"Say no more, Peter," begged his mother. "A father's one thing, a sweetheart's another, and there's naught in reason why they should quarrel if they both hap to be orderly creatures. And if Nancy better liked the thought of biding with her father than joining up with you, then she wouldn't have walked out with you for a month of Sundays same as she has done. You can't have nothing for nothing in any case and, when I hear Matthew's opinions as to the prospects of such a thing, I'll let you know how he looks upon you."

Before this information reached Dinah, however, she spent some hours of an afternoon with another trusted friend. Sunday was a day when Wallabrook people could claim their beauty spots for their own, and favourite regions were the river valley and the waterfall, where many would often go when sunshine invited on the day of rest. Mrs. Blanchard was among them and, during the afternoon of the following Sunday, she sent Gilly to summon Mrs. Chadd and bid her come to tea. But first they walked beside Walla and considered their varied interests.

"You've got your daughter back by now, Unity, and I do hope she's returned home in a cheerful spirit," said Dinah.

"Oh yes, their fortnight by the sea has done both good so far. Very civil to me and Maude glad to get Brian back to work."

"Long may it last," answered Mrs. Chadd. "I wish you could take a few days off for a bit, then it might dawn upon them where they'd be without you."

"They'd find themselves so comfortable they might refuse for me to come back, my dear. But I shan't go till Gilly goes."

"Matt Owlett speaks well of Gilly. He showed the boy his museum. By the same token Peter and me are eating our supper with Matt and Nancy tonight."

"He thinks a lot of you, Dinah."

"I want to know what he thinks of Peter, because things look to be coming to a climax in that direction now. And what touches my son touches me."

They rested together on a rustic seat beside the river, not far from the waterfall, and Unity did not immediately reply. She fell back upon her own thoughts, as always happened when she came here.

"There's places round about you," she said, "that seem to cling a lot closer to your memory than other places. Mostly they happen indoors and belong just to one room, like the room in my old home where John died—the same room where Maude was born. But brighter things than Maude mostly come into my mind here, Dinah. This place don't change; but Lord, what a lot have happened to change me since my husband asked me to marry him on this very spot where we be sitting now!"

"The river's always drawn you, Unity."

"Yes, that's so. Here Walla just quiets again after flouncing down over the fall. There's words I read once—might be in the Bible but I'm not sure as to that—reminds me of the river. Today her voice is like song-birds singing in the branches; and then again tomorrow, when a spate comes down and the snow melts on the Moor, she roars like the floods that clap their hands."

"Just how it happens," agreed Dinah.

"I've sat by her all alone in the dark of a stormy night sometimes," continued Mrs. Blanchard, talking to herself rather than her companion. "Yes, I've crept out all alone and found the din of the flood boiling and bellowing will soothe my nerves when dear John was making me suffer more than usual. If your heart and mind be in a chaos of misery, Dinah, sometimes a greater chaos and misery than your own shows you what a trifle you and your troubles amount to against a whole river howling like a mad thing."

"You might have catched a fatal chill, Unity. I hate to think of you night-foundered and forlorn like that."

The other struggled free of her memories.

"All past and gone now and silly to be chittering about it to you. You were saying affairs were heading for a climax, and you was aiming at Peter no doubt. Well, it looks as if it might be a nice climax for both of 'em. Matt's girl wouldn't keep him on a string so long if she hadn't found pretty much what she wanted to find by now. Thomasina Parsons was wondering only yesterday, when she came to see Maude, why the news hadn't reached her yet. She knows all about it and says it ought to be off or on by now."

"It ain't off and it ain't on," explained Dinah. "Peter's very much took, but he ain't properly tormented over her, else I'd have marked the signs. Still, he likes to be talking about her."

"Not in love, exactly?"

"No, not to the racking stage. I'd say, perfect as he is, that Peter's too young to get married yet and I'll lay my life Owlett will say the same. He'll be talking to me tonight and he may have heard Nancy on the subject. Matt's like to get a lot more out of her than I can get out of Peter. That's why I say things look to be at a climax because, if her father tells me tonight there's nothing to it and he don't wish for his child to marry mine in any case, then it's over and done and I can tell Peter so before he's had time to take failure too much to heart."

"All depends upon Nancy," decided Mrs. Blanchard. "She's got a will of her own and, by now, she knows a sight more about Peter than ever he's likely to know about her; and that's no harm done neither, because she'd never let him down. In fact he'll be lucky to get her."

"He wouldn't be no luckier than what she would, Unity. You don't mean that?"

"Certainly not. You mark happy marriages quite so often as disasters. No news is good news in marriage most times. 'Tis only the failures that make news."

"You was always a hopeful fashion of woman," said Mrs. Chadd. "One of your gifts. I'll tell you come presently what Owlett says."

And, before the day was done, Peter's mother heard. They fell in with neighbours now and presently sauntered back to the village.

"Two free meals I'm taking today," declared Dinah as she drank tea at 'Laburnum Lodge', "and in these times I feel it almost a robbery to do so."

Then she asked Maude as to her holiday.

"We mostly went our own ways," said Mrs. White, "and with people like me and Brian, that was best for us both; but one night he ordained we'd go round the Eddystone lighthouse by moonlight in the little excursion steamer. A queer way to amuse yourself, you'd think. Still, I'm as good a sailor as Brian is, so we went. Not a thing to do twice, as I told him, but just worth doing once in a lifetime, I dare say."

Maude still preserved her holiday spirits and Dinah had never known her so expansive and cheerful.

Mrs. Chadd's day finished with supper at the Owletts', and, when she had apologised yet again for eating so freely at the expense of others, Matthew took the matter in hand, bade Peter go and help Nancy wash up and conveyed his mother into the parlour.

"Now they'll be out of the road for a bit," he said, "and we can talk about 'em if you're so disposed."

"Light your pipe and speak your mind," begged Dinah. "You know what's in mine, and I'd go so far as to say I know what's in yours. It lies in a nutshell for the both of us. You've got one girl and I've got one boy. And I hate to think of losing Peter, just as you hate the idea of parting from Nancy. So there it is."

"If it's got so far as that, then the pair of 'em have overreached me," declared Matthew. "You may be in their secrets deeper than what I am, Dinah, because a boy will tell his mother a lot more than ever a girl is like to tell her father—us being more frank in our youth than ever you are—but I grant there's signs in the air. Has Peter gone so far as to tell you he wants Nancy?"

"Not in so many words; but a mother can read between the lines," explained Mrs. Chadd. "I'd say he was heading to love her, but don't fully grasp it yet."

"Exactly so," agreed Mr. Owlett. "My girl's got that far too, and she has grasped it—so much so that I felt it was time I stirred myself. Nancy holds a high opinion of me, of course, and has always been guided by my views on life in general, so I mustn't disappoint her now. And same with you and your son: you mustn't do nothing to make him feel you ain't all he thinks you. Both our offspring are fortunate in their parents: that's agreed. And having cleared the air, so to speak, you and I must needs know our own minds. First there's what you think of Nancy, and second there's what I think of Peter."

"I've always liked your girl for her fine appearance and good spirits and determined character," said Dinah. "She's the top flower of the basket in Wallabrook, same as Peter is the finest man to my knowledge that ever drew his breath here."

"Then we're agreed about Nancy as a wife-old woman and a thought out of the common. We see alike there. And now you'd wish to know if I see Peter to be such a bright star as you do. That's impossible and outside nature, because no other human being can ever see Peter with his mother's eyes. But don't feel no great fear on that account. I come to Peter same as I come to everybody else. I've got an open mind about Peter and, seeing the importance for me to get to the truth of Peter, I haven't yet reached the point to utter my conclusions upon him. In a general way I'd agree with you and give him full marks, Dinah. I've never heard any unfavourable word spoken against him by a single soul, and Inspector Manley, last time I saw him, said that, from the angle of his business, your boy's making up to be all that he could wish, though still untried in any serious matter."

"You can see his natural goodness in his eyes, Matt. Goodness shines out of his face," declared Mrs. Chadd.

"It may do; but you want something more than goodness to shine out of a policeman's face, or out of a husband's face, don't you? I do. He's got a nice, mild, everyday sort of face, but it ain't hard enough, nor yet understanding enough as yet. Look at my face and allow for my years and my eyelid that droops, which is the result of night-watches aboard ship when I'd got to keep my eyes skinned against every sort of weather. What d'you see as to character stamped upon my face?"

"I'd say there's a lot more to see than I can see, my dear man. I'd say you'd got a mighty sly face and a deep mind behind it. A strong face, but rather a crafty one, Matt."

Mr. Owlett laughed and relighted his pipe.

"I may see more than what you think for in your face," she continued. "I know it so well by now that I can read a lot there; and more still by things you say that puzzle some folk, but not me. You're truth made alive as a rule I well know, and to be truthful just for the love of truth is a bit uncommon. So I won't say you've got a crafty face, my dear, but a watchful face."

"That's better," he agreed.

"But," continued Dinah, "though you haven't said something, I challenge you to deny you've thought it, Matt. You're frightened of his father in Peter. You're feared for Nancy because of my boy's father."

"No, I'm not. If there was a spark showing of his father in him, I'd shut down against him ever marrying Nancy like the clap of doom; but he's escaped his father; and that's a feather in your cap, my dear, because for an ordinary, virtuous woman like you to conquer his father in him was a very clever piece of work. It goes to show, when God wills, that miracles can still be done. I don't mistrust Peter's honesty, nor yet his rules of behaviour, nor yet his mother-taught conscience. They are all in his face and I only want what ain't in his face. He's tender-hearted and not particular strong-willed. To be self-willed is bad, though, seeing the way childer are brought up now, it comes natural to 'em, but you must be strong-willed to show yourself a strong man."

"No call to doubt he'd stand for righteousness, if it was demanded for him to do so," said Peter's mother. "I've tried to lay the foundations, Matthew."

"If the world was full of people like you and me, Dinah, then I'd feel no fear for your boy; but it ain't, and in his job of work he's bound to meet rascals, both plain and coloured, by the score presently. Life haven't found him up against any wickedness to name as yet."

"You ain't going to wait and see how he shapes against murderers and suchlike fearful creatures, are you?" asked Mrs. Chadd somewhat indignantly. "A policeman may do his duty all his working life and never be called to face a murderer."

"Calm yourself, calm yourself," begged Matthew. "I'm not wishful to see Peter after a murderer and I don't doubt for a minute that, if he was, he wouldn't do his best to catch him. I'd say Peter to be so brave as a lion where his duty was concerned, but his duty might come in quite a different shape from a murderer and demand not his courage but his quality and character. Duty's a very downy bird, my dear. And now we'll say no more on the subject. For the present you're not called to lose your boy and I'm not called to lose my girl. They'll both marry somebody some day; but whether they'll marry each other is hidden from all of us—themselves included. Anyway, 'tis them have got to decide, not us, and when we hear their intentions, then we can see as to whether we agree.

That won't make any great difference to them in any case—not if I know Nancy."

"You'd demand to mark time?"

"I'd demand to mark time, certainly, and you'll demand to mark time, I should think. Us Devonshire folk are always famous for marking time, and we fare no worse for that. You and me have got ourselves to think upon, and if our mainstays and supports are to be taken from us, we shall be called to plan our lives different. I don't see myself without Nancy to do a daughter's tasks for me. I've thought to tell her already I shall be glad when she gives up land work and watches a thought closer on my requirements; while you know very well how you'll feel like when Peter marries."

"I thought perhaps him and me might still live on together."

"Then think again," advised Mr. Owlett. "And I'm rather surprised such a clever woman as you thought that. Even a green girl like Nancy knows better."

"She knows what I am to Peter."

"Who don't? Certainly she knows; and she also knows that never is three worse company under one roof than a man and his wife and his mother. Many a misfortunate wretch have died of that, if he didn't escape and run away from the pair of 'em. I've told herself so myself, for that matter. No names, of course, but a bit of common wisdom. The only safe third party to suit the newly married is their first babe, and even that may not be the success you'd count upon."

Mrs. Chadd considered these things.

"Nancy's very fond of me and me of her," she said.

"And long may she remain so."

"Can't you imagine yourself happy enough living along with Nancy and Peter?" she asked.

"There's nothing on God's earth would make me less happy than to live with a policeman," answered Matthew.

It was at this moment that their children returned. They had long since washed up the supper dishes and gone into the garden.

"Come on home, Mother," said Peter. "D'you know the time? Half after nine o'clock."

"I lay father's properly exhausted you with his chatter," added Nancy. "You look cruel tired, Mrs. Chadd."

"He's full of sense, though I don't always find myself to agree with it," replied Dinah.

"And she ain't afraid to tell me so," added Matthew. "However, we've set the world right so far as we can between us. Put the lady's coat on her, Nancy. Getting cold of a night now. What price a spot of whiskey before you flit, Dinah?"

"Not for me, Matt."

"You, Peter?"

"Tee-total, Mr. Owlett, thank you."

"You would be, I'm afraid. Well, God bless the pair of you."

"And both of you, I'm sure. And thank you for a lovely supper," said Dinah.

Then mother and son departed, while her father had time to observe that Nancy was more moved than common. She explained her unusual emotion.

"Sorry if I came back too soon, Dad, but I felt afraid of my life, what with the darkness and his feelings and one thing and another, that Peter was going a bit too far," she said.

"Fear nothing as to that, my love," he replied. "Peter's never going too far. The question in my mind is whether he'll ever go far enough. He'd suit plenty of girls, but you are the high-spirited, ambitious sort, like me, and I'm not over-sure he can top our standards."

"He came on with a rush tonight," she said. "In a most masterly mood he was for once. If he weren't tee-total you might have thought he'd had one over the eight. Oh, Father, I liked him better tonight than ever I liked him! Funny, because I always told myself I'd never take a man under six foot tall, and I do believe, if he hadn't got his outstanding height, I'd never have walked out with him."

"The height is there," granted Mr. Owlett, "and come he's spared into middle age, the breadth will be there too. He'll always be the slow-going, deliberate sort—the sort that put on weight so soon as they are past their prime. Happy folk are prone to grow fat and I dare say Peter will be up sixteen or seventeen stone by the day he's earned a pension."

"He wasn't over-happy tonight. He went so far as to say I was a lot on his mind of late, and coming between him and duty, or so he feared. Then he said he'd got something important to tell me. If I'd pressed him to get on with it, he'd have told me instanter, because of course I saw what it was he meant to tell. But quite enough for one night that he'd reached to the point of offering. 'Next time we go for a walk, you shall say what's on your mind, Peter,' I told the man. 'No doubt it can keep all right till then.'

He fell in with that and, I think, was rather glad he'd got one more chance to turn it over before he took the plunge."

"Love's well known to cast out caution," explained Mr. Owlett, "and if I didn't find that true when I was courting your mother, then nobody ever found it true. Now we know where we stand and you have got time to decide."

"Did Mrs. Chadd have any opinions as to me, Father?"

"There can't be two opinions as to you, my pretty dear. You've got the goods to make any man a lucky husband. No, Dinah was such a lot occupied with her son's virtues that we scarce dwelt on yours. But no doubts about her high opinion."

"Nor yet yours, I hope, Father?"

"I hope not too. You've made up my mind for me now and then, so why not again? You have a great gift to make up your mind, same as your mother had before you. It saves a lot of trouble, and often saves your friends a lot of trouble also."

CHAPTER IX

AMOS HANNAFORD, host of the 'Fisherman's Welcome', was not a typical publican of the more popular sort, and he knew it. "I was called to follow my father, who had the gifts," he would explain, "and I didn't work under him ten years for nothing. I saw where he made his mark, being a genial, easy-tempered man and generous to a fault. As I grew up and grasped the nature of a publican's business, I saw his strength and also his weakness. I found I lacked for his strength and never should have the gift to make friends with my customers like him; but beyond that, I resolved never to make bad debts, or put such faithful trust in my fellow creatures as he did. For the truth is that if you want your business to be creditable, the less credit you give to your customers the better.

"Landlords come and go, but public-houses go on for ever, and though I've heard men say the 'Fisherman's Welcome' ought to be called something different since I took it on, yet no man's had honest cause to fall foul of me. Beer's not what it was, any more than spirits are what they were; but such quality as I can command, I offer, and though you got better whiskey in my father's time for five shillings a bottle than you can look for now at twenty-five, the swindle is done by the Government, not by us publicans."

In this firm and fearless manner Amos Hannaford explained the principles that inspired his thoughts and actions. He was a tall, lean man with a somewhat dour and unwelcoming manner. When customers, new or old, revealed any laxity of morals in the general conversation at his public bar, he instantly rebuked them—a habit which had driven even old supporters away sometimes; but that did not trouble him. He knew that the only rival inn failed his own high standards and that quality was the ultimate criterion. Wandering drinkers almost invariably returned, to be greeted and served as of old without comment. In years long past, the late John Blanchard had once deserted Hannaford; but he soon came back again and explained in his amiable fashion the reason for surrender.

"Here I am once more, Amos," he had said. "The lost sheep's back to the fold, because the inn is more than the innkeeper if you're a thirsty man. Your orderly house and your beer—so near the real thing as can be—is better than a disorderly house and the stuff they call beer and sell as beer down the road."

But two abiding friends and upholders Mr. Hannaford could always number and, on an autumn night, near closing-time, both were in the bar together. Inspector Manley was one, Arthur Brimblecombe the other, and each enjoyed the companionship of his neighbours. Samuel Manley valued the respect his position created; while Arthur—a lonely man—found the atmosphere of the 'Fisherman's Welcome' agreeable when his day's work was done. Politics, rather than local personalities, Amos encouraged.

Himself he lacked humour, yet perceived that jesting never failed to cheer the company and always strove to encourage laughter that was not obscene; but tonight a serious topic occupied the fleeting moment and Inspector Manley expressed regret and wonder at the attitude of Russia on the question of Berlin. The inspector was a stout, black-bearded man with large, owlish black eyes. Always a great reader, he liked to hand on his knowledge thus gathered.

"Time was when we ruled over Europe by right of our wisdom and experience," he said in his deep monotone, "but now we ain't the bell-wether of the nations as when I was born. We'd have our private fights at home under Victoria, and Dizzy and Gladstone would mop the floor of the House of Commons with each other and so on; but now the British lion waits for the American eagle and the French cock before he dares to growl. He dursn't stand up to the Russian bear and make ready to strip the hide off the beast, same as he did in the old days."

"The Russians are our natural enemies, Inspector. They always were and they always will be. I've said it before and I'll say it again here and now," declared Mr. Brimblecombe.

"The world's got to be a lying world," answered Manley, "and I mark a great increase in the habit, Arthur. A man's word ain't his bond same as it used to be, and what's the result? We don't trust nobody much farther than we can see them."

Mr. Hannaford brought the matter back to the Russians.

"History looks to be repeating itself under our noses," he pointed out, "but our leaders don't see, or don't please to see, that the gang of men up top in Russia today are doing just the same as t'other gang that led Germany yesterday. They want the world, and by rights they should all hang for it in their turn, same as the others have done. The mischief is that where the Germans were beat, the Russians may win; and they will win if our Government goes on pretending that Socialism is one thing and Communism another."

"Russia's got right on her side and we know it and haven't got the pluck to admit it, till she makes us."

Thus spoke Brian White, who often took his pleasure at Mr. Hannaford's bar, when at liberty to do so, and rejoiced to oppose the popular opinions.

"Wait and see, my lad," warned Inspector Manley. "Wait and see what the Communists will do to your sort when they get the power. Do you imagine that the railwaymen in Russia see themselves having a five-day week while their wives work for seven? Do you think they get paid holidays to go fishing and dog-racing? You don't know you're born yet, Brian White; but if ever you live to feel the knout of Russia on your hide, then you'll wish you hadn't been born."

"I couldn't care less than for anything you're pleased to say, Inspector," replied Brian. "The likes of you, that draw their living from the pockets of the rich, don't matter to us thinking men. The police force was only created to keep capital safe from the workers that made the capital."

"And what was the secret police force created for in Russia? What was the concentration camps created for? Why's the Iron Curtain clamped down for? To keep the workers safe from freedom and justice and hide their slavery from their own eyes," said Brimblecombe.

"That's right, Arthur," agreed the landlord. "That's where we're drifting to. It's in the air, like a fog or a bad smell, and them who say they couldn't care less will only begin to care more when it's too late and all's lost."

From these gloomy reflections a man brought the interest to local matters personal to himself.

"You haven't heard any news about the gentleman who stole two of my ducks last week, Inspector?" he asked.

"No, Mr. Fern," answered Manley, "not yet, but I'm moving on the case. Did the gentleman have two legs, or four? A lot turns on that. If he had four, then it's for you to deal with him yourself, but if he carries but two, then he comes under my attention."

"I reckon he had but two," answered Farmer Fern. "A fox leaves feathers about, but a thief is careful to hide his tracks."

"I've asked my constable, Peter Chadd, to turn his wits on your ducks, Fern. I incline to the opinion it was a fox, or foxes, myself;

but I may be wrong there, because I've learned of something that might prove evidence to the contrary. Somebody told Mrs. Manley yesterday that somebody else—both shall be nameless for the present—had a duck for dinner not long since. Not evidence, you understand; still, worthy to be called a clue and demand my attention, because the duck-eater ain't such as would have a bird on his, or her, table in the usual course of events. The culprit may be hearing my voice at this moment, or he may not."

The inspector rolled his eyes over the company, but if any sign of guilt challenged him, he kept the discovery to himself.

Mr. Hannaford, who had no need to fear the law at any time, censured this announcement.

"You didn't ought to throw private information about like that, Samuel," he said. "Now you may have warned the very one you're after."

"No, Amos. Fear no such thing. I merely mention the subject to show how a false rumour can get in the air and sound so true that the people believe it as a matter of course. But when I bear in mind who it was that told Mrs. Manley, then—well, then I know that the source of the rumour ain't one to add to its likelihood. Not a word against the unknown, as a fellow creature, but just an argument against somebody as a purveyor of facts."

Mr. Brimblecombe laughed openly and others sniggered.

"We all know our Peeping Thomasina," said Brian White; but Manley had turned to the farmer.

"As to shooting foxes, Fern, though fox-hunters would like to make it contrary to law, there's nothing in the statutes against it, to my knowledge. For poultry-keepers in general foxes are vermin and can be treated as such. A Hunt will pay compensation to the farmer for losses, and once you take the Hunt's money, then, in honour bound, you must let foxes be."

"I shall always shoot foxes, and the Hunt hates me according," said Mr. Fern.

"Hunting looks to become what they call a vexed question," explained Hannaford. "I've heard the fors and againsts argued in this bar scores of times. In reason you can't deny that to get pleasure from torturing dumb animals is a bad mark against a man; but if they stopped killing things for human amusement and sport, such as deer and foxes and hares and otters, then scores of human beings would be thrown out of work—poor folk who minister to sport one way and another and get their living by it."

He turned to a quiet, grey-haired man who occupied the inglenook. He was listening, but making no contribution to the talk.

"What do you say as to that, Toby?" asked Hannaford, and Mr. Trimble of Oakshotts answered slowly but with decision.

"As a gamekeeper all my working life, I'm against foxes, same as I'm against all other creatures that prey upon game—owls and hawks, stoats and rats and crows and weasels and cats; but a fox is different from vermin in general because it's raised to be the animal of all others needful to keep a great industry alive. To shoot a fox would be against my principles in consequence. I've never slain one, but I serve 'em same as I serve badgers when I find they are making their earths and their holts in the preserves, then I turn 'em out and they find they must go some place else if they want to live and increase and multiply. Pheasants first, foxes in their place and the further from the pheasants the better. There's worse evil-doers than foxes or carrion-birds for a gamekeeper."

"And you'd like to see 'em on your rogues' gallows in the woods if you could, wouldn't you, Mr. Trimble?" asked Fern.

"I would," answered the elder. "There's godless scoundrels I'd so soon crucify as the rest of the thieves and robbers, if I could lay my hands upon 'em."

"With our help it may be done, Toby," promised Inspector Manley. "You've got the law on your side, as you well know. 'Tis for you to keep your ears to the ground when there's a raid whispered; and then you can count on the Force to come to your assistance. We'll stamp out poaching some day."

But Trimble regarded the policeman without much favour.

"Lay your hands on their leader, Manley. Lay your hands on their leader," he said. "So long as that man is free, 'twill go on; but words and promises won't catch him."

"Nor yet convict him, my dear man. What we want is evidence, and, so far, neither you gamekeepers nor my constables have got any. Myself, I'm inclined to your opinion and everybody knows him you've got in mind is a very clever man with a lot up his sleeve; but you have to remember that among other things up his sleeve is the trust and support of your employer. You are handicapped against getting a bit of your own back, and, until the man in question is taken red-handed, he'll most likely best you. Anyway, till you can prove him guilty, he's innocent in the eyes of the law."

"I'd say he was dead straight myself," declared Hannaford.

"He's got rather a shifty glance, but there's a quick mind behind it and I've never heard him say any word against plain dealing. He don't care twopence about sport in any case. He's all for natural history. He may have hoodwinked Sir Gerald a bit; but seeing all he gets out of him and the advantages allowed him, he'd be a beastly traitor to steal his master's pheasants."

"Which is exactly what he does and what he is," answered Trimble.

"Some day you'll catch the right one, no doubt," prophesied the inspector, and as he spoke an unfamiliar figure entered the bar. It was Mr. Chave, the Oakshotts butler.

"Evening, all," he said. "Just time for a spot, Amos."

"Who'd think to see you so late as this?" asked Hannaford.

"I'm down here to call up Dr. Bridger," explained Chave. "He'll be along in a minute, and I've got our runabout outside. This evening, after his dinner, Sir Gerald came over fainty. He said it was nothing and he'd eaten too much and he went to bed. But an hour later Fosdick—that's his man—came down and told me he didn't look too good. Then, owing to a chapter of accidents, I was called to get moving. Our telephone's out of order so I ordained to come myself and the doctor's car's out of order till tomorrow, so I'm carrying him back with me in ours. He'll be here in a minute and reckons to bide at Oakshotts tonight."

While Mr. Chave drank his whiskey Inspector Manley expressed concern and trusted that nothing serious need be feared.

"You never can tell at his age," explained the butler, "but I haven't seen any signs of danger yet. His temper's good, and always is for that matter, and he eats and drinks as usual. Food was never a subject that interested him much and he wouldn't know whether he was drinking wine or water except for the colour. I didn't let him know I was coming to Wallabrook for the doctor. If I had, he'd have forbid it; but Bridger's told me behind the scenes to come, or send, at any hour of the night or day if there looked to be a screw loose. Sir Gerald likes Dr. Bridger and he won't be sorry to see him. He says doctor knows him inside out."

Dr. Bridger looked in at this moment to hasten Chave away, while Mr. Trimble asked to go with them.

"You can carry me home to South Gate, Chave," he said. "Save my legs."

When they were gone, the company debated this news and agreed that it was bad.

"Been hanging over the parish a longful time, but bound to come in the course of Nature," said the landlord.

"A most far-reaching affair, because there's none to follow the gentleman, so I understand," declared Manley. "First there's the terrific charges and taxes and duties and a thousand and one expenses demanded by the Law, till the estate's left far too naked to keep up Oakshotts, so the manor will come into the market."

"Who the mischief's going to saddle himself with Oakshotts and half Wallabrook parish nowadays?" asked Brimblecombe. "Nobody in his senses would want to be a landed gentleman under this Government."

Brian White laughed.

"That sort have got their marching orders," he told them. "No more grabbing their rights from the working classes now. The land's ours and, after iron and steel's ours, you bet we'll nationalise the land and send landowners where they belong. Time that such as them gave place to their betters."

"Well may your wife try to save a bit of money for a born fool like you, White," said Hannaford. "A pitiful thing to hear you bleat your ignorance like any other sheep. Wait a bit longer before you open your mouth so wide—wait and see what's coming to you when your friends have knocked the bottom out of the Commonwealth and find how much longer they'll find work and wages to pay your sort."

"I'd trust the State before I'd trust the capitalists," retorted Brian. "You wait till the pubs are national property. Broken reeds—that's what the like of you are, standing against the march of progress."

" 'Tis time you all marched out of this bar anyhow," concluded Hannaford, "else you'll be called to summon yourself for suffering the law to be broke in your presence, Samuel Manley."

CHAPTER X

The anxiety of Wallabrook was brief, for while certain spirits hoped in secret that he might die and with him much that he represented, the majority, long used to his amiable outlook and shadowy rule, felt relief when it was reported that the lord of the manor was going to live. For four days Dr. Bridger wrote a brief bulletin, which was displayed in the window of the post-office, and a specialist from London visited Sir Gerald on the day after his attack. The vicar prayed upon one Sunday that it would please the Almighty to spare His faithful servant's life, while, on the next, he was able to thank God in the name of the parish for doing so. None declared greater satisfaction at this happy issue than Mr. Owlett, while from Oakshotts a sigh of relief ascended and the spirit of security returned. It was reported that the master himself had always declared a conviction that he would recover.

New-born legends sprang from the affair, to support and quicken old ones of late forgotten. Mrs. Parsons reported that the 'Fortesque Bird', always seen on the battlements of Oakshotts when a reigning lord was about to die, had been witnessed by trustworthy eyes, and Mr. Chave admitted noting a white bird aloft on the morning of Sir Gerald's attack, but he believed it to have been a 'fantail' pigeon; while the housekeeper, who also saw it, declared the visitor authentic, but much larger than any pigeon. With his master's return to health, the head keeper rejoiced to learn that things would proceed as usual, autumn *battues* take place and the customary 'guns' attend them.

"As long as we operate together, Toby, the old traditions will be respected," said Sir Gerald, "and our archaic rites persist. Not until November, however, for the fall of the leaf is late: it grows later every year, if my observation can be trusted."

"Most truly the leaf falls later every year," agreed Trimble.

Then Owlett found himself summoned and appeared once more before his supporter. With genuine emotion he shook the hand extended to him and expressed his thankfulness that it continued possible to do so.

"Thank the Lord I behold your honour again," he said. "You've shook the parish to the roots, sure enough, and me amongst the rest of 'em. To think of you dropping out just as the fungi season was coming round again and all! And, when I heard about it, everything looked to be changed and the heart gone out of the fungi and the thought of 'em grown dim."

"A somewhat close call," admitted Sir Gerald, "and for a time I confess I felt only interest in the eternal battle between Nature and science. Nature must often fume with unavailing indignation against science, for we, who are dedicated to truth alone, thrust into her secret places, drag her mysteries to the light, without the least consideration for her feelings. We do not hesitate to correct and even confound her conclusions and intentions regarding ourselves, and when her activities interfere with our convenience, we never fail to suppress them. While recognising where and when she is right, we oppose her instantly when we consider that, from our point of view, she is wrong. She finds, for example, her calculations as to our duration of life utterly upset by science at every turn. Therefore, if she were capable of hating anything, it would be human reason, so prone to overturn her values and draw the sting from those countless perils she has set upon our way.

"Do you suppose," he continued, "that the prehistoric stone-men, who fought out their stormy lives on Dartmoor, ever lived as long as I have, or you probably will? Did the 'three-bottle men' of yesterday often extend their bibulous existence beyond our appointed span? I doubt it. Why, a time may come when centenarians will grow as common as black-beetles and the advance of longevity upset our whole scheme of social civilisation."

"What will happen to our old age pensions then?" suggested Matthew.

"Let us consider a more serious thing," replied Sir Gerald. "Having escaped destruction for the moment, my mind very properly turns to the fungi family, and I know the cowls of these folk are again breaking earth and rising in their punctual fashion. I am no mycologist and never pretended to be, but my modest researches have interested eminent experts. You will remember that I despatched several of your finds to a young scientist already distinguished for his *Handbook of British Fungology* and his study of *Claviceps purpurea*—otherwise known as that pest we call 'ergot of rye'.

"He is coming to see me and, though I cannot show him the habitats of some of our rarities, you will do so, assist his exploration and look after his safety. You must also accompany him to Dartmoor if the weather is favourable. His prime regret appears to be that so much lamentable ignorance still prevails as to the edible fungi, of which there are many quite as wholesome, safe and honest as the mushroom and truffle. These are eaten and enjoyed in France by those skilled in the matter and they are widely distributed in this country and crying for recognition."

Matthew grinned at the spectacle of wholesome and honest fungi crying for recognition.

"What time shall I show up to wait on the gentleman?" he asked.

"Be here at eleven on Monday, my dear fellow. Mr. Pollard —that is his name—arrives on Saturday and will devote Sunday to my collection. Meantime, if you should come across *Tuber brumale* under the oaks, where you found it last year, bring some up on Saturday to greet Pollard at dinner that night."

"The squirrels dig them up," explained Matthew. "I've marked that. So will some dogs; but whether 'tis our red squirrels can find truffles, or the grey squirrels, I couldn't say."

"I often wish the grey squirrels were not so clever or so greedy," declared Sir Gerald. "The wretches are omniverous, apparently."

"I shot two yesterday and gave 'em to Mr. Trimble. I thought he'd pat me on the back for once; but no. He took 'em, yet never thanked me."

"I have tried to shame him on your account, yet I'm afraid he would prefer even grey squirrels to you at Oakshotts."

"Has it ever occurred to Toby that he might retire, your honour?"

"No; but it has occurred to me. However, we will see what another year may bring forth."

Matthew rose to depart.

"You'll have heard of the thanksgivings his reverence put up to church on Sunday?" he asked.

"Most kind, most kind. I was deeply gratified and am very glad to remain on earth a little longer. My regret at going just now was genuine, for I am at the moment making some research into my life-long conclusions and should not like to leave certain minor discoveries unverified for others to correct rather than myself. Doubtless the fear, that I might be proved wrong after my death, assisted me to live. Now depart, my dear fellow, and let it be known in your circle that, when leisure allows, I shall hit upon some gesture of goodwill for the parish, so that all may learn how pleased I am to be still among you."

"Wallabrook don't want, nor yet expect, anything better than your honour in command of it," so Mr. Owlett declared, then hastened away to put on his working clothes and seek *Tuber brumale*.

While returning in triumph with a satisfactory supply, the explorer fell in with two others of his acquaintance who had been collecting the fruits of the earth, but in a different shape and for a different purpose. Beyond the fringes of the forest, on waste land that descended to Walla, there grew a drift of stout blackthorn, and here at autumn time a harvest of sloes clustered upon their boughs for any who might care to glean them. Of such was Thomasina Parsons, famed amid her other activities for the making of sloe gin. She enjoyed this reputation and was at pains annually to manufacture a dozen bottles of the cordial from a secret recipe known only to herself and Maude White. As the widow's first friend, Maude was let into the mystery, but, even so, admitted that her concoction lacked some of the rich and rounded perfection that Mrs. Parsons managed to attain. This afternoon they had gathered a good store of fruit, and though Mr. Owlett felt no admiration for either of them, he yet praised their industry and declared this year's sloes exceptional.

"I'll buy a bottle," he promised Thomasina, "but the mischief with sloe gin is that you need to hoard it so long before it comes to its prime."

"What are you going to charge for it this year, Tommy?" asked Maude.

"To old customers the same as last. Can't go back on 'em; but with Plymouth gin what it costs now, I don't rightly know—not yet."

"Amos Hannaford will decide. No doubt he finds the gin and you find the sloes and you share the booty," suggested Mr. Owlett.

"You can't get anything for nothing in this hard world," replied Mrs. Parsons, "though oft enough you're called to pay good money for what's worse than nothing. I'm faced with a crisis myself at this instant moment. The bettermost people are finding they've got to put down their domestic labour, and, in my small way, it looks as if I must do the same. It's always been a triumph of mine to employ a general servant—a most envious thing; but I doubt if I can afford my maid-of-all-work any longer."

"Surely you don't think to sack Ivy Caunter?" asked her friend.

"Not of my own free will—far from it, Maude. I grant with all her faults she is worth her money—what I pay and no more—but now she demands half as much again! I doubt she'd have thought of such a thing if her father hadn't put her up to it."

"Everybody's worth what they'll fetch for the minute," declared Matthew, "and lots of men and women have waxed in value."

"Not my 'general', however," declared Ivy's mistress, "and now, when I'm thinking to send her off, I fall back upon her faults to console me for doing so."

"I've heard you praise her to the skies, Tommy. You've said you found her worth her weight in gold."

"Not since she's come to find she is herself, Maude," explained Mrs. Parsons. "Allowing for the upheavals all round us, when I hear a chit like Ivy demanding two pounds a week and her fortnight's holiday paid for out of my pocket, then I ask myself exactly what she's capable of doing to earn such awful outlay as that."

"You've said she's a wonder and can put her hand to a lot of things to save your time."

"Yes, my love, I have; but those swift workers have their dark side. You can't have anything without its opposite, can you, Mr. Owlett?"

"What's the opposite of being a quick worker and good all round?" asked Matthew.

"Speed has to be paid for," said Thomasina, "and you can pay too much for it. Ivy will win my applause one day and, before I've done praising her and even thinking of giving her a half holiday for a treat, there comes a crash from the scullery and I know that something I set store upon have gone its appointed way. A towser to work, but too proud of her speed to see the danger. 'I'll do more work in a day than most girls can face up to in a week,' she'll tell me, and it's true; but her pride for haste increases the daily chances of a fall, and she never misses those chances. When I hear her working on her top gear, I know well what's coming closer every minute. She keeps the home spotless, but what's a spotless home if you're always in a twitter about it?"

"It shook your nerves a lot when she broke up that big, white, cloam cow with the red spots," Maude reminded her.

"It did and for very good reasons. Not a week before the end of that cow, a travelling man, on the look-out for china jimcracks and joanies, offered me five pounds for it; but 'No', I said. 'That ornament is a part of my life and belongs to my early history and I don't sell it to anybody.' Then, just while I was waiting for the man to show up again and offer more, she brought the proud object to ruins at my feet. She cried a bucket of tears and said I ought to stop it out of her money. 'I take the blame and the shame, ma'am,' said Ivy; but of course I forgave her. 'Lord love you, you idiot,' I said, 'if I was to pay for your breakage record out of your money, you wouldn't have enough left to buy your shoelaces, you wilful wretch.' "

"You'll have to put her failings in her character if she's going," suggested Maude.

"And the good ones likewise," added Mr. Owlett. "You must be fair, and leave the intending customer for Ivy to decide whether the game's worth the candle."

"What price you?" retorted the widow. "There's a full-fledged rumour flying around that you're going to lose Nancy before you're much older. How would you like to pay Ivy two pounds a week to look after you and all your odds and ends?"

"I'd sooner pay her ten pounds a week to keep away," he replied; "while as for Nancy and your rumours, I set no store by 'em. You start your rumours on the wing a lot too free, my dear, and some fine day one of the ugly ones will come back to roost, and then you'll look a fool."

"When did I report a word that wasn't true?" cried Thomasina. "Are you telling me your girl haven't been walking along with Peter Chadd for the last six months and still continuing?"

"I'm telling you nothing. If you was only to blaze abroad what I tell you, the world wouldn't be no wiser and no worse," answered Owlett.

"None so deaf as them that won't hear," said Maude, taking up the cudgels for her friend. "And what's the matter with young Chadd, anyway? He's all right, by all accounts."

"So's his mother," added Mrs. Parsons. "You ain't going to pick holes in Mrs. Chadd, I'm sure."

"No," admitted Matthew. "I've never heard any false rumours about Dinah Chadd. She's one of them people you can't hang a rumour on, try as you may."

"There's plenty of rumours hanging on you, anyhow," said Maude. "You may not have heard 'em yourself, but everybody else has."

"I've heard 'em," he answered. "I'm a marked man, Maude White, and I often wonder why. There's two points of view taken about me in these parts and one's favourable and the truth so far as I know, and the other is quite the contrary. Strange to tell, them appointed to see the laws are kept take the dark view and think I don't keep the laws; while the rest of Wallabrook, from the lord of the manor downward, feel no doubt but I do. Women like you have heard both sides and published 'em, no doubt."

"Yes," admitted Thomasina, "I've heard both sides. I've heard what Mr. Trimble have told Inspector Manley and I've heard from Ruby Manley that her husband believes him. So you've got the gamekeepers and the police against you, Mr. Owlett, and that would be awkward if Nancy was to marry a policeman, wouldn't it?"

"Very awkward indeed, so now you will be able to launch a fine new rumour and tell the people I won't let Nancy take Chadd because he's a policeman. Then the folks will say there's wheels within wheels and it goes to prove the gamekeepers are right."

"Why would you object to your son-in-law being a constable if you was dead straight yourself?"

"Why indeed? Another black mark against me. But you needn't bawl that out yet, because I haven't objected to my daughter marrying Peter, or anybody else. I haven't heard she ordains to marry Peter, or Peter's asked her to. A man don't run about telling his daughter she's not to marry before he knows whether she wants to do so."

"Would you go so far as to say that, if he asks and she's favourable, you'll consent to it?" inquired Maude.

"I'd go so far as to say that's my business and would depend on a lot of things even Thomasina don't know," he replied, grinning. "Don't know myself yet—any more than your railway porter knows if he's going to make his fortune out of the football pools this winter."

"Talking of them," said Maude, "Brian tells me that a man at Tavistock station made twenty-two pounds last week. Brian says the more you know about football the less likely you are to win."

They pursued this subject until they parted and the old sailor fell in with yet another acquaintance before he reached his home. He overtook Peter Chadd at work and, as his beat took him past Matthew's dwelling, they walked a few hundred yards together.

"Funny falling in with you at this moment," said the elder. "Just heard your name in conversation with neighbours."

"To my credit I hope, Mr. Owlett?"

"Nothing against you. Just a remark from two females concerning your private affairs. Our private affairs are the only things about us that interest most of 'em."

"I don't know so very many."

"More know a policeman than he's likely to know himself. You're a familiar object of the countryside by now. Not only your uniform but your size marks you out."

Peter laughed.

"Sometimes I wish I wasn't so upstanding," he said, "but then again I'm glad, because Nancy favours it. She said once, talking of her future in a general way, that she liked for a man to be taller than his wife, as they commonly are, and never could understand why any man could marry a woman who over-topped him. And I said that a man might fall in love with a woman bigger than himself and feel no shame of it and a woman might see a man so suited to her inclinations that she never minded if he didn't top her shoulder."

"Such things mean nothing where there's true love," agreed Matthew.

"As a matter of fact," continued the policeman, "them that don't feel big, ain't big; and when I'm along with Nancy I never do feel big, but quite the contrary. You'd want to have a smarter mind than mine to feel big with her. In truth, nothing makes me know I ain't all I thought I was so well as a walk and talk with her."

"Nobody ever was or can be all they think they are," answered Mr. Owlett, who loved considerations of this kind. "If you find yourself pleased with yourself, you can bet your boots you're mistaken. Queer but true. A judge of character, like myself for example, don't waste no time on himself; but he can most likely form a righter opinion about other people than they do about themselves. That's because I come to my neighbours with no bias for or against any of 'em.

"But no man ever comes to himself with no bias. The most of us have got a blind eye to ourselves and are ready to find excuses for the weak spots we know damn' well are there, yet believe nobody else has found out. You thought you was made of harder and tougher stuff than you are, I expect, Peter. That's a very common mistake we make about ourselves, and another mistake is to think we are weaker than we really are. Sometimes a sudden urge drives a man to do a really brave, dangerous thing he wouldn't have done for the world, if he'd had time to stop and think. Then he's cheered up for the rest of his life to discover he was more of a hero than he thought."

"I doubt I'd fail in danger," said Peter, "but Nancy says it would all depend on what the danger happed to be. She grants I'd try to stop a runaway horse and risk my life if it was needful to save another life—things she wouldn't and couldn't do herself; but she says there are dangers that might not threat your body, but might threat your good name and your character, which she would face without any fear at all, but which might beat me."

"Like her cheek. Did you tell her not to talk like a self-righteous guinea hen?"

"Certainly not, Mr. Owlett. It was food for thought, as they say."

"Never lost your temper with her?"

"Not to my living memory."

"I suppose not. That's one thing you'll never find difficult: to keep your temper. A great gift."

"Just routine for a policeman."

"And just routine to make other people lose their tempers. That's a policeman's craft, because he knows if he can get a man into a passion some useful bit of information's like to slip. What's said in drink, or temper, may be a policeman's godsend sometimes."

Peter did not reply to this assurance and Matthew summed up gloomily.

"In any case it's luck for most of us we don't know ourselves, else there might be more suicides than we read about. When I hear of such a thing without any explanation of it, I often think to myself: 'Ah! There's another poor devil found himself out at last.'"

Peter hazarded a question.

"Would you say a famous man like Sir Gerald Fortesque knows himself, Mr. Owlett?"

"No, because he's a far better man than he thinks himself. He likes moths better than humans, and why shouldn't he if he finds 'em more likeable?"

"The gentleman never feels to be lonely?"

"Lonely? Lonely, with his insects stacked around him by the thousand? How should he be lonely?"

"If I was an ancient man like him, I'd sooner have my grandchildren stacked around me than moths and butterflies," said Peter.

"Being what you are, you might," agreed the other; "but a man of science knows where he is with things properly labelled. We haven't yet reached the skill to label the growing generation and feel sure as to the truth of them. Be it as it will, you've got a tidy lot to undergo before you're called to undergo grandchildren. Things may happen to make you wish to God you'd been spared any children at all, let alone their children on top of 'em."

Young Chadd braced himself for a request now long on his lips but not as yet uttered. He was very slow in his mental processes and even a resolve, once come to, would often be delayed before its final application. He had long decided to approach Mr. Owlett on this vital question and now took his opportunity, though uncertain still as to whether he did not voice the matter too soon.

"Would you mind if I ask your permission to do a deed, Mr. Owlett?" he inquired. "Whether Nancy has spoke to you on the subject I couldn't say yet; in any case, my mother approached me about it. I hadn't said nothing to her, but she's very quick in her understanding and—well, to cut a long story short—she's discovered me to be in love with Nancy. She wasn't surprised, because she's always felt a great admiration for Nancy herself; but she warned me that any such thing might run contrary to your views."

"Young people ain't given to confiding in their parents as a general plan of action nowadays; but when you confided in your mother what did she advise?"

"She thought it would be a clever thing if I was to do just what I am doing this minute. She said, 'You'll do best to tell Mr. Owlett you want to marry Nancy some day and ask him whether you've got his leave to offer for her.' That's what mother said."

"She would think that way, no doubt—a woman brought up on her fine, old-fashioned ideas," said Matthew.

"She reckoned that if you saw no reason against, then I could get on with it and Nancy could say 'Yes' or 'No' as might happen and no harm done; but if you was opposed, then enough said and Nancy could be spared the sad job of turning me down."

"And you've taken her advice and come to me first? Well, why not? Some might say you were rather a pet lamb, Peter, and didn't have no will of your own. Nancy, for example, might lose heart about you if she ever heard you'd asked me for permission to offer for her. It would sound darned tame to her ear and might even decide her against you. However, that's no matter. You ask me if you may ask her to wed you, and being a free country I know no reason at all why you shouldn't. She's got to speak the last word, not me, nor yet you, so there's nothing more to be said on the subject until you have heard it. She's a very decided piece and won't waste any time telling her views, and you needn't waste any time trying to change 'em when she does."

"Her word's law for me, Mr. Owlett."

"And you'd be the last to break the law—we all know that. So you can go to it with a good conscience and we'll see how the land lies."

"And you wouldn't say nothing against if, by God's goodness, she loves me, Mr. Owlett?"

"If by God's goodness she loves you, Peter, nobody but a fool would waste their wind arguing on the subject. You ought to know her well enough by now to grasp that."

"I'm greatly obliged then—very greatly," declared the policeman. "In fact, a lot of weight is lifted off my shoulders. I don't feel false hopes, naturally, knowing all she is, because the man ain't born who could be worthy of a wife like her; but there's no disrespect in offering?"

"None at all, and if the worst happens, you can creep away with the comforting thought she's forgiven you for daring," promised Matthew.

"We walk out next Sunday and I'll do it then."

"The better the day the better the deed. Tell your mother I'll come over and drink tea with her that afternoon."

"Good night, then, and thank you again, Mr. Owlett."

"Good night, boy."

Matthew had now reached home and Constable Chadd proceeded upon his beat.

CHAPTER XI

WHEN Sunday came the day proved autumnal with fog rolling down from Dartmoor, visibility poor and the prospects of a long afternoon walk somewhat dreary. Peter and Nancy seldom chose other than three expeditions. They were used to visit Virtuous Lady, where once a copper mine had operated near the junction of Tavy and Walla; but sometimes they would turn easterly and climb the foothills of the Moor, while often they selected the river valley and the waterfall. The latter region was traditionally celebrated for lovers' meetings, and Peter, than whom none ever respected tradition more, had already determined to make his fateful experiment on Walla's bank.

He called for Nancy in a new suit of brown tweed that she had never seen before, and a tie of bright orange which made at least one spot of genial colour on that grey and misty afternoon; but she offered no comment on his attire until they were alone, agreed that the river must be chosen since rain promised, and set off beside him ignorant of what awaited her, for Mr. Owlett had made no mention of his meeting with Peter. He saw the pair start, then, an hour later, proceeded to keep his appointment with Mrs. Chadd and presently sat beside her fire and watched her prepare his tea. How much she knew of her son's intentions he could not guess, but thought it probable that Peter would have told her the appointed hour had come. He was right, for Dinah knew all about it.

"They'll have gone on their walking, no doubt," she said.

"Yes; they went along to the river. Never saw your boy looking so grand, Dinah. All dressed up so smart as a courting badger with a yellow tie like a sunrise under his chin."

"Done with a reason, Matt. He bought that suit for a special purpose a month ago, and it took him all his remaining coupons to do it."

"Not a very promising afternoon to show 'em off."

"What's weather to him today? He's far beyond the reach of weather, my dear man. He's always glad to get out of uniform when he's with Nancy."

"And yet I've heard her say he never looks so fine as in his blue and helmet."

"He wouldn't don a new suit unless there was something big on his hands," explained Dinah, and Mr. Owlett laughed.

"I'd say he's always got something big on his hands. A policeman six foot four inches and weighing up to fourteen to fifteen stone has something big on his hands all his life."

"Strange to think at this very moment, while we're drinking our tea, all may be over and his fate known to him," sighed Mrs. Chadd.

"He told me what was on his mind when last we met and I saw no reason why he shouldn't."

"Steadfast he's been from his cradlehood, Matthew. Once an idea comes to Peter it never leaves him, and once Nancy got on his mind I knew, before he did himself, that he'd carry on to the end, bitter or otherwise."

"I can believe that," said Matthew. "I was much the same myself. I resolved to go to sea the first time ever I saw the sea—when my mother once took me to Plymouth to the dentist—me being six years old at the time. And to sea I went so soon as I was adopted to face it."

"You were ordained for higher things, however," so Dinah reminded him. "The love of Nature was in you."

"Nature was always calling. A born naturalist, so Sir Gerald has called me."

"And famous for it, I'm sure."

"So I believe, Dinah."

"Most children change their minds a few times before they come to their true calling," she said. "Peter's elder brother, who died young, poor lamb, wanted firstly to be a chimney sweep, then a railway porter, and then a verger when I took him to church. Last of all he hankered to be a bishop, after one of 'em confirmed him. And now he's an angel. But Peter determined once and for all he'd be a policeman when he was five years old, and now, turned twenty-five, he is one. Inspector Manley thinks a lot of him, Matt, and says he's full of promise."

"Everybody ought to be full of promise at twenty-five, my dear; but, there again, you must take the ways of Nature into your calculations. Peter had a very good mother and you know my high opinion of you and everybody's high opinion of you; but you'll be the first to grant he had a right-down devil of a father, and if you don't know it who should?"

"Thank God his father have never showed up in Peter any more than he did in my first," said Dinah. "There wasn't much wrong with a little boy who wanted to be a bishop, any more than there's anything dangerous about a child who wanted to be a policeman and never stopped wanting till he was one."

"But Peter's sprung from a deep-rooted stock."

Dinah sighed.

"There's changes in the air now about wickedness," she argued. "The Church of England have decided now there's no such person as the Devil, Matthew."

"So I understand. Old Nick's ruled out and hell a thing of the past. But somehow I miss the Father of Lies myself. He had his points, Dinah, beside his horns and his tail."

Mrs. Chadd stared.

"Lor, Matt! You miss him?" she exclaimed.

"Satan was a great preventive, my dear. Thousands of folk who wouldn't be good for the love of God was kept fairly straight by the fear of the Devil. But now he's gone our doubtful ones can breathe again, well knowing there's nobody but the Law to question 'em, and no hell waiting for 'em in any case. All the same, if you ask me, I'd say the Devil ain't dead, and none more like to be his victims in the long run than them that think he is."

Dinah viewed Matthew respectfully.

"You're a deep thinker, Matt," she said.

"No: I only use my wits, and if you can look round the world and fail to see the Devil's hoof-prints everywhere, then you must be sand-blind, I'd say."

Dinah returned to Peter.

"You can claim for my boy like my family—he's the solid, unnoticeable, god-fearing sort."

"That looks to be right," agreed the visitor. "He's got a proper policeman's mind, though if a fault is to be marked I'd say he might be over-given to mercy and a bit yielding when duty demanded for him to be tough."

"His father was tough enough, whatever else he wasn't," said Dinah.

"True, and he may have handed down his toughness without his wickedness," admitted Matthew. "That would be a very fine thing and well within the power of Nature."

"If by chance Nancy was to take him, how would you feel about it?"

"You never know what marriage will bring out in man or woman. Makes some, ruins others. I'd keep an open mind."

This appeared to relieve Mrs. Chadd.

"Fetch the kettle, my dear, and we'll have our tea," she said.

A big yellow cat that had been sleeping at Mr. Owlett's feet woke up and stretched itself, then approached him, erected its tail and rubbed against his leg.

"The creature's wild about you, but won't trust any other man," said Dinah.

"He knows I understand him, so far as a human can dare to say he understands a feline," suggested Matthew.

"You're a crafty pair," she declared, and Mr. Owlett protested.

"Me crafty? You know better. I'm an open book for anybody to read."

But his friend shook her head.

"There's pages in all our books that only God Almighty will ever read," she said.

The visitor approved this sentiment.

"A clever thought that, Dinah. But we were talking of Peter. Very merciful-minded, I grant you—like myself I hope—but if you want to keep your-self-respect and your proper pride, you must have a sense of duty to yourself as well as your neighbour. Now my Nancy has got those gifts from her late mother. My wife was a strong woman. She never liked me, bless her, because she wasn't interested in the ways of Nature and was a lot disappointed with me when I gave up following the sea and came home and stopped home. However, that's in the past, and I never look back. No more does Nancy. She looks forward and looks further than I do."

"Women do look further forward than men," declared Mrs. Chadd. "They've got a lot to haunt 'em that men know nothing about."

"Have they? Well, give me peace and contentment and a mind at rest."

"Have another slice of cake?"

"I will. No cakes like yours, though where you get the fruit and the fat from only you know. Yes, peace and contentment is all I ask, and along with Sir G. and his patronage I get 'em."

"Inspector Manley believes Trimble against you still," said Dinah.

"All jealousy, Dinah. All jealousy and not worth a second thought. I'll instruct Peter in woodcraft myself some day. He don't know a thing about it worth naming and maybe he's too big to be very clever at it. They say a good big 'un is better than a good little 'un; but not always. I've found my small stature and light weight very convenient now and again. I can go where a big man can't and leave no traces. I can mix with a crowd and vanish like a lump of sugar in a cup of tea."

"Not so with Peter. If he's there he can't be out of sight."

Mr. Owlett summed up.

"Well, he's all yours so far, and it's on the cards he's going to be all Nancy's after today. We shall soon know, and I'd say it was about fifty-fifty for or against. If she's turned him down, he'll be back with his tail between his legs pretty soon, I'm afraid; if not, then they'll forget tea-time."

"If it's 'Yes', then they'll forget a lot more than their tea," said Dinah. "But I've got a feeling she's going to take him, Matt. In that case, my dear, what do you ordain to do when your girl's gone? She worships you, Nancy does, and I know what you think of her."

"A very good, faithful daughter, as daughters go," agreed Mr. Owlett.

"Light your pipe if you won't eat any more and sit in the armchair," suggested Dinah.

"Not tonight," he said. "I'll help you wash up, then I'll push along. We may be counting our chickens before they was hatched."

"What do you mean by that?" asked Peter's mother.

"I mean that nothing may have happened after all. How if your boy finds his courage fail him?"

"You needn't fear no such thing," she answered. "He went out resolved, and once he says he's going to act, then the act will be done willy-nilly, Matt."

Elsewhere their children walked by streamside and, after Nancy had admired Peter's new clothes, they fell into a silence for some time. Then she remarked that it was a depressing afternoon and thought the fog seemed disposed to turn into rain. But while admitting the probability, Peter answered that there were occasions in life when weather really made no difference.

"All depends whether you find yourself in tune with it," he said.

"I never find myself in tune with fog," explained Nancy, "and I don't much like the autumn, anyway. Heavy work on the land now and you feel next spring is such a darned long way off."

They had the riverside to themselves, for it was not an afternoon to tempt many from home. A grey mist hung over the falls and above them there stretched a bending tree where the wild clematis had climbed and showered its powder-puff balls of seed shining silver bright through the heavy atmosphere. No wind blew and, save for the murmur of the river plunging into the pool below, all was very quiet. Even the waterfall's riot sounded muffled this afternoon and, when they had passed a hundred yards beyond it, Nancy remarked on the pensive nature of the day.

"Everything looks down on its luck today," she said. "You feel that sometimes on the land, Peter. Sometimes there seems to be a cheerful spirit about even in a patch of purple pickling cabbage; but at other times you fancy the crops are sulking because they know the time's come for them to be gathered in."

These reflections did not challenge Peter. Indeed, he hardly heard them. He accepted the hour for his ordeal and braced himself. First the precise scene of it had to be considered.

"We'll fetch on to the spruce wood and sit in our favourite spot where I cut your initials on the tree trunk. There won't be no damp there and if any folk are travelling by the path they won't see us," he said.

Nancy was thinking also and pursued her own thoughts.

"Funny how you forget just what you want to remember—funnier still how you'll remember what you rather wanted to forget," she said. "There was something I was going to tell you; but I can't call it back."

"It'll come very like before we part. A thought struck me just now too. I was wondering how many chaps had offered marriage to how many maids just here, during the last hundred years or so."

In this crafty manner he prepared to approach the great problem.

"And how many got 'No' for their answer," she replied unhelpfully.

"A hateful word at such a moment," he suggested.

"Why? 'No's' shorter than 'Yes', and often a lot safer. Lord only can tell what danger may hide in 'Yes'. Why, there was Emma Pook—she said 'No' seven times!"

Peter sighed and wished that he had not started thus.

"Who was Emma Pook?" he asked drearily. "Did she turn down the same man seven times?"

"She said 'No' to seven different men, and got so used to saying it that she said it once too often."

Nancy laughed, but her words awakened no amusement in Peter.

"A sad story," she continued. "Too pretty to be happy, Emma

was. It's the plain ones get the best husbands. Perhaps you never marked that? Emma began——"

"Stop!" said Peter firmly. "I don't want no more melancholy news about Emma Pook or anybody else this afternoon."

"Nor do I, for that matter. The weather's melancholy enough."

"To say truth, weather or no weather, I'm come to the high watermark of all my life at this moment—or it might be lowest watermark. We'll pitch here and I'll put down my coat for you."

He doffed his new coat and spread it upon a carpet of brown pine needles that covered the ground beneath a noble tree; but Nancy protested.

"Not your best coat, Peter; that's silly!" she said.

"Couldn't be put to no better purpose and I'm finding myself a thought too warm, anyway," he answered. "And now, for a start, be dead straight and tell me what your father's honest opinion of me may be—if you know it. I've tried to find out, but I didn't."

She nodded.

"Very difficult to get to the bottom of what father's really thinking and I seldom waste time to try," she answered. "I'd say he thinks well enough of you, Peter, in the main, though doubtful as to details."

"Too soft?"

"Not in your bones and muscles. He says you might be heavy-weight champion of Devon in wrestling if you knew how; but he also says that, when you got your man where you wanted him and the man refused to give in, then you'd never have the heart to break his arm, or his neck."

"Break his neck?" cried Peter.

"Yes, if you had to do it to beat him. Father's great on character and he declares that until a man's had a downfall or two, you can't tell the truth of him."

Peter considered this in the light of the moment.

"I may be up against it sooner than Mr. Owlett thinks for," he said. "And you—would you like for me to be more—well, more of a tiger, Nancy?"

"I wouldn't like for you to make a habit of it, but I know what father means. I'd like to know you had the claws, but be very glad if you didn't find the need to show 'em too often."

"A fierce temper always ends in dust and ashes soon or late."

"Well, light your pipe and change the subject," she suggested.

"Perhaps I will light my pipe, and then again perhaps not. If you say 'No' to a question, then I'll light it; but if you answer in the affirmative, that being legal language for 'Yes'—because the Law never uses one word when it can say the same in ten—if you answer in the affirmative, Nancy, I shan't light my pipe."

"Why not?"

"Because I shall be otherwise engaged. That reminds me. If you feel in the pocket of my coat you'll find a present for you."

"I thought I was sitting on something hard," she said, and dived beneath her and found a small package.

"You give me a lot too many gifts, Peter, and I doubt I ought to let you."

He ignored her remonstrance.

"I said to myself, when I was thinking upon this particular walk, that while I did the talking you'd want something to pass the time. And then I said to myself, 'Why the mischief shouldn't she be eating through a box of chocolates while she gives ear to all I've got to tell?' And being in Tavistock yesterday, to see Superintendent for Inspector Manley, I bought a box."

"How like you to think of chocs—my favourite sweets."

Nancy unwrapped her present.

"And what a lovely girl on the lid!" she cried.

"Go to it, then. There's only one lovely girl in my knowledge, and she ain't got tow-coloured hair and a mouth all across her face, thank God. Well, it's like this, Nancy. Things brewing have come to the boil sooner than I expected. So now or never they must out. Still, I scarce thought to say 'em till we was better acquaint."

"We've walked together for three parts of a year almost, dear Peter, so they ought to be ripe for saying by now."

"Eat on, eat on," he begged. "Don't stop. If your mouth's full you can't shut me up, so don't put me out of my stride again."

"Where did you count to be striding to?" she asked.

"I don't know yet. I'm always in extremes along with you and things rise up in my mind that never did before. Now I'll let 'em have their own way."

Nancy smiled upon him.

"Wicked things come into our minds sometimes, I'm afraid," she said.

"Not in mine," he assured her. "A policeman keeps a very orderly mind—both on and off duty—and no wickedness ever came in your mind: that I will swear."

"Plenty. Girls get wicked sooner than boys, I believe."

"I doubt it. Then let me continue—let me continue. You've got to listen, not be talking just now."

"Go ahead, then. Where did you leave off?"

"I'll never leave off once I start—unless you order me."

"Who am I to order you, Peter?"

He started once again, yet dallied by the way.

"You're called to pick your words terrible clever sometimes, and this is one of them. I've rehearsed my speech to you—over and over again I've rehearsed it—in private. Aloud I've tried it out, when I'm on my night-beat and nobody in a mile of me. And some nights it flows pretty well, and other nights it hangs fire."

"Fancy that! What would anybody have thought of it if they'd heard you?"

"Reckoned I was mad, most like. Maybe you will. Anyway, all I invented to say is gone now and only the core's left. I love you, Nancy—yes I do—fiercer and fiercer. I want for you to be my——"

But Nancy's thoughts, in their untoward flight, had turned elsewhere at this vital moment and, with her mind upon them, she did not grasp what he was saying. In any case she knew what he was going to say so well already and had known it so long. His voice was earnest enough, but very low, and a sudden recollection entirely obscured Peter for half a second. As a result Nancy, quite oblivious to what she was doing, interrupted him.

"Oh!" she cried. "I've just remembered what I wanted to tell! It's flashed back! There's going to be the 'new look' in hats for us land girls, Peter. The slouch hats are to be scrapped and we are going to wear green berets—military style!"

Some moments of grim silence followed her announcement and then it was Nancy's turn to receive a shock. She had never heard her policeman roar until this moment; indeed, since he was a baby, it is certain that he had never roared; but now Peter did, and even worse, for his protest included an imprecation.

"Blast it all, where's your decency? Don't you know better manners than that, woman?" he bellowed, and Nancy, with a stroke of genius, made the soft answer that calmed his wrath.

"Oh, darling! Forgive me if you can. Try to forgive me. How horrible! I'll be shamed to my dying hour."

She suited her actions to these repentant words and put her arms round his neck while he sat panting and glaring beside her.

"You were saying?"

"I'd said it so plain as I could speak; and, if there was any chance of a friendly answer, I'd say it again; but since you find a new hat pleasanter to think upon than me, better I shut my mouth and go home."

"When I put my arms round your dear neck, then I must have heard enough to make me do it," she said. "That shows my heart heard what you said though my stupid wits missed it. And I'll never forgive them. Tell over again, Peter, tell over again!"

He thawed instantly.

"If I'm hearing you, you blessed creature, then there don't seem much need to tell any more," he answered. "Out of evil comes good, in that case. If you love me and ain't messing me about to save your face—then thank God."

"Of course I love you and have loved you for a month of Sundays. Sundays and weekdays and working days and holidays and all!"

"What words to hear! I'd sooner hear 'em than any song was ever sung."

"I always dreamed of marrying an outsized man; but I never thought I'd get a chance to do it, darling."

"Well, you have done it now," he told her, "and there won't be no going back. But I wouldn't take any unfair advantages, Nancy. Hard though it is, I'll let you think twice and turn it over. If this has crashed down on you like a thunderstorm and you feel in your excitement you may have gone too far to save me pain——"

"I'll never give you pain again," she promised, "and you haven't crashed on me like a thunderstorm exactly, Peter dear. A girl knows when a man's in love with her by the time she's old enough to put her hair up, and often she'll know it before the man does himself. We're made that way owing to gifts men haven't got and mostly don't understand. But I couldn't do nothing about loving you till you offered, could I?"

"You don't feel no call to weigh me up no longer? Then praise heaven, I'm sure! May I put my arm round you, you blessed marvel?"

"Of course you can if you mind to, Peter. I often wondered what it would feel like when you did."

He clasped her close, but very tenderly, and Nancy shut her eyes that nothing should distract her from the sensation of his embrace.

"Heavens above!" he cried. "Where do we stand now? What

now? I'm going to kiss your mouth next. There! You kissed me back—I swear you kissed me back!"

"Did I? I don't remember."

They babbled in each other's arms for a long minute and then Peter endeavoured to be serious and Nancy tidied herself.

"You've took me for all time—mind that," he said. "You're mine and I'm yours for evermore. I set out an hour ago along with a maiden fancy free—or so I thought—and now I'm going back again with my own maiden—a tokened man and neither of us ever free again."

"I'll never say I was good enough for you; but if you think me so, Peter——"

"Call me 'darling' again."

"Peter darling, then."

"What an upheaval!" he murmured. "What a grand affair to see lovers taking their life in their hands, same as we have, and defying the whole world and the beastly weather and everything!"

"Love makes its own weather, I expect. I'm sure I feel as if I'd got to heaven by a short cut this afternoon. I do then!"

"Every moment I feel my affection so big as the waterfall—properly flowing over!"

"So do I—so do I, darling."

They were silent a moment and then Peter endeavoured to estimate the full splendour of their situation.

"Just dashing along—you and me—and caring naught for anything else on the wide earth but each other! Just dashing along, dashing along heart to heart and soul to soul! Can you beat it?"

But Nancy was collecting herself.

"We'd best to dash along home, I'm thinking—else we'll be lost in the dark, darling. We can't sit here all night like a pair of love-sick rabbits, can we? Stop cuddling and help me up on my feet, my treasure."

She rose and shook herself.

"Here's your coat. I've creased it cruel, I expect," she said, as Peter heaved up his massive frame and took the coat from her.

"I'll keep this to the last minute of my life and hand it down for a heirloom," he vowed. "So like as not my children's children will feel it to be very near a sacred object and tell the folk how their grandmother was sitting on it when she took their grandfather."

"More likely to make a pair of knickers for our eldest, if we ever get so far as that. That's poetry, darling, and Lord send I'm not going to marry a poet. Be serious now and stop thinking of ourselves and give a thought to other people."

"There ain't no other people. Everybody else is but churchyard ghosts compared to us."

"My father and your mother aren't churchyard ghosts."

"That's true," he admitted. "This is like to surprise 'em, you'd say?"

"Not much; but it's like to decide 'em."

He considered this. They were back on the fisherman's path by the river now and dusk closed down.

"There's times when my policeman's habit, to look ahead, comes in useful," explained Peter. "Our job is to draw deductions and act upon them. Then we'll sometimes do what's better than find a criminal: we prevent a crime. Mr. Manley told me that and it's true. Not that it would be a crime for Mr. Owlett to feel kindly disposed to my mother—far from it."

"But what about her?" asked Nancy.

"So far as a woman very unlucky in love would ever meddle with it again, I can't see mother taking a second," admitted Peter; "but your father's different. If by good chance, seeing the circumstances that have unfolded, he thought well enough of mother to set about her in earnest, it might be she would consider it."

"He'll want a refuge now he's going to be separated from me, so we'll pray your deductions turn out right. I can't see no hopefuller refuge for him than dear Mrs. Chadd," said Nancy.

"So convenient, and so simple for both of 'em. We only need to change places—me and Mr. Owlett."

"Your mother comes to my father and I come to you, and there you are, darling!"

"All well inside reason," added Peter, "and he's such a one for the laws of Nature, he ought to see it clear."

The thought reminded Nancy of an experience in her own family.

"All for cause and effect, father is," she said. "He was telling about his sister, my Aunt Margaret—how she spent her whole life working at other people's wash-tubs for a shilling a day and died at fifty-three."

"Cause and effect sure enough," he said and Nancy turned to another consideration.

"Though it sounds mad, I don't believe I could have taken you if you'd lived very far from father, Peter. He's always been my guiding star. Now I'll have two guiding stars—almost too much luck for one girl, you might say."

"Not if she's got room in her heart for the pair of 'em," suggested Peter—"same as I've got you and mother for my guiding stars. Why not two?"

"Especially if they was to become a double star," laughed Nancy. Then he raised an immediate problem.

"Shall we go and break it to your father first, or my mother?" he asked.

"We'll face 'em separate tonight, darling, and tomorrow I'll see Mrs. Chadd and you'll listen to father. We'll fight it out like that."

"Not that there will be any fighting, please God," hoped Peter.

"Not a chance. True love can run smooth enough, for all they say against it."

They parted presently and Nancy went home, to find Matthew had already returned. He was beside the fire in their house-place with a book his employer had lent him and directed him to read.

"Back again, Father!" cried Nancy gaily, and he knew all she had to tell.

"So you've took him? Hasn't he come along with you to tell me?"

Matthew then listened to her story in most amiable fashion.

"Yes, yes—all to the good, my lass. And you'll have him serve you as faithful as he serves the Law. That's right. A police constable for a son-in-law—me! And yet I can't for the life of me see any reason to forbid the banns."

"Only waiting for you to let parson publish 'em, Father."

"All in good time. All in good time. You're better acquaint with Peter than I am yet. Suppose—just for the joke I say it—he wasn't all you think?"

"I don't think, I know, Father. And this is my red-letter day, because all I knew was the living truth."

"Luck's a queer thing and often don't look like what it turns out to be," warned her parent. "I've heard men damn a bit of seeming good luck for ruining 'em, and others who found a proper facer of bad luck to bring out the best they had to offer. I'll welcome Peter, as I always have done, and we'll see how it promises to be while you keep company for the next six months to start with then."

"Six months! Oh, Father!" cried Nancy, staring at the chill thought.

"I courted your mother over two years," he said, "and even that wasn't long enough to grasp her true nature. In fact she left me in doubt, dear woman, to her dying day. In six months you will have time to dip into reality and see if love grows upon you, or loses a bit of garnish with time. In six months I shall have leisure to look round. I wasn't unprepared for this, as you know; but I've got to train myself now as to how I shall fare without you."

"Your word will be the law for Peter in future, same as it has been to me," said Nancy. "He's gone to tell his mother. He wanted her to be the first to know and, of course, I wanted you to be the first to know."

"Then we can leave Providence to keep a weather eye lifting on all of us while we mark time," decided Matthew.

"Oh dear!" sighed Nancy. "My heart always sinks when you say you're going to mark time, Father."

"I often wish I'd learned to do it sooner," he said. "But there again, perhaps if I had, you'd never have been born."

"While we're marking time, time's marking us, I expect," she replied.

"Time flies mortal fast, anyway," he answered. "Time won't draw no lines on your face in six months."

Nancy changed the subject.

"I must look after your supper. Did Mrs. Chadd give you one of her cakes for your tea?"

"She did, and I ate too much, and it follows, like the night the day, I don't want no supper this evening."

"We thought a lot of you both as we came home, Father."

"Very large-hearted, to spare a kind wish for anybody else at such a time. Dinah was full of her son, because she knew he was going to chance his arm this evening and wondered whether it would go round your waist before he came home."

"Peter says Mrs. Chadd thinks the world of you."

"Not this afternoon she didn't. Too occupied with Peter's fate. I told her my opinions of him."

"Somehow I feel I can't leave you all to yourself, Father—a helpless man like you and no cook at the best of times."

"I never was what they call a domesticated man," he agreed, "and Mrs. Chadd is aware of that. She's got to think of herself now in any case when the blow falls, because Peter won't want his mother and his wife under the same roof, worship 'em both as he may. To dwell together would only bring out the worst of both of you."

Nancy had other good news of her sweetheart.

"You'll be glad to know that Peter's a bit more of a tiger than you thought. Something happened to vex him by the waterfall and he didn't only roar: he swore too."

"Did he? That's good hearing," declared Matthew. "He was on edge a bit this afternoon, I dare say, till he found how it was going."

"I'll be near you for years to come," promised Dinah, "and I'd be miserable very far away from you. Peter's told me there's no chance of his promotion yet awhile."

"He's had his bit of luck for the present."

"All the same you'd think a splendid chap like him ought to be promoted, when you see what other policemen look to be."

"He's got to show his betters what he's worth, first."

"He's worth his weight in gold, anyway," she said. "If I don't know, who should? And with me to help him——"

"That's right—'with you to help him'. Much depends on your driving force. He's got the goodness, but it's you that have got the guts."

"He'll go far with me behind him: I do believe that," she said.

"And might go even farther still with you in front of him," suggested Mr. Owlett. Then he suddenly turned to his own activities of the morning.

"I had a very interesting forenoon with Sir Gerald's young friend in Oakshotts today," he said. "Very refreshing to mark any young man keen on his job nowadays, because in general that's the last thing they happen to be. Anything and everything else they'll turn to, but not that. This Mr. Pollard is a man of science and will be a master some day. Sharp as a hunting hawk, though I took him into some soft places and we were muddied up to the eyes before we'd done with it. Fungi were his second nature and he gloried in a lot I showed him. Then he pounced on a peziza—what I thought was just a commonplace, little red chap of no account, and screwed his eyes on it with increasing excitement. And, after he'd soaked it in and made notes about it, he said it looked mighty like a variant and possibly a sub-order—anyway, different from the type and so on. 'I believe I've got something new here, Owlett,' he said, full of joy, and then he went into a lot of deep scientific talk and searched around like a gun-dog to see if he could find another."

"Poor soul," said Nancy. "And to think what the day brought me, Father!"

"He's found a fungus and you've found a policeman. He'll most like get his name hitched on to a new peziza and you'll have your name changed over to Chadd; then you'll both be equally proud of what you've done. Just the point of view," said Mr. Owlett.

CHAPTER XII

SOME few days after the engagement was announced, Matthew received a summons from Oakshotts and learned that his employer would be glad to see him on the following morning at the usual time. He appeared in due course, took his dinner with the staff and received their congratulations at Nancy's betrothal, then attended on Sir Gerald. The scientist, unaware of these personal events, did not allude to them; neither was the matter in his mind related with fungi. He expressed pleasure, however, at Matthew's recent attention to the interests of Mr. Pollard and a hope that the peziza might prove worthy of scientific attention.

"You provided him with material of considerable interest," he said, "and the water-logged woods also furnished him with a bad cold. However, he will swiftly recover from that. Sit down, Matthew, and give me the benefit of your opinion on a question to which you can bring an open and unprejudiced mind. It has nothing to do with science, yet intrudes upon me and I should value your judgment before making my own decision."

"Only too glad if I should have the luck to throw a spot of light, your honour," declared the visitor, "though little like to see different from yourself."

"My purpose," began Sir Gerald, "is to commemorate my return to health by affording some little measure of satisfaction to the parish and indicate gratification at the hope for my recovery which all conditions of men and women have manifested. I will go so far as to say that this universal desire I should live on a little longer has helped me to do so. And now, Matthew, I am confronted with two courses by which to publish gratitude and the form most desirable such gratitude shall take."

Mr. Owlett preserved a respectful silence and his employer continued:

"The enterprises proposed are these: first a drinking fountain at Wallabrook designed for man and beast: a handsome and striking granite addition to the village green with accommodation for human beings, a trough for thirsty cattle at an elevation to accommodate horses and kine, and beneath, not much above ground level, a lesser basin to supply sheep and dogs. As opposed to this monument it occurs to me that a festive and outstanding supply of fireworks—

on a grand scale as yet beyond any such exhibition ever attempted at Wallabrook—would elate the parish and afford an innocent entertainment for old and young alike. I find no little to be said for either gesture. The fountain would be a permanent memento—practical, humane and dignified, and a rational mind would not hesitate for a moment to place this enduring addition before the brief excitement suggested by a pyrotechnical orgy; but one has to remember that the vast majority of every community is not rational.

"Society is built in strata and, if a poll of our inhabitants was organised, it is highly probable a majority would choose the sensational display in my mind rather than the more sensible but somewhat dull memorial represented by a wayside drinking fountain. To what stratum of our body politic shall I appeal, my dear fellow? I entertain a high opinion of your reasoning powers and acumen, as you know, so I wish to learn your independent conclusion and shall most likely abide by it. Speak quite fearlessly. For myself I find nothing as yet to determine me and would even consider some third enterprise if anything better than one of these were submitted to me. What then, Owlett, would you do if confronted with this problem?"

Sir Gerald allowed time for a reply and showed no impatience while the other considered. Then suddenly the light of inspiration flashed in Matthew's eyes; he hesitated a little longer before proclaiming it, then braced himself to do so, took a deep breath and spoke.

"If I was you, your honour—which God forgive me for suggesting—but if I was you, I wouldn't let the drinking fountain quench the fireworks, nor suffer the fireworks to put out the fountain. They're both grand ideas, such as only you could have thought upon, and I'd hate to think Wallabrook was going to miss either of 'em. In a word, your honour, I'd have both! It's very easy, of course, to be clever with other people's money and, if I've gone too far and forgot myself, I beg for your forgiveness, but that's how I find myself to look at the situation."

Much to his relief the ancient scientist applauded. Indeed, the lord of the manor displayed actual enthusiasm and boomed approval.

"A Solomon come to judgment!" he exclaimed. "Once more you give evidence of your capacity and acute discernment. How right you are! How obvious and final a pronouncement! Why on earth, my good fellow, couldn't I think of that myself?"

But Owlett disclaimed any praise.

"You did think upon both fine feats, your honour," he pointed out, "only you didn't hap to see for the moment how they might be two halves of one whole. And when the fountain's finished and in order, you'll be called upon to descend from Oakshotts, come a seasonable day, and unveil it and set the water flowing with your own hands."

The betrothal of Peter and Nancy excited no great emotion at Wallabrook, for Mrs. Parsons had long since predicted it with certainty. Those interested judged that the youth of the contracting parties would mean a lengthy interval before their wedding bells were likely to ring; indeed, Matthew asserted the fact and Dinah told her friends how Mr. Owlett had decreed that a twelve-month at least must pass before any changes were to be expected. Both she and Nancy's father declared the wisdom of such delay, and, remembering Mrs. Chadd's own experience, the folk agreed that she was bound to think so; while for the old sailor, all perceived that, without his daughter, life for him would present a problem and demand readjustment not to be accomplished in a moment.

Mrs. Blanchard knew and admired Dinah. They were old friends and now Unity guessed that Mrs. Chadd might presently confront the question which she herself had recently been called to answer. She was finished with Arthur Brimblecombe for good and all now, but her decision had thrown no cloud on their friendship. Dinah, long familiar with the details of Arthur's romance, knew Unity well enough to discuss them, and deplored Mrs. Blanchard's decision. Indeed, when they drank tea together after the event at Mrs. Chadd's table, she had declared a personal regret at the nurseryman's failure.

"I'm properly sorry to know his hopes were all in vain," she had said. "Somehow I'd always got a feeling at the back of my mind, when your John went home, that Brimblecombe would only wait for a decent interval to pass and then have a dash for you. And seeing how you're situate and the wonderful woman you are, I hoped you might feel attracted to him knowing his trustable quality. You deserve Arthur, in my opinion, Unity, and I'd even go so far as to say he deserves you."

"I haven't got a word against him," confessed the other. "I admire him and he's a most determined chap and I always think that's a very valuable gift for any man; but determination is not enough and I can't feel I'd be of any particular service to Arthur, though I grant, if things were different, he would be serviceable to me. But we understand each other and always shall do so. He's took 'No' for my answer, yet he looks after my creature comforts just the same as when he was hoping, and next year, if Maude's willing, he's quite ready to let my grandson start work in his vegetables. That's far enough forward to look to for the minute."

"For you, yes; but Arthur may continue to look forward also."

"He'll soon tire of that, my love. He's reached to an age when a man don't waste much time looking forward to a future that grows shorter every year."

Unity laughed.

"I ain't the only pebble on the shore. There's a tidy lot of elderly women—widows mostly—that reckon they ain't beyond reach of elderly men. You yourself for an example, Dinah. You've worn a lot better than me and come through a lot more than me. I don't say Arthur for you, because I wouldn't count him to be the type of man to suit you; but seeing what's happened to your Peter, it might turn somebody's eyes in a certain direction."

"It has," said Mrs. Chadd. "You'll be aiming at Matthew Owlett, and to say truth he's touched on the subject. Very lightly indeed, you understand—just toyed with it; but it's moving in his mind, I see that, though he's far too downy to commit himself."

"He's vain, and quite right to be vain, because his cleverness has won the friendship of the squire. To make himself valuable to the lord of the manor was a great feat for an old sailor like Matthew; but I wouldn't say he was a downy fashion of man."

"How might he be like to treat a trusting and loving woman?" asked Dinah. "With most widow-men you can take a line if you look back how they was used to treat their partners; but Mrs. Owlett died before my time."

"I can mind her. She wasn't what you'd call a trusting nor yet loving woman," answered Unity. "Rose Owlett laboured under a very unfortunate failing. She was jealous as the grave, and for the wife of a sailor to be jealous is madness in any case, because what he do or don't do, when he's put half the world between him and his wife, is nobody's business but his own. Her weakness was to make it her business; and another unfortunate thing troubled Rose: she never believed a word Owlett told her. It was contrary to her nature to trust him out of her sight, and so she never did."

"In a manner of speaking she ruled him, then?" suggested Mrs. Chadd.

"Ashore, yes. For peace he gave up trying to answer back and spent most of his time along with his curiosities. There he found his comfort, because they only minded him of foreign parts. Then in fullness of time Rose was gathered in. She shortened her life down to forty-five years by worrying, or so Wallabrook always said, and after she was gone Matt followed his bent and stopped at home and worked at the wonders of Nature. I knew him very well then and John liked him very well, same as most people do; but we all felt tolerable sure that, along of his bleak memories, he wouldn't take another."

Dinah considered these things.

"One side of a tale's only good till you've heard the other," she said. "If Mrs. Owlett was hastened to her grave in her forties, she must have found Matt no better to live with than what he found her."

"She did, without a doubt. I'm not running her down. She was a tough, overbearing woman—rather the type of female my Maude is rightly held to be. There's lots of 'em everywhere, and you'll generally find their husbands have got to lose their self-respect and sing second, if it's only for peace. In your case, Dinah, if things fall out so that Owlett wanted you, I'd say this, knowing him as I do: he'd never give you any cause for regretfulness, my dear. His hobby would always come first in his mind, but it's a harmless one for a wife. His manners, as you've found, no doubt, are outstanding. He's clean and tidy, like most old seamen, and he's got all a sailor's cleverness for odd jobs and the needle if called to use it."

"Can he cook?" asked Mrs. Chadd. "He likes good cooking and praises Nancy because she can cook, which I was thankful to hear for Peter's sake."

"I expect he could if he was called to," answered Unity.

"In that case, then, when his girl goes, he'll have to give his mind to the subject, and if, as you say, he's also handy with his needle, then I don't see why ever, at his age, he'd want to be bothered with another wife at all."

"You may be right, but against that, he's busy as a bee about the ways of Nature, and so long as Sir Gerald wants him, he'll put work first. He'd be lost without service. Time will show. He may perhaps try and see if he can live his life single-handed; but most men who try that darned soon find they can't."

"Time will show, as you say, Unity, and be it as it will I shan't do nothing without consulting you," promised Dinah.

"How do you find yourself to feel about Nancy for Peter?" asked Mrs. Blanchard on a later occasion.

"I've brought my reasoning powers to it," so Dinah assured her. "With a young man like my son—pretty well so near perfection as a human creature can be—I had the right to hope high when it came to his future wife. I can't say Nancy's quite on the same level with Peter, and I should feel the same if he'd took up with a female angel, no doubt; but I've seen this coming for months before it came, and I've sounded Nancy with all a mother's cunning and I wouldn't say I can point to any black spot in her. Of course Matt overrates her, as fathers will their only child; but as girls go, she's sensible and healthy and a worker. She's got a will and that's to the good, and, above all else, she's won the love of Peter, and that's something no other girl ever did. There's a tidy lot have coveted him since he came back; but he wanted a good bit more than a glad eye to win his attention, so I tell myself that where Peter could find himself in love, then I shall also find myself in love come presently."

Thus these elderly women chattered and in a measure served to link those earthly interests each represented. They knew it not, each being concerned with lives that mattered little to the other; but chance now chose to weave their varied preoccupations into a single pattern. Unity Blanchard, her daughter, her son-in-law, her grandson and the nurseryman represented one factor of the approaching fusion, while Matthew and his daughter, with Dinah and her son, stood for the other. None among them anticipated the upheaval ahead, or could have imagined the conditions capable of creating it, yet for these folk and their home-spun interests, Time brought a cyclone that spared not one. But it was no evil hurricane to overwhelm and destroy their accepted certainties and cherished hopes. It came with enlargement of narrow and familiar ambits, with new designs for living, with untrodden paths, challenges and changes unguessed, yet not unendurable, or beyond the powers of native fortitude and common sense to weather.

BOOK II

CHAPTER I

WITH time and consideration of the change that now awaited him, Mr. Owlett revealed some measure of egotism and began, in Nancy's opinion, to be difficult and less reasonable than usual. She rated her father one day over a particularly irrational symptom recently developed.

"Nobody was better pleased than you, Dad, when I gave up the land work and came home, so as I could tend you closer and we'd see more of each other; and now you say that having me by your side all the time only makes it worse and harder and crueller to think what you'll feel like and be called to face when I'm gone for good. And you make a grievance of it and carry on as if I was doing something right-down wicked to desert you, which I never would do and never shall. You knew very well I should marry if the right one came along, and not sooner; and he did come along, so, seeing you couldn't hatch up a shadow of good reason against us being tokened, you're taking it out on me now by pretending that everything I do only makes it harder for you to look forward when I go to Peter."

Matthew considered this and showed no inclination to argue or protest. He even nodded some measure of assent.

"I see your point, my love," he answered, "and there's a spot of truth in it; and the truth, in whatsoever shape it comes, will always demand my respect. Sir Gerald's taught me that much. You must try and understand that though the spirit is tolerable willing, the flesh is weak. The spirit knows you're an outstanding piece and well entitled to a home of your own; but it reminds me that there is much to think upon as to the nature of that home and the man who's going to share it with you. We'll leave him out for the minute. 'Tis easier nowadays to find a husband than to find a home; but time's on your side and I'd always trust the Lord to produce a home for the deserving, though this Labour Government find it beyond their powers. That's by the way. I'll own up I haven't hid my mind when I think of you gone and, since you left the land and came back, the fact you was back, as you have marked yourself, sometimes makes my misery appear when I picture myself without you again."

"There's no call for you to be miserable and you needn't to plead no house difficulty and you very well know it, Father. We've gone a long way past that problem on your own showing, because you've told me in confidence that what you intend is cut and dried. You can't go back on that and you know as well as I do and Peter does that Mrs. Chadd has thought it over and don't feel any doubt as to her course of action when the time comes. It all fits in so comfortable as can be for the four of us and, instead of grizzling about it, you ought to get on with your part."

"I know what Dinah ordains to do when I put the question," explained Matthew, "and because I know, I hold my hand and mark time. Time's my sheet anchor for the moment. I think the world on Dinah; but, after all these long years of liberty and peace, the thought of being under female dominion again strikes a chill. From no disrespect for her, but just because my widowed life along with you has been such a boon and a blessing. Deep things like that you wouldn't understand and I shouldn't expect you to, but when next I see Dinah I'll go further and explain my feelings and why I've hung fire so long. Nobody will understand quicker than her."

"If she could get over her misfortunate first husband and take another, then you should be able to forget you weren't too happy with mother and try again," suggested Nancy.

"Exactly what I'm going to do," he promised. "I'll go so far as to say I look forward to it; but I never was one to be rushed, and them that have tried to rush me always regretted doing so. You can leave the rest to me, Nancy. All will go forward very suent and dignified in God's good time and Dinah can exert herself to restrain Peter's impetuous nature, same as I damp you down now and then. So don't kick against the pricks, but trust the experience of middle age when it puts a drag on youth. We know better than what you can."

"You dodge about so, Father," she answered doubtfully. "I never know if you mean what you are saying, or only getting out of a fix yourself by talking nonsense. But if you promise faithful to ask Mrs. Chadd to marry you, that would be getting a move on."

"I undertake the step shall be took, which ought to satisfy the three of you for the present."

"Peter and I have sometimes wondered if it will be better fit for you to go to live with his mother at her home, or for her to come and live with you in this one, Father," suggested Nancy.

"Wonder no more, then," he replied. "She comes to me. I don't quit my house and my museum for no one on this earth, and if there was a shadow of any fancy I might think of such a caper, then the people can think again."

"That's what I told Peter when he wondered. And his mother supports you. She understands you better than you understand her, Father. I'd go so far as to say she understands you better than even I do. She said to me and Peter that to dare to imagine you and your collection anywhere but here was madness, and when I asked her if she felt she could face up to living with the museum, she said she was prepared to do so and would take her orders from you and none else."

"So I've gathered," replied Mr. Owlett, "and a very proper way to look at it. She told me once that she had her doubts as to whether it might be a clever thing to do. And I granted that. I said, 'If we take this step, Dinah, it must be clearly understood for a business transaction and the betterment of both of us.' And she agreed. Then I said at our ages it would be weak-minded to pretend anything different and she agreed to that too. 'What we may come to feel for each other beyond respect and good-willing, if we adventure to be married, time will show,' I told Dinah, and she granted how only time and experience could throw the true light as to that.

"She said: 'One thing would need to be grasped by both of us, Matt. You must never for a minute think you'll be dearer to me than what Peter is, because he'll always come first above all else in this world; and I shan't for a moment take the place of your curiosities, or be half or yet a quarter so dear to you as your life-long collection.' 'You never said a truer word than that, Dinah,' I answered her. So you can see the way's made clear for me to advance now and put the question. I'm inclined to think that after next Christmas is a thing of the past I shall give her the chance to join me if still so disposed."

Nancy shivered.

"It's a pretty cold-blooded sort of fashion to talk of marriage," she said. "Nobody can say you're an old man in a hurry anyway. You always act as if you was going to live five hundred years at least and Peter admires you for it. He's rather like that himself; but he knows the first step is for you and Mrs. Chadd to come to a conclusion, so he'll be glad you're not marking time much over Christmas. Peter says, in his thoughtful way, that it seems queer to him how young people, with most of their lives ahead of 'em still, should always be for pushing forward and getting a move on—all for speed—and old people, with the end in sight, like you and Mrs. Chadd for instance, take it so easy and let time over-get you and go on looking ahead when there's so darned little left for you to see there."

Her father laughed and rose from their discussion.

"That reminds me to be up and doing this instant moment," he said. "I'm due to go to Oakshotts because Sir Gerald counts on me this afternoon at the appointed time. He ain't got much left either, at his dizzy age; but he sees it clear enough and he's always fore-armed to do his duty. We'll talk this out, Nancy, another day, my love. I've forgotten a lot, but I ain't forgotten what it was to be young."

"How about your dinner, Father?" asked Nancy.

"I shall take it with Chave and the staff before I see the master."

Mr. Owlett went his way and his thoughts were dismissed for those more agreeable which a tramp in the open air always wakened. He welcomed Nature in all her garments, or 'mother-naked' at the end of the year, for to him the skeleton of an elm divest of leaves was as attractive as the same tree at bud-break, brushed with roseal inflorescence, or 'under full sail with all her green canvas set to her top-gallants' in summer-time.

Sir Gerald awaited him and on this occasion, as on many others, offered no formal welcome but accosted him with what was in his own mind at the moment. He would begin at once to talk upon the subject uppermost in his thoughts and transfer the matter from brain to tongue when there appeared one capable of listening.

"A ray of light appears where I least expected to welcome it," said Sir Gerald. "It looks as though the insects of Devon were about to receive a measure of that attention they deserve. This is good news, Owlett, and I welcome it."

"Then I do for certain, your honour. And what's in the wind about the West-country insects, if I may ask?" inquired Matthew.

"Recognition for them, my dear man. The Entomological section of the Devonshire Association has decided to compile a Fauna—an Insect Fauna—conducted along the lines of the Devon Flora! This spells progress and the next step is to create a museum wherein the actual creatures shall appear. That I cannot hope to see, for, at the present day, far more attention is being paid to homes for living people than suitable quarters for defunct birds, beasts or insects. Our national museums, picture galleries and libraries are all utterly inadequate and the increasing hunger for the people's culture lamentably neglected as usual. But a time approaches when this failure is going to startle and shock the intellectual world. You will be staggered to learn, Matthew, that the Library of the British Museum will have no further accommodation for any more books within the space of three years!"

"If Devon can furnish a tidy building for the insect race, surely London did ought to find a home for all the books ever wrote," suggested the visitor.

"Our Government will be called to answer that challenge and many others at no distant date," foretold the scientist.

"For the minute there's more general excitement about setting up homes where you can live yourself and harbour along with your wife and count on a spot of room for your children," explained Matthew. "The young couples are yelping for a kennel all the world over and, in a manner of speaking, the Government is more to blame for the falling birthrate than the people. No self-respecting young man and woman is going to join up till they've got a habitation in sight, and even the fight for 'pre-fabs' you'd never believe."

"They must be as horrible to live in as they are dreadful to see, I'm afraid," sighed the elder.

"For my part I'd sooner dwell underground like a rabbit, your honour, and them that want to go on living, not to say breeding, may have to take to earth in years to come."

"The human race in order to survive might become subterranean, as you suggest," agreed Sir Gerald. "The men of a coming Atomic Age may live like the moles and only peep forth to take the air on moonlit nights. However, these things need not occupy our attention for the moment. I wanted you, as I did last Christmas, for a little inside information. The time approaches when, in obedience to family traditions of long standing, I dispense to the more indigent among us the annual little largesse of coal, blankets and port wine; but Mr. Thornbarrow, my land agent, and I are not quite at one this year on the extent of these friendly gestures. He is of opinion that we should bow to the times, recognise that things are not as they were and that coal, blankets and port wine, even when attainable, can only be secured at a figure far exceeding that formerly demanded for them. He reminds me how the pound sterling is disvalued and bereft. He will harp on its melancholy downfall. I admit this situation, but point out that it cannot alter the physical facts concerning hunger and cold and privation. Such things must not be overlooked to satisfy Thornbarrow. Misery we cannot export, whatsoever else we may."

"Mr. Thornbarrow wouldn't have your high-minded opinions, your honour, because it wouldn't be his place," explained Owlett. "He'd put the manor accounts first."

"For a land agent justice to an estate must no doubt be his first thought; for me my angle of vision is otherwise. The old traditions are going to be preserved and the gifts augmented rather than reduced. You are in touch with Wallabrook and I ask you to see me and inform me of any outstanding quarters outside my knowledge where a Christmas addition is specially indicated. Mr. Thornbarrow, in his present agitated mood, may not be relied upon in this matter; but you can pleasure me with an open mind."

"You will be set on the aged ones no doubt, your honour, because there's none feel the cold like them. And what's took from them in body heat did ought to be put at their service by their fellow creatures, you'd say?"

"Conscience raises the demand, my dear Matt, while circumstance unfortunately limits the response. I much fear there are many more shivering old bones in this post-war world than sufficient coal and blankets to comfort them. But every little helps. So keep it in mind and let me hear in a day or two of any special cases within your knowledge. Let me have such details as you can obtain without giving offence to anybody and leave the rest to me."

The old sailor presently withdrew and on his way home found no difficulty in completing the task set him. His mind then returned to his own affairs, which under Nancy's pressure began to grow urgent, though he set Mrs. Chadd first and admitted to himself that he was not treating her with due respect. Both he and she knew perfectly well that it was time he made a formal proposal of marriage and both also knew the answer to be expected. He was only loitering because he found freedom continue to be so attractive, though common sense reminded him that Dinah would be the last to interfere with his right to pursue life upon the lines he pleased.

Dinah would come to him and Nancy would take her place. Peter was going to have a wife to look after him instead of a mother, while, instead of a father, Nancy would undertake the welfare of a husband. Nothing more simple and obvious could be suggested and Matthew knew it. He told himself that there still remained much to learn of the policeman, but could not in honesty suggest any channel of doubt save Peter's potential inheritance from a disreputable parent. He liked his future son-in-law, yet felt the young man still remained untested.

Elsewhere more pressing and immediate challenges had overtaken a man and his wife, for into the united lives of Brian and Maude White there intruded an unexpected hint of things to come. The man brought it home with him from Wallabrook railway station and both Maude and her mother strove to calm his indignation.

"Here's a damn' fine thing!" he said, and related an activity in contemplation of the Government. Under nationalisation of the railways it was discovered that many more hands were employed than was now deemed necessary.

"They're minded to sack scores and scores," he told them. "By next year they count to carry on with thousands less. We've put the blighters in and now all we get for our support looks to be the sack and our security gone and our money and our pensions and our job of work! That's what they say, and if it's true, then there's a Red revolution in sight. When countless railwaymen find themselves unemployed, then they'll darned soon find employment and bring out them that are left in and paralyse railway transport through the length and breadth of England. Civil servants, mind you! We're all civil servants now, and who the devil ever heard of a government daring to serve its own civil servants same as that?"

"No call to get up in the air till you hear more about it," said Mrs. Blanchard. "The Socialists ain't out to make trouble for working men, Brian. Most like you won't be sacked in any case. The labour ain't less on the lines because they're took from the companies. The only losers, so Arthur says, are them that put their savings in 'em and trusted 'em. The Government only steals their money from folk too weak to hit back. They won't quarrel with your sort, and if they sack any railwaymen it will be the clerks and black-coated ones most like."

Maude had shown considerable uneasiness at this news.

"I hope mother's right," she said. "Maybe you've got it wrong, Brian, because there's a proper huge lot on the railways like you, no doubt, that know their job but never could learn another. What the mischief could you turn your hand to if they fired you?"

"I'd turn my hand to revolution," he answered. "That don't

want no training. If they sack us, they'll find themselves sacked and their jobs and their wage packets gone."

His mother-in-law, who had been of late enlightened from Mr. Brimblecombe's point of view on politics, spoke again.

"Labour may have a nastier problem to face than unemployment," said Unity. "This Government, so Arthur says, have pretty near soaked the rich to the limit now; and the next thing that's like to offer another gold mine for 'em is going to be the savings of the poor. They've kept their claws off that money and will do so till they've weathered the next General Election, then you'll see."

"What's the savings of the small people?" asked Maude. "There wouldn't be much in them to be worth taking."

But her mother laughed.

"Bless your life, Maude," she answered, " 'tis millions on millions, my dear! Small savings mount up in this country to proper huge money."

"If you can't trust the Socialists, who can you trust, Mother?" asked Maude.

"I wonder," answered the old woman. "Maybe we shall live to find out."

They were eating their tea at the moment and when there came a knock at the door Gilly, who had been listening to the high contention in solemn silence, went to answer it. Now he returned with Mrs. Parsons behind him. Thomasina regarded herself as free at all times of 'Laburnum Lodge'; she begged for a cup of tea, kissed Maude and declared herself the bearer of news.

"Good news then, I hope, Tommy, because Brian have just heard a bit that looks bad," said Mrs. White.

"Mine's just news and not what you might call good nor yet particular bad," explained Thomasina. "Just Nature. Have you heard about Mrs. Motherwell, Maude?"

"No, and don't want to. I don't like her."

"I heard she was sick," said Unity, "but don't know her except by sight."

"You wouldn't know her even by sight now, Granny," answered the visitor. "I don't like her myself, but this is different, because I do know her, so I just looked in for sympathy, you understand. I picked it up at the grocer's that she was in danger, so I popped in, and you could have knocked me down with a feather. She's took a frightful jaundice and there she lies, so yellow as a crocus and half dead already! You can't be so yellow as that and recover, so the parish nurse have told her daughter, Minnie."

"Fancy Motherwell going," said Maude. "Who'd have thought it?"

"Dead by morning, I shouldn't wonder."

Mrs. Parsons shone with excitement.

"Needless to say Dr. Bridger don't feel no great hopes and Minnie says her mother's a tidy lot worse than when he was in yesterday."

"Then he ought to be sent for, Tommy," said Mrs. Blanchard.

"So Minnie thought herself," explained the visitor, "and I'm going for Bridger on my way home to tell him the sad news before it's too late."

Brian, who did not admire Thomasina, left them now and Maude spoke.

"So much for your news; ours is a bit different and a good bit more important, Tommy."

"Most news has its important side to somebody. Tell on, Maude."

She heard the railway rumours with great interest and her mind instantly accepted the possibility of Brian's dismissal.

"He ain't what you might call the backbone of the railway station, is he?" she asked. "I should be afraid for him if I was you, my dears, because, though a master of his job without a doubt, there's nothing much else you'd say where he could earn a living at his age."

Maude nodded and her mother reproved Thomasina.

"Why d'you always nose out after news and then take the bleakest view of it you can take?" she asked. "And why do the business of other folk always interest you more than your own, Tommy?"

Mrs. Parsons answered the last question first.

"Just for good-willing, Granny," she said. "I went to see Mrs. Motherwell, not for curiosity but charity, because I reckoned a bright word or two would cheer her up. There's people you don't miss nor yet cry for when they die, and there's the sort that leave a gap you'll never live to see filled again same as they filled it."

"Everybody's got someone to love or hate as the case may be," suggested Maude.

"I keep an open mind myself," declared her friend. "I try for Christian kindness to keep an open mind, because I only want to know the truth about people, not to judge 'em."

"Just a truth-hunter, you'd call yourself," suggested Unity.

"Exactly so! And it's always interesting to know what anybody's game happens to be, Granny."

"Why should they want to tell you what their game is?"

"I often wonder; but it's a queer thing how strange folk like to reveal it. They properly love to tell you what's biting them and what they've suffered and where they've triumphed. When they find you're interested in 'em and their relations and pains and aches and full of human kindness to 'em, then they'll open out and talk even if you're a complete stranger, because to talk about themselves is their favourite occupation and a pleasure that never palls so long as they can find a fellow creature to listen. You learn a lot about men and women that way, for what they say oft shows you what they are. All I've picked up in a bus, or at a bus stop for that matter, would fill a book!"

Mrs. Blanchard regarded the widow with a certain amount of respect.

"You're an artful one," she said.

"If you've got a kind face and a proper touch, anybody can do it," said Thomasina. "Only calls for a bit of practice."

"And comes natural to you, I suppose?" asked Maude.

"Just a gift in my case," agreed her friend, "same as reading advertisements is your gift and knitting is your mother's gift."

"Everybody's got a gift of some sort—good or bad. So long as your gift ain't the bane of anybody else, no doubt it works out to your advantage," decided Unity.

CHAPTER II

It was now, and at the accepted time, as she impressed upon her husband, that Maude's peculiar talent for scrutinising advertisements—and often winning profit from this unusual endowment—produced very startling results. As a rule her investigations revealed new patent medicines or hair-restorers and were applied to herself. Occasionally, too, she met with a promising item that interested Mrs. Parsons and aimed at painless reduction of superfluous tissue, or the simplification of household duties; but now, in print of modest size yet not too small to escape her, Maude found her own maiden name staring her in the face along with possibilities so stupendous that her first instinct was to cry the discovery aloud. She restrained herself, however, checked the cry of excitement ready to burst from her throat and permitted her quick wits to work in silence.

On Sunday there always came to 'Laburnum Lodge' an illustrated West-country journal of high repute, and this privilege was shared among those who dwelt therein. Brian read the *Sunday Clarion* for the football news, the dog- and horse-racing news and the murders, while, after Sunday dinner, his wife spent the afternoon with it and later, on occasions when she did not go to church, Mrs. Blanchard turned its pages for the sake of the pictures.

It was here, while she reclined in her hour of rest, that the fateful appeal met Mrs. White's eyes, rounded them with amazement and brightened them with greed. Thrice she read it, reflected deeply, cast a sidelong look out of the window, where her mother and son were walking in the garden, and then took action. Maude knew that Mrs. Blanchard would probably turn to the *Clarion* after tea and she also knew that the last thing likely to detain her parent was any advertisement great or small; but her mind had operated along the usual channels, and since what she had just read was now digested and understood, as a measure of precaution the remotest possibility of Unity seeing it must be avoided.

This much with lightning-quick perspicacity Maude had grasped and now she acted without further delay. She got a pair of scissors and cut out the words very carefully, leaving a small gap in the sheet from which they came. Nor did it matter if Mrs. Blanchard observed the hole, because, in the remote event of her mentioning it, nothing would be easier to report excision of something quite different. But the need for Unity's complete ignorance had deeply impressed her daughter, because she perceived that this printed request for certain information actually involved Mrs. Blanchard rather than herself.

Only one fear existed in her mind: that others not personally interested might chance upon the appeal. In that case they would very likely call Unity's attention to it. That probability was small, though the possibility could not be avoided, but at least Mrs. Blanchard was not going to discover anything for herself. Maude, however, decided that her husband should hear it. Her first thought was Thomasina; but since secrecy for the present at least must be demanded, she felt that her friend had better not be enlightened until the matter was weighed with Brian. He could be trusted, since he would see in a moment that he had as much to gain as herself in the event of any substantial success.

One ugly fact lay behind any discovery of real importance. Her mother represented the real problem. It was Mrs. Blanchard who stood as a barrier between Maude and the promised land that might lurk hidden in the advertisement. Acutely she understood the situation, and, while entertaining small respect for her husband's wits, yet knew at least that the secret would be safe with him. She had sometimes observed how, though not a clever man, Brian's masculine viewpoint would present a practical line of action where she had failed to find one, and now decided to show him the advertisement and enlighten him as to the difficulties it created. These it was probable he might not see until she presented them. After tea, the night being bright and dry, Unity decided to go to church and take Gilly with her, so Maude found her opportunity and showed Brian the printed words.

"Don't go out," she said. "Give heed to me. A proper wonderful thing happened this afternoon—something the very last to be expected and, coming as it do when your work looks to be threatened, or so you say, makes it all the more wonderful. Read that. I read it in the *Clarion* this afternoon and cut it out."

"Another mess for your skin, or your teeth, or some part of your body?" he asked.

"Read and take it serious and don't be a fool," she answered.

Brian conveyed her scrap of paper to a lamp on the table and read it.

Wanted. If any members of the family of the late James Blanchard of Sydney, New South Wales, Australia, and some time of Wallabrook, Devonshire, will communicate with Messrs. Wilson & Harding, Solicitors, of 7 Pike Alley, The Temple, London, they will hear of something to their advantage.

"Who was the Blanchard that went foreign and no more ever heard of him?" asked Brian.

"He was the brother of John Blanchard, my father. He went to Australia before I was born," explained Maude, "and the only Blanchard left now is mother; but me being her daughter would inherit the lot, whatever it might be, after her."

"Dead sure there's none else?"

"Dead sure. The Blanchards are all down and out years and years ago."

"You would reap nothing before your mother does, however. Have you named this advert to her, Maude?"

"No, I haven't for the minute."

"Don't then," he said. "Not till we've thought it over."

"I wasn't going to."

Brian considered.

"It may be only a flea-bite, in which case no need to bother overmuch about it; but if by some chance there was big money—then?"

"That's how far I've got for the minute," she admitted. "You see how it is. As you say, if it was only a mite, no harm done, and little offering for anybody; but if James Blanchard made good out there and left big money, then we're up against something. It might be. Mother's often spoke of her brother-in-law and father often spoke of him, too, and they used to agree that he was a strong, independent fashion of man and more like to succeed than fail. He's dead seemingly and of course this may only mean he's left a legacy to the Blanchards, if there's any left, and his proper savings have gone to his wife and family; or it may mean that he had nobody out there to consider and willed his money back to any of his own kin remaining. If that's it, then it looks to me, barring mother, I'd scoop the lot."

"She'd come before you?"

"Certainly she would. James Blanchard never heard of me. He wanted to marry mother himself, but she liked John better—God knows why—and he never heard no more about his family after he left England, because he never wrote himself, nor let his parents have any address to write to. He was that sort of man, I expect, and, when he found he couldn't marry mother, he ordained to be quit of his own relations too."

"It's a gamble," said Brian. "We can't say yet if there's anything to it worth thinking about. If there isn't, then you can let your mother know and get on with it; but if it turned out a fortune, what then? She tosses her head quite high enough as a pauper and Lord knows what line she'd take if she found perhaps hundreds of money had fallen in her lap. I'd say keep shut about her and gamble on it yourself."

"Yes," agreed Maude. "For once here's a gamble where you may win and can't lose in any case, except for the needful time and thought given to it. Mother's the snag."

"With my future looking to be in doubt, a gamble same as this might be the way out," he said. "If this turned into proper money for you—which would mean for us—then I could sack the railway instead of the railway sacking me, and then they'd look proper fools and be damned to them; but the teaser for you, Maude, is to know how your mother's to be got off the map."

"I know that."

"That's where the gamble comes in then."

"Everything turns on what this promise of something to our advantage amounts to," she explained. "If we could get a side wind on that, we'd know the size of the temptation to gamble at all. So we needn't to look very far ahead for the instant moment."

"The lawyers will know. If you was to write to them on your own and just fish to hear the advantages without naming your mother, and if they were in a position to tell you what figure they had in mind, then we should see where we stood."

"I'd thought of that myself," she said. "That's where I'd reached to. If mother was a different sort of woman and could be counted upon in any case to do the right thing by her only child, then I wouldn't have thought again about showing her the advert and trusted her, whether it was big or small, to do her bounden duty by me."

"You was wise not to run no silly risk like that," he said. "She don't set no store whatever by you. If she leaves a brass farthing behind her, she'll leave it to Gilly, and in that case it would be hoarded up for him and put beyond his reach and beyond your reach likewise. What we want is a clean sheet. It may be that your mother stands between you and solid money. If she don't, no harm done; but if she do, then we've got a start because she doesn't hap to know a thing about it yet, or anybody else either."

Maude nodded.

"If I write to the lawyers I need to pick my words tolerable clever," she said. "A letter has an ugly way of coming back at you, as Tommy pointed out to me a long time ago."

"For God's sake don't name this to her!"

"I shan't; but if I write asking particulars, the first thing is to keep quiet about mother, because the minute they hear about her, then the game's up for me—to call it a game."

"You'll write as if you was the rightful party to make inquiries?"

"I'll leave them to assume it so; but if it came to cast-iron facts, they'll want to know a lot more, and that's where we need to plan. But what can we plan? You can't pretend there's no such person as mother. She'll be the first to know about it when they hear I've got one. Not all the craft in the world can make folk take it for granted you're an orphan if you've got a mother alive like my mother. Queer to say, Brian, but if there's anything here noteworthy, then it's come along a bit too soon."

He considered and followed her meaning.

"Better James Blanchard had waited to die till Unity Blanchard was gone?"

"Yes—a lot better for us. You might almost go so far as to say, in a manner of speaking, that mother's robbed me of what in common justice should be mine."

They talked on, but hastened to a conclusion as the sound of the returning worshippers came from outside.

Mrs. White summed up hurriedly.

"I'll write careful," she promised. "You always need to go like a cat on hot bricks when you pick up a pen, and never more so than now; but I'll show 'em somebody's seen their advertisement and hear what they've got to tell. And keep your own mouth shut to everybody."

Brian departed as Unity returned the better for evensong. She always put on her best clothes when going to church and never failed to feel interest in the size of the congregation. She was very jealous for her Faith, elated when the flock served largely to fill the house of worship, uneasy and cast down before a scanty company.

"A tidy good rally tonight," she said, "and a promise from his reverence that the church's new heating apparatus will be working before Christmas. He prayed for Mrs. Motherwell, but not in a very hopeful tone of voice."

"Tommy said she was going," so Maude reminded her. "Often the kindest thing you can wish a body, that Nature would get on with it and not play cat-and-mouse with 'em."

But the suggestion, while conveying nothing in particular to Mrs. Blanchard, started a sequence of ideas for Maude. In a subconscious fashion she found herself thinking along old lines and concerned with her past desires to be rid of Unity. In days gone by she had suffered from her mother's existence to a mild extent and, since no natural reason appeared or promised the elder's departure, considered a suggestion of hinting at the only way to hasten it.

Now thoughts of proceeding farther along that road quickened in Maude. She had warned Brian to keep his mouth shut, but found it safe and easy to follow the bent of her own thoughts under this new and tremendous provocation. What looked desirable of old promised to become both necessary and vital now. She looked back that night from the peace and silence of her bed and considered the nature of past efforts to impress upon her mother the bright side of leaving this world for a better. She had as yet done little more than declare her own opinions on the subject of suicide. To tell Mrs. Blanchard to go and kill herself was no part of Maude's technique: she had merely confessed that self-destruction often occurred to her own mind. Even this idea needed delicate conveyance, for her mother knew her too well to credit any such assurance. Indeed, Unity had once rebuked her for certain morbid reflections on the advantage of suicide and spoken words that indicated danger.

"If you want to do away with yourself, Maude, that's your affair and not mine," she had declared. "You may have your reasons, like a lot of other people and, living along with Brian, I can go so far as to understand some of 'em; but you won't get no support from me. There's something up your sleeve, if you ask me, though I can't tell what the mischief you're aiming at."

Scenting peril after this strong rebuke, Mrs. White had abandoned the old line of attack, yet now it returned to her for reconsideration. She saw its weakness and trusted that some more skilful design might presently appear. The need for time and the fear that her discovery would not allow enough worried Maude. Once again she unavailingly wished that James Blanchard had waited to depart until her mother led the way.

When she spoke to Brian again on the subject, his masculine viewpoint impressed her.

"Lawyers are clever at wasting time," he said. "Their money's screwed out of other people's time, and the longer they keep a job dangling, the more there's in it for them and the less for their customers. I've thought of this same as you have, and I wouldn't say your plan to get her in a mood to put herself down ever did promise any results. And I shouldn't start it again. She ain't the woman to do it—not while she's as snug as a bug in a rug along with us. But deeds would be more likely to get her in a mood than words. If she was damned uncomfortable and miserable here, she might be a bit more disposed to get out of it. We could tighten up on her, I expect, if it looked to be worth while. Or we can own up and drive a bargain with her."

"She'd never drive no bargain," said Maude.

"Well, write to 'em, then; but once you've written, then we'll be forced to get on with it. There may be good money for the lawyers to pick out of this for all we can tell, and, if there is, they'll grab it for certain. Once they answer you needn't to write back again in a hurry. Or you could say you'd take up the matter after Christmas perhaps."

"Once I write, the bigger the money the quicker they'll answer me," explained Maude. "They are cunning as rats and they'd smell there was something doing if it was a lot and I didn't show no haste to come by it. They might even send down to look into my *bona fides*, and, so long as mother's here, that would bitch up the whole show."

"Well, I ain't no plotter myself," he confessed. "Direct action is my way to look at things, and that's ruled out. Pity we can't let somebody into the job to advise us, but he'd want his cut off the joint after if we landed anything big out of it."

"It's for us and nobody else, because no honest man would look at this quite the same as we do," admitted Maude. "I'll write, but I won't say anything they can pin on me for a lie till we hear more. Then perhaps all they may have to tell will give us a pointer what's best to do next."

"There's always a dog's chance somebody else who knows about us saw the advert too," he reminded her.

For three days longer she waited and then wrote to London. Meantime her husband declared hopeful possibilities.

"There's a lot of sickness hovering about in this up-and-down fashion of weather," he said. "The papers say 'flu' is got all over France and there's no way to keep it out of England known to science. So, if by chance she catched a dose of that, it might save us a mort of trouble, Maude."

"We want a certainty," she answered. "Chance ain't good enough. We've got our chance. Now it's up to us to turn it into something cast-iron."

Meantime in another family circle Matthew Owlett kept his word and proposed marriage to Dinah Chadd. He postponed the event to the last reasonable moment, drank tea with her on Christmas Eve, discussed lesser subjects and finally offered his hand and heart. Through Nancy, Mrs. Chadd, aware that he might be expected, prepared one of his favourite cakes and greeted him with the usual friendship, but left him to approach the dramatic moment and asked after Sir Gerald.

"I hope the gentleman's facing up to the winter pretty well," she said. "They tell me he's dispensed his gifts very plenteous according to custom."

"I've helped him to do so," explained Mr. Owlett. "He was wishful to know any outstanding cases which hadn't reached his ear, so I was able to give him a tip here and there as to a few of the folk prone to suffer in silence. They've had some surprises and so has Mr. Thornbarrow."

"He's got a lot to thank you for—Sir Gerald have," said Dinah.

"So he says. He sets confidence in me and I rise to it so well as I know. But I put my foot in it now and again and disappoint him."

Matthew laughed at a recollection.

"When he calls me 'Mr. Owlett', then I know I've said something contrary to his opinions, and when he just says 'Owlett', short like that, I feel he's calming down again. When he says 'Matthew', or 'my dear fellow', then everything in the garden's lovely; and sometimes he'll even say 'Matt', or 'my friend', which signifies he's thinking about something deep hidden in his own mind and outside my range altogether."

He praised Dinah's cake and went on to consider her varied triumphs in the preparation of all good food.

"You're such a humble piece, you leave it to others to say a good word for you most times," said Matthew, "but you ought to rate your own valuation higher, Dinah. When anybody's heard to cheapen their own efforts, few folk take the trouble to disagree with them."

"If I've got your good opinions, Matthew, I'm contented."

"Your stock's going to rise when the people hear I want you. For that matter I may say a lot of 'em know it already, because, when your name comes up where I hap to be present, I never hesitate to sing your worth," he assured her. "And now it looks to be the time for me to put a climax on it. I never was one to be rattled by the rising generation, though your son and my daughter have gone so far as they dared to force my hand; but they held strong cards without a doubt and were cute enough to know it. So when Nancy was in a position to tell me there was no fear of a defeat if I advanced and that, in solemn truth, I might count upon a favourable reply and no ugly reverse, which would have made me look a fool and not to be thought of—then I faced it."

"You may look more of a fool for offering than if you'd decided against doing so," she said; but her suitor would have none of this.

"The offer's made and the stroke's struck," he said. "I'm wishful to marry you, Dinah, and I'll make bold to say that if you agree, I shall be the gainer and you'll lose your house and be called to live in mine; but against that, you stand on firm ground and will be perfectly free to run your life as your fancy dictates. Peter won't be out of reach for you no more than Nancy will be out of reach for me, and if you say 'yes' and feel you could do with a new partner and a new name, then we can let the news be known and go on same as we are now—quietly marking time for a bit till our children are older and we all grasp what the future has got in store for the four of us and have planned to face up to it."

"It sounds a bit on the vague side yet, then," murmured Dinah, "but I wouldn't pretend to know all that might be moving in a big mind like yours."

"As to that, I always demand to be trusted, Dinah. There can't be no bed-rock affection if trust lacks from it. I shall trust you with everything but my collection of curiosities, which I never would trust to anybody but myself; but all else will be in your hands along with my goodwill and respect and devotion, and if I get your goodwill and devotion in exchange, then we ought to be a fine advertisement for the married state. Do I understand you to agree, my dear? Because, if so, I should like to hear you say the word."

"Yes, I do agree, dear Matt, and I hope to God nothing will ever overtake us to make you wish different."

"Good!" said Mr. Owlett. "We'll trust each other and feel very sure that God Almighty's going to trust the both of us also."

"That's right, Matthew. I always say that the wedded state ain't called Holy Matrimony for nothing."

"A most broad-minded opinion for a woman like you, seeing what was your first experience of it," said Matthew, "but, be it as it will, I can guarantee to go one better than your Aaron ever did."

"I own to be hopeful, Matthew," she said. "At our ages the word 'love' don't cut much ice and don't mean what it means to our children, of course; but whatever we shall be like to feel to each other, we'll always love them and they'll be our first thought and our brightest thought."

It was Matthew's turn to find a certain obscurity in Mrs. Chadd's outlook.

"I wouldn't say I exactly know what you're aiming at there," he answered. "They've both had their luck, but no need to drag 'em in at a moment like this. They can't have it both ways. You're going to be my first thought and my brightest thought in future, not them, and I expect and demand to be your first thought and brightest thought. So I'd think again as to that, if I was you."

She yielded instantly.

"I didn't choose my words very clever," she said. "I'm a poor talker at best. You'll be first and foremost so long as I live to watch over you, Matt, and I didn't ought to have dragged 'em in as you say."

"No, you didn't. They're all right in their proper place and always will be. They'll understand we're behind 'em and may live to know it was a darned good thing we are. But they don't want us for the minute and we don't want them. We've got quite so much to occupy our whole attention as they have now."

"That's very true indeed," declared Mrs. Chadd. "All they'll want is for us to get on with it, so as Nancy can come here and watch over Peter."

"The time to get on with it is our affair and will be a matter for our dignity," he explained.

They parted with affection and Matthew kissed his future wife, declaring himself grateful for a blessing high above his deserts.

"Same here, I'm sure," answered Dinah rather tearfully.

"Don't cry about it," he begged. "You're a beautiful creature still on your good days, Dinah, but I won't have no tears. When Peter comes back, you tell him the brave news and put a spot of triumph in your voice same as I shall."

He found Nancy waiting for him outside Mrs. Chadd's home. She knew what was ordained to happen and had come to learn particulars at the first possible moment.

"I wasn't going to intrude at such a time, Father, but I counted to be the first to see you when you left her," she said.

They returned in the darkness together and Nancy expressed her joy at the great news.

Free to do so now, and knowing where his routine work would take him, she often joined Peter on outlying beats, where they could converse in private on their own affairs. It was not a practice the policeman favoured, but his sweetheart often surprised him pleasantly by appearing, on moonlit nights, to brighten the monotony of his lonely beat. For the moment, however, Peter was at Tavistock on special duty, but would be returning in the morning by the earliest train, so Nancy stood on the platform next day when, in the sulky blink of a winter dawn, her sweetheart came back. He expressed surprise and pleasure at the sight of her, but chid her for being in such a hurry to meet again. Indeed Nancy found him a little constrained and, reading his simple moods correctly enough, asked him what was the matter.

"Just been talking to Brian White till your train came in," she said. "He's grumpy too. He said it was time railway hours were changed and that, some fine day, he might better himself. Funny talk. I don't much like him—no more does father. But you, darling? You don't sound properly awake yet. Or are you hungry? That's it, I reckon. I'm coming home with you to tell Mrs. Chadd how happy father is about it. She'll be Mrs. Owlett now and I shall be turned into Mrs. Chadd."

"Very good news, Nancy. And none too soon. 'Tis for you to keep your father on the move as far as you can."

Through the early morning silence came the whistle of the departing train and a more shrill and melancholy shriek nearer at hand. The familiar but unpleasing noise seemed to accord with Peter's frame of mind and he commented on it.

"Another good pig gone to his rest," he said. "A strange thing I've often thought on: that a pig hates to die worse than any other living creature."

"What does he know, or can know, about death?" asked Nancy. "Father says that the animals have got a great pull over us there, Peter, because they don't know a thing about death and don't waste a moment fretting on the subject."

"They may not know about death, same as we do, but a pig has got his suspicions when he's handled," said Peter. "He don't understand what's interfering with his comfort, but he's pretty sure it's something unpleasant."

"And I believe you'd think the job just as unpleasant as the poor pig if you had to kill him?"

"I should. A weakness of mine. I never could kill with a good conscience—just a feeling against taking life."

"Awkward for a policeman, because you might be called to—not very likely, but you might. If you'd chanced to be a farmer, you'd soon have got over that."

"Don't you jump on me this morning, Nancy," begged Peter mildly. "I was jumped on to Tavistock yesterday and haven't got over it yet."

"I thought there was something on your mind, Peter," she answered, looking anxious. "Who jumped on you at Tavistock? I'd like to meet him."

"My own fault, in a way. I was talking with some other constables where we put up, and the landlord of the place turned on me after I'd aired my views about justice to the poor. He was an old man and the hour was late and we were all tired and I may have said something silly."

"Not very likely, Peter."

"Well, he thought so, because he said that any man but a fool would try to understand what he was opening his mouth about and not start to explain a subject before he knew a damn' thing about it. 'But you can't make an obstinate man depart from his convictions,' he said, 'especially if he's a young one. And when an ass like you says he's made up his mind, then you can bet your bottom dollar he's got darned little mind to make up.' "

"Like his cheek—to talk to a police constable that way."

"Much what your father's often told me before," confessed Peter.

"Father always says you're a brave man and would stand up to any danger and peril to your skin; but he stills doubts whether——"

Peter interrupted with justifiable impatience:

"If Mr. Owlett will be so kind at his convenience to tell me exactly what he's wishful for me to do, I'll endeavour to oblige him. I haven't found nothing come between me and my duty so far."

"I'll tell him," said Nancy. "He's got to look after his own behaviour now and marry your mother and stop marking time, thank God."

The young man calmed down.

"I shall be on my beat beyond Oakshotts this afternoon," he said.

"Right. So shall I," she promised. "Now go and eat your breakfast and congratulate your dear mother."

CHAPTER III

CHRISTMAS came and still Mrs. White found her letter to Messrs. Wilson & Harding, of Pike Alley, undespatched. Written it was on several occasions, only to be torn up again and rewritten. In private Brian troubled at this delay, though she assured him that, within bounds, delay was entirely desirable. Her mother's existence represented the only difficulty. Maude scanned the pages of the *Sunday Clarion* like a hawk for any further appeal, but saw none, and finally committed herself to paper, writing as vaguely as she knew how and asserting that she was niece of the late James Blanchard of Australia and the daughter of the late John Blanchard of Wallabrook. She expressed a wish that it might be possible to have some details and hoped that Messrs. Wilson & Harding would excuse her for troubling them about what was doubtless a very trifling affair.

Then that happened to cheer Maude exceedingly. The lawyers replied and addressed her with a measure of respect quite beyond her experience. She was told almost exactly what she had hoped to hear as to the importance of the estate involved, and more than that. First she learned that the sum promised to be substantial and secondly that other communications from Australia must now be awaited and further intelligence should reach her upon its arrival. Since a legitimate claimant was now in sight, the lawyers were about to despatch a letter by air to Sydney. Meantime they assumed that Mrs. Maude White would presently forward more particulars concerning herself and furnish responsible directions to whom reference could be made. Elated by these assurances, Maude breathed again, but found Brian not so well pleased.

"The money's there all right," he said, "as I always felt we'd find it, and we've got a bit of time to clear the way. Anything may happen, but there's only one thing needful to happen, and if it don't happen, what then?"

"I know—I know all that," she answered, "and I shan't put pen to paper to 'em again till I must. There's only two things to do—dally so long as they'll stand it, which might suit 'em, because lawyers are masters of dallying themselves. The other thing, which I hate, would be to own up and tell mother and make some sort of a bargain with her—get it in writing so as she can't go back on it."

"That's the last resort," he declared; "but a lot might happen before we're drove into a corner like that."

He elaborated this at a later time and revealed emotions that, as Maude told herself, only utmost provocation could have awakened even in Brian.

"There's only a few things can happen to her and the question is whether we can help to bring one of 'em about," he said. "She won't be reduced to a frame of mind to take her own life, as lots of old, unwanted people have done; but she might meet with a fatal accident. There's only an accident to fall back upon, that I can see."

"We ain't going to put her away, if that's what you're aiming at," she answered.

"What'll you say next?" he asked. "I'm talking of the chance of an accident over-getting the old woman. I'm 'shamed of you, Maude."

She laughed.

"No you're not," she answered. "You're thinking how soon an accident might hap to fall out; but what price if it did? Suppose a fatal misfortune did happen to her? That's all right and everybody very sorry; but how would it look when, on top of her going off the map, 'tis heard I've come into her fortune and mother's just gone too soon to enjoy it?"

"There's accidents and accidents," said Brian. "Granted all you think, it only signifies that the accident would call for something where no chance of any human hand shows in it—least of all yours."

"Best to watch your own step. No call to talk to me as if you were the big noise in my life," replied Maude sharply. "Why for I ever told you a thing about this I don't know. You keep out of it and don't think you'd be pleasuring me if you plotted any harm to mother. More like you'd be risking your own neck."

He scowled at her and they fell into their familiar antagonism when alone together.

"There's many would risk their necks to be rid of such as you," he said. "I never know where I stand with you. Always poisonous just when your common sense should make you trustable. Blast all women: they're never safe till they're dead! We take 'em for better or worse, but don't know the worst of 'em till too late."

"We're the fools most time, not you," responded Maude.

When she was angered her face always turned pale rather than red and her voice sank to a hiss but never rose.

"When a man's wild after a woman, that's the time you can see through him if you've got eyes," she continued. "A man in love's no better than a whited sepulchre anyway—same as you was. A lot you hid from me—just what your cunning told you had better be hid if you was going to succeed."

"So did you from me, for that matter. If you're so keen about a showdown, you can have it."

"If I'd married a decent man, I'd never have been roused to hate him as I hate you, because there would never have been no reason to. You brought out the savage in me, like fear brings out the savage in creatures that never was savage till they got frightened."

He knew what was in her mind.

"When I gave you that black eye, I didn't do it for nothing. You can't pretend I hadn't a good cause to be angered."

"You was angered because you believed lies spoke to you behind my back by one that hated me. If you'd given him a black eye, you'd have shown you was a man, not a coward. A black eye's no matter: it will turn white again, but you bruised my soul when you struck me that day and you did for yourself, though you didn't know it. I forgave your beastliness and didn't take you to court as I well might, but I never felt the same after and never shall again."

Maude always got the better of these exchanges and Brian usually left the last word to her. On occasions of extreme acidity, as in the present, she was apt to sulk for a day or two afterwards and then resume their normal relations of rough-and-ready agreement. So indeed it happened now, for, twenty-four hours later, Mrs. White made a curious discovery, and, since she could impart it to nobody else, acquainted her railwayman. Their altercations, however frenzied, never created any lasting breach, but found them hunting in couples again ere long. Maude had often overlooked Brian's errors of commission, since they only touched his standards of honour, not her own, while he never hesitated to applaud her doubtful dealings in other directions.

Now there occurred certain mysterious and unexpected incidents tending to awaken hope of a fruitful development, for something out of the common happened after Christmas and Maude and Brian took their dinner alone. Mr. Brimblecombe would often come to 'Laburnum Lodge' for a chat with Unity, choosing those occasions when he might count upon seeing her alone, and on one of these visits he earnestly begged Mrs. Blanchard to eat her Christmas dinner at his nurseries, instead of with her family.

"Arthur's wishful to have a spot of company, being a lonely man," explained Unity, "and it would pleasure him out of the common if I went to him on Christmas Day. He's got a turkey from a customer at Tavistock and he says it's a sizeable bird with enough on it to keep him going till Eastertide if he can't find no help, so it occurred to him to ask me and Gilly to dinner, Maude; but I didn't say 'Yes' till I'd unfolded to you, and if you feel how you and Brian would lose your appetites with your son and me at another table, then enough said and I won't go."

Her daughter was aware of a certain irony apt to lurk in Mrs. Blanchard's speech, but the prospect of avoiding appropriate Christmas additions to the household fare much appealed to her, as Mrs. Blanchard knew it would.

"Gilly's never tasted a turkey in all his young life," she answered promptly, "and you'd like for him to have a better feed than we can afford at home, no doubt. Yes, and you too, Mother. I don't see no reason against. Mr. Brimblecombe's a well-to-do man, with no relations, or so Tommy always tells me. She's tried to find out if he's got any, but failed."

"There's no kin to his knowledge nearer to him than Barnstaple," explained Unity. "None so near as would come to his funeral if he dropped. As an old friend he feels he'd like for me to go, and Gilly also."

"We shall miss him and you, too, Mother, of course; but it might be good judgment for Gilly to go, because it looks like as if he'll start work next year at Arthur's nurseries."

"That's so if you come to terms as to the boy's money. He likes Gilly and might befriend him some day if all went well."

"I've thought upon that myself," confessed Maude.

"And why not? Arthur's got none to succeed him, though he swears he ain't doing so well as once he did."

"Prosperous folk always do that," declared Maude. "They do it as a precaution so as they shan't be over-charged and pillaged. Nobody minds dipping into the pocket of a rich man if they can get away with it."

"I'll tell Arthur that we'll come, then," promised her mother.

Mr. Brimblecombe's entertainment proved a great success but now, as another year dawned and January brought weather unseasonably mild, Maude did not find her mother welcome the high temperatures as old people are apt to do. When congratulated upon the lack of frost and snow, Unity showed herself ungrateful, or at least indifferent.

"'Twill be like last year, I expect," she foretold. "A lot of soft weeks and sunshine to bring on the growth and then a deadly frost to freeze the bloom on the boughs and ruin another apple harvest."

Her unusual melancholy persisted at this season. She suffered from a cold, which came to nothing, but cast a continued damper upon Mrs. Blanchard's spirits, and Maude listened to sentiments which amazed her enough to awaken sleeping hopes. An unfamiliar vein of pessimism appeared in Unity's outlook on life. She lost heart and showed occasional impatience instead of the usual amiable resignation displayed over most human affairs as she was wont to envisage them. She grew testy with Brian and exchanged sharp speeches instead of merely smiling and shaking her head at him as usual. Thus, when he laughed at the disappearance of certain parcels containing food from the railway station and asserted that the authorities might save their trouble to find them, Unity uttered stern and sharp comment.

"It ain't good manners now seemingly to call a thing by its right name," she said. "You don't say a bit of property was stole: you talk about pinching it, as if that was just a trifle to laugh at and not feel 'shamed about. I've lived to see most of the Ten Commandments scrapped in my time—the eighth most of all."

She censured Maude, also, and her daughter often found Mrs. Blanchard regarding her with a sort of anxious distrust which she felt at a loss to understand. But Unity grew more silent than of old and began to evince an indifference to life in general which her daughter noted. Thus a dim possibility began to emerge and once more Maude found appropriate moments to hint at another and brighter world.

"You can't help sometimes feeling what peace and comfort there is in the thought of taking leave of everything and everybody," she said once, "and if we found we had done wrong to go when we got there, then there's all eternity to atone in. I do feel everything would be forgiven, Mother, when everything was known. There's many a brave creature have risen up into a public heroine after she'd took her own life. What might look like a deed of darkness in our eyes may seem very different up above. If you put your trust in Providence, same as we do, then we can well trust Providence to lead us right."

"Yes," agreed Mrs. Blanchard. "Providence talks straight. It don't speak with two voices. It's like the waterfall in the vale: it only tells one tale."

"I often think of the waterfall," said Maude. "Sometimes it seems as if it was calling me and Providence using the voice of the waterfall to tell me something."

"If I was to take your tip and launch out, you'd say the waterfall?" suggested Mrs. Blanchard bluntly.

"For God's love don't talk like that, Mother! I only know what I'd do myself if there was naught against."

"You'd go by water?"

"Yes. I'd slip off by night and just give myself over to the pool under the waterfall. All peaceful and painless, you might say, and no wet eyes at the funeral neither. I'm one of the unlucky ones, Mother. There's very few on earth love me but you, I'm fearing."

Unity made no comment as to that but continued the main argument.

"None ever came back from drowning to say it was peaceful and painless; but very like it may be," she admitted. Then her humour broke through.

"I'll think it over none the less, my dear. Maybe some night, when I'm hungrier than usual, I'll rise up and do it."

"I find the idea grow on me, but my instinct bids me to fight against it for my husband and my child's sake," sighed Maude.

"I dare say it might. As for me, I ain't feared of going, mind you."

"You never was feared in your life: that I'd vouch for," declared her daughter very earnestly; "but don't you let yourself dwell upon it too much, Mother."

"I won't," promised Unity. "A lot depends upon the weather, I expect. Winter-time you'll find the most seasonable weather to do away with yourself and, if your health turns against you and the future don't look no better than the present, then no doubt their thoughts point that way for some folk."

"We must fight against it—both of us," decided the younger; but behind her woebegone countenance this conversation cheered

Maude greatly. Nor was that the last of it, for soon afterwards Mrs. Blanchard made another surprising suggestion. On a fine Sunday, while the mild conditions persisted and the low winter sun brought winter beauty to the vale, she suggested a walk and invited Maude to accompany her.

"Haven't been down the river this longful time," she said, "and I feel to be up for a stroll by the stream to settle down my dinner, Maude, so if you ain't otherwise occupied I'll ask you to come. I was always very addicted to the waterfall and find myself wishful to see it again."

"Nothing could be better fit for a Sunday afternoon," agreed Mrs. White. "I'd like to see it too and I oft wish we was nearer to the river because the sound of running water comforts my mind. mind. Here we only get the noise of the railway trains. We'll go, Mother. Thomasina's coming to tea, but we shall be back again before then."

They walked presently beside Walla and found the river deserted today. Unity was very silent and, when Maude began to talk, begged her to desist.

"Don't be chattering this afternoon," she said. "Let me hear the water talking, Maude. 'Tis pleasanter than our voices."

The stream ran somewhat low for the time of year; but the waterfall lifted its usual harmony to heaven and Mrs. Blanchard stood upon the bank beside it and listened for some time.

"A very welcoming voice to me and have run through my life and talked sense ever since I heard it," she said to Maude.

They sat together presently and she indicated that her mind still ran on the river.

"Walla have always drawn me and a lot of the high spots in my life have happened beside her, or in call of her," she said. "It's more than just a river journeying to the sea; and other folk I've known feel the same to other rivers by which they may hap to live. Each one has got its stories and earned its good or bad name, same as we humans have ourselves. Dart now. Dart's earned a bad name. Dart's a killer. Never a year passes but Dart takes the life of man, woman or child. Never known to miss. Dangerous, treacherous is Dart. Same with Tavy, though I never heard Tavy mistrusted like Dart. Yet, in my own experience, Tavy's a killer. It drowned a baby and I knew the mother of that baby. And it also drowned a moor man under Tavy Cleave. He was crossing on his pony and it fell and pinned him under the water and Tavy finished him. But I never heard of no fatal thing done by Walla. Have you?"

"You can't blame natural objects for no felonious intentions, Mother. Water's water, and if you fall in water that's deep enough, then you pass away at God's good will."

"It has been a very pleasant help in time of trouble to mankind, no doubt. Rivers have saved so many lives as ever they've took, I expect, if we knew all there is to know about 'em. Helped to keep alive them starving of thirst and helped to put away them starving with misery."

Then she changed the subject abruptly and continued:

"It's a queer thought that when you get to my age, Maude, you feel the bulk of your friends and them dear to you have gone home and that you'll never see any of 'em again until you go after 'em. There's lots you never want to see again in this world or any other, but there's always a few special ones you'd like to share eternity with. In this world most friendships soon wear thin as a poor carpet, but in the next one—who can say? An everlasting friendship would be an amazing fine thing. Then, again, to see a new creation around you and find yourself where sparkling winged angels harbour! That might be a cheerful change full of glad surprises."

"My very own thought, Mother!" cried Maude. "You do hanker sometimes for something better than your fellow creatures. You'll get a warm welcome, be it as it will."

Unity's mood changed once again.

"Not too warm, I hope," she said.

"You've got good rights to your place up there, so soon as ever you're brave enough to take the journey."

"A journey by water," mused Mrs. Blanchard. "I never was much for journeying, but that looks the easiest way. Don't want no tickets nor time-tables, nor railway trains, nor all the fuss of packing up. The quicker the better perhaps, Maude."

She fixed her eyes on her daughter.

"You always made time your servant, Mother. Once you had fixed up your mind, I never knew you to let time come between you and anything you was wishful to do."

"If a big thing like a waterfall calls you and you hear your own name named, who turns a deaf ear?"

They fell silent and then Maude suggested they should abandon these sad thoughts and go home to tea.

"Must keep up my strength for my journey, you'd say?" asked her mother.

"Don't—don't speak no more to me about any such thing," begged the other. "I'd thankfully go along with you if I was free to; but you'll have a better companion on your road than me, Mother."

Again Unity cast a side-glance at her child.

"That's right, my dear—a darned sight better companion than ever you could be," she agreed.

"But turn your mind away from the rivers for God's love," implored Maude, "and never, never go nigh one of 'em again. You make me hate the name of 'em, Mother."

"'Twas you began about the charms of sudden death, not me," answered Mrs. Blanchard.

They were late in returning home and found Mrs. Parsons already awaiting them. Thomasina proved to be full of the latest news and related it with customary gusto.

"There's times," she said, "if you watch events so close as I do, that you can see what's coming to people even before they do themselves. Now and again you can warn them and get thanked for your trouble if they're nice, sensible folk, and other times you get a flea in your ear, which was what happened to me yesterday along with Matthew Owlett."

"I don't like him at any time," declared Maude. "He always looks to have something up his sleeve and gives himself airs owing to his standing at Oakshotts. He's got more enemies than he thinks for, Tommy."

"Don't I know it, Maude? Ruby Manley's a friend of mine and she tells me her better half, Inspector Manley, has always misdoubted Matthew and reckons he'll take his pitcher to the well once too often."

"I don't care if he poaches or if he don't," declared Brian White, "but I hate the side he puts on, when he looks in at the 'Welcome'. As if Labour weren't his master same as it is over everybody else."

"Well," continued the visitor, "of course I well knew, after his girl took Peter Chadd, the natural and orderly thing for Owlett was to marry the policeman's mother. It stared you in the face from the first—planned by Providence for the comfort of all concerned—and, sounding Dinah Chadd and finding she weren't against it, then I asked myself why it hadn't happened. There was Matt, well known to be buzzing over Dinah like a bee over a clover bed, and her well disposed, yet nothing doing, so when I chanced to meet with the man yesternight, I took the bull by the horns and said 'Good evening, Matthew; when are we going to hear tell you're tokened in a certain quarter, my dear?' Just innocent and well-meaning like that. But instead of answering, he only asked a question himself."

Mrs. Parsons broke off to laugh and drink a sip of tea.

" 'And when are we going to hear you're minding your own business, Thomasina?' " she continued. "That's what he asked next! 'You spend your silly life going round and round like a squirrel in a cage, working like hell and getting nowhere, my poor woman, for how do news-hunting help your body or your soul? You'd better to go rag-picking than what you do.' But then, after I roared with amusement in his face, he relented and laughed too and told me he'd reward me for once. 'You'll be excited to hear that Mrs. Chadd has took me," he said, "and you're the first to know it outside our families.' "

Mrs. Blanchard spoke.

"A very good bit of news, Tommy," she declared. "To call it news. I've well known it was going to happen and I'd say it was better news than you think for, because what Manley thinks and what the keepers say about Matt is all humbug. He's straight enough and got better brains than most of us, a very high standard of honesty and a very good heart likewise. He'd no more do wrong against his employer and steal Oakshotts game than Mr. Manley would, or Toby Trimble either. They're jealous of his mastership and hate to see him advanced."

"I'd sooner believe you than Ruby Manley, nice woman though she is," replied Thomasina. "I always like to think well of a person so long as I can. Time shows up everybody soon or late, and you've only got to be patient and watch what they do next."

"Owlett was right, Tommy," said Mrs. Blanchard, "you waste your time."

"Not if by watching 'em you can help to keep other people right and help 'em to be safe, Mother," suggested Maude.

"It ain't no more a waste of time than going to the pictures and seeing a play, Granny," argued Thomasina. She liked to be the centre of criticism.

"If you've got a joyous nature," she continued, "you can enjoy whatever betides and take the broad view. There's always something to laugh at, wherever you find yourself, if you're built same as I am."

"Don't you ever find yourself cast down and feeling sentimental?" asked Maude.

"Cast down never, my love, but sentimental sometimes."

"And what overtakes you to give rise to that, Tommy?" asked Mrs. Blanchard; whereupon Mrs. Parsons made a most surprising reply.

"Of a Sunday—this very morning, Granny, to morning prayer. I got a sentimental feel in me—not for the first time. Not prayers, because you know 'em by heart if you're a regular worshipper, which I am, but the boys' voices singing. Lord knows why, yet so it is. Just the children singing crystal clear and touching notes only their innocent little throats can rise to—same as the wild birds and caring no more than a song-thrush or a skylark for what they sing. You know all the time they're hard-hearted young devils really, same as all other healthy, beastly little boys, but their voices lifted together always make me get a queer feeling."

"Softens your heart-strings," agreed Unity. "A very clever thing to mark. So it do mine."

"That's it—softens my heart-strings for the passing moment, if anything can."

Brian laughed.

"Fancy a hard-boiled egg like you having any heart-strings at all, Tommy!" he said.

CHAPTER IV

WHEN Sir Gerald Fortesque next summoned Matthew on scientific business, Owlett felt glad, because he also desired an opportunity to discuss a personal question with his employer. It had nothing to do with insects or fungi, but related solely to the old sailor's own concerns. "I'll take his orders," thought Matthew, "then I'll creep to what's in my mind. And I'll begin by telling him I ordain to be married, which, though common knowledge now, won't have rose to his ears."

He kept his appointment, took a preliminary meal with the staff at Oakshotts, learned from Chave that all was well with Sir Gerald and presently went before him. They had not met for some while and congratulated each other on their good health and the continued mildness of the weather.

"With January behind us, my annual ambition to see another spring begins to take shape," said Sir Gerald, "and the greediness of old age revives in me yet again. I have been hoping for just one more spring every January since I passed the allotted span, Owlett, and now I consider the possibility of hearing a migrant cuckoo once again becomes a probability."

"So good as a certainty, in my opinion, your honour," declared Matthew. "Mr. Chave tells me you've took the air daily ever since Christmas and your tubes are working very suent and your appetite not too poor neither."

"He is right. Under other circumstances, Chave might have succeeded as well in the capacity of physician as he has triumphed as a butler. He possesses great natural gifts and, after his long experience, he can diagnose my condition, detect a symptom, take a temperature and hint at treatment in a manner I have often found trustworthy and effective. But now to a more important subject. The larvae of hawk moths, as you have reported, are unusually numerous."

"A proper harvest," agreed Mr. Owlett. "Never remember such a lot of 'elephants' and 'privets'. The 'privet' caterpillars catch the eye with their bright green and violet colours."

"We must not, however, ignore them because they are so abundant," said Sir Gerald. "There will be considerable numbers pupating underground this winter and, if we are to be blessed with high temperatures, we may herald a fine emergence in May and June. But other factors need to be considered, for weather that favours them will also favour their enemies—the ichneuma first among them, for example."

"You'll never be hungering for no more 'elephants', nor yet 'privets'," suggested Matthew.

"On the contrary. Admitted that we must not count our hawk moths before we catch and hatch them; but the paramount importance of the catch is the nature of the hatch. Amid the mass of familiar things, who knows but there may harbour rarer varieties? All must be taken and submitted to me, my dear fellow, for among them may lurk those choice and precious. If one in a hundred rewards us, the ninety-nine can go free, the treasure serving to pay for our time and trouble. A Natural History Society, of which I am the president, reports discovery of a pine hawk moth, Owlett, and an even more important and uncommon capture comes as good news from Cornwall. The silver-striped hawk—celario—has been taken near the harbour of Penzance!"

Sir Gerald pursued this attractive subject and furnished instances from years long past of his personal adventures.

"Thus," he summed up, "year by year do we add data with patience and assiduity, each man of science handing on the torch to his successors and so attaining to more and yet more truth concerning these denizens of another order than our own. We advance from strength to strength, Owlett; knowledge grows and indomitable man wrests her secrets from inscrutable Nature, discovers her purpose, reconciles her apparent paradoxes, arrives at the federation and synthesis concealed beneath the seeming detachment, opposition and confusion presented by her sleepless activities. To these prodigious problems we bring our reasoning powers and our penetration until the inner meaning of the life stream is revealed, its deepest mysteries unfolded, their significance explained."

In his secret heart the listener felt that all this ado awakened by the manners and customs of the hawk moth was needless and little to the point; but he displayed his usual reverent attention.

"I catch your meaning, your honour," he said, "which is that I must keep an eye on the subject and never overlook naught even though it don't seem of importance at the minute."

"Precisely," agreed the older man. "Nothing is of no importance in Nature, and the less we can make top or tail of phenomena, the more important they may actually be. Many a doorway leading to truth has been neglected because some human mind failed at the critical challenge to persevere."

Judging the moment apt, Matthew now entered upon his own affairs.

"Before I go, I'm very wishful to name a matter touching myself, if you'll grant me half a minute," he begged. "'Tis the subject of my future son-in-law, if you'll be so gracious as to turn your mind on him. Not a word against the young man—a good, clean chap and doing well in his calling. He's a policeman and so far has not been required to show what I hope lies in him, but he hasn't got what in my opinion should be a policeman's mind. He don't look at life with a police constable's eyes and is a lot addicted to find himself on the side of the wrongdoer, Sir Gerald."

"Quite a common weakness, but undesirable of course in a guardian of the law. One feels sorry even for a malefactor when he happens to be caught, but we should consider what he has done that made it desirable and necessary to catch him. Mass hysteria rushes to sympathise with any picturesque desperado, forgetting those who have suffered and perhaps perished from the scoundrel's activities."

"In Peter Chadd's case his father was such a man, your honour, and what's in my mind is the blood in Peter's veins. Science shows how such things may be handed down. I've agreed to the marriage because in honesty I couldn't do otherwise, but then again something tells me I ought to wait and see if the blood in his veins is free of his father's poison, before it's too late to guard against it."

"A curious problem," admitted Sir Gerald.

"And curiouser still, because I'm wishful to marry this young man's mother and she's wishful to marry me."

"Science is turning serious attention to human parentage and would control the business of the Law Courts if given power to do so," explained Sir Gerald. "The psycho-analyst demands the entire revaluation of criminal conduct and seeks to establish the fact that anti-social action may result from heredity. Evil-doers are no longer to be retarded as such, but invalids. We should seldom hang a homicide in the opinion of science, but condole and comfort such a sufferer, free him of mental anxiety, clothe him, feed him and restore his liberty as soon as his health returns. First, of course, Law itself must be subjected to the dominion of psychiatry, which I trust may not happen in my time."

"Dear my life! How clever we're all getting and what a world we're like to make of it some day, your honour!" exclaimed Matthew. Then he strove to bring the matter back to Peter.

"There's great confusion of mind among young men nowadays," he continued, "and the war's unsettled 'em so that you'll find, while sound on one subject, they're all adrift on another. Take poaching now. Poaching, that looked to be little better than stealing when I was a young man, is held in no account at all nowadays; but there I'm glad to say my future son-in-law takes a sound view. And yet, while he joins me in condemning it, he's dead wrong on other aspects of crime, and if he was to hear about murderers being no more than hospital cases, most likely he would agree with pleasure. In fact you might almost say you'd only to do a doubtful deed to win his support. That looks to me how his father has come out in him."

But the listener was not interested in Peter's character. He fastened on one word only.

"Poaching, like everything else, is subject to the laws of evolution," he said. "Not long since my neighbour, Lady Champernowne, threw surprising light on this subject, of which I knew little and cared even less. It happens that she cares very much. The old, rough-and-tumble clashes, resulting often in broken heads, occur no more. Instead, gangs of intrepid and skilful fellows avail themselves of science and steal game with increasing success and security. They employ the motor-car and have developed an elaborate and triumphant technique for the black market which is always ready to reward their activities and make poaching as worthy of attention as smuggling once used to be. The old poachers may be forgiven because they were sportsmen and danger was often the incentive behind their achievements; but the new poachers are not sportsmen; they are tradesmen with the somewhat sordid outlook that often accompanies that order of mind. They well know that pheasants are worth fifty shillings a brace, so they see in this enterprise inducements worthy of their attention. I have explained their methods to Toby Trimble, who was as ignorant of them as myself until Lady Champernowne enlightened me.

"One must, however, admire their ingenuity while resenting their abominable behaviour. It is their delight on a moonshiny night, Owlett, to fire warning guns in some remote quarter of the coverts. It is always near a road and, having sprung their decoy, those directed to the task get into the motor-car awaiting them and speed away, so that when the keepers reach the spot they find nothing and nobody. But what meantime is happening elsewhere? Other scoundrels with silenced weapons are shooting pheasants and another motor-car is waiting to receive them and speed off with the booty.

"This trick has been practised with complete success at Oakshotts last autumn, as you doubtless know, and elsewhere all over the country. Everything goes like clockwork and the risks are small, for, even where failure attends them, you will find that most of us game-owners won't be bothered to make a fuss and seek the aid of the Law. We are quite wrong in neglecting our duty, but so it is. While a rabbit continues to be worth five shillings, unscrupulous people who know how to catch them will do so, and also set gate-nets for hares. The fact, however, remains, that professional poachers are common thieves, and another fact her ladyship deduced which is not so self-evident: that the poulterers and fishmongers they serve are receivers of stolen goods and should be treated accordingly."

Mr. Owlett listened to this exposition with due respect.

"The case in a nutshell!" he declared. "No question of sport but just business, and if Toby has got the wisdom to profit by what you learned him, then he didn't ought to lose another bird, your honour."

"In Scotland the theft of salmon has also reached proportions of gravity," continued Sir Gerald. "With this game fish at ten or more shillings a pound, the skilled and organised raiders can and do often net a hundred pounds sterling in a night! The canny Scots are already overhauling their laws in the matter, which, like our own, are hopelessly behind the times. Game stocks are in fact at a low ebb everywhere since the war, and though personally I care nothing, efforts should be made for our national self-respect to catch these fellows and convict a few of them. We will hope your young policeman may get a chance to distinguish himself in this field, but there must be no nonsense about the sporting instinct common to us all; what we have to do is to curb the stealing instinct common to us all. A poacher is a thief and to palter with truth in your life is just as dangerous as to juggle with doubtful explosives in your laboratory. Impress that on the lad. Doubtless there is a great deal you can teach him."

"So I will, then, and my daughter will teach him a lot more still," promised Matthew. "Speaking of Mr. Trimble, your honour, did he mention I'd met him in the rhododendron plantations under the larch wood?"

"He did not, Owlett."

"I was carrying my gun at the time and he marked it. 'There's no call for that, Owlett,' he says, 'and you well know it.' A bright sunny day it was, a week ago, and good light for a quick eye. I didn't answer in words, but put my hand in my big game-pocket and pulled out five grey squirrels."

"Five! Well done, indeed, Matthew!"

"Five by this hand, your honour. Four hours' work and five of the varmints less in consequence. 'There,' I said to Toby. 'That's why for I'm carrying my gun. Now you can nail 'em up in your gamekeeper's gallows along with a lot of other creatures that didn't ought to be there.' He took them without a word of thanks to me, or praise for my skill; but I never quarrel with him now. He belongs to a vanished generation, so all's said."

The elder was tired of the subject and changed it for a recent personal experience that had entertained him much.

"We know how to inflict adequate punishment upon the grey squirrel at any rate, and no psycho-analyst has to my knowledge interested himself on its behalf. Now I'll tell you something to answer you, my friend. Lady Champernowne again. What do you think she said to me after disposing of the poachers?"

He uttered his rumbling, deep-chested laugh; and Matthew, used to these occasional confidences, listened and prepared to laugh also when he learned what there was to laugh about.

"Her ladyship is noted for saying what she means, both on the Bench and off it. She does not hesitate to be personal after all these years, and it pleases her to castigate me still, though a sinner long past redemption now," confessed the old scientist. "'*Noblesse oblige* is a very good motto, as we all know,' she said, 'and I am very sure when you were young, Gerald, your parents and your schoolmasters tried to make you aware of it. All in vain, of course. Apparently the material was not in you to work upon. You were born without respect for tradition, or any reverence for long descent. In another walk of life you might have crept along without reproach and perhaps risen to be the adequate curator of a museum, or some such dreary place. But the obligations of your position you have always and utterly ignored ever since I knew you and probably long before I was born myself. You have employed your brain-power and concentrated your whole active life upon such pitiful interests that, for any social and practical purpose whatever, you might just as well have been a nocturnal moth yourself, flitting about aimlessly in the moonlight and of no earthly use to anybody!' "

Sir Gerald displayed utmost entertainment at this cherished recollection; but Mr. Owlett, aware that he had listened to treason, only shook his head.

"A Justice of the Peace same as her didn't ought to venture on such improper opinions," he said.

"But worse remains untold," continued Sir Gerald, still rumbling joyously. "She finished this indictment by reminding me of my crowning infamy—how that I had shirked my most sacred obligation of all, by evading matrimony and thus extinguishing for ever a famous and ancient baronetcy!"

Awed by an affront so tremendous and bewildered before Sir Gerald's amusement, Matthew rose to depart.

"Females will often let their tongues run freer than us," he admitted; "but to tell such things as that is going too far, even for an uppermost lady like she."

On returning home he related the dreadful tale to Nancy, after warning her to let it go no further; but she tended to share Sir Gerald's attitude.

"Funny things often amuse the very old folk," she said. "They remember all manner of queer jokes in their past; but if the gentleman wasn't shocked, there ain't no call for you to be, Father. What did Squire want? Not to tell you about her ladyship's sauce."

"I took a minute, when he fell quiet, to tell him what I wanted. I said I was going to be married to Dinah and you was taking her son."

"Did it look to interest him at all?"

"Not much. He didn't say nothing against, and if he had ordered me to reconsider doing it I should have obeyed him and dropped Dinah, needless to say. He thought Peter sounded all right in the main, but how Mrs. Chadd sounded to him I couldn't say."

"Not that it matters to us," suggested Nancy. "What we're going to do is our business, not his."

"He was well aware of that, my dear. Naught interests him less than other people's business. He feels that I ought to be a tower of strength for Peter, which is what I wish to be, same as I know Dinah will be a tower of strength to myself. A lot passes in the mind of Sir Gerald that's hid from us as a rule; but you'll never hear him say a harsh word against anybody, whatever he may think about 'em. He's like Peter in some respects and has got a great fellow-feeling for his fellow creatures. In fact he forgives most anything but paltering with the truth. He's tender to the young, but doubts if we educate 'em right. There's a lot they'd be the better for learning, but since their teachers haven't yet learned those things themselves, of course they can't hand 'em on."

"Bound to be old-fashioned at his age," suggested Nancy.

"To be a gentleman is to be old-fashioned now," answered her father. "They've got so rare as white moles and the breed's dying out, same as some rare insects are dying out. Conditions ain't favourable for 'em no more, so they grow to be museum specimens to be put in a glass box and labelled and forgot."

"Did you tell him about Peter and me?"

"I told him I wanted to see Peter put to the test, same as I have seen other men who were not police constables put to the test. Then, as they might succeed, or fail, you'd come to learn the real truth about 'em."

"You will always be making mysteries where there are none," grumbled Nancy. "What more d'you want than what you know and why can't you take my word about Peter and be done with it? You're such a one for the whole truth and nothing but the truth, yet can't believe the truth about Peter, though I've told you often enough the truth about him. I know him a million times better than you do, or his mother either. His worship for me—that's his guiding star, and so long as he's got my worship back, which he has got and always will have, then he's all right. He knows me so well as I know him and never, never, whatever the temptation, would do a mortal thing he knew I shouldn't hold with. If he was up against something or put to any test whatever, he'd bring it to me before he took his final action on it and he'd do what I advised, so if you say my good sense is trustable, as you've told me scores of times, then you can rest content Peter's good sense is trustable whatever was to happen to him."

"But if he's going to run to you when he can't see his way clear, and abide by your advice and leave his mind a sounding-board for your opinions, where is he then? No man under the command of his wife ever got very high up in the world."

Nancy laughed.

"I suppose you know what you're talking about, Dad," she answered, "but when you get in these daft moods I'm beggared if I can tell what's in your head. Peter would no more suffer to be henpecked by me than I'd dare to attempt such a thing. You forget what it is to be in love—if ever you really was, which I doubt more and more. What you've got to do is to get Mrs. Chadd to fix the day, and then, after we're all married, perhaps you'll begin to see what a lot of your life you've wasted marking time."

"The pace have got to be speeded up along with Dinah for her self-respect, if not my own," admitted Matthew. "No doubt we shall soon be finding what the new year brings forth."

CHAPTER V

SOME three weeks later an event of very great importance relieved the strain under which Maude White and her husband continued to suffer. They waited still for a letter from the lawyers and now expected it every day, and they asked themselves how the truth could be longer evaded to their advantage when the definite facts arrived from Australia. A ray of doubtful hope shone from Mrs. Blanchard herself, for her depression persisted, and it appeared that not only was her own vitality at an unusually low ebb, but her thoughts, when she uttered them, continued to be tinged with unfamiliar gloom. The origin of this darkness remained hidden with Unity herself and Maude made no attempt to lighten it. She told herself that her mother's melancholy was the only bright thing to keep hope alive, yet found it impossible to account for such dejection. Then came an apparent *dénouement* upon a morning when Maude stood at the foot of the stairs at 'Laburnum Lodge' and shouted to her mother that breakfast awaited her.

"Mother, Mother—breakfast!" she cried. "Do stir yourself for pity's sake and come down house if you're ever coming. 'Tis seven o'clock."

Brian had already begun to eat.

"Be damned to the woman! I doubt she's awake," he said.

"She's later of a morning since she got so low-spirited," explained Maude. "If she'd die in her sleep—what a blessing! Only yesterday I thought——"

Gilly appeared at this moment and took his place at the table.

"Good morning, Mother. Morning, Father," he said.

They took no notice of him and he began to eat his porridge.

"Granny not down house?" he asked. "That's funny."

"Call her again," bade Brian.

"Come to think of it, I didn't hear her moving this morning," answered Maude. "I'll see to her."

She left the room, and Brian followed her in thought.

"Only three days now before I set to work for you and mother along with Mr. Brimblecombe," announced Gilly. "Then you and me will both go to work of a morning, Father."

The railwayman nodded, but his attention was overhead, and

a moment later he heard Maude call him and rose to go to her. She came half-way down the stairs as he entered the passage, and he marked that she was much moved.

"Oh, Brian! Mother ain't in her room!" she said, her voice sunk to a whisper.

But Gilly had followed his father and heard her.

"Granny not there, Mother?" he cried.

The three of them returned to the house-place, and Maude spoke.

"Her bed ain't pressed. She never was in it last night seemingly, but her clothes stand on the chair where she always puts 'em. What did we ought to do, Brian?"

"Look for her, I should think. Her clothes there and she ain't? Have she gone out of her mind?"

"How could a sharp woman like grandmother go out of her mind all in a minute like that, Father?" asked the boy. "She was all right last night."

"No she wasn't, Gilly," answered Maude. "She's been cast down and queer for days now."

"She took a good supper and praised it," suggested Gilly, then his father spoke.

"Hunt round again, Maude. She must be up there some place. And you look in the garden and the tool-shed, boy. Run and look. She may be wandering in her mind."

"Ah! I'll bet she's there and lost her way in the dark," replied Gilly. " 'Tis a heavy fog outside, Father. The trains will be late, I shouldn't wonder."

He hurried out, and Maude answered Brian.

"It's no use going up over. She ain't there. I'll swear it."

"She wouldn't take much room. You don't think . . . "

He regarded her eagerly as she sat down panting and poured herself a cup of tea.

"Yes, I do think—I do more than think. I can see so well as gospel what this means, Brian."

"No such luck, though time we had a bit of luck sure enough."

"It's come," she said. "It's happened! I believe it's happened. I saw a lot more up there than I said before the boy. Her working clothes are there—old shoes and stockings and all; but her best clothes are missing—all her Sundays down to the only pair of stockings she had that wasn't darned. She slipped off while we were asleep and put on her best to go in—her shoes with steel buckles, Brian, and her bonnet with the red roses."

"What the devil do that signify—except she went mad at the last minute?"

"Oh no, she didn't. I can tell you what that signifies. She's done it! Mother's took her life! I see it clear as noonday and read her mind unfolded, like the pages of a book. Always a great stickler for her clothing, she was. She'd have died for shame before she'd have gone into church, or company, in aught but her best, and she'd never have gone to the next world in her everydays. Her mind gave out last night and she's gone; but her habits clove to her, and she donned her bombazine gown and her agate brooch and silver chain round her neck and all the rest of her adornments."

"Gone to the river in 'em?" he whispered.

"That will be for others to find out, not us."

Maude heaved a sigh and a ray of colour lighted her face.

"All's plain sailing now," Brian said. "You didn't touch nothing up there, did you?"

"I've left everything as it was, and we can't blaze this abroad too soon."

"I'll go to work, then," he declared, "and you can send Gilly to the police station, and when Manley comes round, tell him I'd took my breakfast and was gone before you missed her."

"I can't do that," she answered. "Gilly knows you were here. No use to start telling silly lies about it. The truth's all that we need to tell. Let stationmaster hear she's missing, and ask if anybody's seen her up there on the line. I'll get your food."

Gilly returned at this moment. The daylight had grown stronger, but a white fog hung heavy over Wallabrook.

"I've hunted like a terrier after a rat for Granny," he said. "She ain't in the garden, nor yet the shed."

"Then it's the queerest job of work ever I heard tell upon," said Brian. "Lord knows what's happed to the old soul."

"My, what a fearful odd thing to overtake dear Granny!" gasped the boy, and Maude heard him as she returned with her husband's frail.

"Odd, but not fearful, we'll hope, Gilly," she told him. "Perhaps she's just lost her memory and it will come home to her again with the daylight."

"Well, stir yourself, Maude," said Brian, "and I'll get to work. I'll tell 'em on the line. They may be called to search the permanent way for her."

"She'd never have took her life under a railway train, Father—never—never!" cried the boy.

"You can't tell what a person will do if their mind's faltering," explained his mother, then Brian issued an order.

"Hook it straight off to the police station, Gilly, and see Inspector Manley and ask for him to come here instanter. Just say a very serious thing has fell out at your home last night and I'll thank him to step up and see your mother, because time's all-important."

"All right. I'll speed," promised Gilly. "Poor Gran! Fancy anything important happening to her!"

"Don't be chattering—go," directed his father; "and don't lose your way in the fog."

The boy hastened off and Brian spoke to his wife. "That's that, then! Watch your step with Manley when he turns up."

He stared into Maude's eyes, and then down at the table.

"I can't believe it yet. Takes a bit of time to soak in. Here's her food gone cold, and her colder still herself if you're right."

"I'm right enough: it's all of a piece," she answered. "She's gone, Brian."

"And we'll be gone ourselves before another summer, I hope," he said. "Let 'em sack me now and be damned to 'em! Who'd have thought our troubles was over just at the proper minute? And no funeral expenses to pay out if they don't find her."

"They'll find her all right when Manley hears me," said Maude.

"No need to shilly-shally no more now. All safe now. You can face the lawyer and get on with it at last. You only need to let the people know we're leaving Wallabrook because you've come into money."

"What a born fool you are behind your swagger and noise!" she answered. "You warn me to be careful what I tell the police, and then say a silly thing like that! Not on your life do we talk about leaving, nor yet say a word about the money."

"Why not?" he asked. "You kept back your mother and let 'em presume you had none, and now that's true just in the nick of time. We can touch them for something in advance and get away and look if there's a house to suit you where you want to go—somewhere in the smell of the sea, which is my fancy too. Then I can give in my notice instead of getting it. I'm counting on that a'ready."

"You can count again, then," answered Maude; "and keep the future off your stupid tongue. You'll carry on as if nothing out of the common was happening to us, and not a word about leaving 'Laburnum Lodge', or the railway. And there's another thing you'd best to remember. It's my money coming from Australia, not yours. My money, and it runs into thousands. 'Thousands,' they said. And all mine—every penny. So I wouldn't plume myself to be a gentleman at large too soon if I was you."

"All right! All right! No call to talk like a bitch in the manger," he answered. "I know the money's yours. It's your money and I'm your husband. We've been tolerable good pals as married people go, haven't we? Money ain't going to divide us, is it? You'll be called to write a will now there's money to write about, and there ain't any reason against leaving your money where it ought to belong. If it had fallen to me, that's what I'd do first thing."

Maude laughed.

"A good faithful wife wouldn't be like to put temptations in her husband's way," she said. "You bide on the railway a bit longer, or else find a better job and stick to it. You're the sort, like most men, that's safer at work than idle."

Brian turned very red.

"To hell with that! D'you mean I'm going to be——" he began; but now returned their son and he said no more.

"Mr. Manley's coming up so quick as may be in his police car, but he can't drive very fast because the fog's as thick as wool," explained Gilly.

Then Brian prepared to leave them.

"I must push on, though work's like to be hung up till it lifts," he said. "If news comes in, send Gilly, Mother, and let me know."

"You'll hear first minute after I do," promised Maude. "And don't forget to eat your food."

"Yes, yes—I'll eat," he said. "We must keep hopeful about her yet. I reckon she went sleep-walking most likely. Old folks are often took that way, but sleep-walkers never come to much harm, they say."

"I'll send for doctor if they find her alive," said Maude.

"Spare nothing—spare nothing," he directed, then left them, while Gilly commented on a strange phenomenon.

"Blessed if Father ain't properly sorry about it," he said. "He was never one to put himself about for Granny, or anybody else, was he, Mother?"

"He is put about and every right to be," replied Maude. "You often don't know what a thing was worth till you lose it, Gilly, and now we may have the bitterness to know what our home will be like without Granny in it."

"I hope she ain't in no ugly trouble, Mother. Such a dear good Gran to me she always was."

"No more ugly troubles for her, Gilly. All her troubles are over, by the look of it."

"Oh, I do hope not!" cried the boy. "I never heard her tell about no troubles to me."

"We'll know the best or worst before very long, I expect," she said, and then the grunt of a motor-car came through the fog.

"That'll be inspector. Open the door to him and then clear off, and look where you're going," his mother directed. "You can let it be known that Granny's missing for the moment."

Gilly went his way and a minute later the policeman entered to hear Mrs. White's apologies.

"I'm properly sorry to trouble you, Mr. Manley," she said, "but my husband had to go to work and he ordered me to let you know our bad news at once."

Inspector Manley revealed his usual ponderous and solid method of approach.

"Quite in order," he assured her. "I'm sorry also that the need should have arose and I hope the Law can soon clear up anything that demands attention."

"Sit down, Inspector," begged Maude, dusting a chair. "Will I make some tea for you this ugly morning?"

"No, no. Had my breakfast. What's the trouble?" he asked.

"It's my mother—Mrs. Blanchard."

"Oh dear, Mrs. White! I always say, 'What would Wallabrook be without Granny Blanchard?' She's the one you always hear a good word about. Naught wrong with her, I hope?"

"Something parlous wrong seemingly and we're very much afeared."

"Too bad!" declared Mr. Manley. "Too bad, that is. Must be sudden too. Bright and cheerful enough last time I passed the time of day with her. Only Monday that was. But why me? Why the Police Force? Why not Doctor Bridger, if she's sick?"

"She never would see a doctor. I've been at her time and again to have the 'once-over' from Bridger, but no: her answer was always the same, Inspector. 'I know my innards better than he does,' she'd always say, 'and I've got the proper remedies for 'em if they go back on me.' "

"Remedies for what?" he asked.

"She wouldn't name no weak spots; but watchful as I always

am, I'm cruel afraid I can," explained Maude. "Unknown to herself, of course, she's took to revealing 'em. Often of late she's gone so far as to say it's time she left this world for a better, Inspector. There's voices, she's told me—three times she's told me—voices calling to her from the Happy Land. Sounds mental, don't it?"

"There's nothing particular mental in wanting to go to a better world than this," said Mr. Manley solemnly, stroking his beard. "She wouldn't be the only one disposed that way."

"Very unlike her, however. But 'tis the best and most useful are snatched."

"True enough as to the best and most useful being snatched," he admitted. "I've marked the same, Mrs. White, and found it in me to wonder why valuable men, doing priceless work down here, should be torn away from it."

"One of they mysteries," suggested Maude. "Mother's thoughts have all tended out to the next world of late and the dead folk up there and the quickest road to get to 'em. That's why it looks—but I hate to name such a thing now she's missing."

"Suicide's in your mind—eh? But seeing suicide's a crime and your mother's got in sight of seventy without a bad mark against her to my knowledge, then it's little likely she'd fall at her age. A most orderly character and stood up to her misfortunes like any other good Christian."

Maude sighed.

"She was short of seventy by a few years still, Inspector, but that's neither here nor there and you can't be orderly if your brain's turned. That's what's in my mind about her—the fear she's lost her wits, else she'd never have done such a thing."

The inspector considered and nodded his head slowly.

"The Law's very tender to them that miscarry like that," he assured her. "Too tender sometimes, in my opinion, because, when you inquire for motives, you'll often find a would-be suicide had plenty. Then, when they're caught alive, they plead bats in the belfry and we let 'em off with a caution and give 'em time to try again, instead of sentencing them to imprisonment for committing a crime. Plenty of such people are as sane as me or you."

"But if they bring it off and the coroner's called to sit upon them, he generally finds it was a mind disordered, don't he?" asked Maude.

"He does," admitted the inspector. "He certainly does, but it isn't for the victim's comfort—only to save the face of his or her family. If you happen to be sane, then self-murder's homicide, and folk would rather their relations were found crazy than proclaimed to be criminals. So they don't go into reasons too close."

"Mother had a reason for everything," argued Maude; "and if her mind wasn't upset, she wouldn't have done it, Inspector, there being no reason why she should."

"Never a more reasonable old lady, I grant you, Mrs. White."

"That's why I still hope it mayn't be too late," she said.

"Did your mother ever tell any word to point at such a rash act in your hearing?" he asked.

"Once only she was direct about it. Then she said that for those minded to such a thing, the best plan was to go by water, because water was clean and short and sharp. Then I lost my temper, I'm afraid. I was angry and rebuked her and said some hard things to her."

"How did she take 'em?"

"Only laughed, poor old dear. She'd been walking one Sunday with me down by the river, and she said that would serve the turn very well."

"Serious, or just laughing?" he asked.

"She said the big pool under the waterfall was apt and handy. But don't ask me no more, Inspector. I don't want to think of such a thing. Please God you'll find her and fetch her home before another night. Brian thinks she might have gone out sleep-walking maybe and woke up and found herself lost in the fog."

"Water attracted her, you say. Is there a well on your premises?" he asked.

"No—we draw our water from the pump at the crossroad. But she'd never have chose a well—I'll swear to that. A stuffy end, to go down a well, and she was a great one for the open air always."

"And you can't hazard a guess at any grief upon her mind, or anybody vexing her?"

"Not a soul, to my knowledge. The folk she knew were all life-long friends, you might say. A most unnoticeable old woman without an enemy in the parish, just slipping down the hill unmarked by anybody but us."

"I wasn't aiming at any attack upon her, Mrs. White," he said. "Most innocent people have been murdered now and again and only police work and skilled detection discovered the malefactor and why it was done. When did you find she was gone?"

"I called her as usual before seven, for she was always a good riser, and took her a cup of tea as I sometimes will, and I found she had never gone to bed at all last night. A most strange thing and not in my experience before, because she was early to bed and a sound sleeper. And then I found a stranger thing still. Hunting round for any sign, I discovered she'd gone off in all her Sunday clothes! That was a facer for a minute, but fearful for her, as I felt by now, I yet saw one explanation. It wouldn't have struck anybody who didn't know all I've told you, Mr. Manley, but it struck me."

"What was that, then?"

"It flashed to my mind and I reckoned, with her nice feeling about her garments, she'd never have started to go to heaven except in her Sunday best."

"Folk don their go-to-meeting toggery for many other places than heaven," he said.

"Not in the middle of the night, Inspector."

The idea suggested some ancient lore to Mr. Manley's mind, and he smiled.

"Once they did," he told her. "In what we call the Dark Ages now, the witches would go to their sabbaths to meet the Devil, and you can lay your life they went in their finest garments, though 'twas only on a broomstick they flew."

Maude tried to show fleeting amusement.

"You're so learned," she said, "but mother a witch! Never, Inspector—not even a white witch."

"No, no. There never was any such creatures in sober truth," he said. "They were phantoms born of ignorance, my dear woman. But there's plenty of doubtful characters about to take their place, and never more than now. I'll be moving at once, Mrs. White. We'll very soon get to the bottom of this. And first I'll send a search party to the waterfall and hope they'll find nothing. Then I'll return here and give a trained search to her sleeping-room. Don't touch a thing till you see me again. And keep everybody out."

As though to defy the policeman's direction, somebody now hastened to join Maude, chattering loudly as she did so.

"Oh, my dear love, what's this they're telling? What the mischief——Oh, beg pardon I'm sure. Didn't see you, Inspector!"

It was Mrs. Parsons, full of animation and out of breath.

"Morning, Thomasina. Trust you to be on the scent!" answered the inspector amiably. Then he turned to her friend.

"I'll be seeing you again later, then, and if there's any news of her meantime, let the police station know at once. And if we find Mrs. Blanchard, I'll let you hear so quick as I can."

Maude's voice sank to a whisper as she replied:

"Where—where will dear mother be took to if . . ."

"To the mortuary if the worst has happened—unless you're wishful for us to bring the body home."

"No—better the dead-house, Mr. Manley; but please the Lord she's living yet. You wouldn't say you've given up all hope, would you?"

"No, and for this reason," he replied. "To my certain knowledge them who give out their intentions to do away with themselves are always the very last to perform it. I once knew a man who ran about this place roaring that he was going to cut his throat in two minutes by the clock, and half an hour later he turned up as mild as milk with a lot of silly excuses for not doing so after all."

"No doubt," said Mrs. Parsons, "they'll often change their minds when they're all alone with the next world staring them in the face. I'm sure I should, Mr. Manley."

"So am I," he answered. "I don't feel no fear on your account."

Then the inspector withdrew and Maude asked a question.

"Where did you hear tell she'd gone, Tommy?"

"I met your boy full of news," she answered. "He told me Granny had disappeared this morning and not a sign of her round about, and I couldn't but run to you, my dear, to tell you how sorry or glad I was, as the case might be. Too well I understood what a care and what a drag she was upon your tender heart. But now it looks as if you was a true prophet and she's done what you feared she might. So I hope there's what they call redeeming features. Here today and gone tomorrow, and gone for good, d'you reckon, or do you really think she may be with us still, Maude?"

Mrs. White shook her head.

"Not really, Thomasina, not really, I'm afraid. She's gone where she wanted to go."

"Patience rewarded at last, then, and I'm thankful to know it for her own sake and yours too. Tell me all the details and give me a cup of tea. Thank God I was out early this morning—else I'd have missed this. You're so white as a maggot, my love, but you must bear up. Most everything is for the best in the long run, or so I always find it. Make the tea so strong as you can. Do Brian know, or was he gone before you missed her?"

N

Maude brewed strong tea and told her story with attention and detail, while the widow listened greedily.

"A proper landmark lost," she summed up; "and now I must be off and let the true facts be known. The more hear tell, the better the chances to find her. And see you get her gold chain and agate brooch, Maude. Don't let 'em be overlooked. There won't be much worth money to remind you of your mother, but her gold chain ought to be valuable now, when gold in any shape looks to be a thing of the past. I'll tell the people how well you are standing up to your affliction."

"Every dark cloud have got a silver lining, or so they say, Tommy."

"Not every dark cloud, by a long shot," declared Mrs. Parsons. "I've known plenty that was black as hell all through; but this one—yes."

She hastened away, and Maude allowed her thoughts to outstrip time and look ahead. They fastened finally upon Messrs. Wilson & Harding of the Temple and later in the day, when Brian returned home, she explained her purpose to him.

"I don't want for any mistake to be made," said Maude. "We've got all the top cards now and must play 'em right. As it stands, I've let the lawyers suppose I was an orphan without saying so direct, but I am one now, though not when I wrote to 'em. If they was to find that mother's death and burial didn't happen till after I told 'em she was gone, they might feel I was a twister and I couldn't deny it. So the question is exactly what I shall write to 'em."

"Why say anything?" he asked. "Better wait till it's all over and then go up and see 'em. They'll never think of it again if you don't remind 'em. They'll take your word that you're what you say you are and entitled to the money. What does it matter to them so long as they get the lawyers' share of it? You fuss about nothing. If you did lie in your last letter, what does it matter to them so long as what you suggested then is true now? You can't explain away why you said it, so better leave it alone."

Maude considered this.

"I see your point," she admitted. "The thing is to think out an explanation if they should raise any difficulties and keep shut about it if they don't."

Brian had made inquiries at the police station before returning home.

"No news from anywhere today," he said, "and Manley's

going to drag the pool tomorrow. He told me you was very clear and that when he came back he investigated her room but found nothing to throw any light."

"Did he have any opinions as to what happened?"

"If he did, he kept them to himself. But he asked me what my opinion might be and I said I didn't feel no great surprise because my mother-in-law had looked to be heading for suicide for quite a time."

"What did he answer to that?" she asked.

"Nothing. I didn't stop long. He don't like me. He's heard me express my opinions in Hannaford's bar and don't approve of 'em. He asked me if I was leaving the railway under the national dispensation and I said I might, or might not, but there was plenty of other ways I could earn my living if they didn't want me."

"You didn't hint you had money in sight, or any fool thing like that?"

"I did not," answered Brian. "I can look ahead as well as the next one."

"What we've got to do is to keep shut about the legacy and, when it comes, be as much surprised as everybody else," explained his wife. "That's enough to go on with for us. After they've found her and the funeral's over, then we can come to the future and clear out of Wallabrook for good and all."

"What price Gilly?" he asked.

"I'll see as to him after I get my money. He can bide along with Arthur at the nursery for the present. I've thought of that. Brimblecombe's going to miss my mother a good bit. He's taken Gilly to pleasure her and I made a fair bargain with him over Gilly. No call to worry as to him. Keep our heads: that's all we've got to do. We need to bear ourselves seemly, but nobody will expect us to shed no tears about it. They'd know they was crocodile tears if we did. Mother's lost her mind and took her life and that's all there is to it."

"And she's bundled herself out of the world at the right moment and none too soon. All to the good, and pity more old ones don't go the same way and leave a spot of room for somebody usefuller," said the railwayman cheerfully.

CHAPTER VI

WHILE Wallabrook, now aware of its apparent loss, remained in suspense and waited with some genuine emotion to learn the truth, it happened that excitement and even consternation concerning an event little likely to agitate anybody but himself had confronted the shocked attention of Sir Gerald Fortesque. He read of the outrage in *The Times,* stared with solemn eyes upon the printed words, considered first the reaction likely to result in all men of goodwill and secondly to what extent this assault on the sacred temples of science might act as a personal warning. He knew the supreme sufferer. "And it might have been me!" thought Sir Gerald. Age is timorous and ancient nerves are quick to take alarm before challenges often welcomed by the young; but, to Sir Gerald, this dry record of a tragedy awakened instant fear and a need for action. "It might have been me!" he told himself again, "And it may still be me, unless I take warning from these dreadful facts."

His first step was to send for Matthew Owlett and he directed the butler to do so.

"Some very significant incidents have come to my notice, Chave," he said, "and as Owlett is obviously the man most capable of grasping their significance, I beg you will send for him. I sometimes think that he should be connected with me by telephone and may now take steps in that direction; but for the moment I wish to see him as speedily as possible, so send somebody and direct him to come today."

Chave hesitated.

"There's a chance he may be helping the police over the mystery down there, Sir Gerald," he answered. "Four-and-twenty hours have passed since Mrs. Blanchard disappeared and no sign of her so far."

"That is nothing to do with Owlett, in any case. I want him and he must be found at once."

But Chave's mind ran upon the Wallabrook mystery and he failed of his usual circumspection.

"The butcher was up just now, Sir Gerald. And he says he came by the waterfall path on his pony and they're dragging for Mrs. Blanchard, because her daughter's got a fear she might have took her own life by drowning."

"Don't chatter, Chave. Do what I direct. If Mrs. Blanchard has taken her life, that is her own business probably—certainly not mine. Summon Owlett instantly, or I shall be seriously annoyed. Indeed I am already in considerable concern—not about what has apparently happened in Wallabrook, but things that may quite possibly occur at Oakshotts."

"Beg pardon, I'm sure, Sir Gerald. I'll see to it prompt," promised the butler, and a boy started on his bicycle ten minutes later. He, too, went by the river path and was fortunate to find Mr. Owlett engaged with others in the business of dragging the waterfall pool. It proved a difficult and as yet intractable puzzle how to do so, for the water was ten feet deep and the bottom obstructed with heavy stones. Now, into an argument as to further procedure between Matthew and Inspector Manley, thrust the boy from Oakshotts, and upon hearing his message and the exceptional gravity of some discovery unknown to all save Sir Gerald himself, Owlett acted instantly, abandoned the operations in Walla, took the messenger's bicycle to save time and sped away as fast as he was able.

He arrived out of breath and was greeted by his employer with considerable relief.

"Recover your wind, my good fellow, while I acquaint you with a matter of utmost gravity and moment," he began. "You will see its implications as I proceed and swiftly realize the challenges put upon me. I anticipated none such and am only thankful that power remains to lock the stable door before and not after the horse is stolen."

Matthew dried his brow with a red handkerchief and regained his wind while Sir Gerald boomed on.

"When the public reads, as it has daily opportunities to do in these licentious days, of atrocious thefts conducted often in broad daylight, who cares?" he asked. "Should this woman lose her jewellery, or that woman find herself the poorer by disappearance of a fur coat worth a thousand guineas, not one sympathetic sigh is heard to rise. Some merely censure the victim's idiocy for creating conditions in which such a thing can happen; others may actually display amusement and assume that those who can suffer such misfortunes possess the wherewithal to make them good. I myself on such occasions feel passing regret for the insurance offices which are, one must imagine, the real sufferers. But how different, how serious, how tragic the knavery becomes when something of real significance has been raped from those who not only possess it, but by every moral and social and even international obligation are called to hold the treasure as a sacred trust and acknowledge their covenant with society, science and civilisation!

"I have approached my subject with these commonplaces, Owlett, that you may the better judge its nature as contrasted with those everyday catastrophes with which we are all familiar; but a truly stupendous atrocity has happened on the Continent and it has overtaken no less a man than France's recognised, leading entomologist, Monsieur Eugene le Moult—a pre-eminent savant whose name has long been a household word.

"From his collection of three million butterflies and other insects, which incidentally is valued at two hundred thousand pounds of our money, eleven thousand butterflies are reported as stolen! While he was absent from home the crime has been committed and this great man's brief vacation brought to an end. *The Times* tells us that some of the butterflies have already been traced and recovered, and there is negative satisfaction in the fact that one of the very rarest specimens ever taken—an insect discovered and named by Monsieur le Moult himself—was overlooked and is safe.

"He housed his collection in a flat, where eleven rooms are stacked from floor to ceiling with collecting-cases. I can see them in my mind's eye still, as clearly as when I visited the owner and spent many fruitful hours in his company. We differed as to numerous obscure problems, but swiftly attained to understanding and respect for each other's attainments. No more of that. I have already written to him, and he will well know what this grievous stroke means to me and our colleagues the world over; but now for us—for you and me—arises the personal problem of how to profit from this knowledge—melancholy though it be. We are warned; we learn that our collections—yes, even yours as well as my own—lie in the shadow of this threat. Intrepid devils, if so minded, could enter my museum by night with little fear of any serious opposition and, in your case, a child could steal your butterflies while you slept.

"But such things must not be, Owlett. The peril demands to be met, not only to ensure safety for treasures dear to ourselves, but because these things represent contributions to scientific discovery beyond all price, and we, who are no more than their guardians, cannot retain our self-respect while such wealth remains inadequately protected against potential villainy."

Matthew welcomed a few moments' silence when the speaker

made an end. His private opinion inclined to a belief that Sir Gerald's fears were little more than a storm in a teacup, but he did not reveal it.

"Then you know where you stand, your honour," he suggested. "Of course your collection is worth mighty big money, and where there's known to be big money harbouring, there's always like to be big scoundrels after it."

"Such a supposition is sound," agreed his employer; "but it wanted this terrible illustration to bring me to my senses in the matter. I knew the Oakshotts accumulation to be exceedingly valuable, though never until now considered it in any mercenary light; but the case is altered and this Parisian outrage shows that where the carcase is, there will the vultures be gathered together. The gang that has successfully pounced on Monsieur le Moult may be specialists familiar with my own great collection. There may already exist designs maturing against me. I envisage them and am rent between two alternatives."

"A proper disgrace you should be called to put such a lot of vexations on yourself," said Owlett; "and what I can do to lend a hand to set your mind at rest I will do, your honour, if I've got to sit up night and day till it's done. My little lot of odds and ends is no matter. Only a few folk know about them. Nobody imagines for a moment anything I've gathered would be worth a brass farthing. But Oakshotts is different. You have let plenty of unknowns come and go to see it and never thought crooks was likely to be among 'em; but now you know what humans can sink to. And you say you've hatched two plans to defy 'em and ain't sure which to decide upon?"

"The first is to surrender my museum and permit it to be conveyed to London and take its place at the National History Museum while I still live. It would then be under the charge of an administration, which loves to nationalize everything and would, I imagine, extend a welcome to something of infinitely greater importance than railways or coal mines. That failing, the solemn charge remains with myself, and I must seek to render it impregnable and beyond reach of destruction. Oakshotts in that case should become a fortress, Owlett—a fastness and stronghold to defy even atomic energy!"

Matthew's eyes twinkled at these absurdities.

"The criminal classes ain't got atomics—not yet," he said, "though it's easy to guess what they'd do with 'em if they had.

And one thing I'd beg to mention here and now, your honour. Don't you let any hazard part you from your butterflies. They stand for your joy and your glory and your comfort and consolation, and if they was swept away to London, there's nothing left on earth would fill the blank for you. What would Oakshotts be to you without the collection?"

"Probably a howling wilderness, my dear fellow, lighted only by one minor star of consolation: that everything was safe."

"They are safe," declared Matthew. "Even as it stands the museum would take a tidy lot of professional skill to break into by night; but it will be easy enough for you to make it even safer yet. I'd say turn your big mind to the subject, your honour, and consider what a few hundred tons of concrete and steel will do if properly applied. I'll help—by this hand I'll toil with all my might and main and never rest in my bed till the butterflies be as safe as if they was in the Tower of London."

Sir Gerald applauded these sentiments.

"You are both right and wise," he declared. "It shall not be said that we took the line of least resistance. What I have I will hold, Matt, and you shall help me to do so. I will communicate with the authorities and take the needful steps. Meantime a night watchman must be engaged if we can find one with credentials and courage and experience equal to the task."

They parted then and the old sailor pondered with pleasure at the confidence imposed on him, but felt no alarm at these shadowy perils agitating the ancient scientist's serenity. Matthew went home by the river, where Inspector Manley still proceeded with what he called a routine task.

"It sounds an easy matter to drag a pool no greater than this one, Owlett," he said, "but the plain English of it is we can't do so, because the bottom's all crowded over with big boulders and the drag-net gets fouled the minute you start to draw upon it. In sober truth what I ought to demand is a diver, but the superintendent wouldn't support me."

"You can't expect they'd suffer such an expense, Samuel," declared Matthew. "They'd most likely tell you that 'twas the custom of corpses to bide under for a week or thereabout and then rise to the surface by the laws of Nature. They'd say if Unity Blanchard lies here, she'll appear in due course and proclaim herself without any police intervention and free of charge."

Manley agreed.

"That's so, and I'll go farther," he said. "Granted on Maude White's showing that this was the place in her mother's mind, it don't follow for a dead certainty that this was the place she chose. It adds to the likelihood, but ain't a certainty. There's a lot of deep holes in the river between here and the village and she might have gone under in any one of them; or, again, she might have changed her plans and never gone in at all."

"Now you're getting somewhere, I shouldn't be surprised," answered Matthew; "and I'll go so far as to tell you this, Sam. I knew the old lady very well indeed. I've known her and admired her pluck and patience along with her poor husband for many years. I knew John Blanchard also and was sorry for his failings. And faced with this situation, which you all take for granted is suicide, I say that if ever anybody was likely to be driven to such a way out, it wasn't Unity."

"As to that, we've got her daughter and her son-in-law to witness she'd been leaning towards it for quite a long time, Matthew."

"But why? Why should she be leaning towards such a thing? I grant living along with Brian White and his wife wasn't much fun for the old lass, but she'd unfolded the situation to Brimblecombe, who was her greatest man friend, and also to me. Arthur always wanted to marry her and would have taken her off her daughter's hands willingly enough; but Unity never meant to stop with Maude once her grandson, Gilbert White, was free of his parents and out of 'Laburnum Lodge'. That was her intention, and now Gilly's gone, or going, to earn his living at Brimblecombe's nursery, that was the accepted time when Mrs. Blanchard intended to leave the Whites. She'd got her ideas mapped out and had planned 'em decent and orderly. And I will swear she had no intentions to kill herself last time I saw her. Quite the contrary, in fact. Cheerful and brave and rather bucked by the thought of one of the charity cottages, where she'd be free if she could get it."

The inspector listened.

"I'll own I was deducing she might—well, she might still be alive and hid for her own reasons; but what reason could there be for such disorderly conduct?" he asked.

"There's a lot hid and it's your job to find out the reasons why it's hid," declared Owlett. "Something a great deal out of the common has overtook Mrs. Blanchard, no doubt, and the first thing is to consider whether it happened because she planned and willed for it to happen, or whether it's happened contrary to her wishes.

So far you've took it for granted this queer thing was her own doing—for reasons yet to be discovered; but you may have to take wider views pretty soon, Samuel. You may have to ask yourself if she isn't the victim of those stronger than herself."

"It's early days yet," argued Manley, "but once I was to take the line she isn't responsible for her present position—whether alive or dead—then a pretty wide field of inquiry opens before me."

"It does, sure enough, and I hope you'll be spared it," said Matthew. "I hope you ain't going to find yourself up against a proper teaser, Inspector, and out of your depth without a clue in sight. But you may be. If she doesn't turn up in twenty-four hours alive or dead, and if you don't get any line to follow, then, knowing her nature and her strength of character, it looks to me you'll have to take into account the chance that some unknown persons are behind this."

Such opinions tended to touch the policeman's self-esteem.

"You can leave my business to me, Owlett," he answered. "I haven't been in the Force from my youth up for nothing. I shall take the needful steps and have thought of all these things long before you did."

"No offence, Samuel. I was only pointing out how it looks to me," explained the other. "For what it's worth I don't believe she committed suicide. But something's come between her and her plans and it may be something's come between her and her life. I hope you'll find her, in any case."

Mr. Manley trusted that he might do so.

"Pheasant shooting's over in a week," he said, "so we shan't have to bother any more about my undertakings to help the Oakshotts' keepers. Trimble tells me it's been an ugly season and more birds stolen than he'd care to count."

"Which will continue to happen every year so long as he's in charge. Better you hunt for Mrs. Blanchard than the poachers, because she's like to be easier to find."

With that Matthew went his way and Mr. Manley looked after him doubtfully. The inspector was not among those who placed absolute credit in Owlett; but their conversation had tended to make him uneasy. It opened possibilities which Samuel had never been called to face and he trusted that the mystery of Mrs. Blanchard would be solved with as little delay as possible.

But his hopes of a speedy solution failed to mature; two days passed and there came no information from any quarter concerning the vanished woman, while meantime the inspector's growing fears began to quicken local tongues and add zest to the enigma. It was Mr. Manley himself who unconsciously created such sinister interest, for when his wife learned of the doubts that now assailed him, she hesitated not to acquaint her friends. Thomasina soon heard these exciting suspicions and she speedily conveyed the news where it was least likely to be welcome.

"I've come for a cup of tea, my love," she said, bouncing into 'Laburnum Lodge' on the evening of the third day that brought no news. Seeing her approach up the garden path, Brian, who was at home, had already asked his wife a question.

"What do that chattering magpie want to come worrying you for?" he inquired, but Mrs. Parsons entered before Maude could reply. Her words of welcome, however, sufficed.

"Come in, Tommy—come in," she said. "You're the only true friend ever I had here, or ever I shall have. But you look for a friend at times like this."

"And got a right to do so—now or never, my dear. Keep your tails up and trust in Providence: that's what I always tell the downhearted."

"If they could only find the poor dear we'd be so thankful; but not a clue yet."

"The river will give her up soon or late. You can bank on that," added Brian, and Thomasina broke her news.

"The inspector's whispering she may not be in the river at all," she said.

"If she ain't in the river, where is she?" asked Brian. "That's the only place where she could be hid, because they've hunted everywhere else for miles round."

"Who knows, Brian? But somebody might have hid Granny for their own reasons: that's what looks to be moving in the policeman's mind."

"Hid Granny? What the devil for?"

"For reasons of their own? D'you mean that, Tommy?" asked Maude.

"I don't mean anything, my love. It's what Manley looks to be meaning."

"Where's the motive for such a thing? Naught happens without a motive," declared the railwayman. "You hear of children being kidnapped for ransom, not old women."

Thomasina laughed.

"I'm afraid there's nobody ready and willing to pay big money for dear Mrs. Blanchard—unless it might be Arthur Brimblecombe," she said. "Don't you people waste a thought on the police. They're always full of excuses if they fall down on a job."

"How do you come to know what's in Manley's mind?" asked Maude, and Mrs. Parsons laughed again.

"Because he's married. Every policeman's wife darned soon knows what's in her husband's mind. And the less mind he's got, the sooner she knows it. I met Ruby not an hour ago in the grocer's. Your old lady's the big noise in Wallabrook for the minute and his wife hears what Samuel's thinking and hands it on—in strict confidence where it's safe. But after all, other people can put two and two together as well as Manley. He's mentioned Scotland Yard to Ruby! Yes he has, so any fool can see what's in his mind, because he hates the Yard and wouldn't call it in for a fortune if he was free to choose. But no policeman mentions the place unless he smells crime in the air."

"What will he smell next?" asked Maude. "If not suicide, then there's only one other thing it could be—an accident of some sort."

"Not likely, my dear. Would any old lady put on her Sunday clothes when all the parish was asleep and traipse out on a winter night in the moonshine by accident? There's another thing the inspector said to Ruby—a pretty good point making against suicide in any case. He says that them disposed to destroy themselves nearly always leave behind a farewell note of some sort for their friends, if they've got any left; but most often to the Coroner who's going to sit on 'em after they're gone."

"My mother could write, for that matter," said Maude.

"But always hated doing so," added Brian. "When she wanted to do so, she'd let Gilly write for her."

"She couldn't let the boy put down her intentions if suicide was in her mind," argued Mrs. Parsons. "She'd have wrote herself and told you where to find her and so save trouble. A kindly woman like she was, with such a daughter as you, Maude, would never have done it, well knowing what her fearful end would mean to you. And yet away she flits into the unknown all dolled up in her Sundays and best bonnet! Such things don't happen, and so everybody have a right to say there's a nigger in the woodpile."

"How can you explain things like that—unless she was demented?" asked Brian. "Why must Manley make a mountain out of a molehill? There's the only possible reason staring him in the face."

"He don't think it's the only possible reason. Knowing Granny Blanchard, he doubts—same as a lot of us do—whether she was the sort of woman to go mad. And if she'd had an accident or a stroke to slay her, then they'd have found her body where she was struck down and her poor remains would have told us all we needed to know; but if there was a fearful crime, Maude, then——"

"Have another cup of tea," said Maude. "You'll get dry talking such a lot, Tommy."

"Thank you; but you ain't making no tea yourself this afternoon."

"You give me the shivers to say Manley thinks mother might have been put out of the way."

"Ruby didn't go so far as that; but it was in his mind clear enough."

"And what sort of motive did the fool find could there be for anybody to murder the old woman?" asked Brian. "What sort of motive would a man risk his neck like that for?"

"Man or woman," replied Mrs. Parsons cheerfully. "Man or woman, Brian, and if the evidence pointed for dead certain to anybody and the motive was discovered and no alibis nor nothing like that could be found, then they'd be for it without a doubt. A fearful thought for all of us, I'm sure. There's poor Maude, gone so white as a dog's tooth, poor child!"

"Better stop this talk. It may be meat and drink to you, but it ain't to me, nor yet to her," said Brian.

His wife had followed the implications of Thomasina's last remark.

"In that case some innocent creature might well go to the gallows," she murmured.

"Certainly," agreed the other with gusto. "The innocent are well known to hang sometimes, Maude. There's likely to be plenty of surprises of that sort come Judgment Day."

"I wish to God she'd turn up alive and have done with it!" cried Mrs. White, and Thomasina stared to hear her.

"Be patient, my love, be patient!" she begged. "Them without a motive have no call to shake. If there's no motive, then everybody's safe."

Brian asked a question.

"Who does Manley suspicion? Who does he dare to put a motive upon?"

"Ruby wouldn't divulge even if she knew," explained the

visitor. "I probed her a bit, but she said her husband didn't name any names. Too cautious for that yet."

"If you've finished your tea, you'd best to clear out, then," directed Brian bluntly. "We've heard about enough of this twaddle."

Thereupon Mrs. Parsons instantly dropped her cake and rose.

"You don't gain nothing by being coarse to your wife's best friend," she answered, "but since we're on it, you can hear one little bit more about what Manley said. I shouldn't have named it in this house, because I'm very quick always to withhold any ugly words that might give a neighbour pain, being sensitive for any other body's feelings; but, since you've insulted me, you can jolly well hear it. I was properly shocked myself when Ruby told me and perhaps you'll feel the same. Anyway, inspector said that if he was up against murder and no wandering lunatic responsible, then it looked to be terrible like an inside job. So there!"

Mrs. Parsons prepared to fly after that shaft, but waited in safety near the door and rejoiced at the rage of the stricken. Brian cursed and swore, Maude gasped and moaned.

"Good Powers! He couldn't say a thing like that!" she cried.

"I protested," declared Thomasina. "Yes, I did. I was short and sharp with her as never before. 'If Unity Blanchard was put out of the way at 'Laburnum Lodge',' I said, 'then there's only three souls could be guilty, namely her own daughter and her son-in-law and her grandson; and if this was to come to their ears, I wouldn't answer for their actions.' That's what I said to Ruby Manley!"

Then, panting and agreeably excited, Thomasina sped away while Brian bawled at his wife, "That's a damned libel, and she'll be up against it as well as Manley when I go to lawyer."

Maude waited for him to calm down and strove to do so herself before speaking.

"That's enough," she said presently. "You won't gain by making a row. We must keep our heads because there's a lot to be thought upon now."

"There's nothing to be thought upon," he answered. "To say what she said was actionable and I'll see Manley's superintendent tonight and tell him what the damned idiot's been speaking against us. The police shall get hell for this, if I'm anybody."

"Tommy's torn it, sure enough," admitted his wife. "But, since it had got to come, better we heard it from her than another. We must think, I tell you."

"And I say there's nothing to think upon. What excuse was there to talk of an inside job, or imagine any such blasted thing? Where's the motive for us to do it?"

"Now you're talking," she answered. "You ask me that and I'm the only one can tell you. Manley don't know the motive and why he said what he said I can't guess, because nobody knows any motive but us. And the whole point is that darned soon we shan't be able to hide what will look parlous like a motive!"

"What trash are you telling now?" he asked. "What motive ever existed against us? And if there was such a thing, why couldn't we hide it?"

"Look ahead. See what's going to happen next—something that must happen now, something beyond our power to prevent whether they find my mother or whether they don't. That's the legacy. It will be found that we knew about the legacy long before this happened, because they'll nose out that I wrote to the lawyers soon after the advert was published and never named my mother when I did write. Then they'll find how only she came between me and the money, and that it was big money. And what do that mean if nothing turns up to disprove it? It means there was motive and more than enough for us to clear her out of the way."

"Then we'd be in a spot?"

"What do you think? You talk about giving the police hell; but a lot more like they'll give us hell if mother never turns up again. How can we prove we were innocent with all that evidence against us?"

"They'd want more than that to prove we were guilty."

"I don't know. You can hang on circumstantial evidence, I expect. The body might prove us innocent if she was found along with evidence to show what had happened to her; but if she was murdered, there might be no evidence to let us out."

"Blast the legacy, then!" swore Brian. "Better you never heard of it."

"A lot better, I dare say; but the legacy's fastened on me now and you can't escape that. And if the law was to decide against me, then I shouldn't have it after all."

"Because so like as not you'd be hanged."

"No, because you can't inherit money if you've killed them that owned it. I know that much, and if this ever came to a murder trial and we was brought in guilty, the least coming to us would be a life sentence. Then maybe Gilly might get the money."

Brian was silent and watched Maude clearing up the tea-table. Then he said something to startle her.

"You talk about 'us'," he said. "What d'you want to drag me in for? Suppose you're lying about your mother? Suppose you know a darned sight more about her than I do?"

She looked at him without replying and he spoke again.

"It might be devil take the hindmost then," he said.

"Ah! It wouldn't be women and children first if you was in a shipwreck!" replied Maude. "But don't you worry: we'll hang together if hang we must. You can't desert me: I wish you'd try, then they'd soon catch you and know you was the ringleader."

Brian grinned and remonstrated.

"I was only having a bit of fun, Maude. You never can see my jokes. No sense meeting trouble half way like this."

She peered at him out of her hard little eyes.

" 'Tis every sense," she answered. "When you meet trouble half way, you can nip it in the bud if you're smart enough to do so."

As she spoke her son appeared from his new work and declared great concern.

"There's a fearful thing happened up to Mr. Brimblecombe's," he said. "He's lost, Mother!"

"Lost?" she asked. "What d'you mean 'lost', Gilly?"

"He was thought to be at Tavistock as usual for three days; but he didn't come home yesterday when Mr. Toozey expected him, so he rang up the telephone to Tavistock and he's heard this afternoon that Mr. Brimblecombe haven't been there at all! And Mr. Toozey's gone to the police station."

"What the devil does that mean, Maude?" inquired Brian, and Gilly submitted a suggestion.

" 'Tis known he was wishful to marry Granny," he told them, "and I wondered perhaps if he might have run away with her against her will and got her locked up somewhere till she gives in and marries him!"

The idea apparently awakened others in his mother's mind. Maude's white face brightened for a moment and she even smiled for one fleeting moment.

"For once there's something happened Thomasina don't know about," she said.

CHAPTER VII

It often happened that Nancy Owlett would join her sweetheart on his evening perambulations for the pleasure of his company and the privacy of the empty countryside. His beats were known to her and her father, but on no occasion as yet had they furnished an opportunity for Peter's intervention at the call of duty. Now there came a night when the lovers went together under a cloudless moon upon the high road nigh Oakshotts, where it stretched south of the plantations, dividing them from a tract of barren and heath-clad land, broken only by thickets of furze and occasional solitary trees of spruce or birch that broke the expanse. It lay two miles from Wallabrook and for understanding eyes was beautiful at all seasons; and here, where it glimmered under the moonlight in naked silence, came Peter and Nancy together, full of their own affairs and the paramount interest of Mrs. Blanchard's disappearance.

"It's a black mark against the Force that you haven't picked the poor old lady up before now," said Nancy, and the big policeman agreed with her.

"So I think," he answered; "but, when all comes to be known and she turns up, living or dead as may happen, then good reasons for our failure may be found. Inspector Manley's fretted because he's come to believe criminal action might lie behind the business and he don't want nothing to mar his credit for peace and order and a clean sheet after all these years. But things will be different now the shoooting season's just over, and there won't be more need to back up the Oakshotts keepers. This is the last time I shall travel here by night till next autumn."

"I'm sorry in a way," she said. "I've loved these nights when I could tramp a bit of your beat with you. But I shan't want to much longer now."

"Mr. Owlett don't point to the date yet? I've sounded him but he won't fix it. Now he's as busy as a bee up here at Oakshotts and says first things must come first. Marrying my mother don't look to be the next thing yet."

"He's very evasive. He still talks about the importance of character—meaning you—and he hoped you'd be the one to find Mrs. Blanchard and cover yourself with glory. For the minute Sir Gerald's uppermost in his mind. The gentleman's suddenly got a fear there may be thieves going to steal his moths and suchlike and he's ordained to protect them and make his museum burglar-proof. All sounds pretty weak-minded and father says the place is safe against the powers of darkness in his opinion, but of course he's got to do what he's told."

"He'll jump at anything to put off marrying mother, or so it looks to me," grumbled Peter. "It's either that, and a disgrace to him if it is, or else, now he's faced with it, he can't bear the thought of losing you, Nancy."

"No, he hates my going, and I hate going myself for that matter. I can't see myself away from him and all his mysteries, maddening though he is; but I long to join up with you for good and all—more and more I long to. More and more I want to be looking after you first and last and always."

"Same here, my blessed."

"I can't but feel the end's nearer than we think for. Dad loves surprises and sometimes I fancy he's got one up his sleeve to spring on us any time now."

"I wish I was so hopeful as you."

"There's surely something in his mind for the minute. I always know when there is, because he turns silent and don't answer questions. He's asked your mother and you to Sunday dinner, so it may be he's going to choose that for telling us. There's something hid, but it's not your mother, nor yet me, nor yet the lord of the manor."

"Though mother's took him, sometimes I've heard him talk as though he was feared she might give him the slip," said Peter. "Funny, that, because at other times it looks as if he was trying to give her the slip."

"He's only got to march her to church and marry her. I ordered him last night to tell me what he was brooding about, and all he said was that nothing ever happens but the unexpected."

"Maybe he thinks I'm wanting still, but don't like to mention it," suggested Peter.

"Nobody in their senses ever dared to think you was wanting," declared Nancy. "They'd get a bit of my mind if they did. But he looks to feel there's a climax hanging over our families, and if he marks time a lot longer, we'll make our own climax and you'll have to run away with me and chance it. So you can make your policeman's deductions what would happen next."

The young man was much amused.

"My deductions would be that I should get dismissed the Force with disgrace and we shouldn't have a bean to live on, darling."

"You might turn into a poacher," suggested Nancy. "Father says they make quite a lot of money."

"They do. Old Toby Trimble's mad about the losses this year and thankful to God the season will be over in a week now. But I've never seen a poacher yet; no more's Mr. Owlett, so he tells me."

"There's wheels within wheels wherever you look," she said. "When the young ordains a clever piece of work, there's always the middle-aged to throw a spanner in it."

"The middle-aged can't throw any spanner in the works of the poachers anyhow. Young or old, they're one too many for Trimble. But your father asking me and mother to dinner Sunday was light in the gloom."

"It's cheered me too. You take the bit in your teeth after dinner, Peter, and if he don't talk out straight, you let loose on the dear man, and I'll back you up. He'll like that. Nothing pleases him better than for anybody to disagree with him. Then he'll start chattering like a starling till he's convinced you you're wrong. But he always fights fair. He——"

Peter stood still and put his hand on her shoulder.

"Hush!" he said under his breath. "Harken! I heard something t'other side the hedge!"

Through the profound silence that followed came only the hooting of a distant bird.

"Only an owl," whispered Nancy; but as she spoke a nearer sound—swift and stealthy—reached them.

"That's a man running in the wood," said Peter. "He's following the wood path to the next gate."

"A poacher! Oh, Peter, get after him! Then I can see you to work," she cried as they broke into a run towards a five-barred gate that opened upon the high road.

"Go gently with the wretch: don't put out your full strength against him, else you'll kill him and be sorry after," gasped Nancy.

"If I've got to take a man, you hook it home. No place for you," he said.

They hastened now and Nancy stuck beside him.

The invisible runner enjoyed a good start, but he was hidden only half a minute longer, for as they approached the gate under bright moonlight a small figure appeared, climbing it swiftly. The escaping man saw them when they were but forty yards distant from him and made frantic efforts to climb back over the gate again and get to the woods; but he was too late. Peter had left Nancy and rushed forward in time to collar the unknown and drag him back into the road.

"In the name of the Law," he said, then stared, struck dumb at the situation, and when Nancy caught him up it was she who first found words.

"Father!" she cried.

Mr. Owlett was panting and made no reply for a moment, nor could Peter swiftly recover his voice; but it seemed that horror and dismay rather than loss of breath kept him silent. Matthew was clad in a long working-day jacket and he carried his naturalist's gun.

"God's light!" he said. "Peter Chadd, sure enough! And you, Nancy. And the moon shining so clear as day and the air soft as lambs' wool! What a beastly venture, to be sure!"

He panted and mopped his face, then waited for Peter to comment on the situation; but it was Nancy who spoke.

"Why were you running? Are you all right, Dad? Whatever has happened?" she asked.

"Something very unexpected, I'm afraid," he answered.

"Why was you afraid, then? You always say the unexpected is the only thing to expect."

He did not answer her, but turned to the policeman.

"Better you go on your way and forget this unfortunate job of work, Peter," he said, "and I'll sit here and get my wind back. Then Nancy can see me home. Least said soonest mended sometimes, so you push on your beat and forget it, like a wise man."

"I am on my beat, Mr. Owlett."

"Of all hateful things to hap to us—all of us—and such a wondrous fine night for mid-winter," replied Matthew in a melancholy voice. He laid his weapon in the hedge and sat down beside it.

"Your gun, I see," said Peter.

"Yes, my gun."

Nancy had been looking at his bulging coat.

"Oh, Father! Well might you run," she sighed.

"Not fast enough, however," he said. "You ought to have sighted me sooner, Nancy, and called the man off while there was time."

"What's in your pockets, Mr. Owlett?" asked Peter, now assured.

"Moths—nocturnal moths for Sir Gerald. Ain't that good enough? Can't you give me the benefit of the doubt and clear out?"

"Oh, Father! What's the use of silly lies like that?" asked Nancy. "Own up, that's the best thing to do. Then we can talk."

"You don't go after night moths with a shotgun," said Peter.

"How right you are!"

Then Mr. Owlett, though his face looked very anxious in the moonlight and his mouth showed no amusement, endeavoured to raise a laugh.

"I'm in luck, though it don't look like it for the moment," he said, still breathing hard. "I thought Toby Trimble and his little lot had catched me at last; but you—that's different, and I can breathe again. I'm properly sorry and the season over and all. Little did I think this mishap was going to overtake us. The pitcher's gone to the well once too often, seemingly, and there's naught left now but to pick up the pieces and bury 'em."

He turned to Nancy.

"Since you was doomed to be here of all sad places, my love, then be useful. Empty my pockets, Nancy. There's a brace of pheasants and a very fine hare in 'em, to be exact."

"Oh, Father!" she said again, like a bell tolling, as the game appeared.

"A brace of pheasants and a hare, as you say," chronicled Peter in a dreary voice.

"That's right, or wrong as you look at it," admitted Matthew. "The birds are Oakshotts birds, my dear man, and the hare—well, the hare you may say committed suicide and was caught in a rabbit-wire on a rabbit-run. He ought to have known better; but he may have found life too difficult, like many of his betters do. A hare is beset with many dangers along of the Harriers and coursing, but you don't find 'em weak-minded till March month as a rule."

"The gamekeepers were right about you, then, though I always gainsaid 'em," said Peter.

"And I never guessed nor yet dreamed of such an ugly thing against you, Dad!" cried Nancy, with tears in her voice.

"Why should you, my love? Why should anybody?" he asked. "I never counted upon no showdown of this nature, and I never thought to do such a fantastical thing again. Just came over me, and now we'd best to cut the cackle and play our parts and part. Firstly, Peter's called to remember the underdog was always his strong suit, and that appearances can be deceitful. He's also got to mind a blind eye is sometimes a lot usefuller than a seeing one. Nelson put his blind eye to the telescope and won a lot of glory in consequence; and now it's Police Constable Chadd's chance to do the like and follow a good example."

Then he turned to Nancy.

"I'm tired, I'm tired and cruel thirsty," he said. "Come on home, girl, and be done with this."

Peter was concerned with what had gone before.

"I haven't got a blind eye, Mr. Owlett," he answered, and then his sweetheart spoke.

"It looks like you'll need one, then," she declared.

He was disconcerted and stared at her in doubt, but her father applauded.

"Well spoke," he said. "Don't let's have any more nonsense, my dears. Nothing easier on a moony night, when the world's peaceful and going to sleep, than for us to overlook some unexpected, unlikely happening such as this."

"Not for a policeman, Mr. Owlett."

"And a good policeman at that," agreed Matthew. "Inspector Manley tells me you're a model constable, though I fancy you can't claim to be very promising for the detective branch. But now, my boy, you stand in sight of marriage and are called to look at quite a lot of other things outside earning your living. You've got to think of your life, Peter. Your life's one thing and your living's another; and you look to stand at the crossroads between 'em. You need to forget your trade for half a minute—no more. Then you can go on being a policeman again. In a way I'm sorrier for you and your dear mother and Nancy than what I am for myself."

"That's sense," approved Nancy. "That's truth, Peter."

"Next Sunday as ever was I ordained to let you all into a secret," continued her father. "Yes, I did, and Nancy was going to jug this fine hare for our dinner and all looked like wedding-bells after next Eastertide; but now—what a turn in fortune's wheel! Instead of my girl jugging the hare, you've jugged me!"

He laughed, but Nancy begged him to be serious.

"No laughing matter for any of us," she said.

"Peter must try to laugh for once," argued Matthew. "There's times when a good honest laugh is the best answer to an ugly question. Nature knows that. The hyenas laugh at their dirty work, and when I hear a woodpecker laugh I often think——"

Peter interrupted firmly.

"Excuse me, this ain't no time for natural history and very well you must know it, Mr. Owlett," he said. "If you've got anything to explain about your situation, better do so. And mind this: anything you please to tell may be used against you when it comes to——"

"To what? What the mischief are you aiming at, Peter?" asked the culprit blankly. Nancy also expressed surprise.

"Don't talk so harsh, Peter!" she cried. "Father's right: you'd best to drop your business for half a minute and think upon other people. This ain't no time for self-righteousness, or any nonsense like that. All of us make a slip now and again—even a man like father."

"Ah!" said Owlett. "There's mercy and goodness out of a good daughter's mouth—the girl that's going to be your wife, Peter, same as your mother has promised to be mine. What's one police constable against facts like that? And what's a brace of pheasants and a hare? Less than nothing at all, I'd say. We must turn our eyes on the future and give no heed to fairy-tales of a man like me being caught poaching. Folks mustn't be asked to believe no such thing. Dammy! I wouldn't believe it myself. You and me are up against reality, Peter. We're going headlong into holy matrimony—the pair of us. We can't keep two good women waiting any longer, my boy, and we'd best begin by wiping out this night's work as a bit of moonshine—just something we dreamed, to laugh at when we woke up."

"All this brings you nowhere, Mr. Owlett," replied his captor patiently.

"Don't it? A pity, then. A cruel pity you can't use your powers of deduction better than that."

"It don't want no deduction," said Nancy. "It's a matter of common sense, Peter. If you must harp any more on it, I'll go bail for Dad. He'll promise on his oath never to have no lapses again—won't you, Father?"

"I'll do more," promised Matthew. "I'll put ten bob in the poor-box against these birds and never stop another pheasant, wild or tame, so long as I live. Yes, I'll undertake that on oath."

"And you'll keep mum as a mouse over it," added Nancy, "and enough said."

"Not near enough," answered the young man. "Is that all you've got to tell, Mr. Owlett?"

"D'you want any more?"

"A confession you done it—before a witness," said Peter firmly. "That's how it's fallen out, because Nancy chanced to be here."

"A confession to be used against father?" she asked.

"If need be—yes," he answered.

"You can't make a man's child testify against him—not in England. The nation wouldn't stand for it," promised Matthew, with assurance. "And be that as it may, I've nothing to say that can be used against me, Peter."

"Then I'm fearing——"

"No need to fear anything against father," cried Nancy, with rising anger in her voice. "You'll need to fear for yourself if you don't watch it, Peter Chadd."

"She's right, you know," agreed the elder cheerfully.

"Duty's duty, Mr. Owlett."

"And what do you hold to be your duty? What shape do you count your first duty to take, my dear?"

"Little I thought it was going to take a shape like this," answered Peter.

"You never know what shape your duty will show," admitted the old sailor. "There's your duty to yourself and your duty to your neighbour, and what he is to you and what you are to him."

"They point the same way for me."

"Oh no they don't, else you wouldn't be putting me and Nancy to such grief and pain this minute. If you take me in charge, Peter, then you'll go far to break your mother's heart, or next thing to it, and you'll break my heart on your girl's account. That's what you're up against. Mighty complicated, I grant, but life's a mighty complicated piece of work at the best of times."

"You can leave Nancy out, Mr. Owlett. No call to drag her in."

"Leave me out and take father up? Who d'you think I am?" asked the girl fiercely.

"I'm afraid you don't grasp all there is to her yet," explained Matthews. "'Tis a thousand pities she went spooning with you tonight; but here she is, and it looks that she can't keep her temper and watch her father being led off to the lock-up with his good name gone for evermore, my boy."

"Love you as I have loved you, Peter, and worship you as I always have done, I'll never look on your face again if you're set to ruin father," vowed Nancy.

"And dear Mrs. Chadd," continued Matthew. "Think of your blessed mother, man! What would she say about it if such a thing came to her ears? Ask yourself that. Do she want to marry a second, godless scoundrel like your father? Not her, poor soul. She'd love me no more and sacrifice all her hopes of everlasting security along with me. Take the bird's-eye view, Peter, and mark how your fancied intentions will wreck my show, and your mother's show, and Nancy's show, and your own show worst of all. Then a high-minded man like you will see it's just a trap and the devil himself up against you—not your conscience, nor yet your duty, but a plot to play hell with the welfare of your best and dearest."

"Let him speak, Father," begged Nancy. "I'm sure he sees it now, don't you, Peter? Every word father says is true."

A great gasp of impotence escaped the policeman's chest and he answered them, his deep and stricken voice rolling over the nightly silence.

"Listen to me—the pair of you, for God's sake," he said. "Have done with this, because I won't hear no more of it. I'm not my own master when I'm on duty: no policeman can be. I'm a servant of the State and paid by the State—paid with the nation's money—and I've took a solemn oath to do my bounden duty to the best of my powers. And if my own affairs offer to block the way, then so much the worse for them. Here I stand, and I've took a fellow man breaking the laws of the land and stealing valuable property, and I've got to hold him if all the angels from heaven called out to let him free."

"You said I was an angel from heaven once," said Nancy. "Oh, Peter, am I nothing to you now? Is my fight for poor father nothing to you? Then come to your senses while there's time left to do it, darling. Drop this play-acting and go on your beat and get out of sight for all our sakes and let father come home to his supper and repent in peace."

She approached him, put her hands on his shoulders and looked into his eyes.

"Give me a kiss, Peter, and let me have that gun—you don't want that no more now."

She pretended more confidence than she felt, for her lover was not responsive and kept his hold on the little gun.

"Duty's duty, if I must tell you again, and Lord knows I wouldn't have thought the likes of you was going to doubt it," he said. "You talk of conscience, Mr. Owlett; then what fashion of conscience have you got?"

"Ah! Delicate ground, delicate ground," answered Matthew. "Who can look at another man's conscience, Peter? My conscience is so clear as ever it was in my life tonight and that's the truth."

"You know better. You must know better and you can't send your conscience to heel like that."

"A weak, wilful old man, and his first slip—if it was a slip—his first slip, and his last. That's what my conscience might say most like if I was in your place and you in mine."

The policeman shook his head.

"They'll take into account it's your first offence, if they believe you," he said. "Anyhow, there's no wrongful acts proved against you till now and the only crime that counts is the first the law finds out. What's the use of talking? Come on, Mr. Owlett. Be a man and get it over."

"You're going to run me in, then?"

"Give heed to me, Peter Chadd," cried Nancy. "So sure as you take father, I've done with you for evermore!"

"I know that well enough," he answered. "I'd have known that even if you hadn't been here tonight to tell it. Your father won't be called to wait very long. The Magistrates' Court sits day after tomorrow at Wallabrook."

"A hideous shock for Sir Gerald. That's another side to it," said Mr. Owlett. "Your conscience may shorten the lord of the manor's life, Peter."

"He won't sit on the Bench, because he can't try his own case against you. He'll be plaintiff and you'll be defendant."

Matthew cackled.

"You can't choose but laugh when you look at it from other points of view than your own. What a triumph for Toby Trimble and Inspector Manley! Poor Sir Gerald won't dare show his face to Toby again. Well, come on, Peter. Best we're jogging. Then you can go home and tell dear Mrs. Chadd how you've saved her from another bad lot. Cheer up, my girl. All the same fifty years hence!"

"If he takes you, I'll never see his face again, Father."

"Hard luck your being here tonight. Hard luck for him as well as you," pointed out Matthew. "Now all looks to have gone down the drain for Peter and all's gone down the drain for you and me. What are they like to do, policeman? Imprisonment or a fine?"

"You're like to get a fortnight, Mr. Owlett."

"So be it, then. After that I'll creep away from these parts when I come out and I'll eat the bread of tears and make my peace and work my passage, with my girl to help me."

"Come on, please," directed Peter. "I pray you'll say no more, Mr. Owlett. I'll take the game and you can carry your gun."

"Think twice as to that," advised the other. "It's loaded and vanquished men do desperate deeds sometimes."

"You can shoot me if you've got a mind to," answered Peter. "I ain't particular keen about keeping alive after tonight."

"Your work—not father's," declared Nancy, but Matthew corrected her.

"No, no—mustn't say that, my love. He must go on doing his duty and being rewarded for it. By rights he ought to get promotion for this job of work and I hope he will."

"He ain't worth the breath he draws—no more," she said, and again her father uttered a reproof.

"Don't say that. Good men are scarce, and he's better alive doing his duty and letting his light shine on a storm-foundered world. So you go home, my girl, and lift a prayer to a merciful God."

"I'll pray to Him to put this hard-hearted, stiff-necked, cruel devil where he belongs!" cried Nancy.

"Don't you carry on and make a show of yourself," begged her father. "There's always a ray in the gloom, my dears, and heaven's still lighter than earth on the darkest night. Be hopeful, same as I am. Look at the moon. If the man up there can laugh, why not us? He sees a lot to laugh at, the man in the moon does. Come to Court the day after tomorrow, Nancy, and bring dear Mrs. Chadd along with you. She'll be torn in half, poor Dinah will, between her joy in Peter and her shame over me."

He bent suddenly, picked up the dead hare and passed it into his daughter's hand.

"Here, take this and push for home so fast as you can! Run for it! He can't catch you!"

"If you say so," she answered, then grabbed the hare and was gone. Like magic Nancy vanished into the heath and her father bawled after: "Jug it! Jug it for Sunday dinner!"

The incident took but twenty seconds and Peter knew pursuit would be vain.

"I've got to stick to you," he said, "and she's took evidence. That hare's part of the evidence against you."

"True, but no matter; you've got the birds. Push along now and let me think. I'm tired—very tired indeed. Best I take your arm, Peter."

They started and again the younger sounded his dreary slogan.

"Duty's duty, Mr. Owlett," he said, and Owlett agreed with him cheerfully.

"I'm beginning to believe it myself," he answered. "You've done well, boy."

"If you'd confessed, I'd have let you go home, because I'd have known where to find you tomorrow," explained Peter, "but because you wouldn't confess, I couldn't lose sight of you."

"You've done your duty according to your lights and I'm better pleased with you than you think for," answered the culprit. "Now tell me: is there a tolerable comfortable bed at the lock-up?"

"Inspector may let you go home when we get there and he hears about it."

"Not on your life! That wouldn't be his duty. He'll hold me tight. He'll be shocked too. I can't count up the number of people who will be shocked tomorrow."

After another silence he spoke again.

"Bed and breakfast, then, it's going to be?"

"Inspector Manley will see to your breakfast and convenience in general for certain."

"Shows you've got a good constitution if you enjoy your breakfast," said Matthew. "My favourite meal."

Again both were silent, then Mr. Owlett asked a question.

"Who's like to be on the Bench tomorrow, Peter?"

"The Colonel can't come because he's out of England, and Sir Gerald can't sit, of course, so there will only be Lady Champernowne."

"Lady Clara—eh? Not a soft-hearted woman by all accounts, but full of good works, they say."

"The Magistrates' Clerk looks after the Justices and sees all goes in order."

"Mr. Westover—a good lawyer," commented Matthew, "but likes trout-fishing better than the Law. I've watched him sometimes and he throws a very good fly."

To the police station came Peter with his prisoner and his grim news. Inspector Manley already suffered from acute professional anxieties and now he stared at Owlett as though gazing upon some creature outside his experience.

"Powers of light!" he almost shouted. "What next? Here's a woman missing and a man missing, and now you catched red-handed at last! What's come to Wallabrook? What's overtook the place?"

"A man missing, Inspector?" asked Peter.

"Arthur Brimblecombe. He was thought to be at Tavistock as

usual but now it appears that he hasn't been heard of at Tavistock at all!"

Matthew gazed with sympathy upon the distracted policeman.

"Too bad, Samuel," he said. "Too much to put on the shoulders of a kindly, harmless old man like you. Better you'd retired last year, as you thought to, and escaped the evils to come."

CHAPTER VIII

GREAT news, whether good or ill, flies fast and on the following day Mrs. Parsons, appraised of everything through her own magical technique, was running about and oozing hard facts generously upon every ear that would stop to listen. In two supreme quarters intense emotions were instantly aroused. For Inspector Manley came startling information as a boon and a blessing from one best able to prove its truth; while for Maude White the latest intelligence, though it eased one intolerable fear, yet brought the crushing news that all her hopes were ended. Her goal was lost and her good name promised to be a thing of the past; but against that certain dreadful fears for her husband and herself now haunted her no more.

For the inspector nothing but amazement and satisfaction promised, and after an hour with his informant he breathed again and was soon regarding his surfeit of experiences as little more than a bad dream. Mr. Brimblecombe himself worked this wonder, for Manley had but finished his breakfast on the following morning when Arthur appeared at the police station safe and sound, thereby removing one of the triple causes for disquiet that had ruined the policeman's night. Physically weary, unshaved though not uncheerful, reappeared the nursery gardener. He was wearing his Sunday clothes and full of his long and remarkable adventures. Arthur himself felt exhausted and quite worn out, for a series of unique events had taken toll of his vitality.

"You!" exclaimed Manley at sight of him. "Man alive, I'm properly thankful to see you, though a bit the worse for wear, I'd say. Are you all right? It's knocked a year off my life to hear you was missing too."

"I'm all right, Samuel, but crying for sleep. I've been through a most tremendous affair and come out of it a lot aged, but a winner. Lead me where I can sit down and ask Ruby for a spot of your whiskey. There's things must come to your ears instanter and if I drop to sleep while I'm telling 'em, shake me up and make me carry on till you've heard all."

"One word," said the inspector, after he had called an order to his wife. "You'll not know perchance that Mrs. Blanchard's missing while you were away."

"I'll come to her," promised Brimblecombe. "None knew better than me she was missing, Samuel, nor yet why she was missing."

"Then if you can say whether she's alive or dead, that's all that matters for the moment. You look so down-daunted yourself I can't but feel a doubt. We've searched the county and not a trace, but ugly rumours from her daughter."

"Yes, yes; I can well believe that. Nobody ever got aught but what was ugly from Maude White. Let me talk, Samuel, and be content to listen. Unity Blanchard's alive and in a lot better case than I am, for that matter. She'll put herself in your hands after today."

"Thank God, though she's given a mort of trouble to the Force. Come into my office, Arthur. All's clear now and I can spare an hour, if need be, to listen."

"I'll tell so much as I can in an hour, then."

Ruby Manley fluttered in with a whiskey bottle at this moment and declared the parish would be thankful to hear of Mr. Brimblecombe's safe return; but five minutes later she had sped to proclaim it, while the inspector gave heed to the strange story awaiting him. With a certain sense of drama Arthur drew from his pocket a little letter-case, extracted from it a scrap of printed paper and then launched his narrative.

"You'd never think that all this affair arose from an advert in the *Sunday Clarion*," he began, "but that's the truth and there's the advert. No need for you to con it at the moment. All that signifies is just this: that by the will of God it caught my eye, Samuel, and what followed was worked out by Providence in due course. There was the printed word and it aimed at one living creature only, and if I hadn't catched the name of Blanchard I should never have even stopped to read it. But that held me and I did read it. Do you remember the Blanchard race and how there was two brothers—John that married Unity, and James that wanted to, but didn't? James went to Australia when he couldn't get Unity, and these words in the *Clarion* told that James was dead, and next that his relations, if there was any left, would reap advantage from his will if they could be found. He named Wallabrook as the place where they might harbour and accordingly the lawyers in London published this appeal on the offchance it might be read by a Blanchard, if any still remained."

"And Unity by good chance saw it, Arthur?" suggested the inspector.

"Not her! Take note of this, because all turns upon it. She saw the paper and always did see it of a Sunday, but only to look at the pictures. But 'twas I that saw it, and, knowing she wouldn't and guessing it unlikely that any of her friends would do so, I took a chance, cut out the words but kept my mouth shut till I got her alone on Christmas Day. Then I showed the words to her. A lot rose out of that conversation, Samuel, but the important thing she spoke was that Maude read the advertisements. 'She reads 'em very close—her favourite reading, in fact,' said Mrs. Blanchard, and then she laughed. 'My daughter bought a bottle of medicine a few weeks ago, because she said her hair was falling like corn under the sickle, because of the eternal strain on her nerves. And her without a nerve in her body—no more than a steam-roller have got nerves.' Then I brought her back to the matter in hand. Now you can read what she read, Samuel, and I'll go on to the next step."

Inspector Manley looked at the appeal for any news of the Blanchard family. Then he nodded and Arthur went ahead.

"The first thing Unity remarked after she'd took it all in was this. 'So James is one of the late ones now,' she said. 'Only just gone, seemingly, and must have been well over eighty before he went.' 'There's no other Blanchard to come between you and what he's left,' I pointed out, and she agreed to that. 'Now my husband's gone, I'd be the right one,' she said. 'So there we stand,' I answered, 'and Maude read that advert and never told you?' But she was always dead honest, Unity was. 'We can't be positive sure she read it, Arthur,' she replied. 'Can't we?' I asked. 'Then answer this first: if you was gone, my dear woman, what about your brother-in-law's leavings?' Of course she had to admit that her daughter would come next, because the rest of the Blanchard race was extinct for years and years. 'Maude would be nearest to 'em,' she said. 'First my late husband, then me, being his wife, then Maude, being his daughter.'

" 'And when them words fell under her eyes, she knew all that quite as well as you do,' I reminded her. Upon that Unity admitted she wouldn't have been very likely to miss it, but we couldn't make sure. 'You can't show no evidence she's seen it, Arthur,' she says to me. And then I turned to the past. 'It's a month and more since those words appeared in the *Clarion*,' I said; 'and if you want evidence that Maude read 'em, listen to me. She reads this inquiry and what does she do next? Gives out all over the parish you're failing and advises you to make a hole in the water and, for cunning, pretends she'd like to do the same herself.' Mrs. B. couldn't argue against that. 'I see what you're aiming at,' she admitted. 'It calls for action on my part.' 'Yes,' I told her. 'It properly screams for action, and I'll lay my life that her and her husband have took action.' I couldn't swear they had, of course, but I'd got a strong suspicion Maude was moving behind the scenes, and I'm proved to be in the right, Samuel."

"Just so: I should have deduced much the same," agreed Manley. "No doubt Maude White would have got in touch with the lawyers."

"Next," continued Arthur, "Mrs. Blanchard decided it was her turn to get a move on. 'I'll speak tonight when I go home,' she promised. 'Then I'll have it out with 'em.' But of course I forbade any such a mad thing. 'Not on your life!' I said. 'That's asking for it, Unity. Don't you see the foolishness and the danger? You ask Maude if she'd seen the advert and she'll answer "No". Then she questions Brian if he's seen it, and he answers' "No". Then Maude swears that if she'd seen it, of course she'd have run to you with it and told you all about it. And where are you then?' 'Well, it might be true they hadn't seen it,' answers poor Unity, being one of those too apt to trust. 'You know in your heart very well it wouldn't be true,' I warned her. 'If you let the cat out of the bag and show you know what they're up to, then presently the night comes down and you all go to bed and you're at their mercy! Money's an awful temptation to Maude at the best of times and she may know by now it's big money.'

"Mrs. B. nodded and allowed that was so, but tried hard not to let me harbour no frightfulness against 'em. 'You didn't ought to speak such things to me of my daughter, Arthur,' she said. 'You're the mother of a hen-devil in any case,' I answered firmly, and then she laughed and I ordered her not to laugh, but keep her wits. 'Forewarned is forearmed,' I said. 'You couldn't do anything more perilous than let them know you've seen that advertisement and I dare you to do it. You must use what craft you have got to match against theirs. Look at this from Maude's point of view. If it was only a flea-bite she wouldn't have felt no need to be wicked; but she's up against something solid, and, with you out of the way, would stand to collar the lot.' 'There's nothing shakes your highest principles so soon as big money,' granted she; 'and the thought of losing big money might make 'em both pretty fierce no doubt, but not so fierce as all that, Arthur.' 'So fierce as tigers,'

P

I told her. 'They've done their best to make you go quiet by your own hand, but they've drawn a blank there.' Then Unity showed her true cleverness and began to sit up and take notice about it, Samuel."

The inspector was thankful that Mrs. Blanchard had sat up in time.

"Yes; her next remark showed the quick brains of the woman and how well she can look ahead when she's so minded," continued Mr. Brimblecombe. " 'I'd be under my son-in-law's paw in a minute if I was to rob him of a fortune,' said Unity, 'and Maude might find herself very well content if he did homicide on me and then got hung for it, because then she'd be properly free for the first time since she married him!' "

"Showing how a woman can often look forward into the unknown a lot cleverer than a man can," suggested the inspector.

"For a minute after that fearful speech, I think Mrs. Blanchard felt she might have gone a bit too far," proceeded the other. " 'I may be doing wrong to say that, Arthur,' she allowed. 'We must be fair to 'em.' 'Certainly we must,' I agreed, 'but 'tis better to paint too dark a picture than feel too hopeful till you've learned more yourself. First thing is for you to write to these lawyers in your own hand and ask 'em if they've ever heard of Mrs. Maude White. Then, if they never have, that lets her out and all's well. Safety first,' I said. 'Safety is all I want,' she answered, 'and, if they're guilty of anything wrongful, that's the first thing they'll want themselves.' Then she considered. So I kept silence for the best part of five minutes till she'd got her ideas settled and when she spoke she laughed, though there was nothing to laugh at in what she said."

"Women are apt to laugh at very queer times and very queer things," declared Inspector Manley.

"Yes, they are, Samuel. 'As for a letter, I'm asking myself why write at all? I've got a tongue in my head,' she told me. 'Surely none ever had a better,' I replied, and then she made a most startling suggestion, showing the sort of woman she really is.' "

Mr. Brimblecombe paused to drink and the listener praised him.

"The old lady couldn't have found herself in better hands. Thank God it was you who found that advertisement, else she might have been a lost woman for all time."

"Yes: you'll see how true that is in a moment," replied Arthur, and went on with the story.

" 'Seeing's believing': that was the next thing she said and then asked a question. 'How would it be if they lawyers were to see me in the flesh with all my *bona fides* at their service?' she inquired. 'Suppose I went before this Wilson and Harding in my own person and demanded to know what James Blanchard had left to his relations? Then I should have cleared the air and could see straight.' It was a great thought, of course, and I told her so. 'Just a masterpiece you'd think upon,' I said. 'But London! Would you dare to face London at your age, Unity?' However, she didn't see no reason against. 'Why not?' she asked, as cool as a cucumber. 'There's lots of folk older than me dwell up there and think nothing of it.' Which, of course, was true enough. 'I've never been there,' she granted, 'but if it's my duty to face the place, I'll do so. As I said just now, I've got a tongue in my head.' 'You have,' I argued, 'but not a bean in your pocket, my dear,' and she explained that was where I'd have to come in, if so willing. 'You'll need to show your high opinions of me now, Arthur,' she said, 'now or never, because it's not only a spot of your money I want, but a tidy bit of your time. We must rise above little details like that if I ordain to go. I can't tell Maude and Brian I'm off to London and want a five-pound note for my expenses, can I?' 'Lord, no!' I replied. 'If they got wind of that, they'd plan according.'

"Then she went on as if we was plotting a picnic. 'First thing is to keep 'em in the dark, though we look to be out for a deed of darkness ourselves,' she said. 'To save 'em from doing a worse deed of darkness very likely,' I responded, and then she grew serious again and said she hated to think so badly of 'em. 'We must cut their claws before they can use 'em, anyway,' she promised, 'and no harm in that.' Then I asked how and where I was to come into the picture, and she set me gasping again. 'Because,' she said, 'I'll want a faithful, trustable man of the world to see me through this caper. And who more so than you? To go to London I must need a railway train, but I can't embark at Wallabrook, because Brian White would be dead sure to see me doing so and all the fat in the fire when he did. But if I creep off to Tavistock by night and pick up a train there, none will see me that knows me. So we'd leave here in the small hours long after the people were all to bed and you'd drive us in your Ford to Tavistock and we'd nip into the first train to town from there.'

" 'Me go to London!' I cried. 'Never, Unity!' But she meant it. She can be as hard as moor stone when she's got a mind to be. 'You'll come, Arthur,' she said, 'and never had a better chance in your lifetime to do a good deed and rescue a woman in distress. So you can back me up and watch over me, because London's a busy, noisy place and dangerous by all accounts for a stranger. You'll do that and find the money and you'll have my word that you get it back so soon as possible along with good interest for the loan of it.' 'Lord save us!' I said. 'This want's some thinking on.' 'It do,' she granted. 'But not too much,' I said, 'because while we were thinking it out, you might get your throat cut and spoil all.' 'That's the spirit, my dear man!' she said. 'That's how I want you to feel. All in a nutshell really and only the items to fill in and the night to choose. When that's fixed, you can come in the Ford to lich-gate and I shall be there. And we must carry a few sundries for a night in town.' 'Good powers!' I cried. 'What a nerve you've got!' 'Nerve is everything in a job like this,' she explained. 'The better you plan, the less cause you'll have to fluster when you act. We must go so bright as buttons. We owe that to London and the lawyers. I can never pay you for such devotion as you are going to give me, Arthur, but I'll take mighty good care it won't leave you out of pocket.'

"Then her thoughts sped forward and another queer cause for laughing over-got her. 'I'd give a devil of a lot to see Maude's face some fine morning when she bawls to me to come down house to breakfast and finds I ain't there,' she said."

The nurseryman rested awhile and then drew to an end.

"That's what you may call the first act of the drama, Samuel. She went home soon after that—it was Christmas Day, remember—and we left it so. I promised to call at 'Laburnum Lodge' after a few weeks into the New Year, and then we'd fix the night if nothing happened to change her mind. As for the date, it would be near the time when I was always away to Tavistock for a day or two, so I should not be missed, because it was important in my opinion that there should be no suspicions rose about me."

Arthur rested again and the inspector spoke.

"You'd have done better to confide in me, Arthur, and save the Force a good bit of cash and me a lot of anxiety," he suggested mildly; "but you couldn't think of everything, of course. You'll hear there's been a lot of upstore about this business. The Whites reckon she's committed suicide and I've been terrible afraid there might be a crime behind her disappearance; but that's all over now. And where's Mrs. Blanchard this minute, Arthur?"

"I'll come to her next, Samuel. She's safe: that's all that matters for the moment. She's safe and rich beyond imagination! That's Act Two of the play. But you'll do best to wait for her to tell that herself. She's very wishful for her daughter to hear it from her own lips, because she reckons that the woman must have had a tidy lot of trouble on her mind and don't want for her to be tortured any more. Unity's been a bit deep herself and she helped Maude to think she might take her own life."

"I don't care a button about Maude's tortures," said the inspector sternly. "She's earned 'em, and they have been a bit more fearful than her mother may think, because she's heard what I think—so my wife tells me; but this is where I come in, Arthur, and I'm not going to let Mrs. Blanchard be under the dominion of them people for another day. I wouldn't be responsible for her if she was."

"How right you are!" exclaimed Mr. Brimblecombe. "And I may tell you she's of exactly the same opinion. Her heart is soft, but her head is hard and she's very clear now as to the Whites. She don't press her bed in 'Laburnum Lodge' again and she ain't going over the threshold without you beside her. She's forgiven 'em, but she'll never trust herself alone with 'em no more."

"And where is she now?"

"In my house—safe. If it suits you to do so, I'll drive her here in the Ford this afternoon; then we'll take her to face Maude and Brian."

The inspector agreed to this.

"They'll be tolerable glad to see her alive in any case," he declared, "because it's been borne in upon 'em that if she was proved to be dead, they might find themselves in an ugly spot. Maude's like a cat on hot bricks at present. The worst will be over for her no doubt when Mrs. Blanchard walks in, but where she's going to be next will depend on what line her mother chooses to take. I'd say that if she can prove an attempt to steal her money and rob her of it, that's a crime might well land her daughter in gaol for a tidy stretch."

"Leave it to Unity," begged Arthur. "She finds herself a most powerful woman now and it's acted like a tonic on her. She always felt to want power, Samuel, because her circumstances never gave her any; but now power and dominion has come to her."

"I'll do as you say," promised the other. "You can pick me up round about three o'clock this afternoon and we'll take her to 'Laburnum Lodge'. I'd only raise one point: where does she ordain to go after? She can't very well settle down under your roof, can she?"

"We haven't thought that out yet," answered Arthur. "There's a lot more for you to know, Samuel, which she'll be wishful to divulge herself. I'll leave you now and doubtless you'll be pretty glad to feel this job of work looks to be finished. But Toozey tells me you've got another ugly case where least I'd have expected it. He'd only heard vague rumours and I hope they were false."

"No, there's nothing vague about 'em," replied the inspector. "If you mean Matthew Owlett, it's true enough. Peter Chadd took him and he's locked up till tomorrow. Then he'll come before the Magistrates' Court."

"I'd have bet my bottom dollar Matt was an honest man, Samuel."

"You'd have lost, Arthur. There's no shadow of doubt. You can't get round the evidence. And now the mystery that's always hung over Owlett is cleared. Toby Trimble was right, as I always feared he might be."

"How's Matt taking it?"

"In the wrong spirit, so far. You know Owlett. Just bluffing and making silly remarks upon the lock-up and saying he's never tasted a poorer breakfast than what he had this morning."

"A thousand pities it had to be young Chadd," suggested Brimblecombe. "That's the worst of a crime: it never stops at the criminal. You can't tell who may find themselves drawn in."

"In this case you can tell very well," declared the policeman. "He was going to marry Dinah Chadd and that's off already, because, being a sensible woman and well acquaint with what goes to marrying a bad man, she's dropped him. She brought a letter for Matthew to the police station this morning, looking twenty years more than her age already, and she told me what was in the letter and I told her she'd done very wisely."

"Dear, dear!" sighed Arthur. "Then what price Nancy Owlett?"

"She didn't keep Peter waiting five minutes. She was actually out walking with him when they ran into her father; and after she heard Peter was going to bring him in, she gave him the sack there and then. He told me so much, and I warned him it was just one of those unfortunate things that might happen to a policeman and have got to be faced. But I also said it stood for a good mark to his credit and the superintendent should hear about it in due course."

"The girl stuck up for her father, no doubt, so the four of 'em have all got hell in consequence," said Arthur. "Still, somehow I can't believe he'd have done it, Samuel."

"Why can't you?"

"Because of Sir Gerald. If the evidence is what you say, then not to believe is contrary to reason: but when you think upon Sir Gerald, what does reason say? Is a chap such as Owlett going to bite the hand that feeds him? You can poach now and again without blasting your character and still be left with a rag to clothe you; but if any man was to repay what Sir Gerald's done for Owlett by robbing him year after year and taking his money all the while, then he'd be a mean and dirty blackguard sure enough and will deserve the scorn of the parish."

"That's much what Amos Hannaford says at the 'Fisherman's Welcome'," admitted Manley. "I met him this morning and he talked same as you. He granted that Matthew might pinch a doubtful bird, or fish, and agreed he ought to pay for it if he did; but he refuses to believe he would have wronged the lord of the manor on any account whatsoever. And when I told him what Peter had heard Owlett admit how the pheasants were Oakshotts pheasants, still he could only hope the trial would throw some favourable light on the affair."

They parted then and Arthur proceeded to the inn, where he continued to discuss proceedings with Hannaford.

"As for my affairs, they'll be common knowledge after to-morrow, Amos," he said. "All is well and great events offering for Mrs. Blanchard, and I've been drawn in heels over head myself, much to my own amazement; but she's bade me say nothing till she's spoke herself."

"You look to have caused a lot of needless worry and trouble, but if you've satisfied Manley, then no doubt you'll satisfy the rest of us," answered the innkeeper.

CHAPTER IX

WHILE Arthur proclaimed his return, Mrs. Blanchard sat and rested in the nurseryman's parlour with her grandson for company. She had travelled from London by a night train, arrived in Tavistock at daylight and been conveyed thence to Wallabrook by Mr. Brimblecombe in his Ford car.

Unity, despite her tremendous experiences, appeared none the worse and quite equal to facing the demands soon to be thrust upon her. Indeed, she had already welcomed them and planned a future far more adventurous than might have been suggested for one of her age and traditions. She had risen to her startling translation, enjoyed time to consider its possibilities and planned her future existence on lines the last to be expected by her friends and admirers. To these indeed she had added in the metropolis.

Gilly, who now worked daily at the vegetable gardens, came into the presence of his grandmother after she had eaten her breakfast. He was overwhelmed with joy at the sight of her. He had long accepted his parents' conclusions and the melancholy certainty that Mrs. Blanchard must be dead, but now he recovered from his emotions after seeing her, touching her, hearing her familiar voice and kissing the familiar cheek again.

"The people will roll over each other to shake you by the hand, Granny, for most everybody was sure you were a goner," he said. "Mother for one. She's been whimpering like a whipped dog about you and I heard her tell father how she'd give her soul if she could see you walk in the door again."

"She'll see me walk in the door this afternoon, but not as I was used to walk. I'm travelling a lot stronger on my feet than I was. I haven't known where I was walking exactly for a very long time, but now I do know. Even you may have marked I was queer and cranky and cast down since our Christmas dinner in this house with Mr. Brimblecombe, but that's all over now, Gilly."

"Mother's like to breathe again when she knows you're safe."

Mrs. Blanchard did not answer that, but asked him a question.

"How do you fare up here, Gilly?"

"Very nice indeed. I like Mr. Toozey and he'll be nice, too, now he knows Mr. Brimblecombe's back and safe again. He's been a bit put about, because he couldn't hear where the master had got to."

"There's more astonishments for Toozey too. It's a queer thing, Gilly, for an unnoticeable woman like me to find herself news. Mostly, when the unknown find themselves news, it turn out unfavourable to 'em; but I'm glad to say that my news is good news for myself and also one or two more—yourself included."

"If it's good news for you, then I'm sure it's good news for me, Granny. I feel properly thankful just to see you alive. I couldn't believe it at first, but now I do. All in your Sundays too, though only a weekday. I won't let nothing you do surprise me again."

"There's something I plan to do may surprise you very much," she said. "You'll hear what that is this afternoon, because you will be let off your work to go back with me then. Your mother didn't know I was home this morning before you left to come here?"

"No," he answered. "She gave me my breakfast at seven o'clock. But, come to think of it, I lay she do know now, because I passed Mrs. Parsons on my way. She was fleeting up the hill to see mother in a very excited condition and I wondered why she'd got on the wing so early."

Mrs. Blanchard laughed.

"Be sure she was carrying the good tidings, Gilly."

"If he'd got a flag, then father would hang it out for you when he comes home, Granny. He's a 'Red', he always tells, so, if he got one, it would be red, I expect."

"A white one, more like," she suggested. "White for surrender. He'll be true to his name after today."

Gilly did not comprehend this.

"Such a 'mazing lot of things be always happening at Wallabrook," he said. "A proper whirl of 'em, now good, now evil. You're back and that's the bestest ever did happen; and Mr. Owlett—that wonderful man—has been took up for poaching at Oakshotts."

His grandmother dealt with this information firmly.

"Then the more fools them that took him up," she answered.

"I'm glad to hear you say that, Granny, because I hoped such a wonder as him might be innocent."

"Nobody's innocent. You can't live to middle age innocent," explained Unity. "Nobody on God's earth was ever innocent after forty; but Matt's innocent of poaching Oakshotts pheasants—that I'd swear to if he said he had himself."

During the afternoon four persons arrived at 'Laburnum Lodge'. Mr. Brimblecombe drove his car and Unity, Inspector Manley and

Gilly accompanied him. The boy found growing anxiety mixed with his joy, for his adult companions all appeared unusually grave despite the glad situation as he saw it; but Gilly had become dimly aware that his parents apparently rested under some shadow the nature of which he could not imagine.

No flag greeted Mrs. Blanchard, no pennon either red or white fluttered over her head as she entered the wicket gate and marvelled at the tiny garden, which had always seemed so considerable till now, and the little dwelling-house behind it. Her daughter's face was white enough where Maude stood at the open door to greet her and a note of surrender informed her voice, though the faltering words she spoke were framed to chide.

"Thank God! Thank God, dear Mother! But why did you serve us so bad and grieve us so cruel? How could you, darling?"

She embraced her mother without receiving any return endearment, and Maude turned to the inspector.

"Heaven be praised—no Scotland Yard after all, Mr. Manley! I guess you find yourself so thankful as we do."

Then Brian hove up from the house, loud and hearty.

"A police escort! What have you been up to to give us such a turn?" he asked. "Thank the Lord you're safe, Mother, and I hope you haven't been in no mischief. There's a lot us and the Law wants to know, you bad old girl!"

He made to caress her, but Unity withstood him.

"No. I ain't kissing anybody in this house for the moment," she said. "There's a lot you want to know, no doubt, and I'm here to tell it."

"So long as you ain't a penny the worse, that's all that matters to us," he answered.

Mrs. Blanchard turned to her daughter.

"You can make me some tea, Maude, and the pair of you can listen while I drink it. And don't either of you pretend no more rubbish, but give heed where you stand. I ain't going to feel no sorrow for either of you."

They entered the house-place and her daughter strove to offer some excuses.

"We're both mighty thankful to know you're alive, anyway, Mother. You've made us feel terrified, same as everybody else was, that you might be dead."

"Not everybody, Maude. There was one who knew better."

"We've near broke our hearts thinking you'd took your life, anyway."

"Would I have put on my best gown and my jewels and turned out at two o'clock of the morning for a little thing like suicide? Never!"

"What did you turn out for, then?" asked Brian. "How was we to know? How was anybody to know? Here's Manley himself been chattering round the parish that it began to look as if there had been foul play against you."

The inspector intervened.

"And right I was—foul play sure enough, so hold on there and listen to the truth," he ordered sternly. "As for me, I never put much credit in your yarn about her drowning herself. She wasn't the sort to do it and much too spry for an accident to end her life, so what remained? Only homicide, and if homicide, then a motive; and she's told me bitter clear what the motive was, and who wanted her away, and why."

Mrs. Blanchard then resumed the melancholy tale. She had thrown off a handsome, new fur boa from her neck and was sitting beside the fire.

"When we started our chats about me committing suicide, Maude, and your opinions that it might be a happy release for me if I done so," she began, "I wondered a bit what was hid in your mind; and then came Christmas Day and Arthur told me all about the advertisement. You'd been so dumb as a adder on the subject and I hoped for a while that you was innocent and hadn't seen it, but I marked how you pestered me worse than ever to drown myself, just then, and that made my heart grow hard."

"As well it might," said Mr. Brimblecombe. "Wheels within wheels, as they say. And the wheels of my Ford carried us to Tavistock and the wheels of the railway train carried us to London to hear what Messrs. Wilson and Harding had got to tell. They're both dead, so we couldn't find out, but we saw Messrs. Forbes and Pilcher instead and what we feared was proved by 'em. Go on, Unity."

"First Arthur's car broke down in the dead of night and we were hung up so long that we didn't reach Tavistock till morning and missed the early train for town," continued Mrs. Blanchard. "We didn't get to London before afternoon, then Arthur, understanding telephones, rang up the lawyers and said I should be looking in upon 'em next morning. We were armed for one night if not two in

London and he took two rooms at a hotel near Paddington Railway Station and we slept well. Then, come morning, I took a proper breakfast—not bread and skim milk, Maude, but a sausage with butcher's meat in it and a choice between tea and coffee. Being too early yet for the lawyers, we went in Hyde Park and saw a tree or two looking sorry for themselves in that desert of bricks and mortar, and presently we stood before Mr. Forbes and Mr. Pilcher, and very pleasant, understanding men they turned out to be."

Then Arthur took up the tale.

"We came at a most favourable moment," he told them, "because the lawyers had been waiting for a copy of the late James Blanchard's last will and testament. They said it should have reached 'em by air mail long since, and I said the law's delay had hung it up, maybe. A young boy brought us before 'em—an office boy of no great account—and then they proclaimed themselves to us and Mrs. Blanchard proclaimed herself to them and also proclaimed me as her friend, who, being a man of the world, had come with her to bear witness to her character and look after her interests. They hadn't grasped our names up to now and thought we must be Mister and Missus Brian White, with which they were in correspondence, and Forbes congratulated me and said it wasn't often that a railway porter came into such a legacy, and Pilcher corrected him and said it was White's wife's money, not mine. Then Forbes said that husband and wife were one in the eyes of heaven and the Inland Revenue; and after that Mrs. Blanchard broke it to him who we really were.

" 'If you're a Blanchard, ma'am, then I'm afraid we're in sight of trouble,' said Reginald Forbes, and Unity took a high hand with him. 'Well, what of it?' she asked the man. 'Other people's troubles are your living, ain't they?' 'Not always,' he replied to her. 'It's like this: we advertised for any survivors of the Blanchard family and promptly discovered one in the shape of Mrs. Maude White, who sent us particulars of her existence and relationship to the late James Blanchard. We gathered she was the daughter of deceased parents.' With that I looked at Unity. 'D'you hear that, Mrs. Blanchard?' I asked her. 'Your words have come true sure enough, Arthur,' she answered me. Then she laughed and asked the lawyers a funny question. 'Do I look like a deceased parent?' says Unity, and Forbes granted that he'd never set eyes on a lady with more gracious manners and in better health."

"I told him about Arthur, then," continued Unity, "and we got very friendly until Mr. Pilcher brought us back to the business we was come about. 'Now let us know all you can concerning Mrs. Maude White,' he says, and I told him that I'd known her ever since she was born and suffered from her at the time and ever after. 'Maude's my daughter,' I said, 'I'm her mother, and my late husband, John Blanchard, was her father, and James Blanchard, who left the legacy, was his brother.' Then he explained that under the will, now in his hands, the legacy was expressly left to John and his wife if they still lived, and their children, or grandchildren, if they were gone. 'Nothing could be clearer,' he said, 'but for this unfortunate impression created by Mrs. White that she is an orphan.' "

"I struck in then," said Arthur. "I told Pilcher how Maude had lied and Unity was her mother before the nation and the wonder had always been at Wallabrook how such partners as John and his wife had ever come to breed an only one like Maude.' 'Dear me! Mrs. White's not a success, I'm afraid,' said Forbes. 'At any rate, she appeared to be quite sure she was an orphan.' "

"I told him it was just wishful thinking on my daughter's part," continued Unity, "because the facts was different. 'Arthur here saw your advertisement in the *Clarion*, and he misdoubted Maude from the first. So, finding the signs pointing that way, I ordained to look into the matter myself.' Hearing me say that, Mr. Pilcher asked, 'What signs?' and I told him how I lived with Maude and the signs showed how I was a lot more in her way than I fancied myself to be. 'In fact,' I said, 'my daughter told me it might be a clever thing if I cut my losses and got off to heaven while the going was good'; and Mr. Forbes granted that was a pretty broad hint. 'So when you heard about our appeal and Mr. Brimblecombe showed it to you in the West-country newspaper, you concluded that the legacy was probably considerable?' he asked."

"And I answered," put in Arthur. "I saw the danger ahead—I mean you, Brian White—because you could have snuffed your mother-in-law out like a farthing dip if you wanted to."

"I'll have you up for that, you lying dog!" shouted the railwayman, and Inspector Manley cautioned Brimblecombe.

"Stick to the point and let Mrs. Blanchard tell the story, not you," he said.

"Well, Arthur's a man of the world, as I always thought and think more than ever now I've seen him in action," proceeded Unity. "But I never felt same as he did, that there was no redeeming features in Maude and her husband. I always told him that the poor souls were not the sort to rise to a murder for doubtful money, though I granted the temptation might be there. And then Mr. Pilcher told us it was wonderful what a modest figure will oft prove enough to account for a capital crime. And he also said that Mrs. White had already been informed that a large sum was coming to her. Now let Arthur go on and give my tongue a rest."

Her supporter proceeded:

"Mr. Pilcher next thought that Unity's relations sounded to him more stupid than ferocious," he said, "because the truth would have been certain to appear long before they could touch the money; and after that Forbes came down to brass tacks about the will and explained how Unity was sole legatee—and come into the money and land and everything—all but a few small, outstanding legacies. So he said it only remained for the executors in Australia to be satisfied. Then Mrs. Blanchard told them she expected the lawyers to want proper evidence. 'I've fetched my credentials along with me,' she said, and opened her handbag which contained 'em. She showed her marriage lines to begin with. 'It's clear as can be I was the one that James Blanchard was questing for,' she said; and then she gave 'em the address of our minister and told 'em that his reverence, the Vicar of Wallabrook, could guarantee her, because he'd got her baptismal register in his church and her husband's grave in his burying-ground under the tombstone she'd set over John."

Again Unity took up the thread.

"I shan't keep you much longer, Maude," she promised. "Then, after Mr. Forbes had said he didn't feel no great anxiety over my statements, but would verify 'em in due course, I asked him what he'd have done about it without my appearance. 'If you couldn't ferret out no member of the Blanchard race, how would it have went then?' I asked him, and he said James Blanchard had provided against that, and told us something about James. 'Your brother-in-law was evidently a prudent and able man,' he said. 'He made a fortune by trading in land, over much of which Sydney now extends, and he sold it as the city stretched out larger and larger, and made a generous profit. He left rather more than forty-five thousand pounds, and in addition to that you inherit his private residence and an orchard on the banks of the Parramatta river in New South Wales, Mrs. Blanchard. To answer your question, had nobody turned up in the shape of an heir, then his estate would have reverted to Sydney charities. These institutions will be disappointed it would appear.' Something like that he told us, but I'd only caught hold of one word to interest me so far.

" 'Did you say an orchard?' I asked, and he answered, 'Yes, an orange orchard.' "

Gilly raised his youthful voice.

"Was they Orange pippins or Cox's orange, Granny?" he begged to know.

"Neither, boy," replied Unity. "Honest-to-god real, foreign oranges, always my favourite refreshment! Bursting with vitamines, so Mr. Pilcher said. A grand orange-grower was James. He bought the land years and years agone and cleared it and stocked it with high-class young trees. And he loved the place and lifted a fine stone house upon it and lived and died there."

"What a dream, Mother!" murmured Maude.

"It gives you to think, sure enough," admitted Mrs. Blanchard. "When I was a girl I might have took James and, if I'd decided upon him, I'd have gone down there along with him and been eating his oranges every day of my life for the last fifty years, very near."

"And no Maude to mar the prospect," said Brimblecombe, but under his breath so that none heard him.

"My favourite refreshment," repeated Unity. "The joy of my life when I was a girl and could get 'em. And now an orchard of 'em—all mine and, if I ordained to do so, I could sit in the shade of 'em and smell the flowers and pick the fruits off the boughs by the score and hoard the peelings for marmalade."

"You always said 'waste not, want not', didn't you?" ventured Maude.

"I did," said her mother. "When I was young you couldn't charge waste against the poor. They didn't waste, because they'd got nothing to waste. It's different now. None throws their money about freer than the poor do now."

"It will be hard to find yourself properly rich and begin a new life at your age, Mother," declared Maude.

"Not in the least," responded Unity. "Naught teaches you the value of money like having none. I've had none all my days and now I've got a lot. What do they name, Arthur?"

"They told us you could sell the property for another four or five thousand, because there were plenty out there ready and willing to buy it, and you said, 'That calls for a lot of thought, gentlemen, and I'll turn it over on my way home.' Then Mr. Forbes declared how it was always so pleasant to bring a client satisfactory news and took it for granted you were going to leave the business transactions in his hands, and I whispered to you how in my opinion you were lucky to have such good hands to leave 'em in."

"So you did," agreed Mrs. Blanchard, "and I said, 'I trust you, my dears, the both of you, and you can see me through and earn good money yourselves by so doing.' After which Arthur thought, so far as money was concerned, they'd best to begin by letting me have a spot in advance, because he was paying for the adventure out of his own pocket so far. 'She's only got her old age pension,' he explained to 'em, 'and her daughter takes the lot.' Forbes thought upon this and said that if I lived with Mrs. White—but then Arthur interrupted him and put in that I couldn't fairly be said to live along with you, Maude. 'She's lingered with the Whites,' he said, 'because she felt it was her duty, but it wasn't worthy to be called living.' "

"I did say it, and I say it again," declared Brimblecombe. "Then Mr. Forbes explained he wasn't going to mean anything sinister, but merely advise precautions. After which he told Pilcher to draw out a cheque for a hundred pounds, or give it to us in cash if that would be handier. And next he said he'd write to Maude instanter and catch the country post."

"But I stopped him there," proceeded Unity. "Because I felt myself to be able to express my wishes better than him in that matter. 'You can leave my daughter to me,' I said, 'and I don't intend to shut my eyes in "Laburnum Lodge" again, because God only knows where I'd open 'em if I did. No call to fear for me,' I said, 'and when you send future directions, you can do so to the care of Mr. Brimblecombe, The Early Vegetable Nurseries, Wallabrook. He'll know where I'm lurking to.' "

"I told 'em I'd look after her at this end and they could look after her in Australia," continued Arthur, "but then Unity told us she ordained to look after both ends herself so soon as she cooled down a bit and grasped the position. She declared that most that happens tends to age the human frame, but a come-by-chance such as what had happened to her made her feel ten years younger so far. Then, touching her daughter, she explained we wasn't up in town to wash dirty linen before the face of London and least said soonest mended so far as her family was concerned. Of her daughter and son-in-law she said they'd been wicked enough to go wrong, but fortunately not clever enough to go far wrong."

"Then," added Unity, "I told them that I had a grandson who took after the Blanchard race and, if only for his sake, I wouldn't like the Law to nail this on his parents and shame his mother's family. After which I'm very thankful to tell you, Maude, that the lawyer says if I don't proceed against you, nobody will. 'Leave her for her conscience to deal with,' he advised, and I said I hoped you might have enough conscience left to hurt you a bit, because you deserve it. Then Arthur decreed we mustn't waste no more of the gentleman's time. 'You've found an honest lawyer, Unity,' he told me in their hearing, 'and that was a good day's work for a woman of your age.' 'You've found two honest lawyers,' said Mr. Forbes, 'because my valued friend Mr. Pilcher is quite as honest as I am.' We parted then in a very friendly spirit, and I promised 'em they should have a tidy box of my best oranges some day when I could find the time."

Her son-in-law spoke.

"That lets us out, then, anyway," he said.

"Yes, you ain't going to be locked up and disgraced, Brian," she answered, "and you won't lose your job; but if you do, that will give you a spot of time to count your blessings and turn over a new leaf and try going straight for a change."

Whereupon the railwayman swore at her.

"Blast you!" he growled. "Go to Australia yourself and choke yourself with your bloody oranges!"

Then he left them and, in the silence his wrath had created, Maude murmured a word on his behalf.

"Don't mind him; he was always a bad loser," she said, then turned to Mrs. Blanchard.

"Couldn't you bide here for just a few days, to save my face?" she begged. "And we'll go over all your things and see what's worth keeping, Mother."

But Inspector Manley forbade any such arrangement.

"Not with my sanction, Mrs. White," he said, and Unity agreed with him.

"All I've got worth keeping is on my back, and the rest can go in a jumble sale," she answered, "and I don't stop here with you no more. Once bit, twice shy, my dear."

"That's common self-preservation," explained the inspector. "You can't trust human nature smarting under defeat same as you are now. You heard your husband and most like you're feeling just the same, but clever enough to hide it, which he was not. Your mother ain't going to settle herself down with two brooding volcanoes tonight, and I wouldn't suffer it in any case."

Maude turned to Mrs. Blanchard as the company rose to depart.

"You're my mother, anyhow," she said, "and mothers are apt to return good for evil."

"Well, I have done so. You've got your bit of luck and, so long as I live and where I may hap to be, you can trust me and you can trust your son to me. And if ever your husband runs away from you, then you can come back to me and let the future bury the past, Maude."

"Thank you, Mother," answered Mrs. White, now grown tearful.

"You can trust Gilly to me and better do so," repeated Unity. "He'll be safer with me than ever I was with you. Don't shed no tears. I've forgiven you and I'll see you tomorrow."

"And welcome, I'm sure, Mother."

"There's some of my details here I want, of course. There's that photograph took of your father after he had passed away and a few other treasures from the past. I'll see you tomorrow and you can tell Brian I've forgiven him also and if there's blood oranges in my orchard, he shall have a tidy lot to choke himself with come presently."

In this dominant fashion she took charge of the proceedings while both Mr. Brimblecombe and the inspector listened with approval. They went off, one on each side of her, while she cast a final word to Maude.

"And keep off Tommy Parsons, my dear. Give her a miss. If that woman gets to hear I've been spending a night or two in town with Arthur, she'll trumpet it to the four winds of heaven!"

Then, left alone with Gilly, his mother heard Mr. Brimblecombe's motor-car roll away in the gathering darkness while her son strove to support her.

"If Granny was to take me over," he suggested, "that would cheer you and Dad up a lot, because you'd be rids of me for evermore. And if you can't suffer father much longer, then you can cut loose and join up with Granny and me. Don't cry no more, Mother."

"I'll stick to your father whether or no," she said. "Best for beastly people like him and me to cleave together."

Maude permitted herself further tears and was indeed cast down.

"Poor Mother!" sighed Gilly. "Never see you slop over so bad before! But Inspector Manley said you was more foolish than wicked, and that's a comforting thought for you."

CHAPTER X

WHEN Mrs. Blanchard learned of Matthew Owlett's tribulation, she had declined with scorn to believe one word of an indictment so shocking; but while Mr. Brimblecombe and she supported the old sailor and others also took his part, those most nearly concerned found it impossible to do so. The closer they stood to him, the more difficult it appeared to suppose Matthew innocent. Dinah Chadd and her son were equally afflicted and now, upon the night before her affianced husband would confront the Law, Peter's mother spent some hours upon her knees in supplication. Her mind was already determined, but she prayed long, earnestly and woefully that Providence might be pleased to support it. The point at issue concerned a communication to Mr. Owlett, and now, receiving no celestial message to the contrary, Dinah wrote a letter with sighs and tears, sealed it and next morning directed Peter to give it to the prisoner before his coming ordeal. Her son had told her all there was to tell upon the morning that followed Matthew's arrest, described the pitiful scene and detailed his own line of action.

"There's a lot of ways to look at it," he said, "and if you've got an open mind, you must endeavour to see it and keep your nerve, Mother. Take Nancy. Her mind disposed her to be on her father's side and she was a good bit surprised to find I didn't see eye to eye with her. I quite understood how it looked to her and him, and in that matter she was so dead sure of herself that she sacked me once and for all and left no manner of doubt as to her intentions if I arrested her father. So my position was clear and nothing left for me to make up my mind about. But what you'll need to do is different and I wouldn't presume to advise you. You may agree with Nancy, or you may agree with me; or you may decide against taking any action till after the trial."

"I uphold you, Peter," she declared. "It's a very shattering affair that what you thought to be right should bring such a cruel load of shame and confusion on the rest of us; but I uphold you, my son. The first result is you've lost the woman that was to be your wife, and sorry I am, because she's always looked to be the right one and her father can never make up to her all she's thrown away. And the second result is whether I shall serve Owlett same as his daughter has served you."

"If you must, don't do it for revenge," he begged. "Don't let no feeling of vengeance come in it, Mother."

"No—I shouldn't do that," she answered. "If I turn him down that will be for self-preservation, not revenge, Peter. My business with Matthew is my own affair and I wouldn't take no advice upon it from anybody less than Providence. And I won't wait for the trial, neither. Whether he's been wicked or not lies beside the question. There was always a doubt in my heart if he didn't like his daughter's company better than mine and the trial won't clear that up, whereas, by jilting you in a moment of passion, Nancy's took herself out of reach once for all. It's a lot too dreadful for a woman with my poor brain to unravel in any case."

When his mother gave him her letter on the following morning and begged Peter to convey it to Matthew, he uttered a last word of caution.

"Inspector won't object, knowing the situation as he does, Mother, though he's against Mr. Owlett and believes the evidence all that is needed; but I hope you haven't written anything you'll be sorry for after it's too late."

"I hope not, I'm sure," replied Dinah. "Though I wouldn't trust my instincts in such a mess as this if I'd got a divine message not to do so. But no divine message came through, though I've given Providence lots of time to speak if so willing. So I've trusted my memory of what it was like to live with a bad man, and turned Matthew down for good and all."

"Nobody can utter a word of blame against that, Mother," he assured her, "and if you've put it firm and clear to him, he ought to be the first to bend to it. Mr. Owlett's lost his two best friends on earth, them being Sir Gerald and yourself."

Dinah made no answer to that and Peter left her, but before the morning was past there came another to Mrs. Chadd, and Nancy Owlett paid her a brief visit. The elder was pondering her son's words and reflecting on the enormity that had separated his benefactor from Matthew for ever when Nancy appeared, now collected and calm.

"I won't keep you," she said, "and you've heard this fearful story from Police Constable Chadd, no doubt, so there's no call to tell any more about it; but father sent you a message by me, Mrs. Chadd, and I forgot it yesterday. There's plenty of time for you to hear it and do what he wishes, if you choose; but that's for you to decide upon. It was my duty to bring it over, anyway. He ordered me to go to the Magistrates' Court to hear his trial, which I shall do, and he wanted you to do the like, because he is wishful for all to listen to what may happen before they judge him."

Dinah considered and finally agreed to obey.

"We'll go together, Nancy," she replied. "You and me will sit side by side, my dear, and keep an open mind—so far as we can. I shall put on my black and advise you to do the same," said Dinah.

"It's a funeral all right," admitted the girl.

Some hours later they met and the prisoner's daughter found Mrs. Chadd in conversation with another woman. The sufferers were both gloomily attired, but Thomasina Parsons felt no sense of dismay in the atmosphere of approaching proceedings and would not for the world have missed an entertainment so uncommonly rich in promise. She was telling Dinah of Unity's return and the events following upon it at 'Laburnum Lodge'.

"Heard it all from Maude herself last night," she said. "Old Granny Blanchard's come home rolling in money and property in Australia, and poor Maude's been acting a bit too downy—led away by her beastly husband, I expect—and they may both be in the soup yet if Maude's mother turns nasty; but that's in confidence, Mrs. Chadd, and you won't let it go further. You've got your own troubles no doubt and are feeling anxious, like all of us, as to how it's going to be with your intended. Not too good, I'm fearing, but where there's life there's hope."

She turned to Nancy, who had just arrived.

"Good morning, my dear," she said. "I wish the case looked so bright for Mr. Owlett as the sun is. A beautiful morning; but our affairs don't turn on the weather. We must trust that right will be done. I was talking to Inspector Manley a minute ago. Very busy he is, naturally, with such a lot on his hands. Mr. Owlett's case is to be took first, so you won't be held in no long suspense. The public will be let in a quarter before eleven."

Nancy, who knew Thomasina but little and disliked her much, made no reply, while Mrs. Parsons marked Mr. Hannaford of the 'Fisherman's Welcome'.

"Ah! I thought Amos would be here," she said. "He's one always claimed a great opinion of Mr. Owlett, Dinah. A queer fashion of man and I've often wondered about him. You'll never find him pleased over a bit of good luck or cast down by a bit of bad."

Hannaford approached, ignored her, but stopped to condole with Dinah.

"Don't you take this too hard, Mrs. Chadd," he said. "I wouldn't say, knowing Matthew as I do, and as you do, that we may not find there's something about the case yet to come out in his favour. Character, Mrs. Chadd, will triumph against the evidence of your senses sometimes. That was said in my bar last night by a stranger, and it's true."

"Thank you," said Dinah. "A comforting thought, Mr. Hannaford; but I've heard my son who took him and I'd sooner have witnessed the dear man's funeral than his downfall."

"There's few to take his part, Dinah," sighed Thomasina—"very few. Rats will always leave a sinking ship: it's the law of Nature. We forgive the sinners but can't forget their crimes and don't want to be acquainted with 'em no more after they're found out."

"My father's not a sinking ship while he's got me to watch over him," said Nancy sharply; "and rats are vermin, anyway. Where's the man or woman on God's earth that don't slip up now and again? Justice ain't above mercy, is it?"

"Mercy may be a matter for Providence and I'm praying we may see it to work presently in Lady Champernowne's heart," declared Mrs. Parsons, "but meantime justice is her job, Nancy. You can't look to heaven for no miracles nowadays and in any case not such a miracle as to save a poacher caught red-handed."

"Lady Champernowne's sitting on Matthew, and being a woman, maybe she's got her merciful side uppermost," suggested Hannaford. "She holds the Scales of Justice in Court this morning, and she's a very fair woman and a good sporting character. If there's a favourable side for Matthew, she'll most likely jump at it."

"A little bird tells me her ladyship has had her face lifted not so long ago," reported Mrs. Parsons, "and I said that, at her age, her face should be lifted to heaven and no place else."

The widow cackled at her own humour, as she was wont to do, but none heard her, for Hannaford left them and Dinah was talking to Nancy.

"My knees are stiff because I was on 'em praying off and on till daylight last night between cups of strong tea," she said; "for myself and for your father I prayed, and for your poor Peter too."

" 'My Peter'? He's no Peter of mine and never will be again," replied Nancy. "He's a heard-hearted, cowardly, over-grown beast of a man—that's what your son is, and Lord knows how I ever thought different."

"His duty was his duty and he's always done it. You ought to have found that out by now, my dear," answered Mrs. Chadd mildly.

"Duty!" cried the girl. "Duty, to bully the weak and turn on me and smash up everything I'd hoped and longed to happen and serve his future father-in-law like a dog!"

At this moment the doors of the parish hall opened and a hundred waiting people streamed inside, while a minute or two later Lady Clara Champernowne appeared. She was a handsome woman still and waged successful battle against remorseless time.

Then Mr. Owlett, under guard of his captor and another policeman, arrived, and Dinah, surveying the prisoner's box, murmured to Nancy.

"To see your father in that pen of shame—smote to the earth before all the people—breaks your heart!" she sighed.

"He's not smote to the earth, and he'll go game whatever he's done," answered the younger. "Your son looks a lot more like a guilty man than father does. Look at his face! He's ten years older already and pale as a maggot."

The young policeman did indeed offer a spectacle of massive misery and presented an absurd contrast to Mr. Owlett, for Matthew, though dwarfed as he entered, yet displayed a confidence and well-being out of all keeping with his unfortunate position. A hum of wonderment greeted his cheerful bearing, which Inspector Manley suppressed.

"Silence in Court!" he demanded.

"The charge against the prisoner, Mr. Westover?" inquired Lady Champernowne, eyeing Matthew with a sort of doubtful disfavour. She well knew all that this little man had been to his employer, but strove to approach him with a mind unbiased. The Magistrates' Clerk rehearsed the prisoner's offences.

"Matthew Owlett is charged with feloniously entering and stealing game from the Oakshotts preserves on the night of the twenty-third of January last."

"So recently? Then we shall not hear of the Law's delays this time, Mr. Westover."

"They cannot be brought against us on this occasion, your ladyship. Constable Peter Chadd, upon his beat between ten and eleven o'clock, took Matthew Owlett with his gun in his hand and the game upon him."

"Call Constable Chadd, then," directed Lady Champernowne, and, when Peter had taken the oath, she addressed him.

"Now let us learn what you have to say, Constable, and speak up well so that we can all hear you," she said.

"I was following my beat between ten and eleven, being the twenty-third day of January, and I was travelling down the south edge of Oakshotts forest when——" began Peter; but at this point Matthew lifted his voice and interrupted.

"One moment. Excuse me, Lady Magistrate, but may I be suffered to ask the witness a question?" he asked; and in return found one put to him.

"You are not going to plead guilty, then?" inquired the Magistrate.

"Bless you, no! I'm here an innocent man."

"You will have plenty of time to ask questions later if you intend to defend yourself, prisoner," she answered; "but if your question bears directly upon what the witness is going to tell us, then no doubt he will reply. Is that in order, Mr. Westover?"

The Clerk considered and at last agreed that a question might be put.

"It's this," proceeded Matthew. "Was the witness alone or in company when he arrested me?"

"I was in company and about to say so," replied Peter. "I was talking to my companion at the time when I heard suspicious noises and human feet running t'other side of the woodland's edge behind the earth bank that rises there. I started to follow up the unknown and half a minute later—the moon being bright overhead—I saw a man getting over a gate that opens there out of the forest on to the high road. I was on him as he landed off the gate and I found him to be the prisoner. He was much surprised to see me, also his own daughter, Miss Nancy Owlett—me being in conversation with her at the time, because we were engaged to be married. She'd walk out to converse now and again and did so that night as the weather was soft and fine and the moon full."

"You arrested Matthew Owlett?"

"Not instanter, because he had a lot to say. He allowed it was a misfortunate accident meeting me, and then he unfolded his operations and exclaimed how he's been looking after night moths for the lord of the manor and was authorised by Sir Gerald to be free of the preserves. But, seeing his pockets was bulging, and you don't shoot night moths with a shotgun, and there wasn't any night moths flying at this season of the year in any case——"

The people broke into a laugh and Inspector Manley shouted, "Silence—silence in Court!"

When peace returned Peter continued:

"Seeing the prisoner was talking nonsense, I searched him over and found him to be carrying two pheasants and a hare. Then he frankly granted the pheasants to be Oakshotts birds, and his daughter heard him do so; but he wouldn't divulge where the hare came from. He said he was eating it on Sunday and hoped my mother, Mrs. Chadd, and me would join his daughter and him for the meal."

"I have learned the domestic details behind this case," said Lady Champernowne, "and very painful, not to say puzzling, they appear to be; but they do not concern us here."

"The hare do," ventured Peter, "because it was evidence, your ladyship; but Miss Owlett, seeing her father was under arrest, snatched up the hare at his order and bolted with it. Otherwise it would be here."

"Well, you did arrest the prisoner and took him to the police station at Wallabrook?"

"Yes, because he couldn't offer any substantial and lawful explanation of how he came to be there with his gun and the hare and the pheasants, I was forced to take him into custody."

"Quite so. But he has just claimed to be innocent. Had he anything to say at the time in his favour?"

"A lot to say, your ladyship; but nothing I could honestly feel to be in his favour—quite the contrary, in fact."

"Well, what did he say, Constable Chadd?"

"I can't mind it all now, but in his opinion I was making too much of my business and too little of the human aspects of the affair. He said there was times when a blind eye sees further than a clear-sighted, and this had better be one of them. He reminded me I was under contract to marry Miss Owlett so soon as possible and very anxious to do so, and also that he was contracted to marry my mother, Mrs. Dinah Chadd of this parish. Then he pointed out how it would be a sad pity to ruin four people—two males and two females—and give Wallabrook just such a bit of bad news as everybody likes to hear about everybody else."

Inspector Manley silenced a titter and Lady Champernowne spoke.

"He wanted you to overlook the matter so that these misfortunes should not descend upon your two families?"

"That was his earnest desire—just to by-pass the affair, your ladyship. And he showed up all the arguments with his usual command of language."

"I'm sure he did. And now as to Miss Owlett. What line did she take under these circumstances?"

"Her father hadn't expected her to be there, but she shared his view that I was going to extremes to take him in charge. In fact you may say the Owlett family was a good bit disappointed and surprised at my line of action."

"You did your duty, as you saw it, against their plea for mercy?"

"They didn't plead for mercy; they only pleaded for me not to make a fool of myself."

"I see," said Lady Champerdowne, then turned to Matthew.

"Have you any questions to put to the witness before he stands down?" she asked.

"Yes, my Lady Magistrate," replied the culprit cheerfully. "I commend him most heartily, if you'll allow me to do so, because he's given a very clear statement and all he's said is as true as gospel. He's offered the Court the bones of what happened, and now I'll ask him to put a bit of flesh on 'em."

"He will answer any points vital to the case," explained Mr. Westover.

"Then, firstly, when you made clear your intentions to lock me up, what did I say on the subject, Peter—me a grown man speaking to a young and impetuous policeman?"

Inspector Manley intervened.

"Young he may be, Owlett, but he was never impetuous in all his life and never will be."

The witness turned rather helplessly to the Bench.

"Must I traverse over all that again?" he asked, and the Magistrates' Clerk directed him.

"You're on oath, Constable, and must furnish every detail of the conversation you can remember—not for the pleasure of the prisoner, but the satisfaction of the Court," he said.

"I doubt I can call to mind much more than what I've told already," replied Peter. "It was about the family side of the situation he troubled—not the mess he'd got himself in. Mr. Owlett took that very light. He said he'd put the value of the pheasants in the poor-box, if that was enough to satisfy me, and he thought no sane man was going to shatter his own prospects and smash up his future father-in-law for two game-birds and a hare. We were to eat the hare come Sunday after Miss Owlett had cooked it."

"Do drop the hare, Constable. I don't want to hear any more about the hare," declared Lady Champernowne.

"It ought to be in evidence by rights," murmured the inspector, and Peter continued:

"Well, the prisoner felt that to arrest him would be a great mistake and it might be a lot wiser to overlook his misdemeanours, that being to do the greater good for the greatest number, including myself."

"Does that fairly represent what you said to Constable Chadd, Matthew Owlett?"

"Couldn't put it in better words," replied the prisoner. "There he stood rolling his miserable eyes under the moon, and his sweetheart giving him hell and me—me of all men—seemingly caught in the dirty and shameful crime of stealing Sir Gerald's game and abusing the trust my benefactor put in me. And Peter—poor boy—called to let the world know I was a whited sepulchre and hale me off to clink and lose his appointed wife for ever if he dared to put a finger upon me! I very near wept to see him in such a hole; but I tried to cheer him as best I could. I told him you can't always trust appearances."

"The pheasants were there and the hare and the gun: they were realities, not appearances," said the Magistrates' Clerk, and Matthew reproved him.

"We've been told by the Magistrate not to mention that hare again, Mr. Westover," he said, "and as for the rest of the outfit, of course it all looked real enough and it was a reality in a manner of speaking, yet in truth a proper delusion, all for a purpose and no more than a conjuring trick, you might almost say. But nobody must blame Peter for being beguiled by it. He's an honest man and a most praiseworthy man. I'm proud of him and his conduct likewise."

The people applauded loudly; it was indeed a minute before Inspector Manley could stop their pleasure; while Lady Champernowne stared from the Bench with some bewilderment upon Matthew and the Clerk shook his head.

"Young Chadd," continued Mr. Owlett blithely, "was the victim of circumstances and they were made far worse for him by the unfortunate fact that my poor girl happened to be present when the test came. I didn't expect her, but being on the spot, she suffered too and was tested herself for that matter. Both of 'em were victims of appearance; and you'd do it again tomorrow and act just the same, wouldn't you, Peter? You don't stand there shamed or sorry for what you've done?"

"Mortal sorry I was called to do it—not shamed," replied the witness.

"A first-rate answer and I'll lay my life, if she was asked, Nancy would reply the like," declared Matthew.

Then Mr. Westover spoke.

"You can stand down, Constable Chadd," he directed, "and let the case proceed. You are not under the prisoner's cross-examination, though he appears to think so."

Then he turned to Matthew while Peter withdrew.

"If you have any witnesses on your behalf, let them be called; if not, inform the Bench what your defence amounts to," he said.

"Bless your life, Mr. Westover, I haven't begun to defend myself yet, sir," explained the prisoner. "As witnesses for character I could of course call the whole parish; but they were most of 'em in bed asleep when these things fell out; so I'll be my own witness, please. I'm innocent of what I'm charged and I didn't ought to stand in this box. No blame of poaching can be fastened upon me for one instant moment and I'm going to leave the Court presently without a stain on my record."

"Come, come, Mr. Owlett. Facts speak for themselves, you know," suggested Lady Champernowne.

"There's a lot of lies flying about feathered to look like truth, my Lady Magistrate, and I've been instrumental to loose one or two myself," admitted Matthew, "but only from high motives—motives, you understand, that would never have landed me in trouble. I'll explain my motives in half a minute."

"You admit the pheasants came from Oakshotts and that Constable Chadd was doing his duty to arrest you; then what more can be said?" asked Mr. Westover. "That surely is to admit guilt, not claim innocence."

"All true," agreed Matthew. "Never did a young man do his duty better or braver. Six foot four inches tall, and every inch a policeman: that's Peter. He trusted the evidence of his own eyes, and though the evidence, if accepted, would blast his career and mine, and likewise ruin the future hopes of two innocent women, he bit on the bullet and did his duty; and dead right he was and well pleased we all should be with him. I grant the pheasants came from Oakshotts, because birds from there weigh half as much again as pheasants from any other place. Why? Because Mr. Toby Trimble looks after that. There he sits in Court, I see, my Lady Magistrate, licking his lips because he thinks he's got me at last; but it was the police that got me: he couldn't. A head gamekeeper; but look at his gallows in the coverts and see what he slays and crucifies! Magpies—yes;

hawks and crows—yes; jays and weasels—yes; but owls—a thousand times no! Yet there they hang—brown owls and white owls, screech-owls and little owls—all martyred by a lot of ignorant fellows that call themselves gamekeepers!"

"Confine yourself to the charges against you," directed Lady Champernowne.

"So I will, then. You see what things looked like for Chadd and applaud him for acting according; but how different the truth! What happened was like a spider spinning his web to catch a fly—me being the spider and Peter the poor mistaken fly!"

"This is nonsense, Owlett."

"To the world at large it may sound so," agreed Matthew, "but grim truth notwithstanding. Now I'll give the Law a clue—that blessed word 'clue'. It covers a multitude of policeman's sins and keeps the public quiet. Ask yourself this then, my Lady Magistrate and you, Mr. Westover, and you, Inspector Manley. Would any man so skilled in woodcraft as myself, if he had sunk to knavery and theft, well knowing that a constable was on his beat up there at that identical hour and place, have waited till Peter was abreast of him and then made noise enough to be heard and then pretended to escape and ended by tumbling off a gate into the policeman's arms with evidence of his crime dropping out of his pockets? A child would have known better and sat tight and waited till the course was clear. Then why in the world did an old night-bird like me, well used to the ways of darkness, play a fool's trick like that? Find the answer and you'll begin to see daylight."

"You mean you actually wanted Chadd to catch you red-handed?" asked the Magistrate, and Owlett beamed upon her.

"Ah!" he said. "Trust you to smell a rat! They didn't make your ladyship a Justice of the Peace for nothing!"

Inspector Manley ordered laughter to be stilled and threatened to clear the Court if it was repeated; then Matthew prattled cheerfully on.

"You may go so far as to say that Peter didn't catch me at all in honest truth; 'twas I caught him. I was the bait and he came along and swallowed it, and satisfied me once and for ever of his worthiness to have me for a father-in-law and my daughter for his wife. I'll own it was in me to doubt of his character, so I laid my plans before Sir Gerald himself and, from his store of wisdom, he said there was danger in setting any such a trap for a young policeman, but he didn't forbid me to do it."

"You suggest that the lord of the manor was as downy as you are," declared Lady Champernowne bluntly.

Mr. Owlett grinned.

"Downier—downier, because better educated and deeper skilled in human nature than what I am," he said. " 'Test the young man,' he told me. 'Test him if you feel the need; but you grasp the danger and the severity of such a test.' "

"And then he told you to go into his preserves and shoot pheasants. Are you suggesting that?" asked the Magistrates' Clerk.

"Certainly not, Mr. Westover—not for a moment. I'll come to that. Well, I acted according and the rest you know. Peter withstood the temptation and did his duty. I very near jumped for joy. I could have kissed the young man when he took me up, only that would have spoiled all. It wasn't what he thought I was doing that mattered a button, but only what he was going to do himself."

A feminine voice broke the brief silence.

"Oh, Father, why the mischief didn't you tell me?" cried Nancy.

"Silence in Court!" roared the inspector, and the prisoner smiled upon his child.

"That you, my girl? Ah, and there's dear Mrs. Chadd along with you—both in black, I see. But this ain't a funeral: it's a revel, my dears."

"Order—order!" bellowed Manley, and upon return of peace the Magistrate spoke.

"The facts still remain, Owlett, and we are concerned with the facts alone."

"The facts being a brace of pheasants and a hare killed by the prisoner under conditions which amount to felony. You were not after moths, or toadstools, as a competent field naturalist working for Sir Gerald, and you are in the dock at present for poaching his game. Whatsoever your motives, they do not condone these facts." So spoke the Magistrates' Clerk, and Matthew nodded respectfully.

"The Law's a wondrous contrivance, sure enough," he said. "No, I wasn't after fungi—which are only called 'toadstools' by the vulgar, if you'll excuse my saying so, Mr. Westover. Fungi and humans have a lot in common, sir. Some folk and some fungi are full of charm and clad in crimson and yellow and purple, very pleasing to the eye, but deadly poison under their skins; while others, like myself and the mushroom family, ain't much to look at—just go-by-the-ground, honest little creatures with nothing to make a song about, but good as gold at heart."

"Stick to the pheasants, Owlett," directed Lady Champernowne.

"I will, my lady," he answered. "Do you hap to mind Frank Lemon, the poulterer and fishmonger to Tavistock?"

"Very well."

"He was an old servant of Oakshotts, and Sir Gerald thought highly of him, and when there was a big shoot up over, Lemon would often get a present of some birds for friendship."

"I see. Plenty from the manor go to the hospital too."

"Indeed yes," agreed Matthew. "His honour may be downy, your ladyship, but he's the salt of the earth as well as the lord of the manor. A week ago Frank had a gift of birds, as Mr. Trimble will testify, and I bought a brace over his counter. I've got Lemon's receipt in my pocket at the moment for Inspector Manley if he wants it."

"And that's how you made this elaborate deception look like fact for poor Constable Chadd?"

"That was all the evidence—shaky, I grant you, but enough for Peter."

"Why do you say 'shaky'? What could he have deduced from such evidence but that you were a poacher?" asked Mr. Westover.

"He could have deduced from the birds they had been dead over a week and was long since stiff and cold," answered Matthew, and Lady Champernowne expressed emotion. She put up her pince-nez, frowned upon Owlett and censured him.

"You are a very crafty, cunning and rather cruel old man," she said. "I feel no admiration for this performance and am in fact exceedingly shocked at it."

"But not at the motives, my dear!" he replied, abandoning formality. "Sir Gerald, when he first came to hear of my quandaries, granted that there was nothing like getting the young into the deuce of a mess to find out what they're made of. Those were his very words."

"I shall tell him exactly what I think of him too, when next we meet," she answered, and turned to the Magistrates' Clerk.

"Then that closes the case and we can dismiss it, I suppose, Mr. Westover?" she asked.

"Yes," he replied. "That closes the case, your ladyship. The prisoner has been responsible for unusual and even irregular conduct, but quite outside the Statute Book. The propriety of his actions so far as the Bench is concerned remains a matter of opinion, but he has done nothing indictable."

"There's no call to hold you any longer, Matthew Owlett," said Inspector Manley, and Nancy raised her voice again.

"Then come down out of that hateful box, Father!" she cried. "You don't want to live there, do you?"

The Magistrate had been reflecting and, before calling for the next case, she spoke again.

"One question before you leave us," said Lady Champernowne. "If Constable Chadd had fallen into your horrid trap and let you off, what would you have done about it and thought about him?"

Matthew did not answer instantly, but a shamefaced expression clouded his face and for a moment he was cast down. Then, in the silence that awaited his reply, he spoke.

"I should have gone to my grave a very disappointed man," he said.

"And richly deserved to do so. You have come out of this a great deal too well, so let it be a lesson to you—never, whatsoever your motive, try and catch anybody again."

"Never again—except the night moths, my dear!" he promised. Then the liberated prisoner's friends gathered about him as he returned to freedom and welcomed all.

"Come into the fresh air, you girls," he said; "and Inspector Manley will spare you for five minutes, Peter, because you're the big noise this morning—not me. You take my right arm, Dinah, and you fasten on my left, Nancy. Let's push along. I'm thirsty and we'll drop into 'the 'Welcome' along with Mr. Hannaford."

The little party drifted away and Mrs. Chadd, much moved, whispered to Matthew.

"Oh, Matt, do this mean you've forgived my letter, or have I gone too far?"

"Dry your eyes and think no more of it," he said. "You women don't come out of this so grand as me and your son do, Dinah, and for that matter my tail was between my legs a bit when that fine lady dressed me down, but all will be forgot very quick and forgiven still quicker."

Peter spoke.

"That's right, Mr. Owlett. I must go back now. I'll see you later."

He turned and Nancy turned with him.

"Can you overlook that night, or ain't you going to, Peter?" she asked.

"A thousand pities you was up there," he answered, "but, being up there, of course you were hoodwinked same as I was. You took a very proper line from your point of view—pretty patient you were and a very good daughter sure enough."

"I've jugged the hare anyway," she said, "though little thought you'd ever help to eat it. In fact I doubted who was going to eat it at all. A lot of my tears fell in it, Peter."

Elsewhere, accompanied by Mr. Hannaford, Matthew and his companions proceeded to the inn.

"A man's always innocent till he's proved guilty: that's the bed-rock of English Law," said the landlord, "and gives righteousness and justice a chance to be done. I don't say I saw much light, Matt, but felt, knowing you, there might be a way out. And there won't be no more mysteries in the moonshine hatched by you, I hope."

"That's right, Mr. Hannaford," declared Dinah, who had recovered confidence.

"No, there won't be no more mysteries, Amos," promised Matthew, "but what's life without a bit of moonshine? What's moonshine on earth but sunlight on the moon?"

"You've got peace with honour in my opinion," summed up his friend, "and if there was more like your Peter, Mrs. Chadd, to keep the peace and protect it, then so much the better for the countryside in general."

CHAPTER XI

IN the course of a few days Mrs. Blanchard learned that Mr. Pilcher, from the firm of Wilson & Harding, might shortly be expected to visit Wallabrook in connection with her affairs. She had expected him, but the news that he would soon arrive appeared to quicken Unity into action, for it was noticed that of late she became evasive, introspective, less talkative than usual and apparently suffered from a sort of anti-climax after the storm and splendour of her recent experiences.

In truth, however, her lapse into aloofness arose from no weariness of mind or body, but the demand of great, secret challenges involving her future and a welter of problems to be faced or avoided by exercise of her own judgment alone. Conclusions once come to, she proposed to announce her plan of action and let all involved learn it; but upon one vital particular another than herself must have a voice did her steps take a certain course, and it was the question of approach to this individual that for the moment kept Mrs. Blanchard pensive, preoccupied.

With her family she preserved an armed neutrality, was unprepared to see any of them but her grandson, Gilbert, and directed him to tell his mother that she would pay a visit to 'Laburnum Lodge' at a time to be specified in the future. She also visited the nursery gardens of Mr. Brimblecombe on several occasions, but for the most part remained in the safe keeping of the 'Fisherman's Welcome' as a respected and important guest. There she entertained Mrs. Chadd, congratulated Dinah on the happy issue of her afflictions and learned that marriage was now in sight for the contracting parties; but Unity declined to see Mrs. Parsons, who strove ineffectually to obtain an interview.

Now came the promise of Mr. Pilcher's visit and, when the date was fixed, Mrs. Blanchard hastened her own conclusions, told herself that it would be well to settle everything before the lawyer's arrival and took the vital step awaiting her. She bade Arthur Brimblecombe come to tea, entertained him well, told him to light his pipe when the meal was ended and then laid her wishes before him. He, too, had enjoyed some fame when his achievements came to be publicly learned, but he was quite unaware of the sentiments that already induced observing acquaintance to link his name with another. His private hopes, already killed by Unity before her translation, did not reawaken, for, thought the market gardener, if she could refuse me once and for all, despite her own unhopeful prospects in the past, how much the more must what I had to offer appear but a trifle compared with what she now possesses. But Mrs. Blanchard's theme, as unfolded with her customary clarity, was now to surprise Arthur not a little.

"The longer I think upon all your valuable help over my affairs, the more I feel you was never properly rewarded, Arthur," she began. "All I felt was you must be thanking God it was over and you could now lose sight of me and get back to your proper work and feel you'd done your good deed and would be recompensed for it, if not in this world, then hereafter. But I'd always meant to show my gratitude and only waited to determine what form it would take when I'd settled into my new conditions. That's how it stood till a most curious thing happened and I found myself to be in need of your services yet again."

"And welcome I'm sure," he said. "Once you've tasted adventures, if they turn out well, then you'll find yourself properly hankering for more. I've marked you to be a bit flat the last few days and felt a bit flat myself, for that matter; but you can't go through such triumphant feats without feeling empty when they're over."

"They may be over for you, but not for me," declared Unity. "That's why I asked you to tea, Arthur. I've been thinking hard these last few days; but not feeling no flatness by any means. My demands to look ahead have got to be answered and I've been chasing the answer night and day, ever since I came home to Wallabrook; and now I've caught it, so to speak, and the answer turns out to be you, my dear man!"

Arthur laughed.

"Glad I've given you a good run for your money, then," he said. "And now you've catched me, what next? D'you find yourself planning another rollick and wanting my Ford to start in? You can buy a Ford for yourself now and I'll learn you to drive it."

"Be serious," she begged. "There's nothing comical in what I'm going to say, because my whole future turns upon it, and nobody but a fool takes the future lightly nowadays. I'll tell you what I resolved, Arthur, and I'll show you my resolutions depend upon how you may please to look at 'em. Firstly, thinking upon the advice to sell my Australian property, I reached a settlement as to that in two shakes of a duck's tail. 'Never will I sell a single rood of the orchard,'

I told myself. 'I may be up in years,' I said, 'but what's left of 'em shall be spent in Australia. A Blanchard planted that orchard and built that fine house, and so long as I live a Blanchard shall tend to the one and dwell in the other.' Well, that sounded very fine to me till I looked into the snags. I needn't go over all the ups and downs because it would take too long, but finally, Arthur, just as I was coming to the hateful fear I couldn't launch out all by myself and put half the globe between me and life as I know it, there came my wild idea to ask you to tea."

Mr. Brimblecombe regarded her blankly.

"Go on," he said. "I ain't following your reasoning very close, Unity, but shall see light presently, no doubt."

"I've decided for you to choose whether I go foreign, or bide home," she said. "It depends on you and no other, Arthur. I've shifted off the answer on to your shoulders. If you say 'go', I'll face it and do so; but—here's the point that only you can cope with—if you say 'go', then you'll have to come too. I don't go alone. Wait, now! Don't answer me in no hurry. Don't turn down this huge idea out of hand, because, if you accept the condition I've yet to put before you, I'll be killing two birds with one stone. I'll be showing my gratitude for the past in a practical manner and also able to go to Australia without leaving my best man friend behind."

"You mean by that if I was to come down under and look after your orange trees you'd pay a tidy salary?"

"No, Arthur. Think better of me. What sort of salary, if it was your weight in gold weekly, could pay for all your good works to me? Now give heed, because everything turns on what you answer. When I refused you back along and said once for all I couldn't take a second, I meant it. I had no mind then to saddle you, or any other man, with a worn-out, needy old baggage same as I was. But now the case is altered: I'm ten years younger than a year ago and have got something behind me. What your view of me may be now is not for me to say: but if you still fancy the thought of me as a partner, then I'll throw myself in along with my property and my plantation and fine house out there; but if you don't, then I'll turn down Australia and bide home."

Mr. Brimblecombe had grown redder and redder.

"Do I understand you've opened the sealed book and are minded to marry again along with all your other transactions, Unity?" he asked in a tone of hushed amazement.

"So far as you're concerned, yes," she answered firmly. "I don't go to Australia a single woman and I don't marry again unless it's you, Arthur. But if I marry you, you'll be called to change your manner of life and face the fact that when I die—because I must die some day—then you'll succeed to everything and also to the responsibility of Gilly White, because I shall take him along with us and he will be called to look upon you as his grandfather henceforward."

"You'll marry me at last, then? Fancy that!" He gazed upon her with profound affection, then rose, grasped her hand and gazed, panting somewhat, into her eyes.

"If you'll go to Australia, dear man; not otherwise. Say the word—that's all. At our ages we can bargain, because our affections will best be shown in pounds and shillings and pence, if we've got any. So you have to ask yourself if it's good enough and if you gain more than you lose by it. You've always lost a darned sight more than you gained by your liking for my person, because I've took the cream off your nurseries ever since I was a widow, but if you can revive your old feelings——"

"I can't revive them because they never perished," he assured her. "There's no romantics for you, but for me you are romantical as ever, and if you had still naught else but yourself to offer I'd take you with thanksgivings—orange orchard or no orange orchard."

"Then very happy am I to hear it," answered Unity. "Now we can look the future in the face and I feel no shadow of doubt but we'll make a good job of work out there. I don't call you to take nothing on trust. These ain't times when a man's word is as good as his bond same as it used to be—still less a woman's—because if the Government of the country can go back on its promises and say the thing that is not, where shall the people put their trust? Mr. Pilcher's coming next Monday and we'll tell him what we ordain, and after we're married I shall get Mr. Forbes and him to draw my will and when you've seen the contents you'll know all."

"And I'll make a will also after I'm married, and you will run your eyes over it before I sign."

"Well, thank God that's accomplished," said Mrs. Blanchard. "It's been a good bit on my mind, Arthur, because I hardly dared to think I should have any more luck, and it came over me a good deal that whatever your feelings may have been in the past, they could well have changed after you'd seen such a powerful lot of me on the railway trains and in London and so on, and made you feel glad you wasn't bound to me for ever; but if you're obstinate about me still, then blessed be the Lord, I'm sure."

"Same with me," he declared, and Unity changed the subject.

"I'm going to 'Laburnum Lodge' tomorrow," she said; "not alone, don't you fear that. But now you can come and, if you'd decided different, then I'd have asked Samuel Manley to come himself and watch over me; but now it's your place to do so and we can tell Maude and Brian our intentions."

Arthur dwelt upon the tremendous changes about to overtake his plan of living.

"If anybody had told me I was going to quit my vegetable grounds I'd have called him a liar to his face this morning," he said; "but now that's my first intention. It won't fetch what it would have before the war, yet a tidy prospect for the right man."

"We ain't an old couple in a hurry," explained Unity, "and you must have your price and leave England in a dignified manner."

"Nobody's going to doubt but I've bettered myself," he admitted.

"Nor yet that I have," she declared.

"No call for us to hang about overmuch either, in my opinion," added Arthur. "Our summer's their winter in Australia, so if we hold on for one more summer here, Unity, then we can get over there and catch two summers running."

"A clever thought, and ought to fit in very suent. Come autumn here everything should be in order and Australia warned to expect me," said Unity.

"Us," added Mr. Brimblecombe.

On the following day they went to tea with Maude and found Brian also prepared to entertain them.

Ere they entered her daughter's home Unity, well aware of Arthur's aversion and fearful that in his altered position at her right hand he might be unduly severe, uttered a caution.

"Where you stand now, of course you can dress Maude down more fierce than ever, my dear; but hold your hand so far as you're able and don't rub it in too hard. She's had her dose."

"You do the talking," he said.

They proceeded with a considerable amount of reserve, then Brian invited his mother-in-law to speak.

"We wasn't counting to see anybody but yourself, Mother," he said, "but no doubt you've brought Mr. Brimblecombe for your own reasons."

"And he's very welcome, I'm sure," added Maude.

"For the best of good reasons I'm here," replied Arthur, forgetting his promise to keep quiet. "Mrs. Blanchard has done me the honour to consent to marry me, Brian White, and it was her wish that you and Maude should be the first to know it."

"Not that you are the first," explained Unity, "because three folk have congratulated us already as we came through the village, and I lay your friend, Thomasina, has got it too by now."

"Officially, however, you're the first to hear it from the horse's mouth," continued Arthur, "and I may tell you I'm a very proud and well-contented man; but there's a lot more than that, which you are certainly the first to know, and your mother will tell you."

Brian had been regarding the market gardener with veiled admiration.

"You haven't lost much time, have you?" he asked, and Gilly entered as he spoke.

"Eat your tea and keep your mouth shut," directed Maude. "Your grandmother's letting us know her intentions."

"It's in a nutshell, Maude. After due thought upon such a big thing, we ordain after marriage to go to Australia and bide there."

"Go to Australia, Mother! You, at your time of life!"

"You'll be bed-ridden before you get there," said Brian coarsely.

"Not in two or three days, I shan't," said Mrs. Blanchard.

"Two days! Six months, more like; and think on the voyage and all you'll have on your hands before you can even start, Mother," suggested Maude. "You'll have plenty to help you, of course, because you can pay for service now, but——"

"Be quiet," said Unity. "I'm speaking to your husband now. He may not know it, but an airplane can travel to Australia in two days, and if I so will, Mr. Brimblecombe and myself can fetch over in it."

"You'd trust yourself in an airplane, Granny?" cried her grandson.

"Why not, Gilly? I've as much right to new inventions as anybody else if I can pay for 'em. I shan't be alone, neither. Arthur's game and I trust to take another too."

"I'm in your mother's hands, you people," said Mr. Brimblecombe. "I don't fear the air no more than she do."

"You've got to mind one thing," grinned the railwayman. "Them that start journeying by 'plane don't always land where they expected."

"Curb your hopes as to that," answered Mrs. Blanchard calmly. "The Almighty wouldn't have favoured me same as He has done if I was going to drop out of a flying machine. God don't give with one hand and take back with the other."

"She'd be safer rushing through the air to Australia than ever she was under this roof, anyway," declared Mr. Brimblecombe, but Brian was not discouraged.

"You may not know it, but Australia's properly crawling with poisonous snakes," he said; "and nobody hates snakes more than you do."

"Plenty of poisonous snakes everywhere—Wallabrook included," asserted Arthur, "and the worst sort goes on two legs."

Unity steered the conversation into other channels.

"I shall make a will before I go," she said. "I've never wrote one yet, because I had nothing to write about, but now I have, and when he's my husband, then Arthur will come first in it."

"Same as your mother will come first in mine," added Arthur.

"What they call a marriage of convenience, you and Mr. Brimblecombe, Mother," suggested Maude, "and very convenient I hope it's going to be."

"A lot more than that. However, I ain't here to praise my future husband. It wasn't my uplift made him offer. I'd turned him down so firm such a lot of times that none was more astonished than him to hear I'd changed my mind. More tea, Maude. There's just one other item to name and that depends upon you and your husband. I said a bit ago that, if I went by 'plane, there might be another along with us, and I had your boy in mind when I did so."

Gilly gasped.

"Me fly to Australia in a 'plane, Granny!"

"Why not? You're the kind they want out there. Not the sort of young man who shakes at the knees and looks at his wrist-watch when he's faced with a spot of work. What do you say, Maude? He'll be safe enough with us and free to come back if he don't like it. You can have it all down in writing, Brian."

"Take him and welcome," said the railwayman. "I'll come too, if you like."

"Shan't be wanting you, though Arthur and me will be very pleased to see old friends for a week-end now and again. But I don't ask you, nor yet Maude. You can work your passage and get back your credit at home."

"You've had your bit of luck," continued Arthur, showing spite. "But for the Christian in your mother, you'd have been under lock and key by now—the pair of you."

"Well, that's all there is to it, for the present," concluded Unity. "Now I'll be going, Maude. Mr. Pilcher is travelling down here on my business, to satisfy himself all is lawful and regular; then Arthur's putting our wedding in hand and selling his place, and we count to leave England after corn harvest. Then you'll let me have Gilly—not for my pleasure only but his profit in time to come?"

"I couldn't wish nothing better on this earth, Mother, I'm sure," said the boy.

"He'll be safer with us than his grandmother was with you, anyway," added Arthur.

"If he don't like Australia I'll pack him back," promised Unity, "but I count on it he'll find his feet. And he'll be down in my will with Arthur to watch over him. I must go some day, of course, though never felt less like going than I do just now."

The betrothed went their way and Arthur made a curious comment:

"Her misfortunes haven't made your daughter look no younger," he said, "nor yet more agreeable. Plain as bread always, though that wasn't her fault. Her down-daunted expression comes out of her own wickedness."

"She had a nice open face when she was a little girl," said Unity. "Youth have always got something kind and welcome about it, Arthur."

"Give me middle age," he answered. "Middle age with dignity and sense, like you and, I hope, like me."

"You've kept your bright eyes and your high complexion very well," Mrs. Blanchard assured him.

"Fear nothing for me, my dear. A red face is all right if your blood channels are flowing free, and when I went to Dr. Bridger to cut a lump of flesh off my neck—a carbuncle, he called it—he gave me the once-over and said there was no blood pressure of the arteries and all going well."

"Good, Arthur. Same with me. Now I've got work offering and enough to eat, I'm twice the woman I was."

"You'd have died a natural death by starvation all the same if you'd bided under your daughter's roof."

"Think on her patiently," begged Mrs. Blanchard. "She's young yet in years and have had a tidy lot to put up with—including her own nasty nature. We'll hear how they're faring, no doubt. Brian's going to be kept at the railway and it ain't too late to hope they'll live down their doubtful ways. I've told her if the worst befalls and she feels herself to be in danger from him, to cut loose and come to us."

"I should like nothing worse on God's earth to come to us than Maude," said Mr. Brimblecombe, "but your word's my law henceforward."

CHAPTER XII

THERE came an afternoon when Mr. Chave wheeled Sir Gerald where the snowdrops powdered on Oakshotts lawn, the March wind blew gently and the sun shone. Matthew Owlett walked beside his employer's bath chair and presently they reached a southern-facing summer-house from which noble views of the valley beneath subtended. Here Chave left Sir Gerald in Matthew's company and withdrew, promising to return in half an hour and warning his master that he must not remain longer.

"One should have heard the chiff-chaff ere now, Matthew," said Sir Gerald solemnly, and the old sailor agreed with him.

"More than time, your honour, and I've been hoping for the black-cap also; but not a note as yet," he answered.

"One thing is certain: there must be a reason for such delay, my friend."

"Maybe they've arrived to time but not reached our ears yet, your honour."

Sir Gerald nodded thoughtfully.

"Quite possible; quite possible," he replied.

It was the first time Owlett had been summoned since his arrest, trial and pardon, and now the elder commented on these matters.

"There was a humorous side to your activities without a doubt," he admitted, "but we must examine what lies below. I can assure you that your judge was not moved to any great display of amusement when I saw her shortly after your case came before the Magistrates' Court."

"Lady Champernowne put it across me pretty sharp, your honour."

"She also put it across me pretty sharply," confessed Sir Gerald. "In her opinion the fact that I did not instantly condemn your proposed experiment and forbid it proved gravely to my discredit. And she was perfectly right. She made the enormity of your proceeding only too evident, and to offer as my excuse the fact that I was greatly preoccupied when you spoke to me about it and had failed to give such a proposition the consideration it demanded—to confess to that would have been evasive and cowardly, so I endeavoured to brazen it out and support your effort to learn the truth. She crushed me, however, and showed a philosophic outlook far superior to my own. We are always suspicious of what we do not understand, whether it be some phenomena of Nature or unexpected complexity of human character. And too often, when we fail of an explanation, we grow uneasy and attribute sinister significance to the mystery.

"That is what you did when you still found yourself puzzled by the qualities of Constable Chadd and were disposed to see weakness which he has triumphantly revealed did not exist. Indeed, the more I reflect upon it, the greater my astonishment at my own laxity in supporting you and your irrational failure to trust a young man who must be most unusually trustworthy as young men go. You have unearthed and displayed a remarkably gifted lad; but to dig him out as you did and bring such exceptional probity and high principle to the light was an action that does not redound to your credit and has lessened my own. I am chastened, Matthew, and I trust that you are. We have erred and stand condemned. Supposing that he had succumbed before a temptation so subtle and terrible? Consider the arid desert of withered hope and blighted dreams that must have awaited him. Think also of what a miserable idiot you would have looked in your own eyes, and my dejection and remorse when I learned the hateful sequel."

"Pretty much what her ladyship said in everyday language, your honour," confessed Matthew. "I've been a good bit downcast off and on and quite agree I've had more luck than I deserved; but, against that, you can set the glory of Peter Chadd and the lift his fine performance has given him in his profession. He's got good marks by it, the inspector says."

"To know all is to forgive all, or so we are taught," said Sir Gerald, "though in my own experience, upon the very few occasions when I appear to have known all there was to know about a fellow man, I have found it impossible to forgive him. Certain events will always be utterly unforgivable when the naked truth chances to be revealed about them. Racial fanaticism and superstition, patriotism and eternal selfishness continue to be the curses of humanity, the hotbeds of most of the evils we suffer from, Owlett—you and I as much as everybody else.

"I have turned my museum into a fortress and spent a great deal of money to do so, as you know; you have made an improper experiment with the lives of other people which, had it ended disastrously, would have cost you much more than money and may even as it is have ruined your credit as a responsible man. We are in the same box: our values were mistaken and we have both played the fool—each in his own way."

"I won't have you thinking small of yourself, your honour," declared Matthew firmly. "Granted I did a thing better not done; but when you made the museum secure, you was working for the nation and doing your duty at your own expense, and how many people do their duty if it's going to cost 'em money?"

"Change the subject and tell me about yourself. You were contracted to be married, as I remember. Have your recent activities changed the widow's mind?"

"She withdrew, your honour, but came back when I cleared myself. Same with my daughter: Peter's took her back. The four of us join up simultaneously."

"That is well, and meantime, thanks to this remarkable winter, I am now justified, my dear fellow, in anticipating with reasonable confidence another spring. Thus Providence returns good for evil and I shall hear the cuckoo call and see the bud break once again."

"Also the caterpillars on their food plants and the Death's-head on Toby Trimble's potato patch," suggested Matthew cheerfully.

"You have struck Tobias a mortal wound," said Sir Gerald. "Your devious practices awakened in him the hope that, at last, he was going to get you where he has long wanted you to be."

"Under lock and key, your honour?"

"Had his suspicions proved correct, that is where you would have found yourself; but he was so disappointed that he now proposes to withdraw from Oakshotts, doff his velveteens for ever and retire into private life."

"I'll scrape a friendship with him yet when he's settled down and got over it," promised Matthew, and the other applauded.

"A worthy ambition and I will do the like," he promised. "Toby has never entertained a very high opinion of me, but we must be diplomatic and win his forgiveness if it can be done."

Then came Chave.

"We will return through the glade," decided Sir Gerald. "Thanks to this kindly season, *Magnolia Campbellii* has become a thing of astounding beauty and is at present the wonder of the countryside. I planted it as a stripling of a yard tall. That was fifty years ago, Owlett, and at forty years of age it opened its first blossoms and I prayed that no finger of frost might bring those gorgeous petals untimely to earth. It continues to go from strength to strength—a stranger in a strange land. From the arboreal jungles of the Himalayas it comes and lords it here with the regal good breeding of all its race."

Mr. Owlett gazed upon the noble tree in floral splendour of great, open, shell-like chalices, ivory and salmon-pink. Then he took his leave and Chave, familiar with the old man's ways, kept silence while Sir Gerald regarded the treasure for five minutes. Anon he woke from his reverie and addressed the butler.

"When the Recording Angel is concerned with my meagre credit account, Ned, I think it more than probable that the planting of this precious tree may turn the scale and leave an exiguous balance in my favour."

"Without a doubt of it, Sir Gerald," declared Chave confidently.

Another summer hastened events and brought anticipated changes with it. During the next July, Matthew and Nancy married Dinah and Peter, and while the policeman continued to dwell in his old home, Mr. Owlett's second wife took some little time to fit into her new environment. But the elder pair found agreeable surprise in the success of their union and, weighing the matter some months after the event, agreed the step well justified.

"You've had the fine experience of marrying an honest and clever man, and I've taken a peace-loving and most personable woman," said Matthew, "and we can go on lightening the darkness of our children and help them to face up to married life as well as we do. Marriage has made you braver and hopefuller than what you were. I mark it in a score of ways. You'll utter your opinions with a lot more confidence than what you did, and you've got another interest in your life besides Peter and no call to put all your eggs in one basket no more. You've took a very good line of conduct in my opinion and stand a lot higher in the public eye as my better half than you ever did with your first one."

"That was bound to be," agreed Dinah. "I saw it in the people's faces and heard it in their voices when it was noised I'd fixed the day. A lot pointed out the change in me, and some were hopeful and others felt fear. They weren't feared for me, nor yet you, but they doubted if I would show just the right touch to your museum, or feel comfortable under the same roof with such a lot of fantastics as you'd hoarded and set store by. And I answered 'em that what was precious to you was going to be precious to me also—whether fantastic or otherwise."

"A very fine answer. And another thing pleased me no little.

Last time Unity came back to Wallabrook after her honeymoon, we had a tale up at Arthur's nurseries and she said, touching you, that a thing much to your advantage was you'd got more of a feeling for bright colours than of old. She said you was catching my love of 'em and garbing yourself a lot brighter and in consequence looking a lot younger than ever she remembered to see you."

"Never had the heart to go gayer than grey, or puce at the best, till now," confessed Dinah, "but my fear grows that I'll overdo it some day and look vulgar, Matt."

"Not you. There's very few right-down vulgar folk in Wallabook. Colour ain't vulgar. You wouldn't call a rainbow, or a macaw, or a mandrill monkey, vulgar, nor yet an autumn sunset. Nature's a great one for colour, and I'm all for it myself."

It was a few months later, at the return of another autumn, that the Owletts discussed Unity and Arthur Brimblecombe once again, and while Matthew sat busy overhauling items of his collection, Dinah knitted for him a new scarf of mingled brilliant hues destined for winter wear.

"You want a proper power of imagination to picture that woman nowadays," declared Dinah. "Monday next she flies, along with Arthur and Gilly White, thousands of feet up in the sky heading for the ends of the earth."

"You can imagine her in the mind's eye ascending to the Happy Land some day, but not on an airplane and not until she's finished her job here," said Matthew. "On Monday she will be cleaving the air like an eagle and taking the universe in her stride, but still keeping her nerve same as she always did at her blackest hours."

"What a woman she was, Matt!"

"And is still, Dinah."

"After all, her bones won't lie beside her John in our churchyard, where she always counted for them to go and left a place on the gravestone according."

"She's got Arthur now."

Dinah considered and Matthew continued to dwell on Mrs. Brimblecombe.

"I can see her eating her oranges and dispensing 'em to her neighbours," he said. "She'll never tire of growing 'em, but it's just possible that Arthur may. He was a great one for rotation of crops and, with naught but oranges all the year round, there won't be nothing to rotate."

Then Mrs. Owlett said a surprising thing which came as an echo of her bygone, pessimistic days.

"I wonder sometimes why you didn't take her, my dear. After John died you might have won her, if it was only for all you'd got to offer."

" 'Tis on the cards I could have," he admitted, "and to be honest, Dinah, if I'd known what was hid for her in the future, I might have tried for her, because, in a orange orchard, you can easily guess what the night moths are like to be, let alone the day butterflies."

Dinah sighed and Matthew heard her.

"You can take this to your comfort, my blessed woman," he hastened to say. "A woman who admired Arthur well enough to put her life in his hands would never have looked twice at me. Both good, trustworthy men we are—him and me—but there was that about him turned the scale in his favour and she knew he was the right one, just as you knew I was the right one."

"She came out a lot finer than what I did over that fearful affair in the past," mourned Dinah. "Even when I doubted your innocence—God forgive me—she never did. She stuck to it you couldn't have done such a thing."

"The case was different, you being torn in half betwixt your son and the man you was going to marry," explained Matthew. "A nasty mess you found yourself in, Dinah, and you played for safety, and who shall blame you? Let the past run off like the river—always going, but never gone—never gone. Unity told me she'd miss the river more than the humans. Born and bred in sound of Walla, she was, and old enough to see generations of men and women dance away their lives like the May-flies—here today and gone tomorrow. 'Lord love you,' I said to her. 'Your orange orchard's got a tidy big river flowing close at hand—a proper, boatable river—and behind it the Blue Mountains, lifting up twenty times as high as the tors on Dartmoor.' But she said they might be very well in their way, yet nothing to her compared with the cradle she was born in. Same with Arthur. I lay they'll oft croon together over Wallabrook, of an evening when their day's work's done and the night down and the kangaroos hopping round about in the darkness, and moths so big as soup plates humming in the orange blossom."

THE END

PRINTED IN GREAT BRITAIN BY THE ANCHOR PRESS, LTD., TIPTREE, ESSEX